MW01076040

The Seeds of War

Alaric Bond

The Seeds of War
Copyright © 2021 by Alaric Bond
Published by Old Salt Press LLC

ISBN Paperback: 978-1-943404-33-9
ISBN E-book: 978-1-943404-34-6

All rights reserved. No part of this book may be reproduced or transmitted in any form or by any means, electronic or mechanical, including photocopying, recording or by any information storage and retrieval system, without written permission from the author, except for the inclusion of brief quotations in a review.

Cover artwork shows details from "Engagement Between the USS United States and HMS Macedonian" by Thomas Birch (1779-1851). This work is in the public domain in its country of origin and other countries and areas where the copyright term is the author's life plus 100 years or fewer. It has been identified as being free of known restrictions under copyright law, including all related and neighbouring rights.

Publisher's Note: This is a work of historical fiction. Certain characters and their actions may have been inspired by historical individuals and events. The characters in the novel, however, represent the work of the author's imagination. Any resemblance to actual persons, living or dead, is entirely coincidental.

Published by Old Salt Press. Old Salt Press, LLC is based in Jersey City, New Jersey with an affiliate in New Zealand. For more information about Old Salt Press titles go to www.oldsaltpress.com

Thanks to Kitty, Tessa, Joan, Rick, Antoine, Fred, Chris, Philip, Ken, Seymour, Linda, George and the many others who have helped with this book.

* * *

"May we look upon our treasure, the furniture of our houses, and our garments, and try to discover whether the seeds of war have nourishment in these our possessions."
John Woolman

For John and Deirdre

Other novels by Alaric Bond

The Fighting Sail series

His Majesty's Ship

The Jackass Frigate

True Colours

Cut and Run

The Patriot's Fate

The Torrid Zone

The Scent of Corruption

HMS Prometheus

The Blackstrap Station

Honour Bound

Sealed Orders

Sea Trials

Lone Escort

and

Turn a Blind Eye

The Guinea Boat

The Coastal Forces series

Hellfire Corner

Contents

The Seeds of War

Part One

Chapter One

The sun was shining gently warm amid a clear blue sky and a steady wind blew on their starboard quarter; perfect conditions for a lazy patrol and King was quietly grateful. But then for much of his time on the North American Station he had been fortunate with regards to the weather. Admittedly the previous winter had not been especially kind with one storm testing both his frigate and her crew almost to destruction. In general it was a pleasant climate though and his current duty a thousand times better than polishing enemy rocks on blockade duty.

And he had been lucky in other ways; south of their Halifax base, the Jamaica Station had seen a succession of vicious actions that culminated in Britain invading Guadalupe. It was a brutal, drawn-out affair in which many had fallen yet, throughout, King and his men had faced nothing more taxing than convoy protection and the occasional East Coast patrol. One of the latter was occupying them now and had been since they released the last Indies' convoy ten days before. For the next two months *Tenacious* and her consort, a sixteen-gun brig-sloop, would continue making steady progress up America's Eastern Seaboard as they carried out comprehensive checks on every merchant sail encountered. And despite being a relatively small force, they could do so with an assurance bordering on arrogance, something that came as a result of countless successful naval actions carried out under his nation's flag. Currently Bonaparte was amassing the largest army the world had ever seen and seemed destined to add Russia to his lists of land conquests. But at sea it was a different matter; at sea the Royal Navy had control and could inflict their will on any who chose to sail upon it.

Despite this power, and their apparent lack of haste, King's task remained a complex one. Whatever their flag, no trading vessel could be allowed to carry anything likely to assist Britain's enemies, whilst their crews must also be free of its subjects. Should there be doubt on this last point – a strong regional accent or proof of another nationality that bore the signs of taphouse forgery – the suspects could be pressed. Again, this was a right assumed by the Royal Navy's dominance and easily abused in the hands of a bully, although King trusted he was not of that ilk.

None of the seven ships he had inspected during the present patrol had been seized and, though they must have checked well over a hundred crew members, there had only been two arrests. King knew his attitude was by no means the norm however; even Leyton, who commanded the accompanying brig, was less than exacting unless carefully watched and many Royal Navy captains openly boasted about pressing any man who showed even a cursory command of English.

In addition to the checking of merchants, they must also keep a weather eye for pirates, privateers and slavers. The former was less likely since Napoleon's Caribbean territories had been taken and, after America's official stance against fresh imports, chances of encountering an active slaver should also have dropped. The possibility still existed though; apart from a brief encounter on St Helena, King had little to do with the trade in human flesh but fully appreciated where a demand remained there would be those prepared to supply it, and probably at a healthy profit.

A slaver was a different proposition to apparently innocent merchants and one King felt would be more suited to his talents. There were no forged bills of lading or bogus crew manifests to detect; a vessel carrying live cargo could not be disguised or evade even the most cursory of checks. The only defence was to run and this they did, usually at the first sight of a British flag.

As yet King had not encountered such a craft, at least so he supposed. Several strange sail had been sighted on the very rim of the horizon, sleek vessels that fled so fast even their consort, the nimble *Sparrow,* could not catch them and any or all might have been carrying slaves. Nevertheless he lived in hope for, despite American legislation and assurances to the contrary, the trade continued and might even be growing; several of his fellow captains had been fortunate in seizing fully laden Guineamen and seeing them safely to Halifax. With the prize courts paying handsomely for every freed native, in addition to the value of what was usually a sound craft, such a haul could be highly profitable, although King primly assured himself he had other reasons for wanting to combat the trade.

But despite this lack of success, and a workload that otherwise consisted of nothing more demanding than annoying or escorting those of the carrying trade, King was happy on the North American Station. For he was effectively serving at home, despite his Eastbourne estate lying many miles away. Aimée and the children had moved to Halifax a year before and being so near to his family was a luxury he greatly appreciated. Whenever they made harbour the temptation to abandon the ship and head for their neat little house in Prince's Street was strong, and doing so often came easier than having to explain why he could not. Showing such divided loyalty may hardly be the best way to impress his Commander-in-Chief but King had a competent first officer and felt reasonably secure in his post. For despite having failed to bag a slaver, and even after avoiding any major action, his commission was proving relatively successful. No merchant had been lost in any of the convoys *Tenacious* escorted and past patrols had been more successful. On these a total of three American vessels had been seized following proof of illegal trading and a sizeable privateer was also surprised at dawn and gave up without a fight. All four were currently awaiting assessment by the Vice-Admiralty Court and Sir Alexander Croke, the chief justice, was almost certain to rule in his favour. And even if not, King would still be content as past conquests meant he should never want for money again.

And, probably as a result, neither did he desire action as such. It was more than ten years since the turn of the century had raised hopes for a permanent peace yet, apart from the briefest of pauses, war with France continued. The conflict had already cost the loss of his left arm and, combined with their passage out that proved eventful enough to sate the appetite of any firebrand, King felt he had breathed enough burnt powder. In three, maybe four, years *Tenacious* would require a major refit which may well mean her recall and, when that time came, he had the notion to call it a day. But until then he was content to enjoy the present, walk his quarterdeck and appreciate the fine weather.

He glanced about and considered the ship as she made gentle progress under topsails and fore'. Hardly a line had been touched since sunrise and the watch on deck were sheltering from the sun while they yarned away their trick. Despite having been in commission for some while, *Tenacious* required no substantial work and her people, now well up to scratch in every department, maintained her to perfection. She was a frigate of the fifth rate carrying eighteen-pound long guns as her main battery with thirty-two-pounder carronades to back them up and, though these might not have been used in anger for some while, regular exercise ensured they were always ready for action. Her masts, the tallest of which towered almost two hundred feet into the sky, were solid and proven, her hull was sound and all running and standing rigging well up to scratch. And he was just as certain of his officers; Croft, his premier, had served in the same capacity aboard two other ships under King's command and a more recent, but essential, spell as second officer had only honed his skills further. Lieutenants Cooper and Summers were also well known to him and even a few of the crew had followed from other vessels. In which case it hardly mattered that the current station was proving less than demanding for, if he were honest, King appreciated the rest and sensed he was not alone in doing so.

"Signal from *Sparrow*." Brotherton's announcement brought him back to the present and he turned as the midshipman continued. "Sail in sight, east-nor'-east and heading westerly."

Sparrow was a good two miles off their starboard bow; any sighting would remain invisible for some while, even from *Tenacious'* taller mastheads. King was about to ask the obvious question when Brotherton spoke again.

"There's more, sir," he said, raising his glass and peering at the brig for a moment. "Sighting is a merchant and making good speed."

With the East Coast of America almost in sight, any vessel coming to the end of an Atlantic crossing may well pile on sail, but still King could not afford to relax. What Leyton in *Sparrow* had spotted was probably a fast trader carrying nothing more incriminating than soft fruit, although there was another perishable cargo that could not be ruled out.

4

"Make to *Sparrow*, 'investigate with all despatch'."

Brotherton touched his hat before turning to his team and calling out a series of numbers. King was pleased to note the entire conversation with the brig had been carried out without need of the code book; the lad had turned into a highly competent signal's officer.

"A slaver do you think?" Croft asked, stepping closer. King pursed his lips.

"I shouldn't care to say, though any merchant approaching the coast so is likely to warrant investigation."

"And Captain Leyton definitely seems keen to investigate." The first lieutenant nodded towards the distant brig. "But then he was never one to hold back..."

King followed his gaze and suppressed a smile. Croft was right, Brotherton's message could hardly have been received yet *Sparrow* was already showing more canvas. In no time the extra sail had been set and she was running out her studding booms. King remembered her captain as the antiquated, slightly prissy officer he had inherited as premier when first taking command of *Tenacious*; Leyton's promotion to commander and subsequent appointment as captain of the brig had undoubtedly brought about a change. Now there was fervour in his eyes and his saucy little craft was handled with all the verve and enthusiasm of a youngster.

He glanced across and noticed Croft was also watching with what might have been envy. Much the same could be said about him, King silently decided. Croft and Leyton were both advanced in age yet dedicated and competent sea officers; after seeing the senior man receive promotion and his own command, Croft may now be hoping for the same himself.

"I think we might follow *Sparrow*'s example," King announced and the elderly officer almost sprang to attention before touching his hat and stepping away to let loose with a stream of bellowed orders. On Leyton's appointment it had been possible to re-establish Croft as his first officer; the man had slipped smoothly into his accustomed role and truly was an exemplary second in command. As far as King had been aware, that was the extent of his ambitions although now he was less certain. Just as in Leyton, a spark had definitely been fanned and it would not surprise him greatly if the idea of advancement were hovering somewhere in the elderly officer's mind. Croft continued to perform his duties adequately enough but there had been times when the older man's thoughts were inclined to

5

wander. He may well be thinking of other matters and possibly considering applying for command himself, for there had definitely been something more in that expression.

* * *

"Well, that's us all soundly roused," Lovemore stated with a degree of irony as he flexed his shoulders and stretched.

"I were awake already." Knightly, another seaman, slumped down in the lee of the weather bulwark. "And can do without breaking a caulk to set a pile of canvas that'll only need taking in afore we knows it."

"Dunno why the watch on deck couldn'a handled it." McKenzie, a Scotsman, settled himself a little more gracefully. "Weren't as if there were any rush."

"That's not what old Tommo thinks." Lovemore nodded aft to the quarterdeck.

"'Sides, this lot will be stayin' a while yet," Stokes, their mess captain, added. Of them all he was the last to remain standing and continued to inspect the foremast towering overhead. Partly due to their efforts it now held both topgallant and royal and he seemed proud of the fact. Certainly the fresh canvas was set to perfection and *Tenacious'* speed had already increased perceivably on account of it.

"Think you so, Stokie?" Lovemore leant back against a gun carriage. Like the rest of his watch, he was officially off duty and had been pleasantly dozing below when they were called.

"At least till *Sparra* fetches that slaver," Stokes grunted.

"That what you reckon her to be?" Groom asked while the others perked up visibly at the prediction.

"Stands to reason." The senior man finally looked away and joined them between the cannon. He was older and more experienced than the rest of his mess and an able seaman, which were reasons enough to have been elected their head. "Vessel steering west at speed, an' all on her lonesome; she'll be carrying live cargo for sure."

"No way you can tell that," said Knightly. "She ain't nothing more'n a smudge."

"Maybe not, but you see if I ain't right."

"So you don't think it's worth going below?" Longdon checked.

Knightly shook his head. "Wouldn't be anyway. Up Spirits'll be piped presently and then we all gets to eat."

6

"Providin' we's allowed." Lovemore again. "If what Stokie says is straight we might be in action afore then."

"Nah, we won't be in no action," the mess captain sighed. "Best we'll get is a view of the proceedin's. It'll all be down to *Sparra* but that won't mean old Tommy King'll want to miss out."

"Aye, he'll get as close as he can," Lovemore agreed. "Captain's never been known to give up on a fight, even if he can't take part."

"You think Leyton will catch 'em?"

"Doubt it." Stokes was disappointingly certain. "Well set-up slaver'll show a clean pair of heels to his old tub any day of the week. Mind, I don't blame 'im for tryin', nor Tommo for wantin' to get in close."

"Ebony trade's a terrible thing," McKenzie stated sadly.

"No more terrible than a good deal else." Knightly scratched at his chin.

"Maybe not," Lovemore agreed. "But if she *is* a slaver, and if Leyton *can* catch her, there'll be a regular payout, make no mistake. An' I'd say that's worth stayin' on deck for."

* * *

Midshipman Corbrite clambered up onto the brig's main crosstrees and reached for the support of the topgallant mast. The duty lookout was sharing his scant platform and made space although both knew the lad would not be staying long. Commander Leyton, *Sparrow*'s captain, was as demanding as they came; when the sighting failed to heave to he had sent Corbrite up for a detailed report and would only be satisfied when the boy was almost standing on the mast cap.

With a nod to the seaman he adjusted the glass slung about his shoulder and took a firmer hold of the upper mast. Topgallants were set but fortunately not the royals – even in his enthusiasm, Commander Leyton must have realised the extra canvas would have served little purpose while additional pressure from above might even have slowed them. Corbrite shinned easily up the smooth pine before reaching for the topgallant yard and, with a fifteen year old's contempt for danger, settled himself on the spar, one leg comfortably either side of the narrow mast in the way he had been taught.

Corbrite's instructor had been an able seaman informally appointed as his Sea Daddy when he joined his first ship, a liner in the Mediterranean Fleet. Although elderly by nautical standards and as rough and crusty as any shellback, Seth Scott also proved to be remarkably patient, and the day he chose to desert was one of the bleakest in the lad's young life. But then Corbrite had always expected him to go. Old Seth had been a seaman first and a man-of-war's hand second; he never truly settled to life aboard a fighting sail and probably stayed longer due to his role as mentor. He had taught him well however and, whenever Corbrite remembered certain points, like the correct way to flake a line, or clean kit, or secure himself for lookout duty, it was as if he were still alongside.

His perch was higher than all the ship's canvas so gave him his first full view of the surroundings since leaving the main top. And even though Commander Leyton would probably be fuming below, the lad allowed himself a moment to take everything in.

The sun was almost overhead and lit miles of spangled ocean that might stretch to infinity. And there was *Tenacious*, following in their wake. For a moment Corbrite studied her with more than a hint of envy; she was a fine ship and one he would have been proud to serve aboard, although almost any frigate would be an improvement on his current berth.

When Corbrite first volunteered for *Sparrow* the brig had seemed a splendid proposition; bound for the North American Station with a young and dashing officer in command, she appeared certain to prove his gateway to adventure and promotion. However, her commander had been made post on their arrival at Halifax and his replacement turned out to be of a very different cut.

Leyton was indisputably elderly for the position although, after having learned so much from Seth, Corbrite could hardly see that as a defect. But rather than educate and inspire, his new captain preferred to suppress initiative while holding some decidedly old-fashioned views on how young midshipmen should behave. And there was something more, something subtle yet immediately obvious even to one in his teens; Leyton had a desire to impress that was boarding on the unhealthy.

The trait manifested itself in a number of ways, from constantly carping and criticising his officers, to boasting openly about his own abilities and what he might achieve. It was hardly a weakness and may be expected in a certain type of younger commander although considering his years – the pot belly and greying hair – Leyton simply appeared ridiculous.

Corbrite looked again at *Tenacious*; a proper warship with all the dash of her type. More than that, she had distinguished herself in battle and, despite a captain almost pathologically keen for glory, that was more than *Sparrow* had ever done. Which was another point; Captain King was known to be an excellent commander, one who truly looked after his men and a very different proposition to the puffed-up fool who was a secret, yet constant, source of ridicule in the midshipmen's berth.

But Leyton would be wanting a report before long, Corbrite reminded himself, and he turned his attention further forward. There was the sighting sure enough, and she lay a good deal closer than he expected; in the time taken to climb the mast *Sparrow* had closed considerably. He peered across the sparkling waters, hand flat above his eyes to combat the glare in the way Seth had taught him. She must be less than three miles off their starboard bow and was actually similar in size to *Sparrow*, although her hull appeared sleeker. Reaching back he collected his glass and, with one arm locked about the topgallant mast in the approved manner, focused the instrument.

"What do you see there?" It was Leyton's voice and Corbrite jumped slightly, despite the man being many feet below.

"Two-masted, sir; I'd say she were a topsail schooner." Corbrite's words came slowly as he examined the vessel even though there was little worthy of report. He could see pieces of what might be deck cargo scattered about her waist and three light cannon were mounted to either side. She flew no ensign, or any flag that Corbrite could make out, but there was nothing surprising in that; *Sparrow* was far enough off and could be treated with the disdain most fast merchants hold for warships. In fact the only thing that truly stood out was her rig.

She lay on a broad reach and both her main and foresail were set lower than usual while the jib boom might be slightly longer. Even after having presumably completed an Atlantic crossing, her tophamper appeared in good order and she was making a fair speed. As he continued to watch, the craft began crossing in front of the lumbering *Sparrow* and it was clear she easily had the measure of her.

"And is she a slaver?"

Corbrite paused and blinked; he really could not say. There was certainly nothing to indicate the fact; what should he be looking for?

"She's crossing our hawse and showing no sign of slowing," the lad replied hopefully, before closing his mind to the stream of abuse that erupted from below. He glanced down to the duty lookout still standing on the crosstrees and gained reassurance from the man's wink and knowing grin. Then a shout came from Hudson, the sailing master, and the entire vessel began to heave alarmingly.

Leyton must have ordered the brig to wear; a manoeuvre Corbrite would have appreciated notice of, despite his perch being relatively secure. He clung a little tighter as the yard beneath him was hauled round and waited while *Sparrow*'s stern passed through the wind. And once they were on the opposite tack the position became very different. The sighting now lay off the brig's starboard beam and their relative speed was more apparent; the merchant was visibly overhauling them and, even though Leyton was steering to intercept, would soon be long gone.

But not beyond the range of *Sparrow*'s cannon, or so his captain appeared to think. On first sighting the vessel Leyton had released two blank charges, partly to emphasise his signals and partly to show he meant business, but now it appeared something more substantial was being planned. Even from his great height Corbrite could hear the squeal of slides as the brig's carronades were brought into play. Then, following a curt command, her entire starboard broadside was released in a stuttering roar. The smoke blew to leeward and momentarily hid the sighting from Corbrite's view but all was clear in time for him to register the line of heavy splashes. And every one was short, embarrassingly so; the furthest could barely have reached halfway between the two vessels. If Commander Leyton had wanted to impress the other captain he must surely have failed.

Certainly there was no change aboard the schooner; she held her course and continued as if *Sparrow* had not spoken, or even ceased to exist, leaving her totally alone on the ocean. Corbrite scratched at his chin; it would be interesting to see Captain Leyton's reaction.

And when it came the lad was once more taken by surprise as *Sparrow* was thrown into another sudden change of course, this time back to the starboard tack. Unprepared, Corbrite had to release his glass to seek a firmer grip on the mast. The instrument swung wildly from its lanyard as he steadied himself. Then, with a series of groans, the yard beneath him was hauled back and Corbrite raised his eyes to heaven.

The old fool was at it again, steering for the merchant's stern in the hope he might rake it with his larboard battery. Corbrite knew it was a move doomed to fail and even from the deck it must be clear the schooner would be well out of range by the time she came within the carronades' ark. But as the brig slowly settled to her new heading and the clatter of their guns being readied drifted up, Corbrite supposed such nonsense was what he had come to expect. Exactly why Leyton should be so desperate for action was a mystery; most men of his age would be content to sit by the fire yet he seemed determined to behave like a child with a rabbit gun. And such qualities in an elderly captain were hardly reassuring.

* * *

"If you ask me, *Sparrow*'s making an utter fool of herself!" Croft's remark was made softly and to him alone, while the first lieutenant had criticised a vessel and not her captain, although King still felt vaguely uncomfortable. He could not argue with the sentiment, however; to release a broadside at any merchant was questionable practice and especially so when the craft in question could be a slaver. *Tenacious* was still some way off so King had little way of knowing how near Leyton's shot had fallen but there was no doubt he would have to speak with the fellow when next they met.

"And now she is wearing once more, why I do believe she's trying for her stern!"

"In which case she will fail," King stated gently. Even from such a distance it was clear the fleeing merchant would be well beyond *Sparrow*'s broadside by the time she closed. King glanced at his first officer; he could see frustration mingled with anger written large across the older man's face and felt a wave of sympathy. The similarities between Lieutenant Croft and Commander Leyton were indeed great, both must be considered elderly for their posts and both were definitely products of the 'old navy', with ideals and principles that rightly belonged in the last century. And rather than forming a bond between the two there was resentment, certainly on the junior man's part. For Leyton had undoubtedly succeeded; not only was he superior in rank, he had attained the right to be addressed as captain, with a warship of his own to do with as he wished. But then Leyton was also relatively new to the post and entitled to a few mistakes; King could well remember his first command and the responsibility of being in charge, not only of the vessel but the eighty or so souls it contained. In Leyton's case the change had awoken a belligerent nature common in younger men although strange in one of later years. Rather than the solid officer who had once served as his first lieutenant, he had become a true firebrand and, if the rumours were correct, was equally harsh when dealing with his officers. But King did not expect the condition to last; in time he should see sense, settle down and realise more could be achieved with less effort and greater foresight. Besides, there were merchant captains aplenty who would have baulked at being fired upon by a warship, whatever the range. If the sighting had meekly spilled her wind, Leyton would have been vindicated leaving Croft with no cause to comment.

"Beggin' your pardon, sir, Stokes here thinks he knows the vessel."

King turned; it was Summers, their third lieutenant, and with him was the red-haired mess captain King had appointed able seaman some while before.

"She's *Sapphire,* your honour." The man knuckled his forehead. "It's 'er main what gives 'er away. It's taller than most, yet she's carrying a standard stays'l an' it makes her look slightly off balance. Often see 'er around Halifax and my mess supped with her people last liberty."

"Slaver is she?" King asked and Stokes bit his lip.

"That I wouldn't know your honour. They were a cagey bunch though warm enough with the chink. I'd think it possible."

"Very good, Stokes, and thank you."

The man saluted again then turned away while King considered the vessel once more. Stokes was right, the rig was mildly off-kilter and, now it had been pointed out to him, he remembered seeing the craft himself.

"If that is *Sapphire,* she's British," Croft said, drawing closer. "Owned by a fellow called Fitch; an important man in Halifax, or so I hears."

"The name's familiar," King mused.

"He has several small traders and does extremely well from them, or so they say. Doubt he'll take kindly to Captain Leyton firing on one of his vessels."

"One of his vessels that failed to heave to when requested," King reminded crisply and Croft had the grace to accept this. "Do you know his trade?"

"General shipping I believe, sir. I understand in the current climate it is better not to specialise."

King nodded, they were difficult times indeed and fortunes could be made, or lost, almost overnight. Yet a canny ship owner could still turn a pretty penny without venturing into the slave trade. It was possible *Sapphire* was carrying nothing more illicit than a little contraband but, whatever the case, they had no chance of catching her now.

"Land ho, land off the larboard bow!"

The call came from the main masthead and was enough to settle matters for good as far as King was concerned. They must be approaching a headland and would soon be visible from shore. American territorial waters would not start for several miles but that was as close as he wished to venture.

"Very well, recall *Sparrow*," he grunted to Brotherton before turning and catching the sailing master's eye. "And you may strike the extra canvas, Mr Manton; tops'ls and forecourse will do nicely, thank you."

"Permission to pipe Up Spirits, sir?" Croft enquired.

"Do that Mr Croft, then see the hands fed."

King was conscious of a mild anticlimax; nothing had been achieved apart from a little excitement to break up the forenoon watch. Whoever commanded the sighting was made of strong stuff and had stood up to the bluster of a pair of King's ships with admirable fortitude. His vessel was still heading determinedly for the American coast and apparently taking Captain Leyton's hopes with her. The thought reminded him of an earlier resolution and one that was better faced now than later.

"*Sparrow*'s acknowledging, sir."

"Very good," King nodded. "Signal for her captain to join me at his convenience."

Chapter Two

Actually, Leyton accepted King's reprimand remarkably well. It might have helped that the interview took place in the relative privacy of *Tenacious*' great cabin; a ship he knew well and had once served aboard as King's first lieutenant. And even if not, a senior post captain was vastly superior to any newly appointed commander and later that afternoon the older man readily acknowledged this.

"I have come to realise the autonomy of command can be a dangerous thing," he admitted candidly, "and you will understand the position has come to me late in life."

"I do indeed." King sat back in his chair and regarded the officer. Superficially Leyton seemed little different: he remained the same precise, slightly sour individual King had first met when taking over the frigate from its previous, incompetent, captain. The hair was just as grey and perhaps a few more creases showed the passing of time but these were merely physical indications. Of far more importance was the life that now seemed to erupt from within, the only current indication of which being a faint sparkle to the eyes. However, the change had been exhibited in other ways, his eagerness for all things connected with his command for one. King had never seen a vessel manned so quickly, nor with such enthusiasm. And the entire commissioning process had been achieved with equal speed.

Of course fast did not necessarily mean better; there had been several occasions in their current voyage when *Sparrow*'s captain had been shown to be at fault, and, usually, haste was at the heart of it. But then a degree of recklessness was almost encouraged in those commanding minor vessels: without taking a few chances they would be unlikely to get the best from their charges. And no one who knew him could doubt that promotion had made a fundamental change to Leyton himself. The cautious second officer who had made a career out of protecting less able captains had been replaced by a far bolder spirit and, were it not for the obvious indications of time, King felt he might have been dealing with a much younger man.

"Being a captain is more than simply giving orders," he continued. "Leaders can only function when they have those willing to follow and seeking action at every opportunity is not the best way to achieve this."

"I understand," the older man said. "At least I believe I am starting to."

"Then we will say no more about it."

"And I shall be more careful of who I fires upon," Leyton agreed with the hint of a smile. "Though to see Fitch's vessel make off so was frustrating in the extreme..."

"Fitch? Do I take it you know the fellow?"

"Only by sight." Leyton reached for the cup before him. "After my promotion I spent a goodly time on the beach in Halifax. I took rooms at the George, a lodging house near the dockyard. Fitch and his cronies used the dining rooms quite regularly and it was clear they were in the ebony trade."

"You mean they are slavers?"

"Oh yes. He and his associates have four vessels and most are used for general carrying, only one at any time being sent to sail the middle passage." The man took a sip then replaced the cup. "Such a rotation, and some degree of sleight of hand, is enough to fool any authorities who care to check, though I gather many are happy to be deceived and often emerge the richer for it."

"I see." King was not surprised. Despite the provisions made for Black Loyalists at the end of the American War, Halifax and its surrounding provinces remained awash with slaves as well as indentured servants; a status broadly similar. It was almost four years since both the American Senate and his own parliament had ruled against further importation, yet an industry remained that ensured a regular supply of unpaid labour. But then for as long as one man could legally keep another as his property, money was to be made by providing fresh stock and, whatever the law may decree, there would be those prepared to break it, if the rewards were sufficient. "It is the pity we cannot do more to stop his exploits," he sighed, "though chance our encounter today will have caused a degree of concern."

"I would that you were right, but must doubt it. The only thing that can affect such a man is the outright loss of his ship, and we were unable to achieve that." The elderly commander pursed his lips before continuing. "When next we sight *Sapphire* she is likely to be in Halifax and once more carrying out legitimate trade right under our noses."

"Maybe, though I fail to see what else can be done."

"Why, we could take her now!" Leyton replied as if it were the simplest thing in the world.

King considered him for a moment. "Have we not been talking about judging the correct time for action, William?" he asked. "Chances are by nightfall *Sapphire,* and whatever she carries, will be snug in some harbour many miles from here."

"Forgive me, sir, that might not be the case. Oh, I am not saying she will still be asea; the very reverse. In fact I think I know exactly where she can be found, and it is remarkably close by."

"Indeed?"

"You may remember, it is not my first time on this station," Leyton continued. "On the last occasion there was a large slaving post about three miles up the coast from Doboy Sound. It were legitimate then, of course, though I would chance the place remains and little will have altered as far as its business is concerned."

The man was talking foolishly, of course, yet King found himself strangely drawn in. "So what do you propose?" he asked, despite himself.

"We cut her out," Leyton replied.

"As simple as that? No consideration to the offence we might cause the American government?"

"*Sapphire* is British, as will be a large proportion of her crew. And it is they that are breaking American law; we will merely be addressing the problem."

"Though she lies in American waters," King reminded.

"I am not advocating sailing either of our ships in; from what I remember *Sparrow* would find a safe passage, especially as the moon is full and the tide should be at its highest, but frankly she would be of little use. It must be small boats, cutters probably, considering the long pull necessary."

"Long pull?"

"Yes, sir. At the moment the Jonathans may not be aware we are even close by; only *Sapphire*'s crew know, and those they choose to tell. And however much their undertakings are ignored, they are unlikely to inform those in authority."

King considered this and Leyton took advantage of the pause to continue.

"Our approach must be timed to arrive as near to midnight as possible; the ebb starts about then and should see her out, even if we lack a true breeze. As I said, the moon will be full and high but we cannot help that, though any wind should stem from the south-east and will aid us further."

King went to comment but Leyton had more to say.

"We enter as silently as possible under sweeps, board and carry her; with luck we should be rendezvousing with *Sparrow* and *Tenacious* long before dawn."

"You've been making plans, William," King smiled.

"I have," Leyton admitted. "And do take what you say about not seeking action unnecessarily." He sat back. "Yet when something is handed to you, on a plate as it were, it would be foolish to refuse."

King pondered a moment longer. It was clear a great deal of thought had gone into the proposal and, though to admit as much went against his instincts, it did appear sound.

"What of the slaves?" he asked. "If she is carrying live cargo, would they be aboard?"

"There were pens aplenty in the compound, and they might already have been transferred but more likely that will be delayed until daylight. Or they could be being shipped to another station," Leyton added as the thought occurred. "It is very possible where *Sapphire* currently lies was not her chosen destination. She had just completed a crossing after all and when we gave chase logic would have made her run for the nearest cover. But in any case, the presence of human cargo should make no difference."

"And what if she is not a slaver?" King's tone now held more significance. "What if she carries nothing incriminating and simply did not care to be searched by the Royal Navy?"

"Then we will have made a mistake, although there should be no diplomatic incident," Leyton's reply was remarkably swift. "As we have agreed, she is an English ship, Fitch will have to take it up with our government. But I don't think that to be the case, sir. I think her to be a Guineaman. I think she was steering for that slaving station, which was why she seemed unwilling to make too far to the north, despite the risk of *Sparrow*'s broadside. And I think there will be slaves aboard, which we should be able to liberate. Indeed, I believe it to be our duty."

"You put a strong case," King conceded, "I should like to give the matter further thought."

"Of course, sir, though you will appreciate that time is not our ally. If I may say, we should act tonight; delaying longer will only lead to complications."

"Tonight? Are you serious?"

"I am indeed and would suggest three cutters; *Sparrow*'s is only marginally smaller than both of your own. And I should like at least one lieutenant in support."

"You shall have no such thing," King almost snapped. "You are a commander and have been appointed captain of one of His Majesty's warships. *If* I decide we should go it will be a lieutenant that leads, and I shall appoint him."

"But I know the area, sir!"

"You *knew* the area – some time in the past," King pointed out. "And I'd be bound we've plenty aboard with similar experience, chances are strong there'll be some just as acquainted. Besides, with a full moon and the skies as clear as they have been, an anchored vessel should stand out well enough." He sighed. "I told you, William, take a step back; you're now the captain of a warship: perchance you should behave like one."

Leyton was temporarily stunned. His mouth opened, then closed, and a flush appeared on both cheeks. And then his face relaxed as if in resignation and the elderly officer smiled.

"Very well, sir," he said. "I believe I understand."

* * *

"It's volunteers they want, or so I hears," Groom remarked when the mess gathered for their evening meal. "You never truly know if they means it."

"Aye," Hodges agreed. "Them what choose not to go'll likely miss out next shore leave."

The rest of the table considered these wise words as they bit and gummed their way through their supper. It was Tuesday, a banyan day, so the second time they had mainly dined on cheese, pickled cabbage, onions and slabs of flinty, over-baked biscuit: hard tack that was regularly, and unfairly, referred to as bread.

"This is a straight ship, mind," Stokes grunted from his position of authority. "If the cap'n says volunteers, that's what 'e means."

"Aye," Groom conceded after considering this. "He ain't the type to press no one into doing nowt they don't care for."

"Well 'e pressed me, sure as eggs is eggs!" Knightly said amid a flurry of crumbs.

"Now that's where you're wrong, see," Bovey, who fancied himself as a sea lawyer, objected. "You was sent here from the rondy; Captain didn't 'ave nothing to do with it."

"I were still pressed though, an' me an American!"

"Stow it, Knightly." Stokes spoke with authority. "We all know the story or should do – we heard it enough times."

"Still the truth."

"You was born in Manchester," Groom, a Yorkshireman, reminded him with a hint of disdain.

"An' took the country as me own in the year seven – nigh on four years back! Had papers to prove it an' all, though they're long gone."

"Papers yer doubtless bought in a Portsmouth chop house," McKenzie supposed to a chorus of sniggering.

"They was legal, fair an' square," Knightly declared. "I shouldn't be aboard this barge."

"You could say the same for most of us," Groom tapped his biscuit against the table, "But would be wastin' y'r breath."

"'Sides, if you're so dead against, why d'ya agree to sign?" Bovey again. "They might haul you in but no one can force a man to make his mark."

"Is that right, Bove?" Johnno, the mess boy, asked.

"I do happen to know something of the law," the seaman confirmed primly. "States it quite clearly so it does; a pressed man can go on refusin' to sign, and they still got to see him fed."

"And he 'as to work, just won't get paid," Stokes added. "An' there'll be no prize money neither, nor care from the doctor."

"An' I ain't workin' for nothin'," Knightly declared.

"We're all due a penny or two shortly," said Lovemore. "Soon as the courts decide there'll be a payout from them schooners."

"An' the privateer – don't forget the privateer," Longdon prompted.

"Mr Hanson said it were comin'," Johnno agreed.

"So's Christmas," said Groom. "An' it'll probably be here first."

"Well to my mind the only one who 'as a right to complain is Nearhood," Lovemore declared. "An' he ain't sayin' nothin'."

"Aye, an' I hear he's put 'is name down for the party." Stokes considered the seaman. "Ain't that right, Yank?"

19

All eyes turned to the slight man in a checked shirt who sat at the far end of the table.

"Thought ah'd string along." The seaman spoke quietly before returning to the apple he had been eating.

"Know the place do you?" Stokes enquired but Nearhood shook his head.

"Ah'm from Virginia; never been further south than Franklin, 'cept on the water."

"So you won't be able to point out the cat houses." Bovey gave a look of disappointment.

"It's something I never understood," Stokes admitted. "If you really is a Yank, what you doin' aboard a British ship?"

"Aye," Groom nodded. "Wouldn't you be better off in your own navy?"

"Forty dollars a month, or so I hears," Bovey added to mutual agreement."

"And two months on the capstan head, soon as you sign," Knightly sighed wistfully.

"An' there's no pressin'." Bovey again. "Me brother's in a frigate further south. Seems there ain't no turning over neither. When your ship pays off you're a free man and able to choose your next berth."

"So why's you with us, Nearhood?" Stokes persisted.

"Not that we're objecting, mind," Longdon added in case they'd caused offence.

The American looked up and shrugged. "Ah don't rightly know, an' if I'm honest neither do I care." He placed the core of his apple down and regarded his colleagues. "You see, when you've spent more time at sea than on land countries don't seem to matter much anymore."

"He's right," Hodges declared. "I ain't seen England in years, yet the sea's with me every day and I know which I calls home."

"You got it," Nearhood acknowledged with a faint smile. "So when they picked me up and told me I'd be servin' aboard a limy battlewagon, I thought ah'd may as well give it a try."

"And how do you find it?" Stokes asked.

Nearhood shrugged again. "Ah've known worse berths," he supposed, "an' worse shipmates if it comes to it."

The unexpected compliment silenced them all for a moment and caused several to mutter depreciatingly.

"Mind, I were mainly sailing in the whalers afore," the American continued. "An' you got to go a long way to find folk what smell worse than them."

* * *

There were no marines present, it was something Captain King had been definite about at that evening's briefing and all involved in the cutting out expedition were in complete agreement. Certainly Taylor approved of the arrangement. After serving aboard *Tenacious* as a junior lieutenant he had applied for transfer and followed Commander Leyton to *Sparrow* as the brig's first officer. The move had been made in the interest of self-improvement, as more first lieutenants are promoted than third, although the young man was now uncertain if it had been a good one. But at least it had guaranteed a part in the present mission and given him command of the brig's cutter. And he was definitely happier commanding trained seamen who could pull at an oar or set canvas and still swing a cutlass than a band of stiff-booted sea soldiers.

They had put out over an hour before and been rowing steadily since. Were he to glance behind, the dim shapes of the two British warships would probably be indistinguishable from the distant horizon, although all Taylor's attention was set on the shoreline that drew steadily closer with every breath. He had limited experience of small boat work and, though only third in command of the expedition, found himself envying the midshipman by his side. Corbrite was a good deal younger and even less practised but all the lad need do was follow; it would be up to him as a lieutenant to take the lead.

The entire force was made up of three boats with the two larger coming from *Tenacious*. Between them they held over sixty officers and men with Lieutenant Cooper in overall charge. Taylor had transferred before Cooper arrived and barely knew the officer but all spoke highly of him. He was far more acquainted with Summers, leading the frigate's second cutter. Each lieutenant was supported by a midshipman and everyone, down to the lowest seaman, knew their objective, even if all were equally vague as to how it would be achieved.

For no one could be sure what they would find. A general request had revealed several hands who knew of the station and most were with them now. From the rough chart that had been drawn the approach should not be complicated. With the tide almost fully risen there were few areas where boats might ground and it seemed likely that the slaver – if this was what she turned out to be – would either be moored against the main quay or at anchor a little deeper in the natural harbour. But what might be expected in the way of defences remained a mystery. No one had visited the station after the Non Importation Act came into force; since then anything might have happened. Batteries could have been built and a permanent watch might be in place, or the area may remain unchanged, it all depended on the local authorities and how much they intended to enforce, or ignore, the law.

The only aspect that could be guaranteed was that the British force would be noticed. Each cutter was approaching separately and, despite the breeze, all were under oars alone. Every man wore dull clothes and had blackened faces and not even dark lanterns had been permitted. Yet, as they crept steadily across the moon-kissed waters, Taylor guessed the three ships' boats must be standing out like rooks in the snow.

Attacking under such a bright moon had its advantages of course; details of the bay were steadily becoming more distinct. To the north Taylor could see the outline of a headland, while a lower body of land was also apparent on his left. And the lights glimmering directly ahead were probably from the small collection of buildings some had remembered while a faint outline of a vessel's topmasts could be made out against the starlit sky. That this was the *Sapphire* could only be assumed of course, but the sight had been enough for Cooper to set it as their aiming mark when they changed hands at the oars.

And now, as the small flotilla drew steadily closer, it seemed they would soon discover if their approach truly had been noticed. The distance between them and their assumed quarry was barely a mile, left alone the boats should cover that in minutes but, were there to be cannon fire from either ship or shore, it was a journey they might never complete. A solid hit from even light artillery should account for any light cutter and, with each fully loaded, there would be little prospect of collecting survivors.

"That's her, sure enough."

It was Corbrite. The youngster was pointing forward excitedly and though he spoke in the lowest of whispers, Taylor had to restrain himself from thrusting a hand over the lad's mouth.

"Think you so?" he asked, equally softly, and received a nod in reply that was all too visible in the stark light.

"The rig's the same," Corbrite assured, "and I think I can scent slaves."

Taylor sniffed; there was perhaps a slight taint to the air, but that might be explained if this were an active slaving station.

He glanced forward; Summers, in one of the larger cutters, was half a cable off their larboard bow with Cooper roughly the same distance to starboard. And Corbrite was right, that must surely be *Sapphire* dead ahead; her topmasts were now quite distinct and he even fancied he could see a chink of light from the stern quarters.

Corbrite eased the rudder round to follow as Cooper's boat began to lead them in. A muttered command to Jarvis, pulling stroke, increased their pace until the cutter was positively racing through the water. Taylor felt the tension increase; there was no sign of activity from the moored schooner or those on shore and the longer that continued the better. Already they could only be a few hundred yards off the vessel's hull. It was still time for an effective barrage to be mounted although they must have reached the stage when no more than two rounds from any weapon could be expected. And as the boat continued to speed forward his feelings of hope began to mount. Perhaps this would go smoothly; they would arrive undetected, carry the schooner in near silence and bring her out without a man being lost. Within an hour they could be quitting this hated coast and within two taking a congratulatory glass of wine together. He glanced at Corbrite and the lad grinned back, white teeth grotesque against his blackened face. And then the first cannon spoke.

* * *

Cooper, in one of the leading boats, had been considering their target and so caught the flash of gun fire full in his face. It came from one of three weapons mounted on the schooner and he instinctively turned away, blinded by the sudden glare. A dull whirring sound followed though too far off to cause alarm.

"Not even close," Brotherton, at the helm, chuckled and as his vision slowly returned, Cooper noticed those at the oars were grinning also.

"Step it up there!" he ordered as two more equally ill-aimed shots were released. Lovemore, pulling stroke, dutifully increased their pace until the rowers were positively panting with exertion while their passengers – those who had taken the first trick at the sweeps – began fingering the blades of their cutlasses in anticipation.

And then they had only a few yards to cover. Details of their objective were becoming clearer, aided in no small way by a series of lights that had appeared on her deck along with the stench that told them it was indeed a slaver. Unseen hands must be rushing to reload her cannon, Cooper could hear groans from men and materiel as the weapons were hauled into position then a muffled shout told him it was time to look away once more.

Again the barrage roared out, louder this time and the shots passed considerably closer. Unasked, Lovemore increased the cutter's pace still further until spray was being picked up by the breeze and soaking all aboard. Then they were in the shadow of *Sapphire*'s hull and Cooper began looking for the best place to board as Brotherton brought the boat around in a wide sweep. Splashes rose up as they made their approach – those aboard the schooner must be tossing cold shot over the side – while a faint popping told them they were under pistol fire. But the cutter was very near now and everyone knew they would board whatever.

"Take her in," Cooper ordered and Brotherton swung the rudder back and they prepared to rub alongside. The slaver's freeboard was mercifully low, it would be relatively easy to clamber onto her deck and meet whatever force waited to resist them. And the other boats would be arriving soon. Cooper snatched a look back; yes, Summers in the second cutter, was closing fast, although he could see nothing of Taylor. Then a shout from Brotherton drew his attention and he finally picked out *Sparrow*'s boat.

But this was no trim ship's cutter, more a collection of flotsam drifting half a cable or so off on the brightly lit waters. And there were men amid the wreckage.

Few seamen can swim and it seemed Taylor's lot were no exception. For a stunned second all in the cutter watched as their comrades scrabbled and clawed for a purchase while taking in faint sounds of desperation as the relentless seas closed over them. It was enough to chill the heart though they could do nothing to assist and, with an effort that was more than physical, Cooper looked away. Then a crack, followed by a grinding noise brought all back to reality. They had arrived, the cutter was being secured forward and suddenly all were straining to be the first to board.

"Stand aside, there!"

The tangle of men separated and Cooper was finally able to touch the enemy vessel. Then, as a crowd, they began clambering up, using whales and ports as ledges as they reached for the top rail and finally threw themselves over the schooner's bulwarks.

Cooper staggered slightly on reaching the deck and groped for the cutlass swinging from his wrist. Those attending the slaver's cannon drew back at the sudden onslaught and gathered with others of their kind at the break of the forecastle. Brotherton was next to him and more blackened faces were arriving all the time, but the crowd forming forward was larger – far larger than anyone had anticipated – and more were appearing from below. He cursed silently, their opponents must have been expecting an attack and had supplemented the crew accordingly. More than that; the clean-faced men before them were well built, well armed and clearly meant business.

"We're several short," Brotherton exclaimed, and Cooper looked to his own group. The lad was right; there were several less than there should have been with no sign of more arriving. And then he caught sight of their cutter and realised with a gasp that, rather than being safely secured alongside, it was heading away from the slaver. Some of the sentimental fools must have set off in an effort to save Taylor's lot. He bit his lip then turned back and braced himself, for the enemy were clearly ready to fight.

Chapter Three

The shot that struck *Sparrow*'s cutter had been almost insignificant by naval standards and probably no more than four pounds in weight. But it landed square on the small boat's prow, destroying the stempost and neatly separating those strakes that formed the bows. And as the craft was travelling at speed the seas rushed in, filling her almost at once and dragging the hull under even as those nearer the stern completed their stroke.

Summers had seen the whole thing. One moment the three cutters were part of a concerted attack and the next Taylor's craft had been turned to driftwood. Someone let out a gentle groan and Hanson, at the helm, looked to him for instructions.

"Carry on," Summers ordered, his voice unintentionally harsh.

"But those men?" the midshipman protested.

"We can do nothing for them."

Something of their conversation must have been overheard and a gentle rumble of protest rose up while those rowing still rested on their oars.

"We are already full," Summers explained, "and have an enemy to face. Once they are dealt with I shall send the boat back."

"They can 'ang on our gunnels!" an anonymous voice declared. "We could be with 'em in no time."

"Aye, take us across!" another demanded while Simpson, usually the mildest of fellows, pushed past his mates and made to wrestle the tiller from Hanson.

"Back I say!" This time Summers had no need to soften his tone and fingered his hanger menacingly. "The first that tries to take control will feel my steel and all shall be charged with mutiny!"

The statement did much to cool their fervour. As a body the group settled back and stroke oar began to set the pace again.

"Lieutenant Cooper has made his attack," Summers continued as they gained way. "We must support him but those at the oars may remain." He turned to Hanson. "You shall also and can go back for survivors."

The midshipman nodded although another voice rose up from further forward.

"Won't be no need," it announced, in mild disgust. "T'other boat's already headin' back."

Summers turned to look. It was true, if surprising that Cooper felt able to spare men in the circumstances.

"Though most'll be dead b'now," the voice added.

* * *

In fact Cooper had no thoughts for his boat or the drowning men from *Sparrow*'s cutter: his mind was fully committed elsewhere. The remains of his boarding party had lined themselves against the schooner's starboard bulwark. They were outnumbered, though not by that many and his men were experienced in the brand of rough house fighting that seemed likely. But as the slavers eyed them warily he could hear shouting and whistles from further inland. The alarm must have been raised and reinforcements were on the way, they would have to end this quickly.

"Come on, lads!" Cooper raised his cutlass and, as he advanced towards the mob, knew himself well supported.

The first white face he encountered was clutching what looked like a hunting sword. Cooper's blade was nothing more than an ordinary seaman's boarding cutlass but it was a tool made for the job. He slashed sideways, knocking the lighter weapon from his opponent's grip before hacking down brutally. The man fell to the deck to be instantly replaced by another carrying something more serviceable. He was younger, though – no more than a lad – and lacked sufficient gumption; his slight hesitation cost him dear. Another was approaching from his right; Cooper had to turn and just missed being sliced by a downward cut. He went to respond when a different blade, wielded by Brotherton, caught the man across the chest. One more appeared clutching a pistol but there was light enough to see the lock had been fired and Cooper contemptuously knocked him away with the hilt of his sword.

And then, as quickly as it had begun, all was over and the boarding party paused, slightly stunned. There were several wounded slavers on the deck and those that could began to clamber to their feet while their able-bodied companions scrambled frantically over the schooner's top rail and leapt for the quay. Cooper watched them go; most would be British and might easily be caught and pressed although instinct told him *Tenacious* had no use for any prepared to take up such a trade. His gaze lifted; a succession of lights was steadily growing closer. Reinforcements were definitely on the way and those that had fled would soon turn back.

Three of his own men lay injured, one seriously so; the man was bleeding prodigiously from a wound on his upper arm. But others could deal with that, he must see them underway and quickly.

"'Ere's Summers' lot!" A seaman indicated a flurry of men as they swarmed over the starboard bulwark. Cooper picked out the young lieutenant and made for him.

"We have the ship," the older man announced, "and need to be gone. Have your men show all the canvas they can, I'll detail someone to attend the moorings."

Summers' party had not just been involved in desperate hand-to-hand fighting; they would be fresher and more able to work aloft. Cooper's eyes fell on Brotherton.

"Send axemen to cut the warps."

"It's been attended to, sir."

Cooper gave the lad a questioning look.

"I've already detailed Nearhood and Hodges to cast us off."

"Very well."

Releasing their moorings from the quay was an unnecessary complication when whatever held the *Sapphire* could probably have been slashed through with a cutlass, but at least the midshipman had shown initiative. A rumble from above told him the foretopsail had already been freed; others strained at halyards and braces while, further forward, several were preparing to thrust the schooner's bows away.

And it would be only just in time. The crowd was closing on them fast; musket balls began whining overhead and the shouts of abuse grew louder as their stern line was released. Cooper watched as his men calmly returned the insults while tending to the sheets and braces. Soon the fresh canvas started to fill, then they were properly underway and the shore began to be swallowed by darkness.

"Pongs a bit, don't it?" Summers asked with a grin as he approached.

"She's a Guineaman," Cooper shrugged. "'Tis the nature of the beast."

"We have to pick up your cutter," the younger man reminded. "And if I might say, it were a brave move."

"Brave?"

"Sending your boat back for Taylor's lot when you had yet to carry this little tub."

"There was no such order," Cooper told him stiffly. "At least, not one given by me. I've no idea who took it upon themselves to make for *Sparrow*'s cutter, though do have every intention of finding out."

* * *

At the same time, and not far from Cooper's desperate fight aboard the slaver, Taylor was involved in a very different kind of struggle. As with many of his type, he had little concept of swimming or even keeping afloat, and leather boots paired with a heavy wool tunic were hardly an aid to buoyancy. The nature of their damage meant the cutter had effectively been rowed under the water; from his position at the stern sheets, he and Corbrite had the most warning as to what would shortly happen.

The water was cold, it almost stung as the boat dissolved around them and he gasped as much from shock as the need for air. But the second requirement soon took over as the world he knew disappeared and Taylor found himself dragged down into the dark, clinging depths. His tunic was the first to go, he almost shook the thing from his shoulders and was already releasing the heavy sword belt as it drifted away. Boots were far harder; the left came after a modicum of pulling but by then he knew himself to have sunk deep. Someone kicked him in the side, another struggler, no doubt, and the impact knocked all remaining breath from his body. The right boot would have to wait; if more air were not gained soon he would drown.

The idea of death in such a dark, inhospitable world was enough to focus his mind and Taylor began to scrape and claw his way towards the faint glimmer of light above. His chest heaved and it was all he could do to stop himself drawing in great gasps of water. It might be that he was not moving, it might be that all this effort was simply keeping him from sinking further. It might be better to give up,

29

to allow the sea in and die without wasting any more time or effort, but somehow he continued to fight. And then, as if within a dream, he finally broke surface and there was endless thin, clean air.

One gasp could never be enough, he went to take another which turned out to be mostly water. Then he was sinking once more and the disappointment almost did for him. Struggling as before, Taylor managed to return but this time the precious moment was wasted in a cough and yet again he began to descend.

By now he was not only tired; a strange apathy was starting to take over, one that removed any further fear of dying. But there was an anger as well and this sent him to wrench at his boot again. As if to taunt him it came away at the first pull and he felt a degree of control. With a kick that was very nearly practised Taylor began making for the light once more and, as he broke the surface, finally breathed freely.

His problems were not at an end, however. The boat had disappeared; all that remained was a selection of fittings and the oars, most of which had been requisitioned by clumps of frightened men with white eyes that stared out in horrid contrast to their blackened faces. But each length of spruce could hardly keep a single man afloat so most were kept on the very brink of drowning.

"Over here, over here!"

The act of turning was nearly enough to send him down yet again although with constant movement from his feet and a clutching, grasping action with both arms he slowly brought Corbrite's face into view.

"What should we do?" the lad gasped and Taylor very nearly laughed out loud. Then he realised it was not just the midshipman who was looking to him; he had the eyes of all nearby.

"Keep yourself afloat as best you can." The words were banal and barely spluttered so it was strange and a little frightening when each one was lapped up by his audience.

"Should we make for the shore?" one of the seamen asked and Taylor did his best to shake his head.

"No," he gasped. "No, we're too far off." That must surely be true; if they were having such difficulty keeping afloat none of them would be capable of moving.

"Bennett is gone already," someone told him.

"An' Matthews."

"Gone?"

"Made for the land; they was swimmers."

Taylor supposed that was understandable but infuriating, nonetheless.

"We stay," he repeated between breaths. "Keep yourselves together as much as possible and wait. They'll come back for us; they're bound to."

* * *

Lovemore actually picked up nineteen of the twenty-six originally aboard *Sparrow*'s cutter. If it were assumed that the two swimmers had made a safe escape, that meant five were drowned which, when added to the two dead and two missing from his original boarding party, Cooper supposed was not so very terrible. And he had to admit more would have been lost were it not for the seaman's action. But still there must be an investigation, and the sooner the better while the facts remained in everyone's minds and there was less chance of retelling or elaboration. A brief discussion now would probably be wise and allow him to make a comprehensive report to Captain King on rejoining the ship. Dawn was rising and the dim outlines of *Sparrow* and *Tenacious* had come into view so he may as well see to it straight away. Besides, there was another reason why Cooper was particularly keen for a distraction.

As soon as they cleared harbour and the wounded could be given basic care he, Summers and two well-armed seamen had carried out a comprehensive search of the vessel. It was possible, likely even, that some of her original crew were sheltering below and, as *Sapphire* would likely end up in the prize courts, all were eager to check on the condition of her fabric. No further enemies were found although their inspection naturally included the slaves' quarters and even a short time spent in the airless space had affected him greatly.

The area took up most of the lower deck, an arrangement which ensured the Guineaman could hold the maximum load on an Atlantic crossing yet quite what the place would have been like in the midst of a storm was best not imagined.

For, even now, when presumably some of their number had been lost on passage, *Sapphire*'s live cargo filled every available spot. The place was totally without light and the gleam from Summers' lantern picked out innumerable pairs of morose eyes that watched in

31

silence as the four strangers inspected their hell hole. Wooden staging had been set up to either side that provided a form of mezzanine deck and this, as well as the even darker space beneath, was equally crammed with flesh.

Cooper strongly suspected the staging would be cleared away when the human cargo was unloaded, for any merchant sailing into Halifax, or any American port, should be impounded on discovery of such brutal, and incriminating, accommodation. That was by no means a certainty, however; it might now be illegal to import fresh slaves but the demand for cheap manual labour remained high and he was realistic enough to accept a healthy need, with the associated profits, could turn the minds of many.

The men, and they were mainly men, were shackled in groups of five with their rusted chains secured to the vessel's frame. And though the light was poor, enough could be seen to know this was the most abject squalor. Cooper sensed all in his party were keen to be gone and one of the seaman, a heavy fellow with a broken nose and arms like hams, seemed on the verge of collapse.

But then to be surrounded by so much misery and incapable of offering immediate aid had been awful in the extreme; in under a minute, Cooper found himself struggling for a reason to leave. Though none had been necessary, for each of his party would have gone on the weakest of pretexts and followed obediently when he made for the small door. Yet he had still not truly left; the all-enveloping aroma remained with him still, as did the memory of those eyes.

* * *

"Thought you were a goner," Lovemore told Longdon and the lad laughed.

"Not me," he said. "Take more than a dip in the wet to quench my lamp."

"Didn't seem so when we came for you."

"Maybe not, I'll admit the sight of your ugly mug were welcome."

The schooner was comfortably clear of danger even if their offshore breeze had dropped leaving them barely making steerage way. So although her dim outline could be made out, it would be a while before they were back with their comrades aboard *Tenacious*. And then the usual pantomime would begin with each man competing with the next to boast of their achievements. Yet Lovemore could feel little elation and was quite prepared to wait. Apart from weathering a few random shots, his night had not been so very hazardous, and even Longdon, who had been on the very edge of drowning, could hardly lay claim to any gallant actions. But they had survived, and both were silently pleased.

Their friendship began several years before with Lovemore being Sea Daddy to the young landsman and continued even after Longdon was made ordinary seaman. Now they were tie mates, the strongest bond any seaman recognised. And it was one that extended to all things, even death, when each would attend to the other's corpse, should such a thing be possible. With the same proviso, they were expected to look after the other in life, risking their very beings if need be to see them safe, and both knew Lovemore had done exactly that in heading back for the lad. That and so much more.

As stroke oar he had been in charge, if not of the cutter, then at least those tending its sweeps. And, with the oarsmen being the last detailed to board the slaver, it had been relatively easy to call them back. Not all responded, of course, but enough proved as keen to remain and rescue their colleagues as carry a Guineaman so it had been a simple matter to turn away from the fight and head back for the remains of *Sparrow*'s boat.

And they had arrived in the nick of time. Many of those heaved aboard were all but spent and one died even as he lay on the bottom boards amid his rescuers. Longdon had not been the sole reason for Lovemore to make for them, though a major consideration nonetheless, and when his particular slim frame was picked up the older man felt indescribable relief. But that had long since departed; the lad was safe, as were many of his fellows and, though he was undoubtedly pleased, the fact hardly made up for his current concerns.

For even if Lovemore had saved lives, it had been the wrong move. Many would see his actions as desertion, especially as he had actively encouraged others from combat. And some things could be concealed but not this, for it had been a very public act and the harshest of judgements – and penalties – should be expected.

Yet as he lay back on the slaver's deck and enjoyed what might be his last few minutes of freedom, Lovemore was not sorry. Let them do what they would with him; Longdon was alive and wouldn't be had he not acted. And whatever the law, whatever some foolish list of rules declared, in the seaman's mind that fact outweighed everything.

The noise of footsteps approaching stirred them and they looked up to see Midshipman Corbrite standing overhead.

"Mr Cooper wishes to speak with you," the lad announced with a trace of awkwardness. "He's aft, in the captain's quarters."

Both went to move before Corbrite stopped the lad with a wave of his hand. "It's just Lovemore who's wanted," he said.

Chapter Four

Summers supposed it inevitable that he, as *Tenacious'* junior lieutenant, would be given command of the slaver but, even as the news was announced, he knew it to be a dubious honour.

"Sufficient marines will be detailed to see the natives remain secure," Captain King assured him in the calm of the frigate's great cabin. "And, though *Sparrow* will only remain in company as far as New York, we'll see you all the way to Halifax."

The meeting had been called as soon as the prize met up with *Tenacious* and it was clear to Summers that both the captain and his first lieutenant had other matters to address. But in the hours that had passed since he and Cooper had visited *Sapphire*'s slave quarters, little of the horror felt then had dissipated and the idea of being in charge of such an abomination was daunting indeed.

"You may select whoever you wish for a prize crew, along with two supporting junior officers," Lieutenant Croft added.

"I'd like Brotherton." Summers spoke without hesitation. "And probably Vernon."

"Very well, you can think on it further if you wish." King was looking at him expectantly. "Though I should like us to be underway by nightfall."

Summers nodded. Of course, the sooner they were off the better and he told himself it would be a novelty to be in charge of a topsail schooner – a type known for their excellent sailing abilities. But more than eleven hundred miles separated them from Halifax and the idea of spending the journey in the company of such a pitiful collection of humanity simply appalled.

"If there is nothing else?" Croft hinted.

"No, I shall make arrangements forthwith." Summers stood.

"Perhaps you will ask Lieutenant Cooper to join us?" King added as the lad turned to leave. "He should be waiting in the coach, we will speak with him next."

Lovemore and Longdon had been absent for less than a day yet were still pleased to be back in familiar surroundings and amongst their messmates. Or most of them, for some were missing.

Knightly was one; when all else aboard *Tenacious* had no mind for anything other than the return of their colleagues, the seaman had managed to break into a store room and consume half a pint of white spirits. Consequently, after wasting time in the sick bay when Mr Manning had others to attend to, Knightly was now installed in what had become his customary place on the punishment deck.

Usually the American's absence made for a more pleasant atmosphere but on that particular day all were in a subdued mood as they munched their way through their midday scran. After all, Lovemore and Longdon's exploits were hardly worthy of praise; one might have rescued the other and a few more besides, but all silently suspected rules had been broken and repercussions were likely. And there was more, Knightly was not the only messmate to be absent; two others had failed to return and, though it had yet to be publicly acknowledged, their presence was definitely missed.

"So you were pretty much done for," Stokes remarked to Longdon when Lovemore had finished relating their story.

"Would have been," the lad confirmed. It was a pork day, one of only two in the week. His cut had been especially generous and enough remained to make exploring teeth with a probing fingernail profitable. "Then Curly here shows up in the cutter and starts hauling us all aboard."

"Strange there were no officer involved," Bovey said as he produced an onion from within his jacket and bit deep. "Someone ought to have been in charge," he continued through a spattering of pulp. "It's standard procedure."

"Didn't need no one to tell us what to do," Lovemore grunted. "*Sparra*'s cutter weren't that far off but going down fast, we was there in a trice."

"Unusual, nevertheless. An' didn't I hear Jacky Cooper called you in after?" Stokes added. "Wanted an explanation, did he?"

"He did," Lovemore admitted. "An' that's what he got. I said it were me who took the cutter off, and did so to save lives; 'sup to 'im what he makes of it."

"Not only him," Bovey stated in a learned voice as he

considered his next mouthful of onion. "Cooper'll have to report to the captain; it's Tommo what decides if any action'll be taken."

"Action?" Johnno, the boy, was amazed. "What's anyone gonna do? Lovemore's a nero."

"That's not how the officers is going to see it." Bovey shook his head in apparent sadness. "They was in action, men were needed to carry a prize and Lovemore took a load off without orders."

"Aye, 'ad there been more boarding the slaver it might 'ave been taken easier," Groom, the Yorkshireman, agreed. "As it was, men died who maybe wouldn't 'ave."

"Men like Nearhood an' 'Odges," McKenzie added cautiously. "Curley probably saved Longdon and a few more, but if he'd boarded the slaver like he was supposed, they might have made it back an' all."

There was a silence as the awful truth dawned and Lovemore shuffled uneasily on his bench.

"They weren't in Cooper's lot," Bovey pointed out.

"That's right," Longdon agreed, "they was with Summers in t'other boat an' boarded after the fightin' 'ad stopped."

"Well them's still missin'," Stokes maintained.

"Brotherton detailed them ashore," said Groom. "Jones told me; they was sent to cast the slaver off."

"Which they must have," Johnno assumed, "else she wouldn't have been able to sail out the 'arbour."

"So what happened after that?" Bovey again.

"P'raps they made it back to the slaver and were hit by fire?" Johnno asked. "I heard tell they was shootin' at her when she left."

"In which case where's their bodies?"

"No one were hit," Groom said. "Jonesy told me that an' all; they was lucky."

"They might have been, though it don't sound like Hodges and Nearhood were," Stokes sighed.

"Maybe the Yanks took them prisoner?" Lovemore said.

"Could have," Stokes agreed. "And with Nearhood one of their countrymen, he'll probably be alright."

"Or they might turn against him," said Bovey. "Think how we'd be if we captured a turncoat."

"Well in any case we can't be certain Lovemore's responsible for their deaths," Stokes stated with authority.

"We can't," Bovey agreed. "But you know officers; there's no tellin' what they'll think. Or what they'll do."

* * *

"So let me get this straight." Croft was pulling at his chin, a sure sign he had stared to grow agitated. "You definitely did not order Lovemore to take the cutter back and rescue those men."

Cooper suppressed a sigh, he had already stated as much twice but the first lieutenant seemed unable to accept the fact. "That is correct, sir."

"And would you have given such an order?" the older man persisted.

"Probably not." Cooper's answer came softly. "Though with hindsight..."

"Hindsight is irrelevant," Croft interrupted. "You had been detailed to cut out a slaver; were you confident of being able to do so with the men at your disposal?"

"At the time I was unsure." Cooper paused. "Yet can understand why Lovemore acted so."

"Understanding is not the same as condoning." The older man chanced a quick glance at his captain. Croft had served with King long enough to know he could have strange ideas about enforcing discipline; interrogating Cooper may well be a waste of time. But King seemed annoyingly impassive, so he doggedly stuck to his course. "As it was, you were deprived of several hands who would have been invaluable in carrying the prize. That you were able to do so, and achieve a commendable victory without their presence, goes to your credit, as does speaking up now for those who placed you in such a predicament. However, your success does not confer the right to pass judgement. We cannot ignore the fact that one man took it upon himself to wilfully disobey an order and encouraged others to do likewise."

"He saved lives," Cooper pointed out.

"And may have cost those of others," Croft countered.

"Two from the boarding party fell." Now it was Cooper's turn to look to King, only to be equally disappointed. "Four if you include Nearhood and Hodges who cannot be accounted for. And three were wounded, though are expected to recover."

"Hodges and Nearhood were detailed to cast off the warps?" Croft asked.

"That's correct, sir, and five either drowned in the cutter or tried for the shore."

38

"Which means nine men were lost for the taking of one slaver!" the first lieutenant summarised with a direct look at his captain. Put like that the achievement seemed small indeed, and even King appeared to lose some detachment.

"But twice that number could have died in *Sparrow*'s cutter." Cooper knew he was becoming exasperated yet felt unable to stem the emotion. "Maybe three times – how would those odds look?"

Croft shook his head and sighed. "I accept that, though am still not easy. We might turn a blind eye and not make mention in our report but if the men see us condoning such behaviour, what will they think?"

"They'll think we acted justly and with due regard for their lives." As King finally spoke Cooper felt a wave of pure relief wash over him. "Yes, Lovemore was wrong to take the cutter, yet perhaps we might all have done the same in his situation?"

Cooper nodded, although now it was Croft's turn to appear impassive.

"He was needed as part of a boarding party," the older man repeated, "as were the others."

"So what do we do?" King asked. "Send seven sound hands for court martial? You know as well as I the probable result; put such a case in front of a bunch of superannuated captains and six would be flogged round the fleet while Lovemore must end up hanging from our foreyard."

Croft blanched visibly and Cooper wondered if it was the image of punishment or his captain's obvious displeasure that had caused the reaction.

"I'm sorry, James, this is something that simply should not be done by the book," King continued.

"But it is wrong." Croft was almost whining.

"Wrong? In what manner?"

"Morally, ethically and legally," the first lieutenant insisted. "It is an officer's place to decide on a course of action then give orders accordingly, not a common hand's."

"Maybe so," King allowed at last, and Cooper was conscious of a sudden lessening of tension. "Maybe you're right, James, and we are both wrong. But if it is morally correct to take lives rather than save them I can only think that something is terribly amiss."

* * *

All he had heard about topsail schooners was proving correct and as Summers stood on the tiny quarterdeck of his new command he felt inordinately happy. She was currently under mainsail, foresail and square foretopsail with both jibs set and he had rarely travelled so fast in what was really no more than a gentle breeze. *Tenacious* and *Sparrow* were to leeward and off the small craft's larboard bow but he was coming up fast and would soon pass them. At which point he fully intended to wear and come back on the larboard tack. There was no real need for this, he had already carried out a number of unnecessary manoeuvres and was fast becoming acquainted with the little craft's speed and agility. Still, the sheer joy of handling such a well-balanced rig was addictive and far more attractive than another task he should be addressing.

Then a movement forward caught his attention. Harris, a junior mate from the slaver's former crew, was being helped up the companion way by the assistant surgeon and a loblolly boy. The man claimed to be an American and had been wounded in the upper arm during last night's boarding action. Consequently he was now a prisoner and Captain King had allowed him to remain with the vessel to advise on caring for her cargo. Summers wondered what help a man previously content to abuse so much humanity could offer, and as the assistant surgeon had spent more time caring for his wound than the welfare of the slaves, was already resenting his presence. But he supposed some effort should be made and gave a nod of acknowledgement when the man approached.

"Good breeze for a run," Harris remarked, as he took in his surroundings. "And you're getting a fair speed from the old girl, though I'd recommend swapping a jib for the forestays'l. You see, in such a wind you'll find a flyin' jib is..."

"You are here to advise on the natives' welfare, no more," Summers cut in, and Harris stopped abruptly before considering him with dull eyes.

"As you will, mister," he said.

"And we shall start forthwith," Summers continued, determined not to be intimidated. "I intend clearing out their quarters and giving the chance for fresh air."

"Some might consider it too cold for such a thing," Harris sniffed. "This might be clement weather for Christian folk, though it's a darn sight hotter where them blacks comes from. Better to keep 'em below, they'll thank you for it."

Summers had made two further trips to the slaves' quarters and was now even more certain no accommodation could be worse, but he kept a neutral face and let the man continue.

"Word is we'll be making Halifax in not much more'n a fortnight, I'd leave 'em be, were I you."

At this Summers did give a short laugh. Harris' heavy woollen beard was almost an extension to his positive rug of grey hair and neither could have seen soap, let alone powder, in years. The only clean cloth he wore were the bandages to his arm; his shirt, once white, had mellowed to a dull mottled brown and was barely covered by a stained leather waistcoat that ended a little short of a pair of greasy trousers. Summers was dressed no more elegantly – he still wore the previous night's ripped tunic and was conscious his own trousers had stains from boarding this very ship. But he remained in uniform, and it was one that proclaimed him to be a commissioned King's officer whereas the only allegiance Harris apparently owed was to himself.

"P'raps we're not so much alike," Harris said, apparently realising this.

"I intend starting by bringing some on deck," Summers continued briskly. "They are chained in fives, how many groups should we take at any one time?"

"I'd start with one," Harris told him. "And don't expect a deal of cooperation. Though if the first is treated right you may feel able to try more later."

That made sense although Brotherton had carried out a head count; they had one hundred and forty-eight males below, together with thirty-eight females, nineteen children and what looked like a new born baby. Taking just five at a time would be slow work and not give much space for the cleaning parties he had hoped to organise.

The first group appeared shortly afterwards. Two shirtsleeved marines led a grim procession of five men, four being quite young – roughly Summers' age – and one a good deal older, possibly their father. Together they made an uncertain journey up to the main deck before pausing to wince at the light and look about, clearly suspicious. The order and relative cleanliness of the schooner's upper deck emphasised their squalor; each man wore the briefest of loincloths but was covered in an apparent second skin of filth. And, as Harris had predicted, they were shivering slightly despite the morning sun.

"If you intends givin' them a wash I'd be quick about it," the man advised. "Leave them too long and you'll start a fever that could spread like wildfire. And that, Mr Navy man, will be your main enemy."

Summers considered the slaver, who fiddled with his beard as he continued.

"You might not like our methods, but we know how to keep a cargo fresh. Slaves can be taken bad by what you or I would consider no more'n a cold, and when something truly deadly strikes it's proper devastating."

"What especially?" Summers asked, despite himself, and the man shrugged.

"Don't know the names exactly though I can spot the signs right enough; bloody or white flux, retching, fever sweats, shiverin', yellow eyes; any of them an' you got to act quick."

"Act in what way?"

"Let's just see if it happens," Harris replied guardedly.

With only five on deck there would be no point in Brotherton's team attempting to clean their quarters, but they may as well start with what they had.

"Take them for'ard to the elm pump," Summers directed.

One of the marines, an NCO, reached out and attempted to lead the older man who snarled like a wild animal and snatched his arm away.

"Easy sergeant," Summers warned.

"Easy, sir? Beggin' your pardon, these types don't know nowt about easy."

"He's right, sir," the private added. "They don't even speak the King's English. It's force they understands – that and a superior mind."

"I said easy," Summers repeated with emphasis, and both marines backed off.

"They thinks they're set for a trip over the side," Harris chuckled and Summers turned to him. "It's what we 'ave to do," the mate explained with a shrug. "Not as a regular practice, you'll understand; each of them there hides cost a pitcher of rum to purchase and can fetch over thirty guineas in the right market. But if we finds a case of sickness they have to be ditched; them and those they're attached to."

Summers looked his horror.

"It's on account of the insurance," Harris casually justified himself. "They don't pay nothing when a snowball dies on board, only if we have to jettison do we see a penny and then it ain't the full rate."

"And have you done that this trip?"

"Couple of times," Harris admitted. "It's not just the money we're thinkin' off. As I say, you can't have illness aboard. And some might look on it as being kinder to them below; they're not so likely to go crook."

The slaves' quarters were currently crowded enough, to even think they had been more so, and contained sick amongst the huddled humanity, was terrible indeed. The older native was still resisting the sergeant's cautious attempts to grasp his arm, and those with him were growing visibly agitated. Turning away from Harris, Summers strode down the deck to the small group. The marine stepped back as he arrived, glad to be relieved of his task.

Close up, the men's condition was even more apparent and Summers was reminded of the stench of the lower quarters, but he closed his mind to both.

"It's alright," he said, his voice was loud and distinct and Summers looked directly at the older native as he spoke. "You're safe, and will come to no harm. We just want to see you clean."

The man turned to him and Summers was struck by the fine bone structure and firm chin that were set below hair that had obviously once been well cared for.

"We want to see you clean," he repeated, reaching out and ignoring the look of incomprehension. "You and your companions." Summers continued to meet the native's gaze as he touched both his hands, but did not attempt to take hold. Then, cautiously, the older man brought his arms up and offered the manacled wrists to the young lieutenant.

"Keys!" Summers snapped reaching back and a marine duly passed across a single tool, far larger than he had expected. It fitted into the manacles perfectly though and soon each of the men had been released.

Summers returned to the old man who was holding his hands upwards in a manner both imploring and oddly triumphant. He indicated the elm tree pump and together the pair walked forward with the others dutifully following.

It took no time to see the worst of the grime removed and by then all five were definitely shivering.

"We shall need to wash their clothing," Summers announced

43

as loin cloths were replaced. "And maybe make some more; sailcloth should answer well enough."

He turned back; Brotherton was there, and the two marines, but all seemed too stunned to speak. Only Harris still had a tongue.

"Like I says, you got to keep 'em healthy," he said, "it don't do to let any get too cold."

"Give them some canvas," Summers told the private, "and send for more. And blankets, plenty of blankets." Pieces of linen were quickly distributed and the older man dried himself with elaborate care although at no time did his gaze leave Summers. And when they were finished and the chains had also been rinsed, the young officer held the manacles out once more.

"I'm sorry," he said. "I have no choice. It will mean we do not have to guard you so closely."

The older man considered the chains but made no attempt to offer up his hands. Instead he reached forward and touched the side of Summers' face in the same way that a father might his son.

"It's blackening, Michael," Brotherton explained softly. "He's spotted some of the burnt cork from last night."

"Belike I weren't as careful at my cleaning," Summers replied with a guilty grin, and was unsurprised to notice the same expression on the old native's face. Then both wrists were extended once more, the manacles closed around them and the group was led away.

"Well, that's the first lot done," Summers said a little wistfully as he watched them go. "We'd better look to the next."

* * *

Aboard *Tenacious*, James Croft was a worried man. The captain's decision to suppress the truth about their recent cutting out expedition had been disconcerting but no more. In the years the pair had been together there had been several instances when strict laws that every other serving officer felt obliged to obey had been severely bent or even broken. Consequently he had long since become accustomed to the younger man's almost reckless contempt for form. And, if he were completely honest, neither was he particularly concerned about how the lower deck might take the news.

Every ship King commanded turned out to be a happy one; he had a rare affinity with the lower deck that apparently relied on something more powerful than rules or regulations and there could be no doubting that, whether it be right or wrong, the policy worked. As an officer of the old school this was definitely beyond Croft's comprehension, although he was slowly coming to realise that King at least understood and could be trusted. So, despite having made what he felt to be a necessary stand the day before, the matter could now rest; what truly worried him was something far more serious.

His watch had disappeared. It was not an especially expensive one, and neither did it hold any sentimental value. He was also relatively certain it had not been stolen; he messed in the gunroom – what would be known as a wardroom in larger ships – and the place was shared with other commissioned or senior warrant officers. Most had been aboard *Tenacious* for several years and even the newcomers were experienced men who would never have risen as far with a tendency for petty larceny. Likewise, the stewards had been with the ship since she first commissioned while Dodd, his personal servant and a man who had served him almost twenty years, would probably have defended any one of Croft's meagre possessions with his life. Yet still the thing was missing, and had been for several days. And it was not the first time an item had misappropriated itself.

For almost a week he was without his toothpick. Despite hunting through his housewife and searching the cabin twice it had just vanished, only to reappear when Sturridge, the gunroom cook, discovered it in his pantry. Croft only visited the place during his weekly inspections, so how it had ended up there was still a mystery. And for a while he had also mislaid his turtle shell comb; with a rapidly receding hairline it was something used sparingly and never outside the confines of the gunroom yet an extensive search by every officer had proved fruitless. Eventually he had given the thing up as lost when Hanson, a midshipman, triumphantly produced it; found, apparently, in the boatswain's store. Again it was somewhere Croft rarely ventured and, when he did, would have little need of a comb although, like the toothpick, he could only blame himself for losing it.

And there was more to concern him than just the loss of personal items. Croft felt he was on the verge of losing something far more important: his mind.

While *Tenacious* was shepherding the convoy on the passage down he had found himself unable to remember the name of their fellow escort. Which of course was *Sparrow*, he knew it well enough, just as he knew Leyton, her captain, had been *Tenacious'* first lieutenant – damn it, they had shared the same gunroom for long

45

enough. But on several occasions when he had cause to mention either vessel or man, both names escaped him. Then a week ago he had appeared an hour early for his morning meeting with the captain and twice, inexplicably, forgot the appointment altogether and had to suffer the indignity of being sent for.

All were small points but, when taken together, were proving enough to make him more than a little concerned. Croft had been a sea officer for all his adult life and considered himself reasonably proficient. And though other men might have stifled him in the past, under the captaincy of Thomas King he had positively blossomed, discovering talents and an enthusiasm that had surprised even himself. But, like the mild dizziness that comes before seasickness, these slight aberrations seemed to be portending something more important, something, if he were honest, that felt extremely sinister.

Which was a shame, for he had a ship to be proud of, a position of honour and finally, after many years of enduring fools, a captain worthy of respect. The North American Station was also agreeable and he had already decided would be his home when the time came to retire. But not yet, not for a while; he was enjoying life as never before and didn't want it to end or change in any way. Although he would still keep getting these stupid feelings that it soon might.

* * *

The journey north was probably as uneventful as any could expect aboard a strange vessel with over two hundred souls confined below. It had taken three days to improve the natives' quarters by an appreciable extent and, after introducing a schedule that allowed limited time on deck for all, Summers' unwilling guests had begun to show the benefit. However, he had failed as far as food was concerned. Harris, the former mate, had recommended a diet of horse beans beaten to a pulp which should be served twice a day. These looked to be a form of broad bean of which there was a generous supply and, unsavoury though it might appear, the mash was readily accepted. Nevertheless, after trying a portion himself, Summers decided some variation was called for.

Sapphires' other stores were not extensive and apparently intended only to victual her crew, although enough cheese, apples, stockfish, biscuit and preserved vegetables were found to liven up the regimen. Of them all, only apples found guarded favour; the iron-hard biscuits were viewed with confusion, for surely no food could be so inedible, and the cheese, a particularly robust pink Suffolk, was rejected out of hand. But the worst reaction was saved for the jars of preserved vegetables, a form of sauerkraut, which drew suspicious looks from eyes that were slowly learning how to trust. Despite this slight setback, most apparently appreciated the care Summers tried to extend and, though the atmosphere below could never have been judged agreeable, it did show improvement.

And he had learned much in other areas. The lad was relatively new to commissioned rank and an absolute beginner when it came to command. Not only did he have to care for those confined below, there were marines and seamen with junior officers for both and even the prisoner Harris to account for. And all looked to him and him alone as the ultimate authority on anything from petty disagreements to rearranging watch duties. The fact that *Tenacious* was seldom more than a mile to windward and usually in plain sight proved of little benefit; Summers knew only too well how Captain King would react should trivial problems be referred to him. But somehow they had survived and, once the Sambro Light was finally in view, began to feel proud of his achievements.

There was still one hurdle to clear, though; he had to see the prize safely to her anchorage and for this last duty he was joined by Brotherton and Vernon. The three stood side by side on the small quarterdeck as the schooner made her cautious approach into Halifax harbour. Ahead, *Tenacious* was once more leading the way and for some time had been their only companion, *Sparrow* having left to patrol the waters off Sandy Hook. The frigate's draught was several feet deeper than his tiny command's and it was a generous harbour so all Summers need do was follow in her wake and, with the last of the flood and just enough wind to give steerage, was beginning to see an end to his responsibilities.

"She'll raise a pretty penny in the prize court," Vernon observed as the schooner continued on her gentle way and it was probably significant that this was the first time any of them had considered the vessel's worth.

"There's no doubting she's sound," Summers nodded, "and would make a fine command, were she bought into the service."

"Aye," Brotherton agreed with a wicked glint, "any pup lieutenant would be glad of such a posting."

Sapphire rounded the shallows off Sandwich Point without a hitch before easing past George Island and finally aiming her head for the Navy Yard. About them, the town's brightly painted houses seemed especially welcoming and just in sight was the clock tower atop the sail loft that signalled their destination. Then, even as he was preparing to anchor, another sight caught his eye and it was one that immediately took the young officer's full attention.

Ahead lay a selection of anchored shipping. The majority were commercial craft ranging from tramp merchants – so called on account of their lack of a home port – to far larger affairs that would be comfortable on any ocean at most times of the year. And beyond he could also see a number of warships, members of the British North American Squadron and largely known to him; ships he had served alongside in *Tenacious*, manned by officers, many of whom he considered friends. But one stood out; she lay slightly apart from the rest as if conscious of her individuality and unwilling to catch, or pass on, some strange infection.

Summers studied her even as his own command neared the point where he must anchor. She was a frigate, definitely, though unlike any British vessel he knew. A cursory glance told him she was not quite as large as the six heavy Americans that had attracted such attention a few years back. She did however have the appearance of a well-designed, soundly built craft and as she lay at anchor, slightly squat yet latent with power, he could not help being impressed.

"Captain's preparing to anchor," Brotherton warned and Summers looked up to see *Tenacious* was indeed spilling her wind.

"Very well, keep an eye," he replied reverting to the noncommittal manner he had adopted over the last few days. But even as his own command glided easily in the dying breeze, Summers found himself considering the foreigner once more.

For that's what she undoubtedly was, even if the warship had likely been built less than five hundred miles away and would be manned by seamen who spoke the King's English. The stars and stripes fluttered lazily from her jack and a Union Flag – the courtesy ensign – from a starboard yard, indicating her presence was by invitation or request. So there was no need for concern, Summers assured himself as Brotherton ordered the foretopsail gathered in. Relations between Britain and the United States had definitely deteriorated of late, although most of the ill feeling was in the West; New England and much of the Eastern Seaboard remained neutral and almost benign. And though her gunports were closed and the ship lay at ease, Summers could sense a tension about her and found his mouth drying slightly as the magnificent vessel was left in their wake.

"It's time," the senior midshipman hinted and, as Summers gave a curt nod worthy of any admiral, the anchor was released.

"USS *Delaware*," Brotherton announced when they were finally secure and he could inspect the American also.

"*Delaware*?" Vernon questioned. "Not one of their heavies then?"

"No, only a thirty-six, though she mounts eighteen-pounders."

"So, similar to us," the younger midshipman mused.

"Weightier," Brotherton countered, "and carries more men. They say she's a solid ship, well found and with a weatherly helm."

"You've been reading up," Vernon remarked. "Not thinking of changing services I trust?"

"No fear of that," Brotherton sniffed, "but still I like to keep up on the opposition."

"Does you credit," the lieutenant grinned as the three of them continued to study the warship. "Though she ain't the enemy – at least not yet."

"Maybe, but one thing's for certain," Brotherton continued, "she'd make a formidable opponent, were matters ever to sink so low…"

Chapter Five

"Well I must say it is damned bad timing," King grumbled as he slipped awkwardly out of his shirt.

"*Bien sûr*, but there is nothing we can do," Aimée soothed from her place at the dressing table. She, too, would rather have spent their first evening together at home; they had been separated for such a long time that attending a government reception was hardly on her list of priorities. And to make matters worse, Thomas was in a bad mood. "Maybe you could say you have been detained?" she suggested turning back.

"Hardly, when my ship is lying at anchor for all the world to see."

"Then perhaps you are taken unwell?"

She saw him go to respond then hesitate and, when he did speak, his voice was softer. "Look, Aimée, I'm sorry. This is not of your making yet you've been getting the worst of my tongue."

"It is alright," she said but did not rise from the chair. "And it may be that I am the little to blame."

He waited.

"You see when you are not around I am invited to many such events – it is mainly the wives," she added quickly. "Halifax has a lot of women married to men that do not stay at home all of the time. And they are not just sailors, some are in the military and there are government officials who go looking at the land or those who deal in skins and timber. We keep each other company and are quite the little community; I have made good friends."

She glanced cautiously in the mirror but Thomas seemed pleased, if perhaps a little surprised. "I am glad to hear it," he said. "And they do not mind..."

"That I am French?" she laughed. "No, I should say that is quite popular." Aimée relaxed slightly and began to comb out her long hair. "There are many from my country in Halifax, some I think were once your prisoners though have been released."

"Really?" King grunted. "I had no idea."

"Yes, and your Prince Edward lived here, until he fell off his horse," Aimée continued happily. "He also had a French companion, a Madame de Saint-Laurent; many think you and I are equally wicked and are so jealous!"

She peered into the mirror again. Now Thomas was giving one of his wry smiles as he reached for a fresh shirt.

"I am glad that you have found friends," he said, slipping the thing on and fumbling awkwardly with the buttons. She rose and went across to him.

"And that they think we are wicked?" Aimée asked, brushing his hand to one side and taking over.

"Of course," he said, the smile still very much in evidence. "Who would want to be anything else?"

"Sometimes it is quiet," Aimée explained. She turned away, her job done, but did not return directly to her chair. "And I do like to see people; to go out and meet with others, though not perhaps tonight."

She felt a pressure on her shoulder and looked back, then finally they did draw close, both feeling a warmth that came from shared understanding.

"Then we are of one mind," he said as they held each other. "And will quit this cursed reception as soon as it is decently possible."

* * *

Sparrow had left *Tenacious* and their prize some days before to begin what Leyton felt must be the ideal duty. For the next few weeks, or until he ran out of men, he was to patrol the waters off Sandy Hook and stop merchants of any nation travelling in or out of New York. Once under his control, their manifests and shipping details would be checked and, should either the cargo or final destination contravene Britain's Orders in Council, the vessel would be seized and promptly sailed to Halifax under a prize crew.

For Leyton, with a background steeped in scrutiny and correction together with an attitude that truly belonged in the previous century, it was perfect employment and he proposed to enjoy it to the full. His brig might be small and lightly armed but she flew the Union Flag and that alone gave him licence to be as officious as he wished. And there was an added dividend; as the official representative of an island nation, it was no surprise that some vessels encountered numbered British seamen amongst their people. These could be discovered from the crew manifest or through face-to-face interrogation, and when a fellow countryman was detected he had the power to impress all bar officers or apprentices. Over the past three days he had carried out several inspections with the nett result that two Bremen traders were currently on their way to Nova Scotia and eighteen men lay below under the care of the master-at-arms. Of these, three had definitely deserted the crown and would face punishment that might extend as far as the noose, while the rest had publicly denounced their birthright and claimed themselves American – a crime, in Leyton's eyes at least, almost as despicable.

Consequently, when given the choice of stopping an American vessel against any other neutral, he would always choose the former, and if their inspections took longer and were more severe it troubled him not. For in Leyton's mind the inconvenience and cost he purposely caused was nothing to the betrayal his country had suffered at the hands of such ungrateful children.

And Leyton had yet another reason for conducting this personal vendetta. After a lifetime at sea, much of which having been spent nursemaiding senior, though less competent, men, he finally had his own vessel. *Sparrow* might not figure highly as a warship; there were few smaller in fact and a popgun broadside would not normally bring great riches in terms of prize or head money. But by seizing shipping and pressing men she was steadily clocking up a considerable sum for little apparent risk. The major portion of this would eventually find its way into his pockets and he had rarely been so generously blessed. With the current commission due to last a further three years he should be able to amass considerable wealth, at least enough to purchase a minor estate and live in luxury for the rest of his days.

Or he might choose to stay; Leyton had found commanding a warship to be highly agreeable as well as lucrative. It was not impossible that another vessel might come his way, perhaps even a rated ship that would warrant promotion to post captain.

But however the future panned out, Leyton felt he had finally found a position that properly used his talents. With his trim little vessel and a task both satisfying and profitable, this was truly the ideal posting. And one he intended enjoying for a long time to come.

* * *

Government House was situated on Barrington Street, less than five hundred yards from their home and, as the evening was pleasant, King and Aimée dispensed with a hired carriage and walked. It was agreeing on such things that made them so well suited, he decided as she took his hand; on being invited to an impressive address many women would demand a grand arrival with footmen and flunkies in attendance. And as Aimée's upbringing had been modest, she could hardly be blamed for wanting to enjoy her status as a noted captain's companion. But when they did arrive and were shown into the ballroom it became clear that no pretence was necessary: Aimée had already been accepted by Halifax society and, of the pair of them, was very much in charge.

Still clasping at his arm she led him confidently through the crowd of well-dressed elite, exchanging greetings and small jokes with many wives while charming every husband. The air was rich with the scent of expensive perfume and the genteel strains of a string quartet were being soundly quashed by chatter, laughter and an occasional irreverent shout. Together they processed with Aimée guiding gently while King silently pined for the clean cut of cold sea air and taut lines whining. But though this might not be his world, attending such functions was as much a part of a senior captain's duty as examining merchants or cutting out slavers, and at least he had the bonus of the prettiest of women on his arm.

The lieutenant governor himself was there, someone King had only met twice before and then on the most perfunctory basis. Sir George Prévost was standing with his wife and very obviously only conversing with the invited few, yet Lady Prévost pulled at the general's arm on spotting Aimée, and almost dragged him from his current guest to speak with them.

"King isn't it?" he demanded somewhat awkwardly as the two women descended into whispered chatter. "Delighted to see you, sir. I trust you had a good cruise?"

"Excellent thank you, General." King was reasonably sure Prévost's recognition had much to do with his missing arm and the governor was merely guessing he had recently returned but, whatever the reason, it was gratifying to be noticed. "We were fortunate in bagging a prize."

"A prize you say?" Prévost gave King a careful look. "Not an American I trust? We're doing all we can to improve relations in that department yet you chaps do insist on impounding their shipping."

"No, General, she was British and, I regret, a slaver."

"Then it is a different matter," Prévost agreed. "I think I may have seen her come in, moored by the Navy Yard, is she not?"

"Indeed, sir."

"She should fetch a tidy sum, though I think you'd better be careful who you speak with tonight," the general added with a slight twinkle before nodding towards the far wall. "Fellow over there, by the band."

King followed Prévost's gaze. It was a large room and, although reasonably well lit, much was clad in shadows. But after peering for a moment he did make out a trim, elderly man with an unusually short woman, standing next to the string quartet.

"That's Fitch and you took his boat," Prévost told him with a chuckle. "Can't blame you, mind; if she were slaving it's what he deserves, though there are many hereabouts who think otherwise."

"From what I gather he has a measure of importance," King remarked thoughtfully.

"Oh for sure; whatever his dealings the man makes a mint."

"I do not doubt it."

Sir George eyed him cautiously. "Like it or not, his trade is vital to both the station and our country in general, otherwise he would not have been invited. Though you were totally within your rights to do what you did," he added hastily.

"I regard it as my duty, sir," King replied crisply.

"Of course," Prévost assured and gave a smile that owed more to diplomacy than agreement. A servant passed by offering a tray holding glasses of sparkling wine. The general took one although King shook his head. He was not a great drinker and having his only hand encumbered made introductions awkward. "And there is another unexpected guest," Prévost continued, "though one you would doubtless prefer. A fellow navy man no less!"

King felt he knew all those serving on station and got on reasonably with the majority but the officer Prévost had spotted was definitely a new face. And, when he came to look more closely, his uniform was of an unusual cut, which suggested a newcomer probably more up to date with the current trends. In fact it was only when the man caught Prévost's eye and began to make his way over that King realised he was from a totally different navy.

"Delighted to see you, Captain Walton," Prévost declared, shaking the officer's hand. "Might I introduce Captain King of His Britannic Majesty's Navy? Thomas King, meet Robert Walton."

"Always pleased to meet a fellow seafarer." Walton presented a positive paw which King took guardedly as he considered the man. The American was roughly his age though perhaps an inch or two taller and several stone heavier in weight. But the open expression and genial countenance appeared genuine, if offset slightly by a glint of steel in the bright blue eyes.

"If you'll excuse me, gentlemen," the governor said stepping back. "I really must speak with as many as possible."

"I see you've been a mite careless, Captain," Walton remarked with a grin when they were alone.

"I have," King agreed, glancing briefly at his empty sleeve. "Though all is healed I am pleased to say."

"Glad to hear it and sorry if you think I came on strong. My father told me to say what's on my mind and sometimes it takes folk by surprise."

"I appreciate plain speaking," King assured. "Would that be your frigate lying near the yard?"

"That's her," Walton admitted. "*Delaware.*"

"Had her long?"

"Couple o' months, still shaking down I guess."

"She looks a splendid vessel."

"Oh, I like her fine. Eleven-thirty tons and rated at thirty-six guns."

"Carronades?" King enquired with assumed innocence and received the expected shake of the head.

"Her main battery's long eighteen-pounders, as you no doubt guessed, though we do have twenty of the big fellas as well."

"And is she one of the original six?"

The American smiled again. "Nope. *Delaware*'s smaller than *Constitution* and her like but subscription built so the work was done with care. You must come aboard and take a look."

"That's a kind offer, although..."

"Oh, I don't doubt my commodore would be furious." Now

Walton laughed out loud. "And the president as well, if he got to hear of it. But we're both sea officers – I'd chance there to be an element of trust."

"I'd like to think so," King declared. "Can I ask, what brings you to Halifax?"

"Hackney service; I'm ferrying some officials from Philly who want words with your legislators."

King pulled a face. "That hardly sounds healthy."

"Got the same impression myself," Walton agreed.

"Think there may be trouble?"

"I consider it likely."

King raised an eyebrow and the American seemed to come to a decision before continuing.

"Look, Captain, I was born in the States but my folks came from your neck of the woods. So I've no beef with England and, as a Federalist, would rather have you as friends than any country that regularly cuts off its countrymen's heads. But you got to admit, the RN's been playing fast and loose with our shipping of late."

"I'm not sure I understand what you mean." King was careful not to catch those eyes.

"I mean with enforcing your Orders in Council, as well you know," Walton replied. "Blowed if I can tell exactly what your government's trying to pull but they've almost wrecked our economy."

"I'd have thought your own Embargo Act did that," King countered and the American's smile returned.

"Maybe that wasn't such a good move," he agreed. "Matters have progressed since, though you're still tying us up in red tape and restrictions. The US has the second largest merchant fleet in the world yet still can't go from one port to another without asking permission from the Royal Navy. All you need do is cut us a bit of slack and everyone could be getting along fine."

"And is that what Napoleon did?" King asked.

"Forgive me, Napoleon?"

"When he offered to relax his Continental System? Your government was quick to side with him and drop your own constraints, though there's been no easing from France that I'm aware of. You said you liked plain speaking, Captain Walton, well would you rather deal with those who keep their word, even if it isn't what you want to hear, or a madman that happily promises the earth then delivers nothing?"

56

"I take your point," Walton laughed, "and have to admit diplomacy was never my strong point. Though would still rather fight with treaties than anything sharp."

"An economic war is better than any other," King agreed.

"But surely there's nothing to stop you playin' fair?" the American persisted. "And what's with the taking of our men? Every time one of our ships is stopped they lose a couple of hands; carry on much longer and there'll be no one left."

"We have a right to retrieve deserters, you can't deny us that."

"So how would it go down if I began stopping your merchants and doing the same? For all we know there may be as many Americans serving aboard British ships as Brits in Americans."

"I would dispute that," King said and Walton shrugged.

"Maybe not now, though it might come to it."

"I accept that some captains can be a little harsh..." King began.

"A little?" Walton gave a look of exaggerated surprise.

"Very well, excessively so, but Britain *is* fighting a war; a real one, and not just on behalf of ourselves. From what I hear Napoleon has his sights set on Russia; if he's successful it'll probably be our turn again and, should Europe fall totally under his control, where will he look next? The current restrictions on your trade will be nothing compared to those imposed then, and how do you think he'll regard anyone calling for 'free trade and sailors' rights'?"

"Oh, there'll be no objections from me on that point," Walton nodded, "I simply wish you'd change your methods. We have little use for genuine deserters; scum like that only breed discontent and would be handed back if you asked nicely. Yet the Royal Navy has to carry on as if its ships were the only ones allowed to float while treating us like an inferior species. Times have changed, Captain King, and your John Bull ought to change with them."

"You cannot expect me to go along with that; at least, not officially."

"Of course not, you have your government to support and I mine."

"Then why don't we simply agree to disagree?" King suggested and Walton's expression relaxed.

"Why don't we just do that?" he said. "Got to admit, I've always had a sneaking respect for your lot and frankly, Captain, I like you as well. It'd be a shame to fall out."

* * *

Aboard *Tenacious* a small group of warrant officers were taking their ease in far less salubrious accommodation. The fore cockpit was on the frigate's orlop, a place where daylight was non-existent and the constant scent of bilges pervaded. And the mess on the forward platform was truly unofficial. In effect, it was nothing more than a partition erected in front of several store rooms including those belonging to the carpenter, boatswain and sailmaker. The area it enclosed created a space where five men could eat and sleep in relative comfort and, probably more important, privacy.

The captain was aware of the arrangement and had given it his unofficial blessing, for the work had been done well and even incorporated a narrow door that would not have looked out of place fronting more distinguished accommodation. Inside, all was kept in immaculate order as might be expected with the inhabitants being warrant officers of many years' standing. Some might have found an agreeable spot further aft with the master's mates or been allowed screened-off accommodation on the berth deck itself, but all were of a similar age, status and attitude and appreciated the company of their peers.

The mess had been in place since *Tenacious*' last refit with much of the work carried out by one of its inhabitants; Joseph Morales, the ship's carpenter. He shared the area with Amon, the frigate's boatswain, Regan her gunner, Wilson the sailmaker and Drake the master-at-arms. There was no hierarchy as such, they felt no need; each knew and trusted the others implicitly and, though they might share meals and drink, neither did they try to emulate the rituals and formalities of more senior officers residing further aft. In short, they had created a comfortable, private space amid the crowd and confusion of a ship of war; one where a man might enjoy civilised conversation – or none – and rest easily with others of his type.

Tenacious was currently in harbour and any one of them might have applied for liberty, but none had felt the urge to go ashore. Halifax held no great attraction; there were no family or friends there and neither did they want for supplies. Instead they had enjoyed a simple meal; three of the hens, kept nearby and mutually funded, had made a passable supper for five heavy men who now rested after the effort.

"None of dem were proper layers," Regan, an Irishman, commented a little guiltily as he regarded the mangled remains. "But dey gave us a decent meal in the end, so they did."

"Don't get too used to it," Amon warned. "There's less than a dozen left and the poultry in these parts ain't a patch on those further south."

"Should have bought more in the Windie's." Wilson spoke over the leg bone he was still chewing. "Said so at the time an' were I listened to?"

"If we did we'd have hen every meal and twice on Sunday," Morales told him, not unkindly.

"So, did any av yer get aboard de slaver?" Regan asked.

"I did take a look-see after we carried her," Morales replied. "Sound little craft, she should show a fair return. Though I ain't going back – place stank to high heaven."

"It's the nature of slavers," said Amon.

"I hears young Micky Summers did a bit to clean her up." Wilson had gnawed the bone clean and was now considering his empty plate with satisfaction.

"Well oi took a peep," Regan, the gunner, announced. "Not official, loike."

"Anything of interest, Pad?" Morales asked.

"Nah, dey weren't carrying nothing worth the takin'," the Irishman replied. "But dem slave quarters..." He shook his head in disbelief.

"I did a run aboard a convict ship once," Amon reflected. "All the way to New South Wales and that were pretty bad."

"'Tis was worse than any transport," Regan sighed. "Much worse."

"I saw the natives being unloaded," Wilson said. "They didn't look up to much."

"'Tain't surprising." Amon again. "Spend a couple of months crammed in a tub like that an' we'd all look pretty rough."

"An' they ain't got much to look forward to, neither," Drake added with unexpected authority.

"That so, Francis?" Morales asked as he helped himself to an apple.

The master-at-arms nodded his head. "Sadly. Some'll probably end up in Freetown – that's Sierra Leone – the rest might get a different form of freedom round these parts."

59

"Don't they get given land or something?" Amon asked vaguely.

"Tried it with the Black Loyalists," Drake confirmed. "And it hardly worked out. Government gave the best to some religious society, leaving just a load of rocks and trees. And though the authorities promised to feed them for three years, what they ended up with didn't see them through the first winter."

"So what'll happen?" Morales was losing interest in his apple.

"Majority will end up indentured," Drake said, "which is little better than slavery. And one thing's for certain, they'll never find their homes again."

"You sounds as if you've been learning up," Amon remarked.

"Not me!" Drake's protest was unexpectedly strong. "I've no interest in blacks, be they slaves or free and you definitely won't find me poking round no Guineaman!"

The others considered this; the group had lived together a fair while and been shipmates far longer. The sense of mutual trust was strong and they held few secrets. But neither did they know a great deal about the others' past lives and occasionally it felt better that way.

* * *

There had been several occasions over the previous few days when Corbrite felt his captain was taking matters to extremes. Even before *Sparrow* had properly arrived on station they had begun searching for potential merchants to stop and when the first, an American with a cargo of sugar and hickory hoops, was suspected of having three British seamen aboard, it only acted as encouragement. Of course the matter was heavily disputed. The men, who turned out to be brothers, produced certificates confirming their newly acquired American nationality and vehemently denied ever having served aboard a British warship. But Commander Leyton had been in no doubt; all had broad Scot's accents and a surname beginning with Mac, which was sufficient for him.

The next had been just as rewarding; this was another American and, though her master had documents to prove her destination to be Spain, a comprehensive search revealed mail intended for France. Leyton had immediately arrested the vessel, and placed Lawson, their senior midshipman, aboard at the head of a prize crew. It would be up to the owner to prove legitimacy in an Admiralty Court, something that was bound to take time and, even if she were subsequently released, her cargo would probably be spoiled.

Since then, every hour of the day had been spent searching for merchants. The majority of those stopped were carrying legitimate cargoes that even Leyton could not dispute but there had also been a constant trickle of seizures; men who in the main claimed American nationality and careers that had avoided service aboard a man-of-war. Once more documentation proving their new allegiance had been produced and, once more, Leyton remained indifferent and ordered any doubtful man pressed.

However there had also been three whose tattoos proudly proclaimed them not only British but actually named their former warships. Whether these had deserted or been paid off would be revealed at court martial although Corbrite thought it significant that, of all their captures, they had made the least fuss.

So far only two vessels had been sent for assessment but that could not continue; the young midshipman had an uneasy feeling Captain Leyton would carry on until he ran out of men for prize crews.

Which was why he was present, the lad acknowledged as he and Taylor were solemnly rowed towards their current capture, a brig that had been spotted making a night-time run out of New York. This was his first trick as the junior examining officer but he had learned much of his duties from Lawson and Ashcroft, both of whom were now on their way north at the head of prize crews. Should a suspicious cargo or some discrepancy in the master's paperwork be discovered, the vessel was likely to be consigned to Halifax at which point Corbrite would be in line for his first taste of independent command.

"Seems quiet enough," Taylor commented as they drew closer, and indeed the vessel might have been a ghost ship. No curious faces peered over her bulwarks and the tophamper seemed unusually empty; the brig had only slowed by luffing into the wind and her canvas now thrashed, unrestrained, further emphasising the impression. "But then we usually find the people are reluctant to meet us," the lieutenant continued, adding, "They will be down to you."

Corbrite had been expecting this; Taylor would have his work cut out checking the cargo yet he would have preferred not to be the one to choose who they might press. They drew closer and still there was no sound from the brig and the lad had to restrain himself from shivering. Of course it didn't make matters easier that the whole affair had to take place at night, but that had also been a common factor in his captain's campaign. Leyton reasoned any vessel leaving New York in the dark was bound to have nefarious intents and so their watch had been pretty much continuous. But as they closed further, Corbrite found it hard to believe such a paltry vessel could be a significant factor in Britain's war against France. Or that she might truly turn out to be his first command.

"We're coming aboard!" Taylor bellowed and Corbrite pressed the tiller across until their cutter – a borrowed one from *Tenacious* – came to a gentle halt alongside. The brig's freeboard seemed unusually low for anything planning an Atlantic crossing and Corbrite clambered easily onto the small deck, placing himself beside Taylor, who was definitely experienced when it came to such a task.

"I should like to see your papers," the lieutenant announced, addressing the master, a man wearing rough clothes and an angry look that even the doubtful light of a couple of deck lanterns could not hide.

"Heading for Cadiz," the man informed them curtly as two leather-bound ledgers were produced.

"Look to the crew," Taylor told Corbrite, handing one to him. The lad drew nearer to a lantern and began to peer at the yellowed paper. The muster book had been used for several previous voyages and he flipped through the pages until coming to the last, where twelve names stood out in darker ink. He glanced about, Taylor seemed to be arguing some point with the master; apart from them, and a lanky, long-haired fellow at the wheel, the deck was empty. Even aloft, where a hand should have been stationed above the masthead lamp, he could see no one. But the names were there in front of him and he began to read.

And all were in order he decided as he ran his eyes down the last column. Every man listed was shown as having joined at various ports along the Spanish coast, which was understandable if the vessel made a regular run to the country. It was only when he looked in more detail that his heart gave a slight jump.

Whoever wrote up the muster book had a fair, round hand which was easily read even in such poor light. And it was the last entry that caused him to pause. Seth Scott; a general hand. The name stood out amid the line of Spanish and was one that meant much to the young officer.

He checked the signature; it was no surprise to note the man had made a mark. The Seth Scott Corbrite had known might have been streets ahead of him in sea lore, but was total illiterate. And his former Sea Daddy had deserted in Cadiz, where the brig was currently bound and obviously one of her regular ports of call. Corbrite gripped the book a little tighter. Seth might be aboard and only a matter of feet away; for a moment he wondered about looking for him. If, by some miracle, his desertion could be ignored or covered up they could sail together once more and he might continue his education.

But there was more to it than that. Corbrite didn't just miss his former mentor, the man had been a friend – a father almost.

"We're done here," Taylor announced approaching. "Manifests are in order and I've better ways of spending an evening than rummaging through several tons of salt fish. Vessel's on a regular run by the looks of it and will be feeding Wellesley's troops so good luck to them. How are you faring with the people?"

Corbrite shook his head before trusting himself to speak. "No good," he said at last. "All the regular hands are Spaniards."

Taylor considered this for a moment and Corbrite felt his heart was beating loud enough to be heard.

"That's no surprise considering," the lieutenant finally agreed, adding, "We've likely taken all their Yanks already!"

Corbrite nodded – not too eagerly he hoped – and was careful to keep hold of the closed book.

"Yet it is strange not to have at least one Jonathan aboard, apart from the captain, I means."

Taylor was now looking hungrily at the ledger and Corbrite sensed it would soon be taken from him. And then the lieutenant did reach out for it, but only to place the thing together with the cargo manifest before handing both back to the brig's master.

"Better call it a night," the senior man said turning back. "I dare say our dear captain would have been a sight more officious though I for one am for my cot."

Corbrite followed eagerly but found himself pausing for a moment before quitting the deck. The vessel's master stood next to the man at the wheel and both were waiting for him to leave so they might continue their journey. And below, somewhere, would be Seth. Of that he was now quite certain. The man had left without a word of farewell, but that had been his way. Maybe by now he had found another apprentice, a dew-eyed child as Corbrite had been, to initiate

63

in the ways of the sea – he hoped so.

The midshipman hesitated a moment longer, then turned and swung his leg over the side before descending the entry steps with one hand holding the ledge above in the manner he had been taught. And finally, as he took up his position in the cutter's stern sheets and all about were intent on getting underway, he muttered a quiet, "thank you," that nobody heard.

Chapter Six

"A pint of pure water weighs a pound and a quarter." Manton knew the saying well and had even used it when calculating the layout of stores aboard *Tenacious*. As sailing master the vessel's trim was down to him and working out the exact location for every store, allowing for both access and redistribution, was a regular headache that closely rivalled that of navigating the vessel. So the lack of four tons of the precious liquid would throw all his previous calculations awry, as well as limiting the time they could remain at sea, and yet the captain of the water hoy was adamant.

"Eight tons is what you put in for and eight tons is what you got," he repeated, thrusting the requisition notice in front of Manton's face.

"Yes, I'm certain that to be the case," the sailing master agreed sitting back in his chair. They were in the cramped chart room, the only private space Manton could be sure of and, after refusing to take the other seat, the victualler was towering over him like an angry school master. "But I was expecting twelve," he explained sadly, "and that is what I allowed for."

"Can't help that," the man shrugged. "My tanks is dry, I've given you extra as it is."

"Which is greatly appreciated," Manton confirmed, taking the paper and looking at it more closely. There could be no argument on his part, the slip had been filled in clearly enough and plainly stated eight tons. Croft, the first lieutenant, had even written the amount out in his own hand and signed the form; everything was correct and totally above board yet completely wrong.

"I am sorry." The sailing master looked up and into the victualler's tired eyes hoping for some sign of pity. "There must have been a mistake; is there any way you can allow us another four tons?"

"None that I can see," the man replied, although he did appear to be softening slightly. "We got the water but I've another vessel to fill tomorrow morn'. You'll have to requisition in the usual manner and we'll gets to you when we can."

"But that takes three days," Manton grimaced, "and we are due to sail with tomorrow's high. Is there no other way?"

"Suppose I might be able to get some for tomorra." The man rubbed at his ample stomach in thought. "It ain't regular like, and you'll have to put another chit in. But we're going back to the reservoir now and can take on extra; *Guerriere* only wants toppin' up and won't actually be sailin' till the day after."

"That would be splendid, I cannot tell you how grateful I shall be," Manton effused, standing and shaking the man's hand until he blushed.

"Jus' you make sure you got that chit," the victualler warned, regaining his composure. "And 'ave a word with your firs' luff; fellow makes a mistake like that again and I might not be able to bail 'm out. Make sure 'e knows."

"Oh, I will tell him," Manton assured as the man eased his bulk through the narrow doorway. Then, under his breath, added, "Though doubt the old fool will remember."

* * *

"The ship is now in all respects ready," Croft assured his captain. "There was some confusion with the water but that has been put right; extra was taken aboard earlier."

It was their regular morning meeting and an important one as *Tenacious* was due to sail that afternoon. Consequently Croft had been especially careful to arrive on time.

"And what is the mood of the people?" King enquired.

"Two ran yesterday, which makes five since we put in."

"And it is always the best that choose to go," King mused.

"Though there is good as well, sir," Croft continued. "We're being allowed an additional ten, and all are trained hands. They came aboard yesterday afternoon."

Tenacious had been at anchor six days and could have expected to lose far more, which spoke well for either the ship or her security. But to have their losses made up so handsomely was extremely gratifying.

"Then we are the winners!"

"In theory, perhaps," Croft sniffed. "I should add that all are here against their wishes."

"The Navy was built on such as that," King reminded and the older man nodded.

"Oh, indeed, and I have no doubt Mr Drake will settle them in. Though, it is one thing to press a man for his own country, quite another when he has to serve in a foreign service."

"You mean they are Americans?"

"I mean they *claim* to be Americans," Croft corrected. "Some had protections to prove it, but you know how the Admiralty regards such things. And there can be little doubt most were born in England."

"So not the best recruits." Whatever pressure the master-at-arms placed on the new men they would always be rebels. "And how is Knightly progressing?" King asked, his mind running on.

"Threw his trousers overboard," Croft announced flatly.

"He did what?"

"It was some dispute with a bumboat, or so I understand," the older man grunted. "Claims he was returning them, and you know how volatile he can be."

"I know he's a problem," King agreed, "and one I could do without. 'Tis a pity he was not one of the runners."

"Oh, I think we might win him over in time," Croft said, scratching at his chin, although King remained unconvinced.

"Well at least our next deployment should offer a change and will cheer a few up."

"Indeed, sir; a cruise is always popular. The hands do not respond well to arresting merchants and neither are they partial to protecting convoys."

"With luck we might run into a few convoys ourselves," King replied with a smile, "but of the enemy variety, and we shall also be after their privateers."

"Do you think there'll be many?" Croft asked. "Since Boney lost his Caribbean bases they must have decreased."

"From what I hears the numbers have not changed vastly though those recently encountered have been larger and better armed. A lot have come across from France and are playing hell further south. Quite where they are getting their supplies from is anyone's guess."

"The Americans perhaps?"

"It would seem likely; feelings are running high at the moment and there are many who wish to hurt us in any way they can."

"Foolish," Croft decided, "and totally unnecessary."

"Not what they think," King corrected. "They still believe us to be funding the Indians that cause them so many problems further west."

"And are we?"

"Oh yes," King sighed.

"And there is another addition," Croft continued, glancing at a sheet of paper for confirmation. "We have finally received a further midshipman."

"Good news indeed!" King sat a little more upright. "Tell me of him."

Again Croft looked at the paper before continuing.

"David Godby, eighteen years of age and experienced. Served as a volunteer aboard *Aeolus* and was present when they captured Martinique. Was made midshipman shortly afterwards and Captain Townshend speaks highly of him. He opted for *Tenacious* as she is marginally larger and I'd warrant considered the chances of promotion to be higher."

King nodded, that was all very satisfactory yet Croft seemed to be holding something back. Perhaps it was the matter of promotion? *Tenacious* was known to have an elderly first lieutenant, a factor that usually made advancement more likely, and that may have hit a sensitive spot. "Have you met the fellow?" he asked.

"I have, sir, and will see he reports to you directly."

Again his second in command appeared unusually reticent, although Croft's behaviour in general had been a little odd of late.

"Is there something you're not telling me, James?"

"Nothing pertinent to Mr Godby's career exactly..."

King waited until Croft seemed ready to take the plunge. Then, leaning forward in his chair, the older man's eyes grew wide as if he were about to divulge the deepest of secrets.

"You see, sir, he's as black as the ace of spades."

* * *

Croft was wrong; Godby had colour, certainly, but it was a soft brown that exactly matched his eyes. And the face was strong with prominent cheekbones and a smile that came readily; as he took the seat that Croft had so recently vacated, King immediately warmed to the new midshipman.

"You're from Captain Townshend's command I understand. How is he?"

"I believe him to be well, sir," Godby replied and King was struck by the depth of his tone. "However, you will appreciate that, as a midshipman..."

"Of course," King agreed hurriedly. "Though he has sent an excellent report of your service."

"*Aeolus* was a happy ship, sir. I did enjoy my time aboard her but am looking forward to serving under you. We sail this afternoon, I understand?"

"At three," King confirmed, glancing quickly at the watch on his desk. "Which means we must be brief. I wanted to welcome you aboard *Tenacious* and explain a few points about her and how she is officered."

Godby nodded readily.

"Firstly I do not wish this to be a flogging ship; official corporal punishment does take place, but rarely, and only when other disciplinary methods fail. And I disapprove of starting, or any less formal physical reprimands. That said, the people are hardly made of sugar and we do not treat them with undue leniency or favouritism, either as individuals or a group. Were you to deal with any man, mess or division unusually well or harshly you will get the same reproof from me. To my mind consistency is all, and a quality I value highly."

"I understand, sir."

"Likewise, at all times you will treat your brother officers with respect and consideration; I hope friendships will develop but do not let them cloud your judgement. We are King's Officers first and have our duty to perform; that must always be our primary consideration."

"Yes, sir."

King relaxed in his chair and regarded the new man again. "I think that covers everything. You have yet to be assigned a divisional lieutenant; when you are he will be your immediate superior; take any concerns to him, then Mr Croft or myself if he is unable to assist. Now is there anything you are unsure of?"

"I should like to ask, sir; do you have a special reason for telling me this?"

King paused and blinked slowly before replying.

"Indeed, Mr Godby, and I think you know it well. It is because you have joined my ship and will be one of my officers. I fear everyone has had the same speech or something similar on arrival. As you grow older you may find the habits begin to multiply..."

"I understand, sir." Godby matched King's smile. "And thank you."

* * *

"So how much do you want for these shirts?" Knightly asked as he considered the sample. The lower deck had just been paid but, with no shore leave due or likely before *Tenacious* sailed, the money was burning holes in many pockets. Consequently those of Stokes' mess were not alone in conducting a few last minute purchases from the flotilla of bumboats that regularly collected about the frigate's hull.

"Shirts, Da'?" the girl asked, turning back to the grey-haired man at the loaded craft's stern sheets.

Knightly and his messmates had gathered on the starboard gangway – a narrow platform that linked forecastle with quarterdeck – and most were staring down expectantly, although in some cases their interest was more in the girl's low-cut dress.

"Sixpence each or six for 'alf a crown," the old man grunted.

"You 'eard," she told them, looking up once more and softening her answer slightly with a gappy smile. Knightly considered this, and her; she would have been quite attractive were it not for the profusion of brutal make up.

"What you doin' with buying clothes?" Longdon asked.

"Aye," McKenzie, another spectator, agreed. "I'd a thought you'd ha' learned y'r lessen with them troosers."

"We're heading for the Windies," Stokes added. "They got Yankee cotton there a penny a mile, wait a bit an' make your own!"

"Yeah, well maybe I don't want to wait, or make me own," Knightly replied while considering the shirt, and the girl, further. Two and sixpence was a fair amount of money, though it might be possible to work in a few benefits if the lass was willing.

"You wouldn't find me payin' out for no made goods," Stokes said. "Least not at that price!"

70

"'S right," McKenzie, agreed. "I didna pay more'n threepence last liberty."

"Well I don't get no liberty," Knightly reminded them crossly. "I'm down to me last shirt an' the pusser charges ninepence – when he has any. 'Sides, looks like she's got small clothes an' all."

"Aye, show us yer small clothes, hen!" McKenzie ordered to a chorus of raucous laughter from the seamen.

"There'll be none of that," the old man at the stern announced. "Them's good shirts; made of the finest cloth an' the prices are ripe enough. You don't get no extras from our Jen."

The girl glanced back at her father, then looked up to Knightly again and gave a sly wink.

"Well what about one of these here crowns?" the seaman asked holding up a coin. "What do I get for five shillings?"

"Twelve shirts," she told him quickly. Then, reconsidering, "P'raps thirteen."

"What you going to do with thirteen shirts?" Stokes asked aghast.

"Well I don't rightly know," Knightly shrugged. "Probably sell 'em to you lot when you gets short; that way I makes a profit."

"Won't be much profit on more'n a groat a throw," Bovey snorted, but Knightly was regarding the girl again. To his eyes she promised more than just clothing and, on an impulse, he tossed the silver coin down.

"Crown it is," she announced, biting the money before slipping it into the folds of her clothing. Then, after gathering up a collection of small bundles, she began tossing them up to the line of waiting hands.

Hold hard there!" The voice came from beyond the group and carried natural authority. Knightly paused in the act of catching the last of his purchases and the bumboat man, who was preparing to fend off, lowered his boat hook. Then the small crowd of seamen parted as Godby, their new divisional midshipman, stepped forward and leant over the top rail, a round shot in hand.

"I've a thirty-two-pound ball here," he announced, holding out his load. "From this height I reckons it'll go through your hull easily enough. So stay put unless you wants me to prove it."

The girl looked back to her father who was now wearing an expression of grim resignation.

Godby turned to Knightly. "Show me one of them shirts."

71

The seaman duly held up the sample he had been given.

"Not that, one of the folded."

A tight bundle was selected and shaken out. The sleeves and some of the back were present, but it totally lacked a front.

The midshipman looked down at the boat's occupants once more. "Not much for five shillin' is it?" he asked and the girl had the grace to look abashed. "I think we's due some change."

"'Ave them for 'alf a crown," the old man muttered. "You'd pay that for the cloth."

"A shillin'," the midshipman countered firmly. "Or I'll sell you this round shot for nothin'."

The girl looked again to her father and this time received a curt nod before standing and passing up a handful of coins.

"Is it right?" Godby asked the seaman.

"It's right," Knightly agreed and, at a nod from the midshipman, the bumboat finally drew away.

"That were well done, mister," Stokes announced, as the others gathered around the young officer muttering appreciation.

"I been in Halifax a while," Godby told them. "Them are known rogues."

"Well you sure sorted their hash," Knightly chortled. "Well done, boy!"

The remark had been made in all innocence, which was unusual for Knightly, but still it brought instant silence to the group. The midshipman glared at him.

"My name is Godby," he announced. "You will call me that and nothin' else, do you understand?"

Knightly's face had blanched several shades. "I do," he said, "and am mighty sorry, Mr Godby, sir."

"I'm glad to hear it," the midshipman replied, juggling gently with the iron ball, "'cause it don't do to insult a man when he's carrying round shot."

The laughter was mainly due to relief and Godby used it as cover and walked off the gangway, only to meet Summers who must have been watching throughout.

"You could have had Knightly in irons for that," the lieutenant told him softly.

"I could, sir," Godby agreed, "but think my point was made. And I've been called worse."

* * *

In the two weeks since *Sparrow* parted company with *Tenacious* she had stopped a total of twenty-three vessels and Corbrite, along with all her officers and many from the lower deck, was thoroughly exhausted. Now the senior midshipman, he had been present for most of the searches and some, where the captain had taken charge, involved prolonged physical inspection of the cargoes. Yet despite such vigilance their success rate had fallen alarmingly, due mainly to the brig's presence becoming known. Suddenly it seemed every merchant putting out from New York was the very model of legitimacy, with clear and accurate paperwork, blatantly legal cargoes and crews that lacked even the hint of an Englishman. They had more success with incoming freight; vessels on the edge of completing a safe Atlantic crossing found their path to rest blocked by an officious little warship with a self-important captain. Many proved fair game for Leyton's searching eyes and questions, and minor deviations in their cargoes were discovered although none that justified their being sent into Halifax. Consequently Corbrite had yet to be appointed prize master, even if there were times when he almost longed for the chance, as even the command of a poorly crewed merchant should prove more restful than his present employment.

But finally there had been a change in the weather. The rainstorm that currently enveloped them had been building since first light and now, as dusk steadily gave way to what promised to be a troubled night, Corbrite and Taylor stood together at the conn. Both were clad in oilskins and sou'westers and both were horribly cold.

"Least this'll mean a let-up on the rummaging," the midshipman supposed, his voice suitably loud to combat the sound of falling rain.

"Don't be so sure," Taylor warned. "Them that's in port might stay their side of The Narrows but a fair few at sea will be running for shelter. And they won't take kindly to being stopped by one of His Majesty's vessels."

Corbrite knew he was right. So far their reception had mainly been belligerent. A few of the masters took Leyton's officious ways philosophically enough, but most showed an aggression that ran to the point of threatening physical violence, even in the face of an armed boarding party with their warship close by. The latter cases usually occurred when members of their crew were seized and this had continued whatever their cargo or destination. So far a total of thirty-eight hands judged to be British had been taken from homeward-bound merchants flying the American flag and Corbrite knew the figure could only grow.

But there was less chance of further searches that evening, and for some time to come if a wind followed the rain, although then it was likely the weather itself would provide an alternative source of entertainment.

"Sighting has taken in her t'gallants." Taylor's voice broke into his thoughts and the midshipman brought his mind back to a further problem as he turned to consider the oncoming ship.

It had been mid-afternoon when the strange vessel had first been sighted by their masthead and was identified as a warship shortly afterwards. Corbrite first heard the news from the doubtful comfort of *Sparrow*'s cockpit and had hoped it was *Tenacious*; the frigate was rumoured to be due in the area shortly and supposedly heading south on a cruise. In a perfect world she would collect their tiny brig and together they might cause havoc amid the pirates and privateers that plagued the more temperate Caribbean. Or Bermuda; the island lay not seven hundred miles to the south-east and would provide greater challenges than arresting traders and battling foul weather. But at that point Corbrite's world felt very far from perfect and, when the sighting was confirmed as an American frigate, his hopes were replaced with a far deeper feeling of foreboding.

And now the larger warship lay less than a mile off and, rather than running for the safety and comfort of New York, she was holding her course and seemed determined to close with *Sparrow*.

"I suppose word's got out," Corbrite muttered. "We've been here long enough to cause a stir so they've sent something large to chase us away."

"They might try," the lieutenant replied, "though the captain doesn't seem to be particularly troubled, else he wouldn't have fled to his cabin so."

"Shall I send for him?" Corbrite asked, but Taylor shook his head.

"Not for the time being; Sandy Hook's a good six miles to the east and we've seldom been closer. These are international waters; we've every right to be here, even if some might judge our recent activities differently."

"So what'll the American do?" Corbrite's eyes were still fixed on the approaching warship. "Blow us out of the water?"

Taylor laughed. "I doubt it, even if we pulled a similar trick on

74

their *Chesapeake* a few years back. No, this will just be a warning, official recognition they know we're here and, more to the point, so does the American government. Cleverer brains than ours might use the fact as a bargaining chip in future negotiations, though I wouldn't know about that."

"So what'll *we* do?" Corbrite tried this time, and this time the lieutenant shrugged.

"That'll depend on the captain," he said. "And we'd better send for him now, for chummy here appears to be signalling for us to heave to."

* * *

"What ship is that?"

The call had been timed to coincide with a brief lull in the rain and came over the short distance clear enough to be heard by all in the brig. Taylor looked to the captain who had finally arrived on deck wearing oilskins and a sour expression.

"Damned insolence!" Leyton spat as he glared at the warship that was closing on the brig's larboard beam and threatening to steal her wind.

"Heave to; we are sending a boat."

"A boat he says!" Leyton fumed. "I'll see him in hell first. Lay us off to starboard, Mr Hudson."

"Wind's in the east, sir," the sailing master warned. "That'd take us nearer a lee shore."

"There's hardly a breeze and room aplenty; to starboard I say!"

Even under minimal sail, *Sparrow's* sleek hull manoeuvred quickly and soon she was practically running towards the American coast. The frigate remained with them, however; either her captain anticipated such a move or had an exceptionally well-trained crew for the larger ship easily kept pace and was soon drawing closer once more. Corbrite flashed a worried look at Taylor although his senior seemed unusually composed and, taking his lead, the midshipman quickly adopted an attitude of elaborate unconcern.

"What ship is that?" The cry was repeated but now rain had returned it could barely be heard. Leyton swore again; they were in no imminent danger of grounding yet every second took them nearer to

American waters; should they stray too close with a warship on their tail they would definitely face censure and such an indignity would not be regarded well by his superiors.

"Wear ship!" he snapped and there was a distinct pause before Hudson lifted his speaking trumpet and ordered them about.

They came round easily and were soon taking the breeze on their starboard beam but the American had been no more slow. Even as the brig settled on a more northerly course the larger ship was directly in her wake. And then, steering closer to the wind and carrying a degree more sail, the frigate began to close until she was coming up and would soon be dangerously close to *Sparrow*'s starboard quarter.

"Heave to and await a boat." Again the same voice and each time it seemed to excite the brig's captain more. They were no longer in danger of the lee shore although to have a larger vessel so close definitely threatened his command and Leyton was treating the situation with deadly seriousness.

"We might answer, sir?" Taylor's suggestion was pitched against a sudden flurry of rain so had to be shouted, something that only served to annoy his captain further.

"Reply? To an upstart colonial? I'll do no such thing, Mr Taylor, and will thank you to keep such inane suggestions to yourself!"

In the light of such a response nothing more could be said and all on the quarterdeck lapsed into an uneasy silence as the frigate closed further and Leyton began to simmer gently. Even Corbrite, undoubtedly the least experienced officer present, knew the captain was running out of options. They may continue on the current course and possibly wear to larboard once more but if the larger vessel remained intent on closing there was little they could do to stop it. And *Sparrow* was not blessed with a robust hull, should she come into contact with a frigate the brig was bound to come off worst. A forceful collision could see her sent to the bottom while all the protests in the world would do little against an American defence of bad weather. And that was assuming there would be anyone left to protest; it was not inconceivable – likely even – that *Sparrow* would sink with all hands.

Yet just as the midshipman was resigning himself to a damp and dismal ending, Commander Leyton did react. As if charged by a sudden bolt of electricity, the man spun round, glared at the oncoming ship, then raised one fist and shook it impudently in the air. All waited. There would be more, that was certain, and they were not disappointed. But rather than ordering the brig to heave to, or replying to the challenge, their captain showed he could still surprise them all and turning to his first officer he gave a grim smile.

"I think they've pushed us far enough, Mr Taylor. Clear for action if you please. And when that is done you may beat to quarters."

Chapter Seven

Despite appalling weather and the myriad of doubts that radiated down from their officers, those of *Sparrow*'s lower deck took to the task with a will and within fifteen minutes their brig was ready for war. Taylor reported the fact to Leyton with the slight hope his captain might have had a change of heart, but the man was resolute.

"Very well, Mr Taylor, we'll see how our friends behave on discovering us to have teeth!"

Both men looked back at the pursuing frigate; she remained off their starboard quarter and was steadily forereaching. But even at the current range the American could have found *Sparrow* with her forward chasers and the fact that they were holding back was reassuring, to Taylor at least. It meant that, however aggressively the other captain was handling his ship, and however much he intended to intimidate their little brig, this was to be a warning and he was not spoiling for a fight. When it came to escalating matters, Leyton was totally on his own.

And Taylor was genuinely concerned. The pair had served together in *Tenacious* when he was third officer and Leyton first. Then, the older man had appeared the model of restraint and not for the first time Taylor wondered at the changes promotion and command had brought. That hardly solved the current problem though. The American seemed determined to press them to the limit and if his captain remained equally stubborn this would not end well. Of course the idea of any unrated vessel taking on a powerful frigate was ludicrous in the extreme, but Taylor knew what Leyton was capable of. With the belief that right lay on his side, the man might do anything, and the only factor in their favour was that the physical act of firing on the pursuing frigate would not be easy.

For, apart from a couple of swivels, the brig only carried broadside cannon; if Leyton truly wanted to bring the larger ship to battle he would have to manoeuvre, and do so quite dramatically. The

78

easiest option would be to wear once more, and return on the opposite tack, then engage the frigate with their larboard battery. The move would be well signalled but it remained unlikely their pursuer would think they had any intent other than to shake them off. It would be sheer lunacy of course, although a well-timed broadside might even be successful and, should an important piece of the American's tophamper be carried away, they could indeed be free to make their escape. The alternative, luffing up and literally throwing the brig into the frigate's path, was far more serious; as soon as they were seen to turn, those aboard the warship would be alerted and, though they may not be cleared for action, could at least make preparations for receiving shot. Quite what damage *Sparrow* might do with her popgun broadside was another matter, even if an important spar were hit it remained likely the brig would be crushed by the oncoming ship. But in both cases, whether every shot was made to count or all missed their target by a mile, the damage they caused to diplomacy would be far worse.

A few years before, HMS *Leopard*, a fourth rate, had attempted to stop the *Chesapeake*, an American frigate fresh from harbour and on passage to a foreign station. The British commander had intended to search the warship for deserters but Barron, the *Chesapeake*'s captain, refused to submit and received a two-decker's broadside for his trouble. Still shaking down for an Atlantic crossing, the Americans were taken by surprise and quickly surrendered, but not before three of their crew had been killed with several more wounded. Four supposed deserters were then recovered but the incident caused a furore with American public opinion and was a major reason why the two countries' relations had since turned sour. And now it seemed Leyton was about to repeat the exercise, although in his case with scant chance of success.

As his captain studied the oncoming vessel, Taylor watched in silent hope that sense would win out but when he finally turned back the old man's face bore a look close to rapture.

"It seems the Jonathan is intent on running us down," he said, addressing the quarterdeck in a tone close to triumph. "Time he were taught a lesson." Then, after catching his first officer's eye, "Prepare our starboard battery!"

Taylor instinctively touched his sou'wester as he took in Leyton's words although the doubts were now mixing with dread. Using the starboard battery meant the old fool was intending to luff, surely the most dangerous option and one that could easily see them collide with the heavier warship. An order was an order however, and to disobey would do little good other than see himself disciplined, yet still he felt obliged to protest.

"Begging your pardon, sir, she is close to; if we luff we may place ourselves in danger."

Taylor glanced about, Hudson was near and listening with apparent dispassion while Corbrite bore the look of concerned deference common in midshipmen. But there was no doubting Leyton's feelings or how he would react.

"Do you presume to question my order?"

"I-I think you should reconsider, sir," the lieutenant replied, his eyes flashing again to the sailing master. Some support from that quarter would have been welcomed but Hudson remained a mute and impotent witness.

"I shall deal with you later, Mr Taylor," Layton informed him crisply, "right now there are more important considerations though you should not expect to walk my quarterdeck for very much longer."

Taylor struggled for a response although Leyton was apparently in no need of one, instead he turned to the midshipman. "Mr Corbrite you will prepare the starboard battery, they are to fire upon my word – and see that they do!"

To his credit, the lad paused and Taylor both hoped and feared he might also say something in protest. But for a midshipman to defy his captain would be twice as foolish as a lieutenant, and Corbrite dutifully made his way forward to take command of the guns.

"Prepare to luff, Mr Hudson," Leyton continued in a more normal tone once the boy had gone.

"Very good, sir." The sailing master touched his hat in respect.

Then, turning away from Taylor as one unworthy of notice, Leyton looked back at the oncoming American and gave a smile. "It is time to show our American friend it does not do to intimidate one of His Majesty's warships."

* * *

The gun crews were waiting patiently at their quarters and, as he made his way forward, Corbrite knew he had the eye of every man.

"Prepare starboard battery," he shouted. It was a repeat of his captain's order but now heard by all and, as it came from his lips, they reacted. In common with most warships, *Sparrow* did not carry sufficient gunners to fully man both broadsides, instead her gun crews were made up with some who remained with their weapons and others that would go to the opposite battery if needed. Those that could be spared from the larboard cannon moved across and, ignoring the rain and the patchy light, began to work with silent efficiency. Their weapons had been loaded some while before – when the sun had shone and the current conditions were just an unpleasant possibility – now they just needed to be primed and prepared. Securing tackle was released and the tompions removed, then each gun captain opened his gun lock and dosed their weapons with a generous charge of powder and spirit before closing the lock once more, in some cases sheltering it with their cupped hands. Powder monkeys that were little more than children scampered down to the magazine, there to collect fresh charges for subsequent rounds, others rousted out specialist shot, the short tight clusters of bar and stools of canister, while those with handspikes and crows of iron stood ready to lever their weapons to any angle necessary.

Corbrite considered them as they worked, each carrying out his appointed task with care and an element of pride. And all in the quiet certainty that whether they opened fire or not would depend on their captain, an officer deserving of their total respect and one who must surely work with the same dedication. And as he watched, the midshipman could not suppress a feeling of impending betrayal.

* * *

"On my word, Master." Leyton had one arm raised as he considered his adversary. The rain was continuing to fall, although perhaps not quite in the same quantity, and as a quarter moon began to rise the frigate could be seen in greater detail. A figure stood at her prow, the glint of brass from his speaking trumpet clearly visible, and once more the call came for them to heave to.

"Hark at the fellow!" Leyton huffed. "Perchance he is about to get an answer he does not expect. Now, Mr Hudson!"

As Leyton's hand descended, *Sparrow* was turned sharply into the wind and soon began to stagger as she was caught aback. Taylor watched in silence; they had made little headway before being brought up so should not block the path of the frigate, but that was a minor consolation. Were the Americans in anyway primed and not stopped by Leyton's lunacy, *Sparrow* would shortly face the full force of the frigate's heavy cannon on her prow.

"Fire, Mr Corbrite!"

The eight gun broadside snapped out sharply and for a second the brig's quarterdeck was enveloped in a cloud of acrid smoke. But it cleared as swiftly as it came and they could see the result of their action. The frigate's larboard anchor was struck and now hung at a strange angle, and there was no longer any sign of a man at the prow. Apart from that the vessel appeared unharmed and continued to bear down on them.

"Take her back, take her back!" Leyton roared, apparently realising their situation only then and Hudson obediently ordered them round. But they had hardly begun the manoeuvre when the larger ship passed by their bows and revealed a row of raised gunports and grinning cannon.

They had no way of telling how prepared the American had been and, whether by chance or design, the broadside she delivered was not complete. However, her long guns were potent indeed and each one that spoke found a target. Within seconds sufficient eighteen-pound shot had been received to wipe away any further thoughts of action on behalf of the brig.

Her starboard forechains were struck, releasing support for the mast and causing a series of ominous groans, and two jagged holes punctured her fragile hull. A cannon, barrel warm from recent use, was sent spinning sideways against those who had served it and the mainmast itself received a glancing blow that removed a fair chunk of pine. Other shot found flesh and timber with equal dispassion as a cloud of splinters and debris rose up amid the screams and groans. But it was one of the last shots that proved truly decisive and wiped out any remaining fight in the vessel.

Much of the damage had been taken forward although that single ball made it as far as the brig's quarterdeck and would have passed harmlessly over if chance, possibly influenced by poetic justice, had not guided it elsewhere. On noticing the frigate open fire, Taylor had instinctively taken cover, only to rise when the last shot had been fired. And it was then, when looking about at the devastation the American had caused, that he realised *Sparrow* now lacked both her captain and sailing master.

* * *

The majority had abandoned their guns in favour of seeing to the most urgent damage although, even with a full battery primed and ready to fire, nothing would have persuaded Taylor to continue the fight. They would have to strike, there was really no option, and it must be done quickly, before the American decided to fire again. The frigate had rounded on their bows before spilling her wind and now lay perfectly positioned to deliver the *coup de grâce*. And Taylor was very conscious several of her cannon were as yet unfired.

"Let go the sheets," he roared, "and sound the bell!"

He noticed Corbrite hesitate for a second but Rogers, the boatswain, was already releasing their canvas. Then the midshipman ran forward to the belfry and a loud clatter rang out amid the sound of rain and wind. Taylor turned back; the remains of Leyton and Hudson still lay mingled on the sodden deck but they would have to wait. The quartermaster was trying to hold the ship steady although without pressure from any sail *Sparrow* wallowed dreadfully. Taylor reached for the jack halyard and released it with a twist, before snatching their ensign down. The moon was not bright and, in the confusion of thrashing canvas and driving rain, this final gesture might be missed. For several seconds he waited, silently dreading the first sign they were to be hit once more, before the American appeared to take the hint. A whistle sounded and a voice called out far off – too far off to be understood. Then lights began to appear on the frigate's deck and soon it was obvious they were preparing to lower a quarter boat.

"It was the only thing you could do," Corbrite announced, joining him on the quarterdeck.

"We should never have opened fire," Taylor replied. "I don't know what the old cull was thinking of."

Corbrite glanced down to his former captain's remains then back at the lieutenant. "Never mind," he said, "I doubt he'll do it again."

* * *

"As I see it, Mr Taylor, we had very little choice." The American captain was large – he seemed to fill the small cabin by himself – but, though his tone was rich with regret this was by no means an apology.

"I quite understand, sir," Taylor told him. "I believe our captain overstepped the mark."

"Somewhat," Walton agreed. "When fired upon I had to reply, you must understand that."

"I do, sir, and appreciate it were not a full broadside."

Walton gave a wry grin. "That was more by accident than design, to be honest we weren't expecting a full-blown action. Your late captain had been making a nuisance of himself for some while, my instructions were only to see him off and possibly deliver a taste of his own medicine. But what concerns me now is how we can clear this mess up."

The two men were in Leyton's quarters and both sat the same side of the dead man's desk, Taylor having felt uncomfortable about taking his former captain's place. Dawn had broken and the storm was easing; *Sparrow* now rode more comfortably although whether she would take a sail without extensive repairs was still being assessed.

"I fail to see how such an incident could be concealed," Taylor said. "We lost men other than the captain and have several wounded."

"Oh I wasn't suggesting we hide what happened," Walton declared. "I also suffered casualties and have lost a good friend in my second officer. And they were needless deaths, Mr Taylor, and will be made the more so if our two countries fall out further over the incident."

"So what do you suggest?"

"Initially we must be certain of the facts," the American replied. "And I should make it clear straight away that if there is any suggestion that my ship fired first I will dispute it."

"There is no question of that," said Taylor. "As I have stated, Captain Leyton was unquestionably exceeding his orders; I challenged him on the fact just before we opened fire and would probably be in line for disciplinary action were it not for..." Suddenly he felt unable to continue; it had been a long night.

Walton nodded in understanding. "I'm glad to hear you protested," he said. "It will count in your favour and should make some difference."

Taylor looked up, surprised. "Difference? In what way?"

"When a captain is disgraced it is not uncommon for the shame to equally fall on their junior officers. I should not like that to happen to you, Mr Taylor, and will do what I can to avoid it."

"I should appreciate that."

"As I see it we must work together to see such a foolish episode is not escalated."

Taylor was about to reply when there came a knock at the door and Rogers, the boatswain, entered in a flurry of oilskins and spray. Both men rose as the warrant officer touched a damp hat.

"Beggin' your pardon, sir, we've had a good look at the tophamper and it ain't good."

"We cannot get underway?" Taylor asked.

"Carpenter's checkin' the forechains again though 'e ain't hopeful; gonna need a lot of work and probably a dockyard to sort everythin' proper."

"What about the main?" Taylor felt his spirits falling further.

"That's another matter, sir, and no more promisin'. A fair amount's been knocked away and the whole mast's weakened, see? Chips thinks we might be able to batten it, but it's anyone's guess how long that'll hold."

The lieutenant nodded; should a vessel the size of *Sparrow* lose her main it could tell for her.

"Then we will take you under tow," Walton announced.

"Into New York?" Taylor asked, his voice tinged with horror as he considered the reception they might receive.

"I were thinking more of Halifax," the American added more gently and Taylor's relief was instant.

"That would be preferable," he said, "but we are your prize."

Walton shook his head. "There's no need for that. Like I say, we should play this down as much as possible, and parading a captured British warship along the Hudson would hardly do that."

"If you are certain..."

"I am positive; come, we'd better make a start."

* * *

But the *Delaware* had hardly towed the stricken *Sparrow* more than a few miles when another vessel was sighted on the horizon and soon *Tenacious* was sweeping towards them, sails trimmed to perfection and a glorious curl of water at her bows. On his quarterdeck Walton waited patiently while the vision steadily closed then, as the British frigate came alongside and spilled her wind, he collected the speaking trumpet from its becket and made for the weather bulwark.

"Good morning to you, Captain King," he announced genially.

"Captain Walton, a pleasure to meet once more," came the cautious reply. "Though I wonder..."

85

"I seem to have acquired one of your warships," Walton continued, "and would be happy to explain further."

"Very well, but shall have to visit *Sparrow* first."

"Of course, and when you have done you might care to join me aboard *Delaware*. There is an open invitation as I recall, perhaps we might discuss this over a meal?"

* * *

"From what you say, and all I have learned from Lieutenant Taylor, there is no argument," King said as he finished the last mouthful of pecan pie and collected his glass. *Delaware*'s great cabin was extremely comfortable and the meal the pair of them had just eaten was one of the best he had tasted afloat. "Commander Leyton's performance with the merchants is questionable but he was definitely exceeding his orders by firing on an American national vessel. No state of war exists between our nations and I trust it never shall again."

"This is not the first time a British captain behaved in such a manner," Walton reminded as he wiped at his mouth with a cloth. "I hope it will not become a habit."

"It is a hope we share."

"I am delighted to hear you say so," the American beamed. Then, with a flash of wickedness, "So perhaps we shall see an end to your seizing of our men?"

King gave a wry smile. "I cannot speak for that," he replied. "Indeed, when it comes to government policy I find I am rarely consulted."

"Sure, and it is the pity." Walton gave an elaborate sigh as he tossed the napkin aside and reached for his drink. "For there are those who say your navy behaves worse than Barbary pirates."

"Come now, that is a trifle strong," King protested. "Barbary pirates make slaves of those they capture."

"And what do you do with the men you seize?" Walton enquired innocently over his glass.

King shrugged. "Those we believe to be deserters are sent to trial; the rest are pressed into our Navy."

"Exactly." The American slammed his drink down on the table. "Forced to work against their wishes and if any disobey they get beaten or worse; if that ain't slavery, I don't know what is."

"Your navy is still manned entirely by volunteers?"

"Exclusively," Walton confirmed with a hint of complacency. "Only those who choose to serve do so. We believe all men to be equal and have a right to life, liberty and happiness, however they wish to pursue it."

"There are more slaves in America than England," King pointed out.

"Think you so?" Walton blustered. "You limey's have your share, if not in Great Britain then any one of your colonies."

King sighed. "I suppose we may as well face it, both our countries might have banned the trade though that hasn't stopped either continuing to benefit from it." He took a sip of his own spruce beer. "This is truly excellent," he said.

"Glad you like it; I make it myself on board."

"Impressive."

"Oh, *Delaware*'s quite an independent ship; that rabbit you just ate was home grown as well."

"Really?"

Walton nodded. "We have a veritable herd of the critters and they make better eating than any hen."

"But not so good for eggs, I'd chance." King replaced his empty glass as his mind returned to the current problem.

That Leyton should have behaved so came as no great surprise and he supposed himself partly to blame for leaving him to patrol alone in such a sensitive location. But then he hadn't promoted the man to commander, nor made him captain of *Sparrow*. And at least he and Walton agreed on keeping the matter as low-key as possible. There were obvious differences between them although the similarities were far greater, while he had to admit to enjoying the man's company; it was just a shame they should have met again under such unfortunate circumstances.

"It has been a pleasant meal, Captain," the American told him. Then, unintentionally mirroring King's thoughts, "Maybe next time it will be a more joyful occasion?"

"I assume you had no intention of returning to Halifax?"

"Only to see Mr Taylor and his ship safe; you've a good man there, he should go far."

"Indeed, I have high hopes for him. If you'll permit me to take over the tow I shall continue from here."

"That would be appreciated; perhaps we should make arrangements now, before the sun gets any lower?"

Chapter Eight

Godby's arrival had been generally welcomed by the midshipmen's berth. The lad was obviously well qualified as a seaman having served aboard another Royal Navy vessel, and quickly adjusted to the routine. A ship the size of *Tenacious* warranted six young gentlemen but few suitable candidates could be found in an outpost like Halifax. Not that there was a shortage of those eager for the post, although most were inexperienced and held fanciful ideas about the life while others relied too much on good connections. Consequently they had been surviving on half that number for some time and, in a matter of days, it was as if Godby had always been part of their team. And in a ship that already counted nineteen blacks, two lascars and a Polynesian on her lower deck, his colour almost went unnoticed. It was only Hanson, senior of the berth, who took exception and even with this Godby showed himself to be capable. True to his way, Hanson's bigotry was mainly revealed in muttered asides and obtuse references to his father's plantation that initially were allowed to go unchallenged. But one night, when Vernon was on duty and the three remaining midshipmen shared a late supper in the cockpit, matters came to a head.

Tenacious was at anchor off George Island, having just delivered *Sparrow* to the Navy Yard's tender mercies, and the lads were resting back after consuming copious amounts of spotted dog. The pudding had been cooked by their steward and Hanson was viewing the portion saved for Vernon with covetous eyes.

"That's Simon's," Brotherton pointed out. "He'll be off watch and down at any moment, it'll be an agreeable surprise."

"Surprise, yes," the older lad agreed, drawing the bowl nearer. "So we had better act quick. As I see it, Vernon has no idea of the beast's existence so can hardly be disappointed. Besides, I'm relieving him so will be facing a four-hour anchor watch; this'll do to keep the chills at bay."

"It belongs to Simon," Brotherton maintained. "You can't eat it."

"Not alone, maybe," Hanson chuckled. He had retrieved the spoon from his own bowl and was about to dig deep. "Though I dare say such a thing might be achieved. Anyone care to join?"

"No!" Brotherton insisted with rare authority. "Touch that pudding and you can forget about the loan of my hat for shore leave tomorrow."

Hanson paused although the smile remained. "Come, it is nought but a mouthful. Join me in a share and we'll have it polished off before the cove appears."

"You cannot eat another man's food," Godby announced. He had been a mute witness to the entire conversation but as soon as he spoke all humour vanished from the older midshipman's face.

"Do not presume to give me instructions, *Mister* Godby," he spat. "As far as I am concerned you are here on sufferance."

"Sufferance?" Brotherton questioned.

"You know what I mean, you both do." His eyes darted towards Godby then quickly returned to Brotherton. "There are certain fellows who should not breathe decent men's air, let alone tell them what they might or might not eat."

"Certain fellows?" Godby repeated.

"And you know what that means as well." Now he faced the new midshipman directly. "My father owns more than two hundred like you. Feeds them, shelters them and pays out for the doctor when needs be. But they know how to behave and their proper station; he gives the orders and they obey."

"I ain't no slave," the midshipman stated softly.

"Maybe not now, though I'd chance you have been. You or your parents – assuming you knew who they were of course..."

"That's enough," Brotherton declared, standing and looking down on Hanson. "Vernon's due to be relieved any moment, you'd better get yourself on deck smartish before this deteriorates further. And leave that pudding."

Hanson glanced up at Brotherton with the spoon still raised and an expression that could have melted lead. But, before further words could be exchanged, Vernon did appear. The lad entered with a blast of cold air and an innocent smile that vanished as soon as he sensed the atmosphere.

"What's about?" he asked.

"Merely sorting a few differences." Hanson spoke deliberately. "In a moment Brotherton here shall apologise and all will be well."

"I have nothing to apologise for," Brotherton replied as clearly. "And neither has Godby."

"Well never mind that." Vernon looked to Hanson. "Croftie's askin' for you. Cove's in one hell of a paddy, I'd get yourself up there were I you. I say, is that a spotted dog?"

Still staring hard at Brotherton, Hanson stood. Then, with a sneer for Godby and a sweep of his hand that sent the bowl spinning, he left.

"Whatever's been going on?" Vernon asked, seating himself and calmly claiming his pudding.

"It's Hanson," Brotherton explained, as he and Godby sat also. "Called Godders here a slave."

"Or came mighty close," Godby agreed. "You may as well eat your pudding while there's still warmth in it."

The lad glanced at his two friends who were behaving remarkably oddly, then collected a spoon from one of the empty bowls and set to with a will.

"Of course he was not wrong," Godby stated after a while, and Vernon began to eat a little more slowly as the midshipman continued.

"Both my parents were slaves; belonged to a man name of Jennings," he announced. "And he were a good Christian by all accounts; a Quaker or so I believes."

"I had no idea Quakers kept slaves," Brotherton muttered and Godby turned his brown eyes on him.

"They did then," he said. "You see this were South Carolina; it gets mighty hot in them parts. Whites can't take the heat so they used natives to do their work."

There was a pause and Vernon finally laid down his spoon.

"Well, it seemed Jennings cared for his people and they were happy enough. Then he took ill, whether it were on account of the heat or just chance I don't know, but he was close to death and Ma and Pa were worried. You see he had no family; if he died all his possessions would be sold. That included my folks and chances were strong they'd be separated. At the time America was fighting the British and word got about of a high-up Englishman. He offered freedom to any slaves that reached British lines."

"Dunmore's Call," Brotherton suggested and Godby nodded.

"They figured it to be a way out and Jennings were in no state to go lookin' so my folks took their leave. They made it north without too much trouble and for a while Pa served in the British Army while Ma helped out in the barracks. Both were treated well enough and allowed to keep in touch. Then, when the fighting was over, they were reunited and taken to New York for a spell before being shipped to Shelburne County."

"I know the area," Brotherton announced. "Least, I've seen it from the ship; Cape Sable Island's usually our first sighting of Nova Scotia when we approach from the south."

Godby nodded. "Anyways, the King gave my folks seventy acres of land and promised food for the next three years. The idea was to keep them supported until they could feed themselves. Turned out the land weren't up to much and the first year's supplies didn't last more'n two months. With a bit more time they might have made it work, though you knows the weather in those parts. And some things, like eatin', can't be put off so Pa found work building roads or tending other folks' property."

There was silence in the cockpit as the midshipman gathered his thoughts. Even the regular grumblings of a ship at anchor seemed to have been suspended. And then he began again.

"Their home was a pit house dug deep in the ground with a canvas roof and blankets for walls. Smoke from the fire found its own way out and the place was precious damp. Seemed Pa weren't alone in wanting work and those that needed help found they could get it for near to nothin'. They all but starved the first winter, then those in charge got to realise things couldn't go on much longer. Pa was told he could head south and sign up as a soldier in a West Indian regiment, that or move back to Africa."

"Their home?" Vernon chanced, but Godby shook his head.

"Further north – Sierra Leone where they were establishing a settlement for former slaves. By then my sister had come along and I don't think my folks could stand the thought of starting over, besides Pa had already seen enough of army life. So they moved to Halifax instead and found employment as domestic servants, which is when I turned up."

"So you were born in Nova Scotia?" Vernon exclaimed and Godby flashed a quick smile.

"It's why I'm sailing in this ship and not the *Delaware*!" he said.

"And are they still in Halifax?" Brotherton asked gently.

"Pa is, Ma died a while back; sister took her place. Their people are decent, they work in the fishin'; that's how I first went to sea and found I liked it. I crewed for them a spell then they let me go."

"Let you go?"

"Servants in Halifax aren't like most others," Godby explained. "They're indentured."

"What, like an apprentice?" Vernon this time.

"Similar. Person signs up for a length of service and is paid at the end of it. Mostly it works though some are prepared to cheat; a man who can't read or write is told he's signing for five years then finds it's fifty, or gets let go just before they comes up for their money."

"So it is truly a form of slavery?"

"Can be," Godby agreed. "Though not all are as bad and we was lucky. When Ma died our people took pity and let me join the Navy. More than that, the master was friends with a serving lieutenant and persuaded him to take me as a volunteer. It were against his better judgement, I'd wager, but turned out well in the end. And that's how I got here," he added, the grin returning. "Pa and Sis get a day off every three months, which ain't much different to those that are truly free, an' I know they are better off than most."

"And you have a career in the Navy," Brotherton reminded him. "One thing you can say about the RN, it doesn't care who you are or where you come from; if you can hand, reef and steer, and are willing to work, you'll get on."

"Pressed men have been known to become senior officers," Vernon agreed, "and there's supposed to be an admiral who was flogged when a lower deck hand."

"Oh I likes it fine," Godby assured them. "Last ship were decent and this looks like being as good if not better. Captain King seems a fair man and you folks are tolerable to work with." He beamed at them both then suddenly grew more serious. "Jus' not so sure about our friend Hanson."

* * *

"I'm afraid it will be another escort duty," King announced. It was their first morning meeting for almost a week, King having been ashore on other business. And it had come as a relief to note his first lieutenant was on time, although it appeared the older man had omitted to shave.

"'Tis the pity," Croft sighed. "Had such a time not been wasted on Commander Leyton's foolishness, we'd be off the Indies b'now."

King switched his mind from the first officer's stippled chin and considered his comment. Leyton had certainly been at fault and he supposed there was nothing wrong in Croft voicing an opinion, especially in the privacy of *Tenacious'* great cabin. Still it felt strangely wrong for him to speak so, probably because William Leyton had paid handsomely for his folly. Besides, if anyone had been inconvenienced it was King himself. He had spent the past two days attending a board of enquiry called to investigate the incident, an exercise that all attending had known would be futile from the start.

"It should not be so terribly onerous," King said. "Only seven ships and all reasonably fast, or so we are assured. They are assembling as we speak and should be ready to sail by Thursday morn'. *Tenacious* shall be the only escort."

"Where bound?" Croft asked and King realised he had omitted the most important piece of information. If he did not take care he might slip into Croft's forgetful ways.

"Antigua."

"So another West Indies run," Croft mused.

"And if nothing requires shepherding north, we shall be free to pick up our promised cruise."

"Though the chance of any sizeable prey will be much reduced."

"Reduced?" King questioned.

"By the time we are on station it will be well into the hurricane season," Croft continued. "No slaver will intentionally arrive at such a time."

King smiled. "Lord, James, I don't believe those parts have known a wind worthy of the name in thirty years!"

"Maybe not a full-blown hurricane," Croft allowed. "Although I have seen some heavy storms that might have been called worse – why we passed through one ourselves not so very long ago."

"But that were hardly a hurricane," King said. "Besides, I don't recall our coming to any major harm."

"Perhaps not," Croft grudgingly agreed. "And if we stay out long enough we may even see the season through."

"I should say there was every likelihood."

"In which case we shall be on station when the traffic begins to flow again." The older man was brightening visibly now. "Even if we are running short on some provisions there should be plenty of time for a reasonable haul."

"And plenty of time until Thursday," King added more pointedly. "I assume the ship will be ready?"

"Of course, sir." Croft's reply was sharp and unusually formal for their morning talks.

"There was a problem with the water last time," King reminded, equally firm.

"Which will not happen again."

"I am glad to hear of it." King referred to the notes he had made while listening to the interminable evidence at the enquiry. "And what of the people?" he asked.

As Croft considered this he went to pull at his chin but stopped, quite suddenly, as if shocked. For several seconds the lieutenant stared down at his hand before feeling more cautiously at his face once more. King looked away and waited until the older man finally answered.

"Three more have run," he began uncertainly. "There were four but Collins was recaptured almost immediately."

"And what action have you taken?"

Croft was quickly recovering his composure although still seemed slightly flushed. "All were from the starboard watch but I immediately cancelled liberty for both. Collins is on the punishment deck and due to be brought up at my report later today."

"Very good, but that would seem a mite hard on the larbowlines."

"We must do all we can to discourage desertion," Croft declared a trifle primly.

"Undoubtedly, though I have a notion that might serve." King looked at his notes again. "*Guerriere* is currently in port. Sam Pechell has her – we served on the board of enquiry together. His ship is due for minor repairs but the yard cannot take her until next month. I gather he is under pressure to grant the wedding garland and understandably reluctant to fill his ship with women. He asked if we'd be interested in a spot of ship visiting."

"Us to visit them?" Croft checked.

"Oh yes."

"That is much the better course," the older man exclaimed brightening again.

"Indeed." King was privately pleased to be able to provide such an ideal solution. "*Tenacious* is due out first and Sam might attend to any damage caused while they are in refit."

Now Croft nodded eagerly. "I've known vessels suffer worse from a ship visit than enemy action," he said.

"Well, you needn't worry, *Tenacious* will remain intact and at least half her people can have a spree at someone else's expense. What say we allow the larboard watch?"

"It would be apt – a most agreeable solution in fact."

"There's no reason for them to be punished for the other watch's failings, and though most will return three sheets to the wind, at least we should not suffer any more runners."

"What man would desert from one king's ship to another?" Croft agreed with half a smile.

King pondered for a moment. "Tell me, James, the men we did lose; I don't suppose Knightly was one of them?"

"Knightly?" Croft seemed taken aback.

"The one who claims to be an American."

"Yes, yes, of course. No, he is of the larboard watch. Besides, we consider him likely to desert so have denied liberty on that account. But I'm afraid he has been up to his old tricks; bo's'un complains of him trying to squirrel a length of two-inch line."

"What on earth would he want with that?"

"Sell it to a bumboat I should imagine," Croft shrugged. "And Mr Summers sent him to me citing insolence. I set him to cleaning the heads and promised a further offence would lead to a stoppage of grog."

"He truly seems unable to settle." King pursed his lips. "Sometimes I wonder if it would be better to allow him shore leave, if only to be rid of the man."

"I think that would be a mistake," said Croft. "And serve as a bad example to the others."

"Maybe so. There is no problem between him and Mr Godby I hope?"

"You are speaking of the black?" Croft enquired.

"I am speaking of the midshipman," King snapped in reply.

"Nothing has been reported." The older man seemed unabashed. "Which is strange as Knightly has fallen out with most of his type."

King closed his eyes briefly. "Mr Summers is the divisional

lieutenant for both men I believe?"

"Indeed," Croft agreed. "Though I understand he considers Mr Godby able to take care of himself."

"That is a consolation I suppose, yet I still consider Knightly to be more trouble than he's worth."

* * *

"There's one thing I knows for certain," Stokes told Knightly, "you're more trouble than you're worth."

"Can't see how you make that out," the American protested. "I only said I weren't loaning no shirts."

"But you got more 'an a dozen," Lovemore pointed out. They were in their mess with the majority changing into tiddly suits, the smart clothes saved for rare occasions when shore leave was allowed. Although it was actually a ship visit that had come about and at quite short notice. Out of the blue the *Guerriere*'s lower deck had invited *Tenacious*' larboard watch to join them for refreshment and sport. Such times were highly valued; if *Guerriere*'s hands steered the normal course all in their watch would be treated royally with grog, sweetmeats and cake, along with riotous games that only the generous would classify as sport.

"Maybe I has," Knightly conceded. "Though they need cloth, which the pusser ain't got. I been cutting some up and adding to others but have yet to sort them all."

"Longdon only wants the one." Groom was tying a red scarf about his neck. "An' jus' for the day."

"Just for a watch," Longdon corrected hopefully.

"Aye," Johnno, the boy, added. "Can't see what we can get up to in four hours."

"You'd be surprised," Lovemore smirked while squeezing one foot into a gaudily buckled shoe. "I known some rare old times aboard other vessels – 'specially when they 'ad the weddin' garland a flyin'."

"Well I can't wear this!" Longdon had removed his current shirt and was holding it up for inspection. The cloth was deeply caked in grey slime and smelled worse than any man present. "Messed it when we shifted anchor, and me spare's still in lye."

"Someone else can lend you one," Knightly's eyes fell on Lovemore. "You're his tie mate."

"I only got what I'm wearin'," the seaman protested. "We was

96

waiting for the next southerly trip to buy fresh cotton; no one were expectin' to go a visiting."

"Aye, we're all short, every one," Groom confirmed. "Slop chest is all but empty and there won't be no more till we fetch the Windies. Nor no cloth neither."

"But Longdon ain't got to worry." Stokes spoke with authority. "It only needs one messmate to have a surplus and he'll be fine, ain't that right, Knightly?"

"Not to my mind." The seaman reached into a ditty bag and removed three shirts.

"Any of them would do," Longdon hinted hungrily.

"I don't doubt it," Knightly sniffed, before replacing two and slipping the third, a blue checker, over his head.

"You mean you ain't going to loan?" Groom asked, amazed.

"Got it in one, though I'm always open to a bit of business."

"Business?" Stokes was disgusted. "You mean you want to charge to lend a mate a shirt?"

"Not lend," Knightly corrected, "but purchase would be a different matter."

The silence was only broken by a sigh from Longdon. "So how much do you want?"

"Half a crown."

Now there was a mutual roar of protest.

"'Alf a crown?"

"Fur one crabbit sark?"

"Man's a filch!"

"There it is." Knightly seemed pleased with the reaction. "Fresh shirt, never been worn and with additions by your 'umble servant. All for only thirty of your worthless British pennies."

"You only paid a bob for the whole lot!" Groom exclaimed.

"Like I said, I done a bit of work."

"You're a rum one an' nae mistakin'," McKenzie informed him.

"Some might call me that," Knightly allowed, "and some might call me a man of business. But 'alf a crown's the price, and you can takes it or leave it."

* * *

Despite the short notice, *Guerriere*'s hands had gone to a great deal of trouble. The forward part of their berth deck had been swept clear to provide a space for dancers and, as Stokes cautiously led his mess down the companionway, a small band was already playing a selection of popular forebiters. Further aft, mess tables were laid out with a selection of bread, cakes and scones that came with a scent suggesting most were freshly baked, while outside the doors to the frigate's gunroom a cask of ale had been broached and was already attracting a line of interest.

"Never thought it'd be like this," Longdon told Lovemore.

"I were forgetting, this is your first ship visit." His tie mate treated him to a grin.

A red-haired seaman approached. "What cheer?" he asked, shaking Lovemore's hand as if it belonged to a long-lost brother. "Make yourselves at home, lads. There's food an' drink and sport later."

"Kind of you," Lovemore replied but the man had already moved on and seemed to have forgotten them completely.

"So why they doing this?" Longdon gestured vaguely.

"Honour of the ship," his mate explained. "They put on a good show and we respects them more on account of it – least that's the intention. You wait, once we start laying into their scran there'll be stories of how fast they can set up topmasts or clear for action. Officers cooperate an' all – that's why they got the extra stingo," he added, nodding towards the beer. "By the time they comes to take us back most of our lot will be half seas under, with *Guerriere*'s lower deck laughin' at them for a bunch of chits."

"Take a seat, there matey," another unknown face pointed to a form. "'Elp yourselves to anythin' you likes an' we got a show for you later."

"A show?" Longdon asked.

"Aye." The man's chin was square and he had a nose that must have been broken at least twice but the jovial smile made him appear quite agreeable. "Better than any penny gaff ashore. Middies mainly, an' a few of the monkeys: most scrub into the fairest wenches you could wish for."

"Is this both watches?" Lovemore asked.

"Nah, starbolines got liberty," the bruiser explained quickly. "Be our turn tomorra, an' they gets to clear up – hey, take a seat there matey!" he added, abandoning them and moving on to another pair.

98

Longdon and Lovemore exchanged glances. The band finished the current selection and there was a pause before it came crashing back with a hearty hornpipe.

"So what'll it be?" the older seaman asked. "Beer, cake or do you fancy a jig?"

Longdon glanced forward to where a group of men were already throwing themselves into the dance to whoops and cheers from their mates. He gave a cautious smile. "I think I'll start with some cake," he said.

* * *

The invitation had been extended to the larboard watch's junior officers and Godby and Brotherton were glad to take advantage. But on being introduced to *Guerriere*'s midshipmen's berth both were mildly disconcerted to find three of their opposite numbers dressed as women.

"Never mind them," their guide, who was in full uniform, advised. "Some of us are putting on a show later."

"Not that they need much excuse." An older, and equally correctly dressed midshipman was seated at the single table and made the remark over the book he was reading. "What with rehearsals and performances it's a wonder some uniforms ever get worn."

"Can it, grandad," a boy, disturbingly attractive in a bright floral dress, directed before taking a deep draught of beer from a pint pot. "Show went down well enough with the lieutenant governor."

"And Admiral Warren," another agreed as he flashed his painted eyes at the visitors. "Grosvenor's only jealous 'cause he can't hold a tune to save his life."

"Why don't you join us?" a third, sporting a blazing red wig, asked. "Ain't nothing to it, we got any manner of costumes an if you gets your lines wrong they likes it all the more."

"I'm not one for the theatricals," Brotherton explained.

"Me neither," Godby agreed.

"Suit yourselves," the first shrugged before taking a further dose of beer.

* * *

"All have returned safely enough," Croft reported to King at the start of the second dog watch. "Except for a few that are being purged by the surgeon."

"Barrel fever?" King assumed.

"In some cases," Croft admitted, "though Mr Manning believes the Guerriere's might have laced their beer."

"An unpleasant trick."

"But hardly surprising, there has long been competition between the two ships."

"Well the time away should have cooled a few ardours," King supposed. "I'd chance no lasting harm has been done and at least we have them all back," he added more cheerfully.

"We have, sir, though only just; one did try to desert."

"Desert? Who would do a thing like that?" But even as he asked the question King thought he already knew.

"I fear it was Knightly, sir." Croft was as solid as ever. "They found him hiding in an empty hogshead. With *Guerriere* due for refit and most of her people expecting to be billeted ashore he probably figured there would be a better chance of running than on another convoy duty."

"I see." King spoke sadly. "And he is back with us now?"

"He is, and on the punishment deck. Even in so short a time he made himself thoroughly unpopular with *Guerriere*'s officers; they were only too pleased to return the fellow."

"Well, that answers one question." King leant back in his chair as Croft looked enquiringly. "This morning you asked what kind of man deserts from one warship to another," King explained. "And now we know."

Chapter Nine

The journey as far as Bermuda was uneventful. Their charges, which had miraculously increased from seven to nine, proved both seaworthy and obedient so a creditable pace had been possible; so much so that, when the island finally came into sight, spirits aboard *Tenacious* were high, at least on the lower deck.

For nearly every hand knew what appeared to be no more than a dull grey mound on the horizon was actually as close to paradise as it was possible to get. And, though Bermuda might be closed to them, their final destination would not fall far short. To those accustomed to judging their position through hearsay and scuttlebutt, seeing the island told them they had already completed nearly half their journey. Antigua might be several hundred miles to the south but, to simple minds that only survived through eternal optimism, it might almost be in sight. Once there the delights of shore leave and cheap goods surely awaited them while the sun, which grew hotter with every southerly mile, only increased their good tempers and encouraged what came close to a holiday atmosphere aboard the warship.

However, the mood on *Tenacious*' quarterdeck was very different. Her officers knew more and had greater concerns. They were now in the midst of the hurricane season; winds truly deserving such a name might be relatively uncommon although storms that came close could occur at any time and even the mildest would endanger their small collection of shipping. And there were other perils far more deadly; pirates and privateers roamed these latitudes as well as the occasional stray enemy warship. Meeting either of any size while caring for such a vulnerable burden was something they would rather not consider.

But King was unable to share his officers' detachment and, as he witnessed the departure of two of their number – the latecomers who were only staying with them as far as St George's – he sensed the hands' jovial atmosphere and knew it could not last. Speculation about larger privateers had been the staple dinner table gossip amongst his fellow captains for some while and recent reports of ravished convoys and merchant captures confirmed this. It seemed that, despite losing their Caribbean bases, the French were continuing the constant harassment of British shipping that had already cost his country dear. *Tenacious* would be lucky to arrive without encountering at least one of these newer, larger predators and, despite having less merchants to escort, protecting a convoy single-handed was never pleasant.

Given the choice between fighting privateers or national ships, King definitely preferred the latter for, despite the majority being smaller than his own command, a private warship usually made an extremely tough opponent. Perhaps it was the element of commerce; a privateer fought for material gain rather than honour and capture would mean personal ruin instead of paid imprisonment. But whatever the reason, combat with a private warship usually turned out far more grisly while there was something vaguely honourable about meeting an opposing country's warship in battle. To King it was as if he were not personally involved but carrying out the wishes of a distant sovereign, yet there could be no such subterfuge when fighting a privateer. He might regard an enemy officer with esteem and possibly respect, but could find little to admire in those who steered a course so close to common piracy.

King had been lucky earlier in the commission, a small cruiser was surprised at dawn and fell to *Tenacious'* overwhelming power without protest. That had been an exception, though; singularly or *en masse*, privateers generally made robust opponents and ones he would rather not meet while caring for seven tempting merchants.

However, all would change once they fetched Antigua. He had already decided that, when their hook was set in the sandy sludge of English Harbour, there would be no granting of liberty for the hands. *Tenacious* must water and take on minor provisions, and a topman who had recently fallen from the fore' may live long enough to be transferred to the naval hospital but, if Croft were up to the mark, everything should be accomplished in a matter of days. And then, providing no convoy awaited or any other mundane work demanded their attention, he could finally begin his cruise.

With no stodgy traders steering out of line or hauling in their wind to hamper his actions, King could truly go on the offensive. *Tenacious* was well up to the mark in every department and would probably handle two or even three of the larger corsairs with relative ease. And, though it might not be an honourable fight or one that brought much in prestige or prize money, he would be freeing the seas from a particularly unpleasant nuisance. But that must wait, first he had to see this convoy safe. Then, when *Tenacious* was charged, primed and ready, the hunted could finally turn hunter.

* * *

Eight bells had sounded to mark the end of the second dog watch and the inhabitants of the fore cockpit were at rest. Earlier they had eaten a substantial meal of lobscouse followed by plum duff and now the warrant officers were agreeably listless. And if justice were served their repose should last all night, as most were officially idlers; only Amon, the boatswain, was in danger of being called for duty and he was prepared to take the risk.

As senior petty officers they were allowed to draw their daily tot neat, meaning the rum would not spoil on prolonged contamination with water and could be saved for just such an evening. And, so strong was their comradeship, each man's ration for the previous three days had been poured into a communal pot that any were free to drink from with no accounts kept. So, as the level of their spirit gradually decreased and the shielded candles added an extra cast to already heavy air, they had all relaxed into a feeling of mutual conviviality.

However, the mood was not as settled as it might have been; the captain's steward had just tipped them the wink with important news: there was to be no shore leave at Antigua. This did not affect any of them personally – each had spent many days at English Harbour and missing liberty on this occasion would hardly be the end of the world – but the rumour had yet to reach those on the lower deck; quite how they would react was a different matter and one that did concern them all.

"If yer man want's ter spend his time ashore, he should never have opted for de sea." Of them all, Regan was the only one who had made it as far as his hammock, and taken his cup with him.

"That's just the trouble," Amon remarked after a sip of neat rum. "Most didn't choose to be here, and won't like being kept aboard one little bit."

"A twelve-hour spree would not have gone amiss," Wilson, the sailmaker, agreed. "My lads could do with a decent wetting, and then there's the cloth."

"Cloth?" Drake enquired. He was one of those still sitting at the table and, so small was their accommodation, it was an easy matter to tilt his chair back and rest both shoulders against the bulkhead.

"Purser's been low on duck and cotton for the past month or so," Wilson explained. "Been pesterin' me for number ten sailcloth."

"Dennison'll be allowed ashore." Morales had drunk more than any of them and, although still relatively sober, now rested his head sideways on his arms.

"Yes, and will doubtless buy up all he can," Wilson agreed, "then pass it on at a tidy profit."

"It's what he does," said Drake.

"The lads like to buy their own," the sailmaker persisted. "And if they don't get shore leave we can expect trouble."

"You mean *I* can expect trouble" The master-at-arms stretched. "Though this ain't a bad lot, there's no one me or me corporals can't handle."

"Knightly?" Amon suggested.

"Especially Knightly," Drake replied. "The chuff ain't nothing but a bag of wind. If the captain had any sense, he'd make an exception; give him shore leave and good riddance to the old bugger."

"Sure, but isn't dat what he's bankin' on?" Regan was lying back with the tin mug balancing on his generous belly.

"Whatever, there's no point in worrying over it." Amon helped himself to more from the communal pot. "We've a way to go afore we raise Antigua and are likely to meet privateers, or so I understands."

"Privateers?" Wilson remarked in surprise. "Surely a ship like this ain't got a worry there?"

"From what I hears, there's a new kind," Amon informed before taking another sip. "Larger and better manned, more like corvettes and some as big as frigates."

"Ah, piffle," Drake snorted. "Them's just stories to frighten children."

"Oi wouldn't be so sure; a vessel's got ter be a certain size ter make a crossing," Regan stated with more consideration. "Stands ter call."

"Aye, and the more men they carry, the more prizes they can take," Wilson added. "Catch them at the start of a cruise an' they'll be crammed full of men."

"Well I ain't afeared of no privateers," Drake assured them. "Or Knightly, if it comes to it."

"Maybe not," Wilson agreed. "Though I know who I'd rather fight..."

* * *

Cooper glanced up at the masthead in disbelief although the call had been clear enough, as was the ever-brightening sky. Dawn appeared almost complete, in fact, and at such a time it should be no surprise for several sail to have been sighted.

"Firs' looks to be a warship," Jennings, the duty lookout, continued. "Least she's showin' royals an' has what seem to be gunports. Can't be certain, mind, she's barely hull up."

"And what of the others?"

"Rig's simla'," the seaman replied after a long moment's consideration. "Though only the next in line 'as any hull visible and what there is comes an' goes."

The lieutenant drew breath. A line of shipping was closing to windward of a poorly protected convoy; from their rig and course they were likely to be privateers and *Tenacious*, the only escort, was considerably out of station. This must be one of the classic nightmares of every officer of the watch and the fact that it had happened to him was doubly annoying. For he truly should not have been on duty; the morning watch that included dawn, when new shipping or fresh weather would frequently be spotted, was usually the first lieutenant's responsibility. But, the night before, Croft had claimed sickness and requested an exchange which Cooper felt unable to refuse and his soft-heartedness had landed him in one hell of a mess.

"Set t'gallants," he snapped, "and add the main stays'l." The extra canvas would improve matters though not instantly; they would still be a good distance astern of the convoy when he sounded the alarm, but there was no helping that.

"My compliments to the captain," he said, turning to the messenger of the watch. "We have a sighting off the larboard bow. Five vessels, possibly warships, are steering to intercept."

Even the lad paused for a moment and when he did scurry off it was without his usual light-heartedness. Watching him go Cooper drew little comfort; this was Johnno's first ship: the child could not have been aboard more than a few months, yet even he was aware of the importance of such a message.

Movement caught his eye and he noticed Manton had come on deck. Cooper couldn't be sure if the sailing master's appearance were down to luck or from overhearing the lookout's report, but was relieved to see the more experienced man.

"Over there – to the south-east," he said by way of greeting and Manton peered out at the small dark shape that was barely in sight. "Masthead reports four more beyond," he added.

"Think they're raiders?" the older man asked and Cooper gave an elaborate shrug as he handed over the deck glass.

"Might be at that," he said, his tone artificially free of concern.

"The one we can see don't look too large," the sailing master muttered, "though it's always difficult to judge at such a distance."

Cooper said nothing. Size actually meant little; whatever the type of vessel, if these were cruisers they were likely to be faster than a fifth-rate frigate. Faster, more nimble, and there were five of them...

Tenacious might deal with any single vessel though she would have to catch them first. And while doing so, while concentrating on robbing one of their tophamper or buoyancy with a carefully aimed broadside, there would be four others free to destroy their precious convoy.

It may even be worse; a frigate could annihilate any single brig or sloop with ease, but if several were met simultaneously they would prove far more formidable opponents. Besides, the raiders need not be small; any warship crossing the Atlantic must have a sound hull and be not only capable of withstanding shot, but strong enough to mount serious artillery. A well-found corvette could easily carry eighteen- or even twenty-four-pound carronades and be fast enough to deliver a thorough pounding, then be gone. Such weapons, and tactics, would play merry hell with *Tenacious'* timbers and, properly orchestrated, could easily disable the ship before relieving her of the convoy. It would be like a bull being taken down by hounds and they might be heading for a devastating battle indeed.

"You're well out of station," the sailing master observed as he lowered the deck glass.

"I were chivvying up *La Bella*," Cooper said with a backward jerk of his thumb. "She sprung a yard late yesterday even' and has been dragging throughout the night. Her master was hoping to start repairs come sunrise."

"And you thought you'd check?" Manton glanced back at the

merchant.

"It was a mistake," Cooper admitted. "Truly I didn't think a mile or two would matter and, if they hadn't a spar to hand, we might have provided."

"Seems reasonable to me." The older man turned his attention back to the sighting. "It wasn't as if we was exactly expectin' company."

Cooper nodded, only slightly reassured. His usual watches were the forenoon and first; one took place in daylight, the other mainly dark, so he was not used to encountering dawn, the most dangerous time in any ship's day.

"Mind, I'm not the one who passes judgement," Manton continued more softly and with a nod towards Captain King, who had just made his appearance at the aft companionway. "It's this fellow what has the say."

* * *

He had been a fool to take that draught, Croft decided as he pulled himself up in his cot. The headache that had begun several hours before was still very much in evidence although the effects of Manning's potion – the one the surgeon had hoped would deaden the pain and encourage sleep – remained and was now a major problem. He tried to focus but strange images were swimming about the tiny cabin and he felt physically sick. For a moment he considered calling for his man but the act seemed strangely beyond him. He opened his mouth and tried to clear his throat; there was no sound, just another wave of nausea that swept him back, leaving his body cold and sweating in the bed's damp embrace. And then, mercifully, sleep claimed him once more.

* * *

"She'll take royals as well," King remarked while still examining the strange shipping through his personal, foreshortened, glass. Manton duly touched his hat before issuing the appropriate order. A flurry of topmen made for the windward shrouds and Cooper, apparently the only man aboard not fully employed, fidgeted uncomfortably.

"Why so out of station, Jack?" the captain asked when he finally lowered the telescope.

"One of the merchants had been flagging," Cooper explained. "She lost the use of her foretop yard in yesterday's squall and was hoping to start repairs."

107

"Then you had good reason." King was raising the special glass again. "Our primary concern is protecting the convoy," he added while continuing to study the sighting. "And the only way we might do that is if all shipping is kept together." He glanced round at the second lieutenant. "Is she able to sort the spar?"

"Her master thinks so," Cooper replied. "And if not they have another that might serve."

"Well let's hope they can, and quickly," King continued. "To my mind we have some fancy sailing ahead of us."

* * *

By mid-morning the situation was far clearer. *La Bella*'s master proved as good as his word and the brig was able to rejoin the convoy under a full suit of sail. As *Tenacious* had an hour or so earlier, the extra canvas quickly bringing her up to a more defensive position. Now she lay on the windward station, slightly forward of her charges. And the merchants were definitely behaving themselves; the seven remaining vessels had grouped together in almost parade ground formation and currently sheltered behind their protector as sheep might a shepherd when wolves threatened. Equally there was no doubt about the raiders, there were, indeed, five in all; each a warship of sorts with the nearest three being corvettes. And it was these minor frigates that were causing King the greatest concern.

He knew the type well, had faced their like before and even commanded one very similar. Carrying at least nine-pounder long guns and possibly something considerably heavier, they would be fast, agile and potentially deadly. One alone would be no holiday even for *Tenacious*' heavier frame, but if two or three struck together he would definitely be facing a superior enemy.

Yes, a consolidated attack would be hard to defend and might result in the capture of several merchants. Or worse; were his own ship to lose a mast, or even a vital spar, the enemy would literally run rings about him. Only one would need to position themselves off his bow or stern and *Tenacious* might also be taken.

King brought his glass down and looked away, although his thoughts remained on the advancing enemy. Automatically he sought out Croft but the first lieutenant was not on deck, nor had he been that morning; instead a message had revealed him to be in the hands of the surgeon.

"No further word from Mr Manning I assume?" he asked Cooper.

It was a foolish question; the second lieutenant had been on duty since four that morning with King joining him a few hours later. Neither had been below since and any report from the sick berth would have been heard by both.

"No, sir, and it has been a while now."

King nodded, Robert would sort Croft out, although it was strange and mildly annoying for his second in command to be taken so. The man might not be the best when it came to fighting tactics but in situations such as this he had come to rely on his presence, if only as a sounding board.

"Would you say they were privateers, sir?" Cooper asked, "Rather than national ships, I am meaning."

King jumped slightly. It was surely well known that he disliked direct questions from anyone other than the first lieutenant, yet here was Cooper deliberately breaking the unwritten rule and risking a hefty reproof as a consequence. But there was more to the young man's action, as King swiftly realised. With Croft indisposed it was the second lieutenant's duty to take his place, which probably included becoming the captain's confidante. And the fact that Cooper had both the gumption and insight to do so brought King the first real comfort of that day.

"I think it highly likely, Mr Cooper," he said, conscious that the pressure of command had lessened slightly. "And that might actually work in our favour."

"Indeed, sir?" Cooper was really playing his part very well. "How so?"

"Much will depend on how they are managed," King continued, although now more vaguely as his attention had returned to the oncoming enemy. "And by that I mean overall command. Were they national ships there would be a commodore or the equivalent in charge; someone to manoeuvre his forces to the best advantage. But with luck this will be a disparate band with each only interested in feathering their own nest."

"There are no ensigns." Cooper unconsciously glanced up to where their own battered pennant and colours streamed in the gentle breeze.

"No, indeed," King agreed, slightly less enthusiastically.

"Would you say they will make for us, or try to avoid and take out a merchant?"

"We shall have to see." Now the tone was quite flat. King felt Cooper had done enough by setting his thoughts in motion; no further conversation was required. And then there was another distraction; someone had mounted the quarterdeck steps and, with relief, King noted it was Croft.

But not the Croft he knew. This one had a faintly faraway look in his eyes and pale lips that trembled slightly as he presented himself.

"Are you quite fit, James?" King asked, and there was a flicker of a smile on the ashen face.

"Quite well, thank you, sir," he said.

* * *

"Mr Cooper, you will take charge of the starboard battery long guns; Mr Summers shall control the larboard battery. Mr Hanson and Mr Godby will give support."

They had cleared for action and *Tenacious'* officers were assembled on the quarterdeck and facing their captain.

"Mr Croft, you may handle the quarterdeck carronades with Mr Brotherton and Mr Vernon's assistance."

As signals officer, Brotherton might need to communicate with the convoy although that need not take all his time. And despite Croft not being on top form, with a pair of midshipmen working under him he should still be able to manage both batteries of the heavier, but shorter range, cannon.

"These arrangements are necessary as we shall have to choose our targets carefully," King continued. "I will be directing the fire myself and expect few full broadsides; one side's for'ard or aft batteries will be despatched independently. Do I make myself clear?"

Coping with five fast warships would indeed mean conserving shot. A barrage from every bearing cannon might totally devastate a target, but could just as easily miss and there would then be several minutes when one entire side of the ship was impotent. Time enough for an enemy to close and deliver their own dose of poison.

He glanced up; the raiders were far closer, less than two miles off in fact and maintaining the same line-ahead formation that suggested they were under some form of overall command.

"Much will depend on range," he resumed. "With luck the

110

enemy will be armed with carronades so must come in close to make their shots count. Should that be so I shall order you to load with bar and we can try for their masts. But if they keep their distance we must assume they are carrying long guns, in which case it will be round shot throughout."

There was a murmur of understanding. A long-distance action was the last thing any of them wanted; the frigate's main battery of eighteen-pounders were remarkably accurate at anything closer than half a mile though less so when used at extreme range, while small, fast moving targets would be far harder to find than the more stately *Tenacious*. King let out a gentle sigh; it would soon be time.

"Remember, this is one situation when overall control will be vital," he said. "We cannot afford to release shot without reason." Again there was a general muttering of appreciation and King turned to the sailing master.

"I shall be controlling the ship, Mr Manton, but relying on you to implement my orders," he added. "Kindly be sure to have a mate available to take your place if..."

"If I fall, sir?" the older man grinned. "Mr Penny should be on hand."

King nodded briefly before switching his attention back to the oncoming enemy. The French had only struck their royals and were still moving fast; too fast for him to be sure of disabling more than a couple before the rest set upon the convoy. But then they might have other plans, for there was a very viable alternative.

En masse the force was more than strong enough to take on *Tenacious* and, if they kept their distance and picked at her with long-range shot, should steadily wear her down. Then, once the only escort were accounted for, it would be a simple matter to carry every merchant pretty much at their leisure. He glanced about; his officers remained close by and were talking excitedly amongst themselves. All seemed intent only on seeing off a group of cruisers and he was reasonably certain none had yet considered such a dreadful alternative, although most would do so before long.

"Very well," he said, almost to himself. "Then let us do battle."

Chapter Ten

Tenacious was on the larboard tack and steering as close to the wind as she could bear; the raiders had formed a rough line of battle with the first, a corvette that looked to be mounting twelve guns a side, just forward of her arc of fire. King found he was gritting his teeth and forced himself to relax; about him the ship was as quiet as any vessel sailing so could be, only the sound of her stem cutting through the dark ocean and a humming of wind through taut lines broke the silence although another kind of tension was equally apparent. For his earlier predictions had been fulfilled; not only were the French apparently ignoring the convoy, all now realised this would be more than simply seeing off privateers, and *Tenacious* was very likely to be taken.

"Prepare for'ard larboard!" he ordered, his voice was strangely distorted by the speaking trumpet but clear communications would be vital and Summers, stationed by the break of the forecastle, immediately touched his hat in response. The nearest target was roughly a mile off their larboard bow and the long eighteen-pounders of his main battery should cover the distance although there would be little chance of accuracy. Yet King was eager to fire the first shots as an exchange should tell him what ordnance his enemy carried.

Many privateers were equipped with carronades as the short-range pieces threw a heavier shot and needed less powder as well as a smaller crew. Long guns remained common, however, and were his worse fear; the more traditional cannon fired a lighter ball but could do so over a greater distance and with more accuracy. Were even a few of the raiders carrying such weapons this would remain a long-range fight which would put *Tenacious*, with much of her broadside weight made up with carronades, at a disadvantage. The forward larboard gun captains were beginning to raise their hands indicating the target within reach, so there seemed little sense in delaying further.

With a simultaneous crack the cannon were despatched, their

112

smoke clearing almost instantly and passing back over the ship. All aboard waited and the sigh of disappointment when the cluster of splashes landed considerably short might have come from the ship herself.

"Ready aft larboard battery!" King ordered, and Summers ran back, dodging the forward teams as they loaded their warm weapons, to take charge of the sternmost guns.

"Mr Croft, you may also prepare your larboard battery." King spoke more softly as the man was barely feet away. "But wait upon my word." By the time both batteries of long guns were ready for a second airing the carronades should be coming into range and might be fired then.

"Very good, sir," the first lieutenant replied and King noticed his words were mildly slurred.

Now the leading raider was turning and may even be intending to wear; prime time for another try and with a curt order to Summers, King released his aft long guns.

His aft long guns *and* the quarterdeck carronades, or so it turned out. The sudden thunder close by startled him, even though it formed part of a barrage that included eight heavy cannon from the deck below. He spun round and glared through the vanishing smoke to see the worried face of Vernon staring back at him. Croft must have released his battery by mistake, an error that was inexcusable in the present circumstances. A rumble of appreciation broke into his thoughts and he glanced back to see Summers' weapons had neatly bracketed the leading enemy, even if there was no apparent damage. But nearer, considerably nearer, a second series of splashes showed where the carronades' shot had fallen erratically and dismally short.

"I gave you no order, James," King snapped, returning to the larboard carronades, although Croft appeared not to have heard and was concentrating solely on seeing the guns reloaded. He repeated the statement a little lounder and still to no response, apart from an increasingly worried look from the midshipman. King was taken totally aback; it was as if the first lieutenant had simply lost his mind.

"We're ready to tack, sir," Manton hinted, and King brought his attention back to the job in hand. Yes, they must turn, then continue to close on the enemy, this time releasing their starboard batteries. The raiders were wearing in succession while holding their fire, which either meant they were armed with carronades or simply saving their long guns. The line of battle was relatively orderly but could not last, soon they must break formation. That being the case he could not risk another fiasco; the next shots must be made to count.

"Very well, Master, take us about."

Tenacious swept easily into her turn which had been fortunately timed and caused the leading raider's opening broadside to miss by some considerable distance. The shots had been well grouped, though, and covered the distance easily, so one at least of the enemy was equipped with long guns. King swallowed dryly as he absorbed the information while there was also the knowledge of another, more personal, blow that he must shortly deliver. As the ship settled on her new course and her starboard gunners began to signal the target in reach, he called Croft and Brotherton across.

"I shall be requiring the starboard carronades shortly," he said, his tone intentionally flat. "Mr Brotherton, you shall command the battery; Mr Croft, I require you with me at the conn."

It was not an unusual order, midshipmen were accustomed to taking charge of small groups of cannon and Brotherton touched his hat in brief acknowledgement before departing. Even Croft seemed to accept the change and stepped away from the heavy weapons.

"Go below, James," King told him gently, drawing the man aside. "You are clearly ill and not fit for duty."

"I am perfectly well, your honour," the older man replied, although his eyes were focused elsewhere and a thin trail of saliva trailed from the corner of his mouth.

"Go below," King repeated. "Present yourself to Mr Manning and say I sent you. But go and go now."

The leading raider was close enough for their forward battery to reach and King knew he must concentrate on that. He ordered a half broadside and was pleased to see the corvette's fore' stagger and fall. Until a jury mast could be rigged the ship would lack both speed and control making her useless save as a floating battery, which was surely a victory of sorts. And when he turned back it was a relief to see that Croft had indeed left.

* * *

The older man's departure cleared the air to some extent; King found he missed his sounding board but was equally conscious of not having anyone else to worry about. His second in command had been behaving oddly for some while and it came as an unexpected relief to finally acknowledge the fact. There was no time for deeper thought, however; he had an action to fight.

Tenacious' starboard aft long guns and carronades remained unfired; he could almost choose his target. The disabled corvette was closer now and a further barrage might be in order. But then less than a cable behind something larger was steering to pass her and that must be his next objective.

Although not yet. King accepted the first three barrages had been at long range; he was fortunate to have caused one instance of severe damage, but that was probably the result of a single shot and a lucky one at that. The final three enemy ships were starting to fan out and looked likely to descend on him simultaneously, it would be wise to make sure of this second target if *Tenacious* was not to be overwhelmed.

"Mr Summers is signalling both larboard batteries ready." It was the voice of Manton. As sailing master he was officially a non-combatant, his only responsibility being the management of the ship. But the elderly warrant officer was clearly stretching a point, and King was silently glad. The second corvette was passing her wounded consort now and, yes, she was definitely larger – even without the use of his glass he was sure she showed more gunports.

"Ready long guns starboard aft!"

Cooper gave what was almost a jolly wave in acknowledgement as his gunners lined up their weapons.

"Fire!"

The barrage was despatched neatly enough and the wind might even be freshening as the smoke was instantly whisked away. And there was a stirring sight indeed; a cluster of splashes grouped about the oncoming raider with only one going wide and long, the result probably of a miscast shot. But no damage could be detected on the nearest enemy while the last three were definitely breaking formation.

He glanced across to the convoy, all remained in close company although fresh canvas was being set on some and King guessed a change of course was imminent. So be it; from what he knew of merchant masters, when one chose to run the example would quickly be followed. And it was no bad thing, sea room may be needed in order to fight this pack of predators while Brotherton was now responsible for both aft batteries and could not concern himself with signals.

"Frenchie's wearing!"

Manton's warning brought his mind back to the nearest corvette which was now well beyond its wounded colleague. And yes, she was flying into a speedy turn, raising royals as she went; an impressive piece of seamanship that King fully appreciated. But the change of course and extra pace would mean she would be aiming for *Tenacious'* stern, while the remaining craft made for her bows.

"Starboard forward now loaded," Manton added.

"Three points to larboard," King ordered. The new heading and their current canvas should be enough, he had no wish to add more. "Be ready forward starboard!"

Cooper was once more in position, as he expected, and for a moment King was tempted to add Brotherton's starboard quarterdeck carronades. But the sight of the earlier wasted shot was still on his mind; better to wait.

"Fire!"

There was a general sigh; the range had been well estimated but the splashes fell in such a wide arc that King felt an element of panic had been allowed to creep in, which would not do at all. The corvette had finished her manoeuvre and was speeding through the water on a new course; in time she would be threatening their fragile rump while the following warships, one of which at least was another corvette, had also increased sail and were bearing down on their hawse.

Tenacious had picked up speed slightly with the change of course although she would still be easily overhauled; everything depended on her firepower. He felt like Gulliver fighting the Lilliputians; his frigate, usually so slick and speedy, was like a lumbering whale when compared to the sharks that now descended upon it. Half a broadside might deal with one, but delivering an effective blow had already proved hard and was likely to grow more so when the remaining warships arrived.

"Can you reach her with your carronades?" he called to Brotherton, but the young man shook his head.

"Not with much hope of accuracy, sir," he replied.

Glancing forward, King could see Godby supervising the loading of their starboard forward guns. He supposed he might turn steeply to starboard, and maybe even return to the larboard tack, but that would only bring *Tenacious* nearer to her tormentors. No, better to wait and allow his gunners to serve their weapons, even if it meant turning down the chance of a closer action.

"Frenchie's firing!"

Manton again and King looked up in time to see the last of a ripple of flame flash along the nearest corvette's side. The very act told him she was also armed with long guns, which was bad news in itself, while her captain clearly had no qualms about taking on a fifth rate. But then why should he not? Even with one of their number temporarily disabled, the French outnumbered him on nearly every level.

Seconds later the enemy's broadside began to land and with the first sickening thud King knew it had been well laid. *Tenacious* was comprehensibly bracketed, with shot landing along her entire length and puncturing both hull and canvas. There was a chorus of shouts and several whistles; Amon, the boatswain, was calling for lines to be spliced and two marines had been wounded by the same shot and were announcing the fact in a decidedly unmilitary fashion. But even as King assessed the damage he noted the starboard forward battery were signalling their pieces ready and, at a nod to Cooper, they were released in a ragged half broadside.

And there was no time to assess its worth; the corvette that led the second wave was threatening them now and closing fast, seemingly intent on raking them.

"Can you reach now?" King shouted at Brotherton, and the blessed boy nodded in response.

The starboard carronades rang out as one and King followed their shot in his mind. Then the Frenchman was suddenly surrounded by a circle of turbulence that looked likely to sink the ship on its own. But the corvette rode through, apparently undamaged, and King had to suppress a groan of despair.

"Take her to larboard," he snapped at Manton. "I want her running before the wind."

It might not be the frigate's best point of sailing but with two swifter vessels intent on their bow and stern, he had little choice.

The manoeuvre was completed in seconds and the raiders' superior speed immediately became apparent. Both corvettes were closing visibly with clouds of spray issuing from their prows while the following pair joined in what had become a general chase. And those in the van would have been in range, except King had no gun that might bear on them; he could turn at any time and effectively stand and fight although that would limit him to one broadside and there was still the chance the leading ships would close to either side. He would be trapped in their crossfire but might at least have full use of his own cannon.

However the thought was instantly quashed. Even as *Tenacious* settled on her fresh heading and began running before the rising wind, the leading corvette wore and, crossing behind her colleague, proceeded to aim for their larboard quarter. And she was no sooner past when her compatriot also altered course and made for *Tenacious*' starboard flank. Unless King did something quickly he would soon suffer an unanswerable bombardment from two cruisers and the result would not be pleasant.

* * *

"Reckon the captain will be turning again shortly," Cooper told Summers. Both batteries were fully reloaded now and the officers had been idle long enough to assess the situation.

"How can he not?" Summers agreed, stepping closer to his colleague.

"The real question is, whose battery will he choose?" Cooper supposed.

"We can make up either with the deployable gunners."

"Oh, that is beyond doubt. And if we makes a stand, might beat them off – provided they came one at a time, of course."

"And if not?" Summers asked in a lower tone.

"If not, if they choose to surround us, it will be very different," Cooper replied equally softly. "Every man shall be needed on both broadsides, and even then it might not be enough."

* * *

King actually opted to turn to starboard, although there was little science in his choice. And, since this was to be a stand, he immediately ordered the topgallants in and the ship hove to. The nearest corvettes were less than a mile off; if he continued to split his broadside there should be time to allow three, possibly four barrages for each before the cruisers closed. Yet, even if he were successful, even if both were blown out of the water before they could bring their own cannon to bear, two more lay close behind. And then, with a sudden drying of the mouth, he realised what the enemy were about.

As soon as he made his turn the leading raiders had begun to spill their wind. Now they lay dormant and, though officially in range, beyond the truly accurate reach of his long guns. They must be waiting for their fellows to come up, at which point a line of four could be formed and they would doubtless descend on him in force.

"Mr Cooper, fire as you will!"

That was the best option; the nearest ships were barely making steerage way; *Tenacious* must send the maximum amount of iron in their direction before the rest joined and that could only be achieved by her gunners being given a free hand.

The frigate soon began to tremble to an almost constant rumble of gun trucks and explosions as her long guns were served while, nearer to those on the quarterdeck, Brotherton's carronades added their own sharp barks to the cacophony. The latter would have far less chance of accuracy but a full bombardment must serve as a distraction and should hearten the men. A steady stream of acrid smoke was being carried back by the breeze, stinging eyes and drying throats, while the flare of gunfire made heads spin and constant thunder obliterated all reason. Yet throughout it all King kept a steady watch on the two corvettes as they lay amid a turmoil of boiling water. Each seemed annoyingly impervious to the British shot but had turned slightly and were having the audacity to send a peppering of lighter ball in return. Much of the enemy's fire proved as futile as his own, although *Tenacious* was a larger target and received several hits to her lower hull while a twelve-pound round shot landed squarely on one of Cooper's cannon, making the warm iron ring like a bell. And all the time the final two Frenchmen were growing steadily nearer, strengthening the force that must shortly swamp them by sheer numbers.

In fact it was only at the end, when the last two vessels had joined and the leading corvettes were springing back to life, gathering wind and speed and setting vaguely disparate courses, that one was hit, and even then it was a new arrival and the smallest. The brig, probably less than two hundred tons and carrying nothing heavier than nine-pounders, turned in the wind as her mainmast was taken from her and soon fell behind. But the three remaining vessels, two corvettes and a sloop almost as large, were untouched and one had already proved she carried weapons heavy enough to do real damage.

King looked about in desperation. He could not blame his gunners; the range remained long and with continuous fire it was hard – impossible even – to judge exactly where any individual shot was landing. Still he had hoped for more, indeed he had banked on it. Now they must continue with *Tenacious* aiming at moving targets, ones that jostled for position before they made their attack.

And it seemed that, either by direction or habit, the enemy was once more forming a line of battle, with the sloop that had been last to join in the van. King watched with apparent detachment as the three vessels joined formation on the larboard tack and began to sweep towards him, apparently aiming for a point just beyond his ship's stern. Which must never happen; if his current rate of success continued, he might incapacitate one, probably the smaller at the head, and still leave two powerful unharmed corvettes to deal with. And it would only take a couple of lucky shots to disable his own ship and bring the contest to a disastrous end.

"Take her further to larboard, Master. Wear ship and bring us onto the larboard tack."

To turn so now would mean exposing his stern for several dangerous minutes before the larboard cannon would be given a chance, but bearing away from the enemy must buy a little time. The remains of the convoy were clearly visible; a group of desperate ships showing dangerous amounts of sail as they attempted to escape. King knew he may only be putting off the inevitable, yet, in the time it took to wear, a plan may even form, some clever ruse to confound his enemies and bring him to ultimate victory. Such a thing had happened in the past, he had been in many situations just as dire and the ghost of a scheme had usually appeared; something that could be formed into a more solid, workable tactic and go on to save the day. And he had every reason to expect just such a ploy to occur to him this time, at which point he would know exactly what to do. But until that happened he was very conscious of being at a loss.

* * *

The turn was made without incident and soon *Tenacious* was on the larboard tack once more with the wind comfortably on her beam. And she was making a fair speed, even under topsails alone, although the enemy were faster and gaining on them visibly. The nearest was coming up on their larboard quarter. She was smaller, though well set up and a beautiful sight with graceful hull, stiff canvas and a tophamper so tight she seemed in danger of being lifted physically from the waves. In no time the sloop was almost beam on and had sent a speculative broadside of medium round shot through his frigate's rigging, any one of which might have brought down an important spar. But *Tenacious'* guns were the heavier and King sensed her larboard battery would have sufficient range to account for the nuisance.

Which it did, even as he watched. One or possibly two guns from their next forward barrage found a mark in the cat's cradle of line and canvas that gave the vessel life. Instantly the sloop fell away and must be forgotten for she had been masking another danger; close on her heels and off her quarter was one of the corvettes.

She was considerably heavier and King had considered her for a target but the closer threat had carried more immediate danger. Still, as the larger warship fought to take up her former comrade's position and began a far harsher bombardment, he sensed it would take more than a single well-placed broadside to stop her. And all the while the last raider, another corvette and just as deadly, had altered course and was preparing to sweep down to starboard of them. King smiled grimly to himself; he had intended to divide his enemy, though not by allowing one to descend on his vulnerable stern.

A surprisingly heavy ball came crashing through the larboard bulwark between two carronades, shattering the fixings for one and sending deadly splinters slicing through the air. One caught King on the side of his face and he felt the blood flow down his left cheek but gave it no further thought. For Summers' most recent barrage had also caused damage; the corvette was now missing part of her jib boom and had lost forward support for her foremast while he was reasonably certain her starboard mainchains had also been weakened. The latter would make little difference while she remained so, though should be a consideration if he could only force her onto the opposite tack.

But that seemed unlikely as he would have to tack also and the idea of leaving *Tenacious* prone and vulnerable in such company was unthinkable. Another barrage was despatched, this time from the aft larboard battery, and King was sure he saw debris fly from the corvette's side although she continued to hold her course and seemed determined to run his ship down.

"Be ready, Mr Cooper!"

From further forward the lieutenant gave his customary acknowledgement. The second corvette was now approaching their starboard quarter and getting just a little too close for King's liking, he would have to abandon the first in order to see her off, even though that must only bring them deeper into trouble.

"Very well, Mr Manton, four points to starboard!"

With the weather in her favour, *Tenacious* manoeuvred swiftly and her speed increased further as she took the wind more on the quarter. For a brief moment King wondered again about adding further sail but nothing had changed, even with topgallants raised, the corvettes would be faster while any extra exposure must make his ship more vulnerable. The enemy that had been to larboard now lay off their stern and was steering to follow her fellow in attacking his starboard side. They remained a good distance off, King reckoned less than half a mile, yet even the slight reduction in range was to his favour. Now he must try to properly split the pair, take each with either battery and close further; *Tenacious* was stronger in both firepower and frame, and such a move must surely optimise both.

"I propose to wear ship." He was speaking to Manton though in a voice loud enough for all on the quarterdeck to hear. "We will be in danger for a spell but then able to steer between both Frenchmen and hopefully separate them."

There was a pause while the sailing master absorbed this, then the older man gave a nod of comprehension, if not approval.

"Advise Mr Cooper if you please."

The messenger knuckled his forehead before dashing off to deliver the news. King watched him go as he continued to think. Clearly Manton was not convinced by his plan and it might indeed turn out to be a mistake. But the continual long-range harassment by smaller, faster craft had done them little good. Admittedly three potent raiders had been temporarily taken out of action although, for as long as they insisted on keeping their distance, his ship must be gradually worn down. If he could only close, then bring each to battle on his terms, King might still turn things about. Or so he hoped.

Chapter Eleven

Once more the turn proved to be smooth, *Tenacious* was performing perfectly as were her officers – King must remember to mention the fact when this was over.

When this was over; it actually seemed quite a depressing thought as the likelihood remained that any who survived the next few minutes would end up in the hands of the French. But there was no time for such notions, the odds might not be in their favour but King knew his part in the bargain was to use the excellent tools he had been given to avoid such an outcome.

"Ready both batteries!"

At the command, those gunners deployed on the opposite battery swiftly returned to their own. Which was an important consideration; *Tenacious* was certainly capable of firing both broadsides simultaneously but the work would be harder with reduced crews and made worse if any were called for duty aloft. Yet King knew that was the only way to maximise his ship's potential; his sudden wear must have taken the two remaining Frenchmen by surprise and there was the chance – a slim one perhaps – that he could force *Tenacious*' prow between the pair. And more than that, turning as they had would close the range rapidly; one, the corvette to larboard, would feel his next broadside far more sharply while the other, currently fine on his starboard bow, must move quickly unless they wanted to share the same fate.

"Deck there, sail in sight, sail to windward!"

A while back King would have seized the news with the eagerness of a drowning man, though now it only served to distract. The sighting might be friend or foe, though the latter was more likely, and with two definite enemies close at hand he must deal with them first. The time for partial broadsides had passed, they were due to clear the nearest Frenchman by less than a quarter of a mile and it would be strange if serious damage could not be inflicted at such a distance. Of course he must expect some punishment in return; his opponents had already proved they were carrying heavy weapons and if *Tenacious* were badly damaged it might prevent him dealing with the second raider.

"Sighting's a frigate," the masthead continued, and there might have been a measure of disappointment in his tone from being ignored. "She's running under studdin' sails and comin' up fast."

The nearest British frigate should be many miles away and his was the only convoy likely to be in the area. It could well be reinforcements for the French, in which case so be it; King could address that problem later. First he must silence the two corvettes, the nearest of which was creeping steadily into their arc of fire – Summers already had his arm raised and all were waiting expectantly.

"Fire!"

Tenacious' larboard broadside spoke as if a single gun, the combined roar making her heel slightly as if in approval while deafening most on deck. But as they waited for the impact, the Frenchman proved himself game and an answering salvo was launched from the lighter craft.

The British shot landed first and had been well laid. Holes appeared in the corvette's driver and a cloud of dust and debris erupted from her hull while the vessel itself fell off the wind for a moment, suggesting some element in her steering had been affected. But even as King took this in, the French barrage enveloped them and it proved just as deadly.

Tenacious had seized the windward gauge, so the enemy's fire could be expected aloft, but it was not so. Clusters of twelve-pound shot came whining over their hammock netting snagging men and materiel as they went. Their neat line of marine snipers was broken in three places, and there came a deep reverberating twang as the main mast took a glancing blow. Splinters flew about, fittings dissolved into little more than dust and men fell screaming. But through it all, those of the larboard battery that could, continued to attend their weapons.

"Two points to larboard!"

King had long since closed his mind to the carnage all about, his thoughts only being for the enemy before them. It was important – vital even – that they strike at the same ship again, although the corvette to starboard was steering to cross their hawse and he must keep the pair separated at all costs. Summers' gun crews were hard at work and already half way through preparing their weapons while, closer to, the larboard carronade slides squealed as they were also run out. Two men staggered past carrying the uneven bundle of a wounded gunner but King had no eyes for them either. Already one of the gun captains was indicating his piece ready and soon several more had joined him.

"As you will, Mr Summers!"

There was no longer any point in directing fire from the quarterdeck when a trained officer was on hand. The broadside rolled out, perhaps a little more raggedly this time, yet for the guns to have been loaded amid such chaos was a miracle in itself. And the shot landed with a good deal of success; the corvette's driver was hit again: this time its gaff being knocked clear, taking what was left of the sail with it. And there was further evidence of hits to the hull itself although, so intent was he on noting the Frenchman's damage, King completely missed the tell-tail flashes that showed he was fighting back.

"A further two points to larboard."

The forward corvette was still creeping across, he would deal with that shortly but first wanted to be certain the larboard enemy had been silenced. Manton repeated the order, the wheel was put across and *Tenacious'* braces adjusted. Meanwhile King was starting to relax. It was better: by closing so he had redressed the balance. What followed might even be simple; all he truly had to do was keep his head, fully disable the current target then make for the final raider – which was likely to turn and run on discovering herself effectively alone. But before *Tenacious* had even leant into her turn, the nearer corvette's broadside arrived and this time had been pitched slightly higher. Which proved a good move on the Frenchman's part as the wave of iron that swept overhead neatly removed the British frigate's main and foretopmasts.

* * *

Both Summers and Cooper were on hand and reacted instantly. The main topmast had been struck a few feet above the top and came crashing to the deck in a tangle of wood and rigging that also dragged the foretopmast with it. Those beneath – and there were plenty, both serving the larboard battery or standing ready at the starboard – found themselves instantly embroiled in a nightmare of dust, splinters and canvas. Several were struck or crushed by numerous pieces of heavy tackle and, in two cases, the remains of the topmasts themselves.

"Axemen, cut away that cordage!" Cooper's voice rang out with rare purpose amid the shouts and screams of those who had been enjoying relative normality moments before. The body of the main topmast had landed with its bulk over the starboard side but the fore' was more inboard and lying across the ship's boats. Canvas from both topsails still covered those stationed at three starboard cannon and the remaining yards had distributed themselves randomly about the waist and spar deck. "We must heave both masts over the side!"

The shout was general and Summers was the first to respond. "You there, Hanson – assemble a team to bear a hand on the main. Sergeant, have your men assist!"

Scraps of canvas were already being gathered up and Godby was leading a group of waisters in hacking madly at the shrouds and halyards that effectively pinned the wrecked foremast to their ship. The main topmast went relatively quickly but the fore' was proving more of a problem.

"Party for'ard, take the weight!"

Enough line had been cut to at least move the bulk of the mast further to starboard. With a succession of shouts and curses, the massive chunk of pine was heaved up and dragged further across while others severed more line as it became taut and jettisoned lesser pieces of wreckage. The captain's gig was totally demolished although its shattered timbers could be readily ignored. Of greater annoyance was the launch which had been partially crushed and her hull, so recently filled with water as a reservoir for firefighting, had become tangled in the remains of the fore crosstrees. Eventually it was done and, even though an entire section of filled hammock netting went with it, the remains of the second topmast were finally despatched into the sea amid a chorus of grunts and sighs.

Summers went to speak to Cooper but the senior man's mind was focused elsewhere.

"Back to your stations!"

A brief look about was enough to see he was right. During the time they had been dealing with the wreckage, *Tenacious* had slowed to the point where she was almost stationary. Meanwhile the nearest Frenchman had altered course dramatically; having turned hard, she was now bearing down and would shortly be alongside while her companion, the corvette previously on their starboard bow, had also worn and was closing. In no time there would be a warship to either side or – potentially far worse – off their bow and stern. In such a position the British would be unable to fight and must surely strike.

"Starboard battery, train forward!" Cooper again, clearly he was anticipating the latter threat.

Summers' guns were still being loaded and most of his crews lacked at least one man and in some cases several. But already two of the heavy weapons were being run out and it should shortly be possible to bear on the larboard enemy.

"It looks bleak, Michael."

Summers turned and saw he had been joined by the second lieutenant who now seemed more ready to speak. His face carried a broad cut that was bleeding freely and the front of his tunic had been ripped to reveal the linen shirt beneath.

"We must get underway," the younger man replied but Cooper shook his head.

"Mainyard's sprung," he said. "They're setting the forecourse; other than that it'll have to be head and stays'ls an' anything Amon can add."

Both men looked up to where the boatswain was indeed rigging temporary stays from the remains of their maintop to the base of the foremast.

"Once that's done we might gain way and a little steerage," Cooper continued, his eyes wide and white amid the dirt that surrounded them. "Except this fella will arrive first," he added, nodding toward the nearest Frenchman who was indeed drawing close. "An' his mate for'ard won't be far behind."

Summers knew he was right; once the French took up position what followed would be a mere formality. But several of his gun captains were signalling their pieces ready; they would be able to release another broadside shortly and he must attend to that.

* * *

From the quarterdeck the situation appeared just as dire – more so if anything: King, Manton and the midshipmen had been mute witnesses to the clearing of their damage, as well as the enemy's reaction to it. The nearest corvette was drawing closer while steering to larboard to avoid their arc of fire. Clearly she intended to beat her compatriot in taking station off *Tenacious'* prow and there was little they could do about it. Amon had yet to rig the necessary canvas that would provide them with steerage and, even with boats already in the water, it would be hard to tow the frigate's hull about to such an extent.

"What of the sighting?" Brotherton's question had been unusually blunt and it was proof of their desperation that a midshipman should address his captain so.

"Sighting?" King asked vaguely. His mind was focused on the current dilemma and had been for some while.

"Masthead reported a frigate, sir," Manton stated more steadily. "It were some time back."

"There – to windward," Brotherton added, pointing towards a faint grey shape just down from the horizon. The vessel must be a good ten miles off but should also have been noticed by the French.

"Frigate for certain," the sailing master confirmed as he stared through the deck glass. "And I think's I seen her like before though cannot place it."

King's look to Brotherton was enough, within seconds the lad had grabbed Manton's telescope and was heading for the mizzen shrouds.

"If that's rescue, she'll have to get a move on," the sailing master muttered as the midshipman departed.

"Indeed," King agreed, although it was hard to keep the dejection from his voice. Manton was looking at him strangely and King felt obliged to explain.

"Our shipping is committed elsewhere, Master," he said. "I fear it more likely to be another Frenchman."

"What, part of this lot?" the sailing master waved vaguely at the enemy.

"Or a national ship sent on a similar mission."

"Might it not be a neutral, sir?"

"Maybe, though that would be of little help."

"She's coming at speed," the sailing master pointed out.

King shrugged. "Perhaps I am wrong, but our recent exploits have hardly made the Royal Navy popular with other nations. In truth, when a British frigate is in peril, I can understand any foreign warship wishing to be in at the kill."

* * *

But before that could happen *Tenacious* had some fight remaining and was ready to demonstrate the fact. The boatswain had succeeded in setting a jury jib which was drawing reasonably and, in conjunction with the forecourse and mizzen topsail, gave them some forward motion. And as the frigate slowly gathered way under her ungainly rig, she could also turn to some extent while enough cannon remained to deliver a hefty punch. And because they could turn, the nearest Frenchman was no longer so much of a problem. Soon she was off their larboard bow once more and they were drawing closer. It could only be minutes – seconds – before the first of the British broadside guns were brought to bear.

"I have the sighting!" Brotherton's voice drifted down from the mizzen masthead but, once more, King's mind was elsewhere. If *Tenacious* could have managed another point into the wind they would be firing by now, although Summers had his hand raised and was clearly on the verge of releasing his guns.

Then, with what was almost a shock, the hand descended and *Tenacious'* broadside roared out. Once more it was ragged and several ports now lacked serviceable cannon, but the effect was still impressive and, with the diminished range, they could soon judge the results.

The corvette had been angled with her prow slightly towards them; not so much as to allow a full rake and any shot striking her sides was likely to be deflected. Still, sufficient iron pounded into her bows to cause real mischief. Her dolphin striker was swept away along with an anchor, cathead and part of her beakhead. King knew further internal damage was also possible but, if nothing else, they had given the impudent little ship a bloody nose. And she had not fired back; indeed, as the first shots began to rain down the cruiser appeared to be in the process of pulling away, although her turn might only be intended to bring her own broadside cannon to bear more fully on *Tenacious*.

"She's the *Delaware*!" Brotherton announced over the rumble of gun trucks and King started slightly at the news before allowing himself a private smile. So Walton was close by; he could not be expected to join the fray, for an American interfering in such a contest would be tantamount to an act of war. However, the man might be of use if *Tenacious* were taken. News of her capture could be relayed to Halifax and a force summoned to avenge the defeat. But before he could think further the nearest Frenchman did finally speak.

Apart from some of her forward guns, presumably damaged by the British ship's recent barrage, it was a full broadside and, following the partial destruction of *Tenacious'* tophamper, the aim had been low once more. Twelve-pound shot dug deep into the British frigate's hull and added to the confusion on her forecastle. Yet probably the most important injury was caused to a single length of line; Amon's jury jib was robbed of support causing the sail to fly up and, without the forward pressure, *Tenacious'* bows turned into the wind making her a more tempting target still for the second raider.

But at least the first was rapidly losing interest. Her load delivered, the corvette had continued to turn and was soon running before the wind, directly from her prey. And her partner was proving as coy; the French captain would have every chance and reason to close off *Tenacious'* starboard bow before delivering a series of punishing barrages, although she too was steering away and following the first. As she passed the frigate's jib boom a raking broadside was delivered, but it was at a reasonable range and, though several men fell and a deal of damage was caused to her stem and hawse, *Tenacious* survived.

King watched in disbelief; both of the enemy raiders had the wind on their tails and were presumably intent on rounding up the convoy. Which was logical enough; when it came to it, privateers were men of business and any one of his former charges would bring a greater return than the battered hull of a wrecked warship. Yet when such a prize lay waiting and apparently within their grasp, it was a decidedly odd move.

"*Delaware* is drawing closer," Brotherton continued.

King turned to look over the starboard top rail; the American was indeed in clear sight. Now no more than five miles off and still under heavy canvas she was making excellent speed. Then a part of her rig caught his attention; an odd flag blew out stiffly at her masthead. With the wind as it was he could not be certain although, rather than the white stars on blue of *Delaware*'s own nation it looked remarkably like a Royal Navy commissioning pennant. He lowered his gaze and there, on the jack, the Union Flag was flying just as proudly as on any British warship. The French may not be familiar with the vessel, but must spot such signals; to all intents a powerful, untouched and potent British frigate was running down towards them, and it seemed Walton had saved their bacon.

Chapter Twelve

"Are you there, Captain King?" the American's voice was unmistakable even through a speaking trumpet. King stepped towards the weather bulwark and waved. *Delaware* may have been spilling her wind, but the frigate was still travelling at speed and steering to pass their stern at no more than pistol range.

"We noticed the party," Walton continued on seeing him, "and thought you'd not object to another joining."

"Your attendance was most welcome," King confirmed, although he had long since lost his own speaking trumpet.

"I guess we'd better see those fellas don't take advantage of your convoy; give me a moment to round them up and I shall return."

"Obliged to you."

"Think nothing of it." The two ships were at their closest now and King could see the grin on the man's face as *Delaware* began to collect the wind once more. "Happy to help out. Remember, whenever you're in trouble you can always count on your Brother Jonathan!"

* * *

"So what gave you the clue?" King asked several hours later when they were safely installed in his quarters. *Tenacious'* great cabin had not suffered significantly; shutters now covered the panes that had been smashed, a thick layer of dust shrouded every surface and the air was tainted with sulphurous fumes from the two long guns that shared the space. But in the candlelight only the latter could be noticed and was soon disregarded.

"We sighted an injured sloop on the horizon so made for it," Walton explained. "Though before we could close saw your smoke and what frigate captain can ignore such an invitation?"

"Well I'm certainly grateful. They were only small fry but taken together proved a tough opponent."

"You don't need to tell me." Walton was holding his wine glass to the candle light. "I spent three years as a lieutenant aboard a sloop off the Barbary Coast. Some of them pirates are no larger than row boats but a group'll swamp a warship before you can say knife."

"It was quite a trick you pulled off."

"You mean the ensign?" the American turned back and beamed. "Seemed the best solution while not hurting anyone's feelings. With luck the French will never get to know *Delaware* wasn't a limey, and I don't intend making any mention of it in my report."

"I'm equally thankful for your dealing with the merchants."

"That came easy; your French friends thought I was after them so paid the convoy no attention, instead they made for the horizon like a couple of salted crows, though I reckon one or two British masters won't sleep so well tonight. They're all happy to follow you back to Bermuda, by the way – providing you have replacement spars, that is."

"We have sufficient on board to see us safe and are based at Halifax," King replied. "Spare masts and yards are the one resource we can be certain of. My carpenter seems confident the housings weren't damaged so should be able to set up new topmasts come daylight, then it'll just be a case of rigging spars. With luck we should be underway the following day."

"And your hull?"

"That's going to need a dockyard, yet should still be pretty straightforward. Both pumps are sound so we can keep any ingress at bay."

"And a spell in Bermuda is usually an acceptable diversion," the American added.

King shook his head. "To be honest, I'd rather be with my family in Halifax, though we might at least see out the hurricane season in relative safety."

"Don't be so sure," Walton warned. "I've known some pretty strong winds blow up well past December. They might not deserve the name officially but the damage they cause can be just as great."

"Well thank you for that," King grunted and Walton laughed.

"A little wind don't bother us East Coast men," he said. "When you live with such weather you kinda get used to it. Just make sure you always have plenty of sea room, and I'm not talking about our three mile limit. Providing a ship's well found and her captain has a measure of sense she'll usually survive the worst; in truth it's often

132

just a case of waiting it out."

"Thanks for the advice." King returned the smile. "I'll remember it if I ever get caught."

"Happy to oblige."

"And I'm truly grateful for your action today," King added more seriously.

"Must say, I were glad of the diversion." Walton rose and downed the rest of his wine in one. "That's a nice drop, makes a change from spruce beer."

"We took several cases out of a privateer a good while back. I'd be glad to send you a dozen," King offered, standing also.

Walton considered this. "Kind of you, but my wife knows me too well and ain't keen on me carrying too much liquor – I have to keep my own brew well hid whenever she's aboard."

"Well maybe you can hide a bottle or two of wine as well?" King suggested. "I'll ask my man to put a case in your boat."

"Grateful for that," Walton said as they shook hands.

"It's little compared to the favour you did me."

"Like I said, think nothing of it," the American grinned.

* * *

Once King had seen Walton back to his boat he knew there were many things to attend to about the ship. The carpenter and his team would be hard at work plugging holes and replacing fittings while the boatswain was equally involved setting up fresh line and preparing to install the new topmasts. Working at night would be no great hardship, especially for Morales as much of the damage was inside the ship, yet an encouraging word from the captain never went amiss. There was another department that he should visit first however, and it was the one he dreaded most of all.

His officers were organising the work and seemed to be doing it well, even in Croft's absence, and it was this that had to be addressed without delay. So when King turned from the entry port he did not hesitate, but made straight for the companionway that would lead him down to the orlop.

And when he arrived things were very much as he had expected. In the scale of things, *Tenacious* had not suffered terribly. The line of corpses on the forward grating had been mercifully short – six in all – not counting those despatched during the height of action. But the wounded were more numerous and, as soon as his foot touched the orlop's dark deck, King knew the visit would take some time.

"Nothing so very unusual," Robert Manning had told him as he began to inspect the injured. And he was right; as King moved from one splinter wound to another, occasionally encountering a broken limb or crushed foot, he knew all were to be expected after any long-range battle. Had there been a boarding or musket fire the injuries would have been different and probably worse although that was little consolation. The very smell of the place sickened him and if forced to mutter one more reassuring platitude to a man whose stitches covered most of his chest, or tell another seasoned shellback he might certainly continue to serve, even without the use of a foot, he felt he would break down. And at the end of it there was still one more casualty to be considered, and to do so Manning guided him into the relative privacy of his small dispensary.

"You'll be wanting to know about James Croft," the surgeon supposed, and King nodded.

Without a word, Manning pointed to a grey shape beneath the counter that King had missed. Grabbing at a lantern he knelt down and looked closer. It was the first lieutenant; the man was lying on a makeshift bunk and appeared sound asleep.

"It seemed the best place for him," Manning explained standing behind. "Fellow presented himself in one hell of a state. For a while I could not make head nor tail of what he said. Then I realised the fault truly lay with him and he was simply unable to communicate."

"A seizure?" King asked looking up.

"Possibly," Manning mused. "I've seen several and all presented differently; such things are in need of research. With action imminent, I decided he must be sedated and prescribed an appropriate draught."

"Did he take it?"

"It were a mild sedative; he refused anything stronger. Once that started to take effect I was able to coax a little laudanum to follow."

King closed his eyes. Robert Manning was probably his closest friend although Croft could not be far behind and to hear one discussing the other with such dispassion was almost as upsetting as interviewing the wounded.

134

"Once he passed out, Siemes and I made up the bunk and brought him in here. He hasn't moved since."

"And what do you think?" King asked. "Will he be well again?"

Manning shook his head. "It's too early to tell. I have known those suffering from conventional seizures recover and be as good as new, though they are the rare ones. And, as I have said, it was not conventional – that is supposing such a thing exists. Between ourselves, Tom, I do not think it to be a seizure at all, but rather a condition more associated with old age."

King nodded; that had been his impression as well. "So what is your official prognosis?" he asked.

"I do not have one," the surgeon admitted. "Of late we have made great strides in treating physical ailments and now regard ourselves proficient in most remedies that do not require an opening. Illnesses of the mind are another matter and an area still to be fully explored."

King looked down again and studied the face that appeared far older in the flickering light. They had served together for a relatively short time and Croft was not the only officer he had grown to like and respect, yet there could be no doubt that, of late, the man had been losing his edge. Nevertheless the cove meant a great deal to him and he felt he would do anything to ease his pain.

* * *

Knightly stared at the warrant officers as if they had come from another planet.

"I'm to do what, matie?" He had been clearing up the debris that was once their belfry and almost dropped the pile of splintered wood in surprise.

"You're to join the holders," the sailing master repeated.

"And you will address Mr Manton properly," Godby, Knightly's divisional midshipman, added.

"But I'm a seaman," the hand blustered, looking from one to the other. "Ordinary maybe, but I don't do nuffink in no 'old, not when there's plenty of proper work needed topside."

"And that's the problem," Godby explained. "Long as you keep breaking the rules and causing trouble no one can trust you, so you're bound to get the worst jobs."

"We lost three holders in the recent action," Manton added. "Two might make a recovery but Danton were put over the side yesterday morn'. He ain't coming back and we still need to shift stores."

"So why not someone else?"

"Like I says, you can't be left to work alone," Godby repeated.

"So this is down to you, then?"

"No, it's down to Mr Cooper," Manton clarified. "He's standing in while Mr Croft's in sickers. There's still a stack of repair work but the ship's also down badly at the head, and with her current rig that ain't healthy."

"The holders are a fair bunch," said Godby. "They'll show you what's about."

"Though there's not much to learn," Manton added. "It'll be shifting wet stores mainly and only for the rest of this trick. Beef is marked with an H, pork NH and anything with oatmeal in has an O. The lads will tell you the rest."

"The lads as you calls 'em are built like oxes," Knightly protested. "Look at me, I'm no clod."

"Then you'd better not give them any trouble," Manton advised, "like you seem to with everyone else."

"You'll find the work easy enough," said Godby.

"This *is* down to you, ain't it?" the seaman persisted, staring Godby in the face.

"I told you, it's Mr Cooper's orders," Manton repeated firmly. "And I should address Mr Godby properly an' all or you might find yourself stayin' an holder for the rest of the voyage."

* * *

It was two days later, when fresh spars had replaced her topmasts and *Tenacious* was leading an untidy clump of shipping towards Bermuda, that her captain was surprised by a shout. The call came from the sentry posted at the entrance to his quarters and was accompanied by a clump as the marine's musket butt struck the deck. Yet it was only when a slight and faintly apologetic figure entered the great cabin that he really believed his visitor's identity.

"James, how good it is to see you – please make yourself comfortable."

The sight of his captain rising and helping him to a seat was enough for Croft and he gratefully settled into one of the two easy chairs placed next to the entrance to King's sleeping cabin.

"I have been following your progress of course," the captain announced when his guest was comfortable, "but Bob Manning always claimed you asleep and did not wish to worry you with a visit."

"Indeed, I have slept much," Croft agreed ruefully. "Though now regard myself as fully recovered and, if I am not mistaken, it is eleven of the clock."

As if to support him the ship's bell rang out six times and there was a rumble of feet from the deck above as the ship's speed was measured.

"Why you are right, of course," King beamed, taking the seat opposite, "and the time for our regular meeting, though I had truly considered you on the sick list."

"Well, as you can see, sir, I am fully recovered."

King made no comment. Croft's frail, grey figure appeared anything but; even the eyes that usually shone so bright were strangely dimmed.

"Ship's business can wait a while," he temporised. "Can I order you some refreshment?"

"Thank you, sir, I need nothing. And indeed would prefer to return to duty. The main and foretopmasts have been replaced, I collect; what spars were used, pray?"

"A main and foreyard were found to be adequate and will certainly serve until we fetch St George's."

"We are bound for Bermuda?" Croft seemed surprised.

"We had to turn back, James," King explained. "There was the action..."

"Of course, yes of course; I recall now." The older man went to raise a hand to his head, but stopped and replaced it firmly on his lap. "And continuing south would definitely have been futile."

"Indeed," King agreed, although his concern was growing. Whatever Croft might claim, and however much he must have boned up on the ship's condition, he was clearly a long way from the alert, almost aggressively attentive officer King had known.

"I am hoping for a speedy refit," he continued cautiously. "Though cannot be certain until we put in and are assessed. Frankly, James, were we forced to wait it would be no great concern; we could both use a rest."

"But I have never felt better, sir," Croft declared. "Perhaps a little muzzy still, but that must surely pass. Mr Manning believes I may have eaten something that disagreed."

"He said nothing of the sort to me." The sharp retort had been surprised out of him but this farce could not continue and King felt no regret at speaking so. "James, you must accept you have hardly been yourself for some time. And I have to say your condition was growing steadily worse, until..."

"I feel I must have let you down, sir."

"I was taken aback, no more," King sighed. "In truth, your health concerned me the most, though it were hardly the time to say so with an action imminent."

"It concerned me also," the lieutenant confessed and if anything his voice was slightly stronger now. "I could not be sure how you would view my absence. Many captains would regard it as..."

"I ordered you from the deck, as I recall," King interrupted. "And there was no thought that you wished to avoid action; you were ill, man, and needed to be below."

Croft appeared to acknowledge this although King was sure his words had not fully registered.

"And I must say I believe you still to be so," he continued. "I fully appreciate your presence here, and respect such attention to duty. But when we put in at Bermuda I shall be sending you ashore."

"Ashore?" That word was definitely understood.

"I am sorry, James but you truly are not well, nor have been for some while. A spell of rest may do wonders, and there is no reason why you cannot resume your duties at a later stage."

"Aboard *Tenacious*?"

"I hope so," King answered with blatant honesty. "And if I should move to another ship, should want you there also."

"Thank you, sir. Thank you, that means much."

Now the eyes were misting slightly and there was a danger the elderly officer might let himself down so King quickly moved on.

"Yet you have to be fit for duty. I need the old James Croft beside me; someone who knows the ship as well as I do and her people better."

This time it was as if every word and nuance struck home and the man seemed stunned and slightly frightened. Then, with a faint look of awakening, he focused on his captain again.

"We were a good team, were we not?" he asked.

"We were indeed," King agreed. "And shall be again I have no doubt. But first you must get yourself properly well. And that will mean a spell ashore."

* * *

Strangely, the lack of their first lieutenant's presence in the gunroom had encouraged a more subdued atmosphere amongst *Tenacious'* senior officers. In the past, small jokes or gentle teasing had been quickly stamped upon by the executive officer and entire meals would pass in cautious silence. And with a battle fought, if not convincingly won, together with the prospect of time ashore in Bermuda, Summers would have expected his brother officers' enthusiasm to be hard to control. Perhaps Bream and Rushlake, the marine officers, drank a little more wine than was usual and Cooper, an enthusiastic reader, had been inclined to bring his current book to the table, but apart from these exceptions the mood was definitely restrained.

And it had been no different at that day's main meal, which was taken at the traditional time during the afternoon watch. With the prospect of gaining further supplies on the morrow, the gunroom cook had excelled himself using much of their remaining fresh meat and offal in a splendid beef and kidney pie. The pastry had suffered somewhat from its flour being spoiled by damp while both carrots and cabbage were showing sign of deterioration, if not rot, although that had hardly stopped the dish from going down well with Summers' colleagues. As had the following course; once more replaceable provisions were generously used to create a spotted dog of truly gigantic proportions. And this was still settling in the stomachs of those about the table with the result that what light conversation there had been was now totally stifled. When the first pot of coffee appeared, Bream, the senior lieutenant of marines, retired to his cabin, while the surgeon and purser made for their respective places of work. With Manton covering a watch, only the junior marine lieutenant and Cooper were left, and as the latter had his head down in a book, Summers found himself growing restless.

He withdrew his watch – an extravagance bought with his first ever prize money. There was still over an hour before the first dog when he would be on duty and, as it was Cooper's turn to be daily officer, he wondered about turning in himself for a spell.

"An appointment, perhaps?" Rushlake, the junior marine officer enquired.

"I was considering a caulk," he replied with a polite smile.

"Would that I had such luxury," the youngster sighed.

"Is there a problem with your accommodation?" Cooper asked.

"Not the accommodation as such." Rushlake cocked his head slightly. "More that which is alongside."

In the silence that followed his superior's opening snores could be plainly heard, and Rushlake had the adjoining cabin.

"Believe me, gentlemen, it sounds far worse from my little hutch."

"To be sure, we are not blessed with space." Cooper turned a page.

"But the first lieutenant's cabin is free," the youngster pointed out, "and has been for some while."

"How does that figure?" Cooper enquired, regarding the marine over his glasses.

The lad shrugged. "It's alright for you: sea officers berth to the other side." He nodded towards the starboard bank of narrow wooden doors that lined both sides of their quarters. "You must hardly hear the racket Mr Bream makes when asleep. Sometimes it goes on much of the night."

"I fail to see how that concerns Mr Croft's accommodation," Cooper replied vaguely.

"It's to starboard, like all the commissioned men," the youngster explained. "You don't know what we has to go through."

"Mr Bream's snores may still be heard on our side," said Summers.

"Not at such a volume," the lad countered. "Sure, there are times when I think he's going to blow the partition down. I tell you, gentlemen, having a quiet cabin lying empty is annoying in the extreme."

"Well I fear you cannot avail yourself of the first officer's quarters," Cooper told him as he returned to his book. "It has its own head, and such luxury is not for junior men."

"Besides, we are hoping Mr Croft will make a full recovery," Summers added. "Why I saw him up and dressed this morning."

"Is that so, Michael?" Cooper asked, looking up once more.

"He was leaving the captain's cabin, though did return to the sick bay shortly afterwards."

"Then it is decided. Mr Croft will soon be with us once more," Cooper summed up before preparing to immerse himself once more. "You will just have to put up with Mr Bream's snoring."

And at that moment it seemed the second officer's words were correct as the gunroom door opened and Croft himself appeared.

He stood for a moment, framed by the doorway, a figure so hunched and frail that it seemed to exude defeat.

"Good afternoon to you, sir." Cooper was the first to recover and stand. "Please make yourself comfortable. Shall I send for coffee – or tea perhaps?"

"And there may be some spotted dog remaining," Summers added as he and the marine stood also.

Croft was carrying a pile of clothing, presumably the bed things he had been wearing while in the sick bay, and as he entered deeper into the gunroom seemed concerned about dropping them.

"Can I take those from you, sir?" Rushlake asked, stepping forward.

"Leave them be!" the older man snapped. "And me also!"

The unexpected order had been delivered with unnecessary volume and shocked all present, including Croft himself.

"Forgive me," he said, lowering his head in flagrant remorse. "Forgive me, it has been a trying day and I need to rest."

"Of course, sir," Cooper agreed, standing aside.

But Croft did not hear the words or, if he did, was uncertain who had spoken. For a moment he looked from one to another while softly repeating his need to rest before finally making for his own cabin.

"Allow me, sir." Cooper opened the light deal door and the older man squeezed his bundle through the narrow opening. And then he was gone, with the door closed once more it was as if he had never arrived, and those remaining looked at each other with the only sound being that of Bream's gentle snoring.

Still without speaking the three officers returned to their seats, although all were disconcerted. For there had been something in that sorry figure, something so pitiful and unutterably pathetic, that had shocked them all. And Summers had noticed another detail. Amongst Croft's pile of laundry there was an item so decidedly out of place that its presence puzzled him still. For what possible use could a first lieutenant have for an ordinary seaman's pistol?

Part Two

Chapter Thirteen

In the long months HMS *Tenacious* had spent in the hands of Bermuda's Royal Naval Dockyard she had been made new again and Cooper, her first lieutenant, was rightly proud. For the time had not passed easily and those first few days following his predecessor's self-murder were undoubtedly the worst.

The unofficial investigation had been bad enough with the port admiral and his retinue visiting the ship on several occasions and once – somewhat ghoulishly Cooper felt – insisting on inspecting Croft's cabin. Then there had been the two-day board of inquiry, a process that asked questions of many and instilled doubts in more before judging their former first lieutenant to have died whilst suffering from lunacy brought on by melancholia. This was common in such circumstances as a verdict of *felo de se* would have entailed the forfeit of Croft's possessions to the Crown and caused his funeral to be conducted without the benefit of clergy. The board's recommendations were readily accepted by Bermuda's official coroner and shortly afterwards the frigate's senior officers attended a brief ceremony in St Peter's, a pleasant little whitewashed church near the harbour, where their late premier was laid to rest.

However, that had not been the end of Cooper's responsibilities, nor indeed his relationship with James Croft. In taking over as first officer he had needed to refer to countless reports and journals compiled by the man. Most had been kept in impeccable order until the last few months when some astonishing and irrelevant entries were discovered that often took an age and much investigation to set right. Then there had been the not inconsiderable hurdle of moving into the late man's quarters. The gunroom stewards had been unusually sensitive; Croft's former cabin was both cleaned and painted, with much of its furniture replaced or rearranged. Yet still Cooper would occasionally awake in the darkness of the middle watch when there seemed no limit to the places his troubled thoughts might lead.

But by then *Tenacious* had been taken in hand by the Dockyard and most of Cooper's waking hours were focused on her refit. St George's had no dry dock as such and, even when lightened, the damage to her hull could not be adequately addressed without the ship being laid over. It was a process that required the removal of all ordnance and stores as well as a total evacuation of her people. He and his fellow officers had been accommodated well enough in a lodging house while junior men and the lower deck were billeted in the nearby barracks, but it had been a complicated process that tested Cooper's organisational abilities to the full.

The one aspect that had been especially pleasing was the support received both from fellow officers and more junior men, while even some of the common hands had shown a degree of understanding he would never have expected. But then James Croft's death had taken them all by surprise and there was a good deal of genuine grief. Though by no means a popular officer – especially amongst the lower rates – he had been respected, while the manner of his passing left many feeling vaguely responsible. And it appeared this energy was put to positive use; despite the confusion and upheaval of stripping a ship of stores and men, most took to the work with a good heart and there was an unusually positive atmosphere throughout. So much so that, with Captain King's agreement, Cooper had arranged for selected members of the lower deck not directly employed with the refit to be granted regular shore leave. This was received with general approval; in an island base where naval and military forces dominated there was little chance of anyone successfully deserting, and the shore patrols reported far less trouble in the pot houses and pushing schools than Cooper had anticipated. Then, once the ship was refloated, her artificers were also granted liberty so, by the time she could take to the sea again, *Tenacious* had been strengthened in both fabric and morale.

And now, with fresh tophamper and a sound hull, though somewhat lighter in stores than he would have liked, they were making for Halifax once more and Cooper could finally experience being first lieutenant of a viable warship. It was daybreak and now he officially stood the first watch – one of many of his new responsibilities. There were others he had been unaware of, as well as an equal number of disadvantages.

For a start he had noticed far less general conversation in the gunroom; individually he might speak to Summers or Manton in the same friendly manner yet during group discussions his opinion was usually accepted as final judgement and inclined to end further debate. And the morning meetings with Captain King took some getting used to. Previously he had felt he knew the man well, and even regarded him as a friend, but in the hour or so before Up Spirits a far more complex character had been revealed. No less likeable, perhaps, though undoubtedly daunting.

Of course, once they fetched Halifax and a fresh lieutenant could be taken on, all this might change, and there was every chance he would revert to second officer. But Cooper hoped not, if for no other reason than it would mean his performance thus far had been acceptable. The time was still some way off, though. With the lengthy delay needed for refit, they had been forced to abandon the promised cruise and return to their home port, although that had not stopped King closing with the American coast at the first opportunity. It was in sight now, as Cooper stood on the quarterdeck; a faint grey line off the larboard beam that had just been picked out by the rising sun. To those used to deep ocean passages the proximity of land always gave a mixed impression of both danger and security. Navigation might be more simple although there was always the lingering worry that disaster lay but a few miles distant. But Cooper knew King had another reason for hugging the coast so; he was hoping for another slaver, one similar to *Sapphire* that he himself had cut out the previous year. She had been a sound ship and should by now have received adjudication in the prize courts. Or if not a slaver, perhaps a merchant. In the current climate of punitive sanctions, such vessels could prove fruitful without a shot being fired and, as with most sea officers, Cooper was partial to the odd spot of prize money. But so far all they had met with were empty seas and he strongly suspected that would remain the case until they raised Nova Scotia.

Or perhaps not totally empty, he decided, as the sun continued to rise. There were clouds to the north-east and dark ones; even at such a distance they seemed unusually leaden, and moving quickly. Furthermore, though it had yet to cause him to shorten their modest sail, he was also aware the wind was steadily rising. That, combined with an increase in swell and a falling glass which had been commented upon as long ago as the previous evening, seemed to suggest they were in for heavy weather.

But not for that day, Cooper assured himself. Whatever might

144

be bearing down on them would wait at least twenty-four hours. For now the sun still shone bright, and he was finally starting to enjoy being a first lieutenant.

* * *

However, by the time the lower deck's midday meal was piped a day's grace seemed optimistic. With the ship under the care of the seven bells men, several off-watch junior officers had taken advantage of the relative peace to gain some fresh air on the quarterdeck.

"That's a hurricane or I'm a Dutchman," Godby declared on first seeing the grey cloud that had continued to grow off their starboard bow.

"Is that the case, Mr Butterbox?" Brotherton enquired politely.

"I mean it," the lad maintained.

"But we're long past the season."

"Maybe so, but I seen the like before, though never at sea."

Manton, the sailing master, was close by. He had finished taking the noon sights and was now writing up his journal using the binnacle as support.

"What say you, Master?" Brotherton asked. "Would that be a hurricane?"

The senior warrant officer looked up and grimaced. "Unlikely, though that don't mean we ain't in for one hell of a blow."

"So what are we to do about it?" the midshipman enquired.

"What would you have us do?" Manton snorted. "Order the wind to stop and the waves be still?"

"Could we not find shelter?" Brotherton persisted. "I take it the Americans are not our closest friends at present, yet they might surely provide a harbour in bad weather."

"A harbour you say?" The sailing master beamed as if the lad had just produced the best of japes. "And you think such a thing would save us?"

Brotherton looked to Godby for reassurance but his friend simply appeared smug.

"Were we in harbour and that little lot was heading my way, I should wish to quit as fast as we might raise our hooks," Manton assured them both. "Only place to be in such a state is the open sea, and even then there is little chance of safety."

At this Brotherton swallowed and even Godby began to look apprehensive.

"So you can thank your stars we won't be in the midst of it," the sailing master continued. "As soon as them below 'as finished their scran we're changing course, least that's what I suggested to the captain."

"You mean turning back?" Brotherton asked.

"It's what I wanted," the older man said. "Head directly away and under all the canvas we can carry, though that went down as well as a case of bedbugs during daily rounds. You see Captain King has commitments, an' one of these is to raise Halifax."

"I thought we were in no rush to return?"

"We're not," Manton agreed. "St George's might have left us light below yet we've still wet provisions for six weeks or more, and bread that'll last a while longer. But there's one thing in making slow progress as we look for game – a few neutrals or another slaver like last time – quite another in heading in the opposite direction entirely. You see once we're home we has to hand in the log and journals, and them with big hats don't like it when a ship turns south when she's supposed to be steerin' northerly."

"But to avoid a hurricane..."

"I told you, it won't be no hurricane," Manton sighed. "Besides, bad weather's the oldest excuse in the book. Mind, I'm hardly saying we're not going to avoid it. Captain's no fool and won't place his ship in danger, not when there's a compromise to hand."

"Which is?"

"Hour from now it'll be five points to starboard and make all the sea room we can. With luck we'll only catch the edge and it'll be triple-reef the tops'ls and hunker down. If that little beauty continues west it should pass us by, and we won't feel no regrets." The older man considered the storm for a moment, then added, "Though if he decides against, we might be in for a deal of fun."

"What sort of fun?" It was Godby this time, and all thoughts of superiority had been forgotten in his growing concern.

"That'll come later, first we have to prepare for heavy weather and much of it you'll know already."

"Batten down?" Brotherton assumed.

"'Ventually, though there's a bit to be done afore that. First we have to look to our steering. Start with the wheel ropes; see they're sound then grease the gooseneck and sweep. Relieving tackles'll be hooked on and the spare tiller'll have to be rousted out from the orlop. Then we'll place the portable compass below so them working there can steer on their own if needs be. Gunner'll see to the ordnance, there'll be a double breaching for all guns with muzzles lashed above and ports sealed tight with oakum. Preventers'll need to be clapped on the anchors, jackasses stuffed in the hawse holes and plugs for the scuppers. Capstan'll be wedged tight and t'gallant masts and yards sent down. Then we check the lightening conductor and rig paunch mats."

Brotherton and Godby caught each other's eye, but the sailing master had more to say.

"Storm sails'll be rousted and laid ready and, when it does start to hit, *then* we'll batten down, though there's always a corner left free so men can come and go if they needs."

The two lads exchanged nods at this wisdom as Manton resumed.

"Lifebuoy'll be made fast to the deep sea line and trailed aft so if some poor bugger gets washed over the side he might find his luck improves. Drain holes in all boats'll need to be opened and the deck-gripes hauled taut. Then it's just the hammocks to send down, weather cloths rigged in the shrouds to keep those on deck dry and lifelines all about. And after that..."

The boys looked on expectantly as the sailing master smiled.

"...And after that we can just sit back and enjoy the blow."

* * *

For Acting Lieutenant Hanson the prospect of an oncoming storm felt like one hurdle too many. He had been made up to his current rank on the first lieutenant's death and, though the promotion was welcomed and attracted unexpected congratulations from his former peers, the bald truth was he had yet to fully settle in the post. This might be down to having spent so long in the cockpit; of late the prospect of becoming an oldster midshipman had seemed increasingly likely and he was well aware that much of his frustration had been taken out on those beneath him. But then some he had originally signed on with were now captaining their own vessels and, after already failing several boards, Hanson had begun to doubt promotion would ever come.

And now it was here he felt genuinely scared. As a midshipman he had been competent if uninspiring while, however well he knew his duties and however often the same task were repeated, help was always at hand: someone of more senior rank who knew every answer and would take responsibility should it be necessary. Now, though not yet in receipt of an official commission, he had effectively become that officer and Hanson would finally have to become accountable for his actions.

Which was daunting indeed and a totally new experience. During the refit he had been shielded to some extent as competent men from the dockyard supervised much of the work and, even later, when the ship was working up after her time in harbour, mistakes had occurred that could be excused. For all – from the captain down to the third class volunteers – needed to adjust to sea duty and were almost expected to be slightly out of practice. But that period was continuing for Hanson; he still made the most rudimentary mistakes, issuing wrong orders or mishearing those given to him, while whenever he opened his own mouth in the gunroom he made an ass of himself.

Some might brush such foolishness aside and move on, although Hanson was not of that type. For him a mistake was far more than an opportunity to learn; he viewed each as a major defect that, if repeated, must eventually lead to disciplinary action and his dismissal. Consequently, any progress was slow and painfully cautious while at the back of his mind lurked an additional fear. For it had been so long since fresh responsibilities had come his way it seemed likely he had simply forgotten how to learn. All of which made him overly wary as he sat down for meals in the gunroom, and this particular one, taken as it was in prospect of a storm, was proving especially difficult.

So far the talk had centred on the impending meteorological conditions; a subject that had dominated the senior officers' conversation since the previous evening. And, though he had ridden out countless squalls and one or two proper tempests in his time, Hanson remained painfully aware he was not a natural heavy-weather sailor.

Which might be said for all present, he told himself while running his eyes around those at the gunroom table. For all he knew even Cooper, occupying the president's seat at the head, might abhor a blow, and he was quite certain Summers, currently on deck and a lad of roughly his own age, held a healthy regard for storms.

But Summers also had a natural advantage: he knew how to be a lieutenant. Not only did the cove have all the swagger of a commissioned man, he could speak with seaman or admiral alike with the confidence of his position. Summers even knew gunroom protocol; which knife to use for fruit, when to help himself to food and when it should be served, which way to pass the port and when lighting a cigar was acceptable; etiquette that foxed Hanson still, even after many weeks.

And, as conditions topside grew steadily worse, he felt almost entitled to be concerned. After *Tenacious* turned seaward, the swell had increased to the extent that her galley fire needed to be extinguished and spirit stoves were prohibited – their sea pie had been served barely lukewarm. But even that had failed to dull the mood of his fellow officers, men for whom a tropical storm appeared little more than tiresome and, rather than an atmosphere of gloom and foreboding that Hanson would actually have preferred, the company seemed determined to make light of the prospect.

"Should test the work of them riggers at St George's," Marine Lieutenant Bream chuckled as he laid into his meal with the appetite of a lad.

"That's another consideration," Manton agreed. "I was speaking with Amon earlier; he reckons three quarters of our line is fresh and not sufficiently stretched. He'll need to take in as fast as it lets out if we want to keep hold of our spars."

"Should keep his team busy," Cooper agreed over the book he was reading.

"I note Wilson is having to resew one of the storm stays'ls," Dennison, the purser, added.

"Serves him right, should have seen to it afore," Manton replied curtly.

"Well I am glad he is addressing it now," Dennison said. "Last thing we want is a seam running in the midst of a blow."

"Anyone spoken with the carpenter?" Rushlake this time.

"I had a word earlier," Hanson found himself volunteering. "He sounded the well when I were on watch and all was dry." The ordeal of speaking had made him flush slightly, which he hoped the poor light would disguise.

"Dry?" Manton grunted, apparently oblivious to the younger man's discomfort. "I'd be surprised were that the case!"

"'Twould be a first for sure!" the first lieutenant smiled mildly over his book.

"I misspoke," Hanson flustered, colouring more from the general amusement. "There was water for sure, though only what Mr

Morales expected; all was as it should be."

"He'll have to do that on an hourly basis from now on." Cooper calmly turned a page. "And I'd chance we'll have both pumps running by nightfall."

"The old girl always did work a bit," Manton agreed, "and laying her over like that wouldn't have made an improvement."

"Old Joe said the extra caulking needed lengthened our refit by as much as a month." Dennison again.

"Well let's hope it fixed matters," the sailing master sighed. "Layin' over puts a terrible strain on any hull; plenty of ships have broken up in the first blow after."

"And that's the ones you knows about..."

The conversation then moved from approaching storm to the stress of refit but Hanson had ceased to listen. Though cold, the sea pie was better fare than any tasted in the midshipmen's berth, and even if mean and dark by some standards, so were his surroundings. And he was now an acting lieutenant and had taken a step to the first of only four commissioned ranks in the Royal Navy. Yet despite this being a necessary stage, and the next was by no means guaranteed, Hanson felt a faint longing for his former home and position.

To be a midshipman might be the lowest of the low, but he had been senior in the berth. More to the point, he could speak with experience and knowledge knowing his word must be respected by those beneath. There were even times when he had been something of a bully – times he now regretted more than anyone would ever guess.

He glanced about furtively. Summers had the deck but, even so, Hanson knew he was not the youngest present; he could give Rushlake, the junior marine lieutenant, at least a year. Yet every member of the gunroom seemed comfortable and performed their duties with competence and ease. None made fools of themselves on a regular basis and all would doubtless go on to glowing careers and successful lives. And, with regards to the more immediate concern, no one seemed in any way intimidated by the prospect of a coming storm, or that the ship might not stand up to it. Worse, they seemed to regard the possibility almost with amusement. He sighed and took another bite of cold pie. There was much he had to learn about being an officer, and some aspects Hanson sensed would never be mastered.

* * *

The rain began at the start of the second dog watch and from the first drop all knew it would last for some time. And Hanson actually had the watch but for once the responsibility sat lightly as every senior man had gathered on the quarterdeck along with the standing officers; even the surgeon and purser had come up to take in the approaching weather.

Which was to the north-east, a low dark mass capped with unusually bright light giving all the appearance of a truly supernatural phenomenon.

"There's been a change in direction," King shouted after they had watched in silence for some time. "I now have it moving southerly."

"That would seem to be the case, sir," Manton agreed, equally loud. *Tenacious* lay hove to under triple-reefed topsails while the wind had already risen to the extent that normal conversation was difficult. "An' if you'll forgive me, it won't be so easy to avoid."

King nodded; the sailing master was undoubtedly right. His plans for neatly skipping past the storm were now shown to be deeply flawed. Worse, with the heavy weather moving so, he had actually placed them in danger. In a poorly run ship such a mistake could have been costly; were those about him to lose faith in their captain the lower deck might just as easily start to mistrust their officers with disastrous results. But that would not be the case aboard *Tenacious*; in the main the people were solid with many having been aboard since he had taken over several years before. Even without Croft's reassuring presence he felt he had a strong crew; one that would understand every captain has to cope with the vagaries of the weather, and might be allowed the occasional mistake.

"And do you believe it will continue so?" he bellowed back.

Manton's shrug was difficult to detect in his oilskins. "Hard to judge, though would think it likely."

King considered further. An added disadvantage of coming too close to the storm was that it was now harder to avoid; he would have to guess again and this time must be right.

To continue east was now likely to run them straight into the tempest's path and, however sound his ship, she should be lucky to survive without serious damage. And turning south would be little better with the likelihood they would continue to be chased and probably overtaken. Steering north could be preferable, if the bad weather continued on its southerly course they should clear it more quickly, although doing so would bring them perilously close to the storm's very heart; it would only need a slight variation in direction for it to swallow them completely. So he was left with little option and, even though it signalled his earlier error more strongly while also carrying the added peril of land nearby, King knew he must take it.

"Very well," he said, although mainly to himself. And then, far louder, "Take us back to the west, Master!"

The rain was driving hard yet still he could see the sailing master's eyes as they searched his face while those officers within earshot also began to regard him with particular interest.

"That would be towards the shore, sir."

"I am aware of that, Mr Manton," King agreed. "But west it is."

Chapter Fourteen

By the time darkness fell the wind had risen considerably. Even standing on deck required two hands and a strong grip so King had long since allowed himself to be strapped to the mizzen fife rail. But there was good news to balance this mild indignity, for the storm itself was continuing to head south.

The thought that it might change course once more had been haunting him for several hours yet, even though *Tenacious* was heading for the American coast and at a speed out of all proportion to her meagre canvas, she should not be gobbled up by the tempest. There ought to be time aplenty to change course before they grounded; by his estimation at least twenty miles lay between them and the nearest danger which in this case was not land in the conventional manner.

"Diamond Shoals'll be dead ahead."

It was no surprise that Cooper's words directly followed his train of thought, for the motley group of men that crowded about the frigate's mizzen had only one subject in mind. The Diamond Shoals was a line of sandbanks that lay eight miles off Cape Hatteras. For centuries they had been a hazard to mariners, their constant shifting defying all forms of survey while the number of ships they had caused to founder had earned them the nickname of Graveyard of the Atlantic.

"We can hold this course for another hour, no longer," King roared back. "Before then it should be possible to make a more northerly heading."

Cooper nodded briefly; both knew the circumstances well enough. Providing the heart of the storm continued south, what King suggested should certainly be possible. And if not, if it stayed firm and there was no chance of turning to starboard, they would simply have to bear away in the opposite direction. Then it would be a race and no mistaking, with land to one side and a tempest the other, even if the frigate didn't take the ground she might still be battered to pieces.

But that should not be the case, as King hurriedly assured himself. Even in the last few minutes the storm had moved noticeably and was continuing on its southerly heading. Before long they might try a point to starboard, then another after that, with each minor deviation buying them further time. The only danger lay in the storm suddenly deciding to stop or, perish the thought, head west once more, in which case they would simply have to take their chances with the sandbanks.

The wind continued with a constant howl that soon became tiresome on the ears and drove the rain nearly horizontal. And then, finally, King began to feel his luck was starting to return. After a further ten perilous minutes Manton was able to give the necessary order and *Tenacious*' bow shifted slightly to starboard. King glanced at the elderly quartermaster who, with three men to assist, had been holding them steady for the past few hours. It was clear the man had been born to the task and duly swung the wheel across, then centred it with practised ease before turning to the officers.

"She'll take a couple more!"

Without waiting for confirmation Manton ordered another point then another after that until slowly, and with apparent pain, *Tenacious* began to steer a more northerly course.

"That was close," Cooper sighed when they had finally settled. With no land actually in sight and scant chance of a star, they only had the compass and dead reckoning to go by, but for a while at least they must surely be safe.

"She's on the very edge of a luff," Manton muttered to himself as they continued to watch the quartermaster. Indeed that had been the case since beginning the turn while the fact that it could have been made at all was the clearest indication the storm was truly passing them by.

"We'll keep her as she is for at least another hour," King bellowed. "After that any room we can make to starboard should be taken."

Manton nodded in agreement. From this point on the coast fell back and didn't creep significantly east again for at least another hundred miles. Yet *Tenacious* was still being pounded by both wind and waves and deserved a little respite.

"Beggin' your pardon, your honour, but I seen a sail."

King turned to see a sodden seaman clinging to a lifeline as he knuckled his forehead respectfully.

"Where away?" In the atrocious conditions the man's tarpaulin hat was pulled well down and King had no idea who he addressed.

"Ahead, sir, though several miles distant. Them's no danger to us."

"What course?"

"Same as us, sir, an' I'd say she was a frigate, or maybe somethin' larger."

A warship; that should be no surprise. In such weather only the boldest master would stay out in a private vessel, although anything over five hundred tons would probably be safer at sea than cooped up in harbour.

"Very well, who is at the masthead now?"

"Daniels, sir," the seaman replied. "I sent 'im up to take my place as no one on deck were hearin' my calls."

"Go back and keep him alongside," King directed. "Soon as you get a firm sighting, one of you come down to report. And make sure you are replaced by two more at the end of your trick."

The man knuckled his forehead once more then made a cautious crossing to the starboard main shrouds before racing up the sodden ratlines with an agility that impressed all with time to watch.

And King's thoughts were definitely on other things. The likelihood was the sighting would be British, so at least they would have company in the current torment. Still, to come across any other warship on such a night was unusual. And to his mind, vaguely worrying.

* * *

"There's something else out there," Godby shouted to Brotherton. "Stokes just came down from the masthead, he reckons it to be another frigate."

"Well jolly good luck to them," his friend replied.

"It's ahead an' on the same course though little chance of our running it down."

The pair were in the waist and gaining as much shelter as they could from the lee of the quarterdeck and weather gangway, but even so the wind howled about them and they still suffered from the driving rain.

"With luck we'll be making further to starboard shortly," Brotherton bellowed. Though they may be minor cogs in *Tenacious'* complex order of command, both lads were fully aware of the situation, along with what might still go wrong. Then a larger component approached.

"We need a man at the masthead," Acting Lieutenant Hanson announced.

When they shared a berth, Hanson's arrogant manner had caused him to be the butt of countless midshipmen's japes, but on promotion all such frivolity ceased. Besides, this was not a laughing matter.

"At the masthead?" Brotherton repeated in horror.

"You heard. Don't mind which but whoever it is should take this with them." Hanson handed a night glass across. "There's a ship out there that the captain wants identified."

The lads looked out at the storm-ravaged deck; even though firmly battened down, the hatch covers still billowed in the wind and streams of water flowed freely from the stored boats.

"And he'd like to know now," Hanson added more firmly.

Brotherton looked at Godby and each seemed equally reluctant; then the senior man said something that surprised them both.

"Very well, if you prefer not, I shall go."

"There's no need for that," Brotherton assured him hurriedly. "It's just not a duty anyone would wish for."

"I understand entirely," Hanson replied, surprising them further. "And neither of you will suffer for it. Now if you'll excuse me..."

And with that the man was off and making for the weather shrouds with the glass slung loosely about his shoulder.

"Well, who'd have thought?" Brotherton asked, although Godby was too surprised to answer.

* * *

In fact Hanson had very good reason to take the masthead duty and, even as he clambered up the main shrouds with the wind nearly pressing him through the tarred line, did not regret it. For the past few weeks he had been struggling with divisional reports and journals, while trying to find his place in the gunroom and effectively pretending to be a lieutenant. But masthead duty was something he did understand and, though he might never have done a trick in such appalling weather, and however much he hated storms, it felt good to be on familiar territory once more.

The glass battered against his back as he swung nearly upside down from the futtock shrouds while *Tenacious* continued to corkscrew in the terrible conditions. Then he was back almost upright and setting out on the next run of shrouds that led to the main crosstrees; the fragile perch that would provide dubious safety for the foreseeable future.

And he was not to be alone; two seamen were already there and both had dressed for the occasion in heavy tarpaulin jackets and sou'wester hats. They stood to either side of the mast, each with a line passed about their waists securing them to it.

"Where away?" he shouted and one, who might have been Daniels, pointed over the larboard bow. The other, Stokes probably, was offering him the free end of another line but Hanson shook his head. With two already secured there would be no space for another if he was to use the glass. Instead he rested against the pair and, feeling the reassuring pressure of a heavy hand on his shoulder, proceeded to scan the torrid waters with his telescope.

Even with its shade out the lens clouded quickly and, as the ship continued to buck and fall in a manner just short of predictable, a systematic search would be impossible. Luck was on his side, though and he came across the mystery ship within seconds.

It was a frigate for certain, and one he had seen before although at that moment Hanson could not remember when. She was under storm staysails, as was *Tenacious*, and close-hauled on a similar course though perhaps a mile ahead and three cables nearer the shore. Which must still be a good five miles off, the young man told himself as he continued to look. And she seemed to be making heavy weather of it; her hull might be denser or perhaps the ship itself simply larger, it was impossible to be sure in such conditions and without some point of reference, although *Tenacious* was definitely closing and would be level in less than an hour. And then, as he continued to hold the vague shape in his glass, realisation dawned. There was no single distinguishing feature as such, rather several small points that Hanson's brain unconsciously noted until the vessel's identity was finally revealed. He withdrew the glass and looked to the seamen.

"One of you'll need to drop down," he said. "Tell the captain we have *Delaware* in sight about a mile off our larboard bow. She appears sound and presents no danger for now."

The two seamen exchanged glances and Daniels shrugged before beginning to release himself from the mast.

"*Delaware*, you have that?" Hanson checked.

"*Delaware*," the man confirmed. "The Yankee."

Then he swiftly transferred himself to a backstay and, with a nod to his mate, began a far swifter, and possibly safer, descent than could have been made by the shrouds.

With Daniels gone there was more space by the mast and Hanson gratefully accepted a rope's end from Stokes. Once the line was about him he began to feel more secure and the knowledge that he had passed on important information warmed him, despite the wind and rain. It might have been a small matter but this felt like his first true contribution to the ship since leaving the midshipmen's berth. Then a nudge from Stokes caught his attention and he looked round.

The seaman was offering him something; Hanson instinctively extended his hand and a hard cold lump was pressed into the palm. He considered it; a plug of tobacco with one end obviously chewed. He glanced his thanks at Stokes before bringing it up to his mouth and biting off a small portion. The dried leaf unrolled in his mouth, instantly filling it with both flavour and a strange numbness.

"Thankee Stokes." He spoke unconsciously as he handed the tobacco back yet the words had been sincere; the seaman's small consideration had meant more to him than any gunroom cigar and, as he brought the glass up once more, he felt a warming that had come from something other than the drug.

* * *

King had not left the deck and, for as long as his ship remained in danger, neither would he. But the tempest was still heading south and there must surely be an end to these terrible conditions before long. Due to the storm's movements and their own steady progress, it would shortly be possible to steer another point or two to starboard. The shore was no longer a real threat, although any sea room must be taken in such conditions and he was just considering ordering the turn

158

when it happened.

The gust came from nowhere; one moment *Tenacious* was bending to the steady pressure of a known wind in her canvas, the next she had been laid flat by a sudden bolus of power that could have been the hand of God himself. Secure in his bonds, King was probably the first to recover and glanced about. All officers were present and clinging grimly to their lifelines while the quartermaster and his team also appeared sound. It had been a freak blast; such things were common on the edge of a tempest and should have been expected. Had it not been for a length of two-inch line he might have been washed away. Then, before he could reproach himself further King noticed a seaman making unsteady progress across the angled deck.

"Mr Hanson reports *Delaware* in sight, sir," the man bellowed as he knuckled his forehead.

"Where away?"

"'Bout a mile ahead an' off our larboard bow," the lookout reported before suddenly snatching at King's fife rail for support. "She's steering as we is an' he don't reckon there's any danger, sir."

"Very well, return to your post."

Another quick salute then the man was gone and King allowed himself a private smile. So Walton was out there and facing the same conditions. It was a strange notion but simply knowing the American to be close by was oddly comforting, even though neither could do much to help the other. And then a different sight caught his eye, something that wiped all foolish notions from his mind. Another figure was approaching and this time it was unmistakably Hanson, their probationary third lieutenant. The man had clearly made the same descent from their maintop as the lookout and King briefly wondered why; he had asked Hanson to send a lad to the masthead, not go himself.

"It's *Delaware*!" Hanson announced by way of greeting; he was obviously out of breath and grabbed at the fife rail as if it were life itself.

"I was aware," King began, but Hanson had more to say and no difference in their rank was going to stop him.

"She were blown down," he bellowed, and there appeared to be something in his mouth although King could not imagine what. "An' when she came up her topmasts were gone. Most are trailing behind and she's being driven westwards."

That was important news indeed. The nearest land must still

be several miles off but a helpless vessel would move quickly in such conditions. Within an hour, possibly less, Walton and his ship would find themselves on a lee shore unless something was done about it. Yet, at that moment, King could not think what.

* * *

"No change, sir," Stokes announced as Hanson struggled up to the crosstrees once more. The climb had felt harder than before although it could be the conditions had worsened slightly – that or he had become used to the indolence associated with senior rank. He took the telescope from the seaman and once more refused the offer of a rope's end. On raising the glass he found *Delaware* almost immediately, she was much closer but had already drifted a fair distance to the west and was currently rolling and wallowing with all the control of a twig caught in a cistern. Of her staysails only one, the fore, remained; if *Tenacious* were to do anything to assist, the Americans must rig at least another. But that was assuming something could be done. The storm was still heading south and, though they were very much on its periphery, that hardly lessened the wind, while there was the added disadvantage of an occasional surge similar to the one that had almost accounted for the Jonathan.

"Don't look good."

Hanson nodded as he finally squeezed himself between the seamen and felt Stokes' fatherly arm encompass him. Indeed, *Delaware* did seem to be in an unenviable situation – they all were when it came to it. Yet strangely Hanson had not felt so secure for some time.

* * *

King knew he must start by surrendering some of his sea room. With a shout to Manton, *Tenacious* began to bear away until she was taking the wind more on the beam and then almost her quarter. Nearby, Amon, the boatswain, had roused out a hundred fathom of hawser and was currently splicing a shorter length of grass rope to one end. A young lad stood by, one who had joined them in Bermuda. King only knew his name – Lindsey – although Amon had spoken well of him and he appeared confident of the task ahead. Further members of the boatswain's team were taking what shelter they could from the weather; they would see the line paid out and finally secured.

But King wondered if it would all be a waste of time. There was still no sign of *Delaware* from the deck; when ordering *Tenacious* westward her actual course had been part intuition and part guesswork. Chances were strong they would be swept by without even catching sight of the American ship.

And then suddenly there she was. A chance break in the weather showed her rolling hull less than a cable off their prow; if they weren't very careful they would run her down.

"Starboard a point." Manton's command had not been prompted by King though there was no harm in that. In the next few minutes much must depend on instinctive seamanship: there would be little room for protocol.

He peered into the rain-filled night; *Tenacious* was bearing down on the stricken hull and must pass it by in seconds. The American was lying broadside to the wind and they would be lucky to clear her jib boom by more than ten feet, although there looked to be space enough to allow a line to be passed. And time, but only just.

"Can't see anyone ready to receive!" Manton bellowed and King nodded. That was surely to be expected. Walton and those aboard his ship might not have been aware *Tenacious* was even in the vicinity and, after being blown down, all their attention would have been spent on stabilising their ship. When a British frigate came powering out of the gloom it must have come as quite a surprise.

And then there was a figure. No, two – in fact a group of seamen were standing at *Delaware*'s prow and clearly hoping for a line.

"Ready, sir," Amon announced, and King could see Lindsey, supported by two of his mates as he swung the weighted grass rope.

Then the rolling hull was upon them. In the short time King was distracted, *Tenacious* had closed almost to within touching distance of her bowsprit and, as he looked back, Lindsey had thrown the line. For a moment it seemed to disappear into the dark prow of the American warship and then the hawser began to race out through an aft gunport.

Which might mean nothing, the line could have become entangled in *Delaware*'s rigging and be unreachable, or possibly missed the ship completely and was now hurtling down to the ocean floor. But Amon and his team were assuming otherwise; the end of the hawser had been secured to one stanchion with the main bulk coiled past and round another, allowing it to be paid out as needed while retaining a goodly amount for later freshening.

They were passing *Delaware* now and the next stage must begin if the line was not to be plucked from either ship.

"Very well, Master!"

Manton began to bellow and *Tenacious* crept back towards the wind so she would be broadside on when the critical moment came. And it seemed the tow was secure, with a rumble that could be heard above the wind the line suddenly began to pay out even faster and then, just as the British frigate took her first point into the storm, they knew they had her.

"Secure?" King bellowed.

"Secure," Amon confirmed. The line had stopped paying out and instead snaked back with only the slightest of dips until it reached up to *Delaware*'s prow. As he watched, King could see the American ship pull round and come close to the wind. She was under his control and, for as long as the tow held, would be safe.

But they were not; *Tenacious* was only steering marginally into the wind, the bulk of her hull lay almost side on, which was dangerous indeed. King looked to Manton and the sailing master seemed fully aware of the situation.

"A further point to starboard!"

It made sense to take the turn in stages, for they were steering for two now, and a sudden jerk on the tow might well part it. But the manoeuvre was completed with the rolling hull of *Delaware*, now stabilised to some extent by a fresh main staysail, proving obedient. Being encumbered so meant they could not return to their previous heading though, some room must be left to ensure the ship could always be controlled. Yet everything had gone as smoothly as any could have hoped and, as *Tenacious* slowly drew further from the storm, her motion began to subside and King almost relaxed.

Then suddenly there was danger once more; as the British frigate settled to her new heading a sudden blast hit her again. Manton went sliding across the deck and was only just caught by Cooper while even King had to grab at the fife rail to stay upright. But this time *Tenacious* was not fully laid over and it proved to be the final crisis; the storm's parting shot. When the gust passed there was a slight lull that lasted long enough for them to claim their previous heading and the tow continued, with both ships gradually becoming more stable.

Steering as they were, any leeway should be counteracted by

their forward progress; as long as that continued all must be well and, with the coast receding, it ought to be a case of simply waiting out the storm. They were Walton's words – King smiled at the memory – and it was then that he noticed a greatcoated figure on the American's prow. The fellow was waving and, even though there was no way of telling who it might be, King felt he knew and returned the greeting.

"Beggin' your pardon, sir..."

He turned; there was the hand who had originally announced *Delaware*'s presence; as he removed his sou'wester, King could finally tell it was Stokes.

"Another sighting?" he asked.

"No, sir." The seaman was holding his hat before him in respect, or what might have been supplication.

"What then?"

"It's Mr Hanson, sir," Stokes continued. "He's just been washed off the top."

Chapter Fifteen

"May I offer you some more of this excellent wine, Captain?"

King didn't usually drink more than a glass at any time but still nodded and Walton reached across with the bottle. For it really had been a splendid meal and, after several days of seeing out the storm then attending to essential repairs, so good to relax in convivial company. And all the better for not being planned; King, Cooper and *Tenacious'* boatswain and carpenter had been aboard *Delaware* at the time of the ship's midday meal and Walton suggested they dined together in his quarters. The other three were with him now, as was *Delaware's* first officer along with a couple of her midshipmen who, in company with both British warrant officers, had initially been in awe of the occasion. Yet this was no gathering of admirals, more a simple meal taken amongst friends; the eight of them sat to either side of a dining table with no distinction between rank or country.

And it probably helped that *Delaware's* great cabin was still mildly dishevelled. One of a set of prints fixed to a bulkhead had a cracked glass, there were stains where the two aft gunports had let in a great deal of water and the sliding door to one of the quarter galleries appeared to have come off its runners – something that Morales had been eyeing with professional interest since their arrival. Such untidiness only seemed to add to the charm, however, and there was no doubting the atmosphere which was relaxed and comfortable, while the substantial meal just enjoyed had proved excellent indeed.

Which was strange in itself, for it was relatively plain fare; a stew made from pickled beef with what tasted like pumpkin and a whole cob of corn that King found particularly hard to manage. The hasty pudding that followed was equally nothing out of the ordinary yet, content in such pleasant company, all had laid in like starving wolves until there was little remaining apart from nuts and apples.

"With luck we'll finish our fixes by tomorrow even'," Walton continued as he filled his own glass with the last of the wine. "And I must say you folks have been real helpful."

"Delighted to be of assistance," King grinned while Amon and Morales made depreciating noises. For the repairs they had helped with were basic indeed although should prove sufficient to allow the frigate to see harbour again, which had been their sole purpose. In addition to topmasts, the American warship had lost her boats and all spare spars but King had been able to contribute enough of the latter, as well as more practical assistance, and between them the two crews had produced a working jury rig.

"Of course, we should have known there was a storm a-comin'," one of the midshipmen announced to the surprise of all present. After their early shyness the youngsters had been steadily gaining confidence until they were in danger of dominating the conversation.

"And why would that be, Mr Jackson?" Seymour, the American lieutenant, enquired.

"We saw a petrel," the second chipped in before his friend could reply. "Bo's'n spotted it first and the beast stuck with us for several hours."

"Several hours," Jackson confirmed.

"You always catch a gale after sighting a petrel," the second added apparently in triumph. "Everyone knows that."

"Do they indeed, Mr Bazzard?" Walton sniffed as he reached for his glass.

"You don't take to superstitions, Captain?" Cooper asked.

"Indeed not, sir. 'Always step on deck with your left foot first', 'whistle for a wind and shed blood to still a storm'," the American began reciting, "and point not at the horizon, lest your finger acts as a lightning rod for evil spirits.'" He gave a short laugh. "I tell you, gentlemen, it's all so much bilge."

"Still, you have a faith, surely?" Amon, the boatswain, enquired.

"Not in that sort of fiddle-faddle, or any of your gods and 'life hereafters' if it comes to it," Walton assured them. "Though I suppose I do have a faith of sorts, but it is a faith in real things – physical things: things that make sense. My ship, my people... and my friends," he added, treating them to a grin. "And faith in my country – it may be young but is shaping up nicely and I believe will be one to reckon with in the future. Though beyond that, I fear I must disappoint."

"My family holds much by superstitions," the younger

midshipman confessed a little sadly.

"Then you must follow them, Miles," Seymour assured him, adding, "and let no one tell you otherwise," with a poignant look to his captain.

"Oh, for sure," Walton agreed. "Believe what you will, it is a fundamental right."

"The day my uncle died his clock ceased to tick," the boy added, encouraged, "and has not done so since."

"Remarkable," Cooper commented politely.

"And it was definitely his clock?" Walton clarified.

"Indeed, sir, he bought it when new and was his prized possession."

"Then perhaps it was him who used to wind it?"

A wave of genial laughter flowed around the table just as the steward appeared with two further bottles of wine.

"These are the last, sir," he said.

"Never mind," Walton replied as he collected one. "It would be a shame to spoil such a party – we shall have another glass, shall we not?"

All seemed in favour and Walton dealt with the cork.

"Sure, your gift was well received, Captain King," he added as he filled Cooper's glass, "and 'tis a shame if this truly is the end, I have taken quite a shine to the stuff."

"So tell us, where do you gentlemen go from here?" Cooper asked while Walton passed the bottle to the warrant officers.

"Back to Delaware," the American replied. "Dockyard facilities aren't up to your British standards – there ain't a dry berth in the entire US – but they'll attend to the tophamper well enough."

"Should you be telling us this, sir?" Amon enquired as he helped himself to wine.

"Pardon me?"

The boatswain shrugged. "When we left St George's the talk was of war; for all we know it might even have been declared."

"In which case you're all in my custody," Walton grinned, reaching for a handful of pecan nuts. "How did you like your rations?"

"The prisoners ate a hearty meal," King said. "But when did you last touch land?"

"Oh, some weeks back, though we close up to our signalling stations on a regular basis; if there'd been any developments I would have been informed."

166

"I wonder what might happen." King set his glass down again. "As far as I can see our two countries were pretty much on a collision course."

"It's the War Hawks," Walton declared. Then on noticing King's incomprehension, added, "They're a bunch of youngsters recently elected to Congress. They mainly come from the South and West and are mighty aggrieved at having missed the last bout with you fellas."

"An odd regret."

"Maybe, but that's not all. They have high hopes for expansion."

"Expansion?" Cooper questioned. "Surely you have enough land?"

"Ah, they have their eyes on Florida and parts of the North-West." Seymour, the lieutenant, had also started on the nuts. "And would hardly say no to all of Canada."

"Canada?" Amon gasped.

"It's on their list and is ripe for the taking," Walton nodded, "or so they believe."

King collected his glass once more. "Bold ambitions," he said.

"Well, they have a fair amount of support." Walton reached for more pecans. "Although not so much in New England."

"Do they want war in New England?" Cooper asked.

"With you folk?" The American captain considered this for a moment then shook his head. "I would say not. Despite the sanctions, Britain remains their main avenue for trade; sure a war would do both sides harm. And strangely they seem to take your antics at sea a darn sight better than those further inland."

"Antics?"

"Your stopping our ships, stripping them of crews and generally behaving like the absolute bastards all Englishmen are." The nut broke with a decisive crack and Walton glanced up in apparent innocence. "You'll take no offence I am certain."

King grinned. "How could we when so much is true? Though I would point out your merchant trade only became established with the use of British hands."

"Many of which are now American," Seymour pointed out.

"But were trained in our navy," King countered. "And Britain is already fighting another war, one that will change the course of history for the entire world – we can't afford to let valuable assets go

167

to waste."

"Who said anything about waste?" Walton laughed. "Your countrymen are truly welcomed and put to good use. And we reward them well, with American citizenship, decent wages and the choice of whether they serve or not – which might be why so many wish to join us."

"All know you treat your people well, sir," Morales chanced, not looking at his captain.

"Why even your rondys have good food and music," Amon, the boatswain, agreed.

"I'd hazard there are better ways to get a man to work than forcing him," Walton said.

"As I have said, we are already fighting a war," King maintained, breaking a silence that had lasted for several seconds. "Our need for hands is so great we cannot risk the carrot but must revert to the stick."

"That hardly gives you the right to press from our merchants, Captain," Seymour insisted.

"Maybe not, and I'll readily admit some of my fellow captains take matters too far. But our supply of fresh hands is a long way from here yet every time we touch port we lose a few to your navy. And who can blame them when they are encouraged so to do? Why I understand in Virginia it is a crime to arrest a British deserter and few, if any, have been handed back."

"I guess there's right and wrong on both sides." Walton finally laid his nut cracker down. "Right now our merchant shipping is at an all-time low, and some are blaming the British, even if much of the problem has been caused by our own legislation."

"Aye, the Embargo Act was a disaster," Seymour agreed, "and what followed seems hardly better."

"So why were they imposed?" Cooper asked.

"Ah, that was down to your Orders in Council," Walton sniffed. "If you fellows hadn't brought up that little beauty we might all be getting on fine."

"And as it is...?"

"As it is I think it will be war, Captain," Walton announced with more than a hint of reluctance. "At least war on a different level."

This time all seemed unwilling to break the silence.

"How so?" King asked finally.

"Well, let's be real," Walton suggested. "We've been fighting each other with economics for years and little good has been done; the War Hawks think it time to change weapons."

"And do you think a physical war will fare any better?" Cooper this time.

"Now, that I simply cannot answer." The American captain spoke with genuine sadness. "Though I've an inkling we are about to find out."

* * *

With the ship due to be underway shortly, Godby had much to do and was hurrying as he made his way to the midshipmen's berth. But not so quickly as to collide with the solitary figure who emerged unexpectedly from the stewards' room. The lad instinctively dodged, bending his head further to avoid the deckhead that dropped even lower as it reached the ship's side. But whoever it was failed to see him or simply hadn't bothered to look; Godby found he had to squash hard against the scantlings to avoid a collision.

"Who goes there?" Godby shouted, instantly annoyed as the heavier man made off in the opposite direction without so much as a look or comment. The figure walked on several paces then slowed for two more before finally coming to a reluctant stop.

"I said, who goes there!" the midshipman repeated.

The man turned and was now partially visible in the dubious light, although Godby already had a good idea of his identity.

"Back here, now!" he ordered, pointing at the deck, and after the briefest of pauses Knightly drew closer.

"What do you mean by barging so?" Godby asked, his suspicions confirmed.

"Beggin' your pardon, mister, I didn't see you," Knightly replied.

"Is that so? Yet I could make you out well enough!"

"And credit to you for it," the hand acknowledged. "Though you've younger eyes. And besides..."

"Besides what?"

He sniggered slightly. "Well you got to admit, it were harder for me."

Godby drew closer and the seaman appeared to square up. "In what way harder?" the lad asked.

Now Knightly fixed him with his gaze. "Black man in a monkey suit," he said. "What chance did I have?"

169

Whatever Knightly had been expecting the fist that landed squarely on his mouth came as a surprise. And it was thrown hard, bursting lip against teeth. The seaman staggered slightly with shock as much as impact and brought his hand up to a chin that had already started to redden with blood.

"There were no need for that!" Knightly exclaimed and for a moment Godby thought he might return the blow. In the darkness and privacy of the orlop the man could even do worse; he would not be the first midshipman murdered by a member of the lower deck, before being furtively dropped over the side. But Knightly had more sense and merely stepped away.

Watching him, Godby sensed something more should be said. It was an odd situation; were it reversed and Knightly had struck him, the seaman would probably end up swinging from the end of a rope. As it was, no offence had been committed and, even in an enlightened navy, officers could still strike hands pretty much at will, especially those showing insolence. Nevertheless, Knightly was morally correct; there had been no need for violence; Godby had overreacted and used his rank to punish him. It had been the blow of a coward.

"The next time you pass a midshipman you will show the necessary respect," he huffed, stumbling over his words only slightly.

But Knightly did not respond. The blood was now flowing over his hand and seemed comment enough as he slowly turned and moved on.

* * *

"I need to be clear on this point," Cooper declared. He had only just returned from the meal aboard *Delaware* and his head was still decidedly groggy. "Did Mr Hanson rejoin you at the masthead?"

With so much to do aboard their own ship and the American, there had been little time to analyse exactly what had transpired during the storm. But damage to *Tenacious* had undoubtedly been caused and men lost; in such a situation it was the duty of any executive officer to compile a report for his captain.

King had yet to ask for this although Cooper knew the time would soon come. And as one of the deaths had been that of an officer, the investigation must be as formal as possible as it may become evidence presented at court martial. Consequently he had summoned Stokes and Daniels to the relative privacy of the gunroom where he was currently questioning them.

"He did, sir," Daniels agreed. "And we made room for him on the top."

"Offered a line an' all," Stokes confirmed sadly. "Several times."

Both men stood in front of the gunroom table and waited while Cooper made a note.

"Which I presume he did not accept?"

"That's right, sir, he were keen to keep a check as we took the Jonathan in tow."

Cooper looked up sharply. "Could not he have watched while being secured to the mast?"

"'Tain't as easy as that, beggin' your pardon, sir," Stokes replied. "You see there ain't a great deal of room and only the members of the crosstrees to stand on. Two men can find a safe enough perch and three might be squeezed in, though it would be hard to use a telescope or move about much like Mr Hanson wanted to."

"I see," Cooper muttered, glancing down. And he could, all too clearly.

Hanson might easily have ordered one of the men down, at least as far as the fighting top. But that would have made him unavailable if communication were needed with the deck and, in such weather, one man alone could not maintain an adequate watch. Of course there had been further lookouts at the fore', although that position was several feet lower and, remembering they were on the very edge of a tempest, such a distance might have been important.

Then there was the question of why Hanson had even been up there in the first place. Brotherton and Godby had already given their evidence; they had been asked to go but were daunted, as might be expected when given such a posting. Cooper was in no doubt either would have gone if Hanson had chosen to insist; the very fact they admitted their reluctance seemed proof enough of that. With Hanson dead it would have been a simple matter to deny they were even asked. The point remained, however, why did an acting lieutenant choose to carry out a midshipman's duties?

He had done so well, of course; it was possible neither of the younger lads would have identified the American frigate so quickly, nor noticed she had been partially dismasted and have the gumption to warn the captain themselves. In which case the *Delaware* would probably have washed up on some Yankee beach with the loss of most of her people.

But that was beyond the scope of his investigation; he needed to find out how Hanson had died and let those more senior draw their conclusions.

"So when he returned he did not secure himself," Cooper confirmed.

"No, sir," Stokes agreed. "Like I said, he were more interested in watching us take the Yank in tow."

"And then?"

Daniels shrugged. "By the time we 'ad the line aboard he were preparing to go down. It was like there was no need for three on a crowded top. He turned to me to speak and it were then that I clocked the gust headin' our way."

"You can tell by the way the rain comes at yer," Stokes added.

"I called a warning but by then it were upon us and the whole ship went over, like it were going to be rolled."

Cooper nodded, he remembered the time only too well.

"And when she had righted 'erself, there he was, gone."

"Washed away?" Cooper supposed and both men nodded in unison.

"Very well, thank you for what you've told me. If I need to know more you will be sent for."

The pair left and Cooper looked down at his notes. It all seemed a terrible waste, even if it could be said that Hanson had died saving lives rather than taking them. And it was sad on another level; though he might never have risen further than lieutenant, the man had been turning into a very usable officer. A little hesitant on occasions, but that was no bad thing. Cooper remembered his own time as a junior man and how long it had taken to adjust to an entirely new world. And he was fortunate, his brother officers were supportive, the first lieutenant especially so. Perhaps if Hanson had received a little more attention it might have helped?

But it was no good thinking so, Cooper decided. He had also been adjusting to a new regime and could not be expected to have eyes for every man under his command. Besides, whether Hanson was succeeding as an officer or not would have made little difference to his presence on the crosstrees, and neither would it have stopped him from being washed away.

He assembled the papers into a neat pile and reached for a fresh sheet. The report could have been written in his cabin, indeed he might have interviewed the two lookouts there although something about the place still worried him. And besides, there was far more space at the gunroom table.

* * *

And there has been no contact since?" Brotherton asked.

Godby shook his head. "It only happened a few moments back."

Following the incident Godby had made straight for the berth and relating the tale only increased his shock.

"There's nothing to say," his friend sighed. "Knightly is just trouble; I don't think he has it in for you in particular."

"Maybe." Godby rubbed gently at his right hand which was just starting to swell.

"You'd better tell Jacky Coops though," Brotherton supposed. "As first luff he ought to know, and might mention it to the captain. But whatever, you can be sure Knightly'll be brought up for lack of respect – they're both pretty hot on that sort of thing."

"And what good will that do?" Godby asked. "Man's had more punishment than the rest of the hands put together. Thought we'd finally lost him at St Georges, then that fool of a marine brought the cull back."

"It won't do no good at all," Brotherton agreed, "but we got to do it, if only for the sake of the others. And though you might not think so now, your reaction was exactly right. He'll remember that blow long after any stoppage of grog or even a stand at the grating."

"Maybe so." Godby still rubbed at his knuckles, and was by no means convinced.

* * *

"I'm gonna miss that little tub, bloody marvellous it were," Morales enthused as he entered the mess and slumped down at their small table.

"The Jonathan?" Drake looked up from his seat.

"Aye, never seen a vessel like it. Live oak for scantlings and all as solid as the rock of Gibraltar. The Yanks can sure teach us a thing or two about makin' ships."

"Designed and built by Quakers, or so I hears," the master-at-arms commented. "And them what's never laid eyes on a warship in all their days."

"Well whoever it were, they did a good job, and used some fine materials."

"Amon were sayin' as much 'bout her cordage." Regan, the gunner, was polishing his hat's brass buckle, a task he undertook on a daily basis. "Though Wilson weren't so happy 'bout deir canvas."

"They back?" the carpenter asked.

"Both came aboard aboyt an hour ago," Regan replied, before spitting on the pot of brick dust and wiping it with his cloth. "An' found a deal here to do which I've naw doubt you will an' all."

"I'm sorry you couldn't come," Morales told them both.

"Yankee navy's different, is it?" the Irishman asked.

"Set up's much the same, 'cept there's no messes an' the people aren't bossed about so."

"Ah, there's nothin' wrong with a bit a discipline," Drake told them all sternly.

"Maybe not, but it seemed to work." The carpenter picked up their teapot and discovered it to be empty. "Like I say, it's a shame you couldn't take a look-see."

"Oi probably wouldn't ha' gone even if needed."

"Why's that, Pad?"

Regan shrugged. "Stands ter call, if what we heard in Bermuda turns oyt, we'll be milling wi' dem soon enough. I've naw wish to fix me enemy's ship."

"They ain't an enemy yet," Morales declared. "Most is British anyway, at least that's how they started. And there were even a few familiar faces."

The man stopped polishing and Drake became alert. "In what way familiar?"

"From *Tenacious*," the carpenter replied.

"You'd be talkin' runners?" the master-at-arms checked.

"In the main."

Regan pulled a face and went on with his work. "Well they can stay dare for all oi cares. Fella what deserts 'is ship is bad enoof, fella what takes up with an enemy is somethin' else and oi've naw time for 'em."

"I told you, they ain't our enemy."

Regan stopped work again and eyed him over the hat. "Maybe not at de moment," he allowed.

"Aye," Drake agreed. "Like the barber said when the monkey cut off his tail; it won't be long now."

The following day *Delaware* was indeed ready to set sail and King, who had come across to finally inspect the work, nodded in approval.

"You might not be able to raise royals, but those spars will carry tops'ls readily enough."

"And I'm obliged to you for the loan," Walton replied. "You must tell me where they can be sent when we've done with them."

"Let's call it a *quid pro quo*," King grinned. "I seem to remember you pulling us out of a hole in the past."

They began a slow walk to the entry port; the sun was starting to lower in the sky and both men should be on their way yet were oddly reluctant to part.

"I would also be happy to lend a cutter," King suggested.

"Kind of you, though I think we should manage; if this wind holds we'll make port in a matter of days and should anchor without trouble."

"I hope we meet again soon, and that all this talk of war comes to nothing."

"It is a hope we share," Walton assured as the pair shook hands.

Despite the storm having passed some days before, the swell remained heavy and a boatswain's chair awaited King. He made for it and was preparing to submit to the indignity of being hoisted off his friend's ship when a familiar face caught his eye.

"Hodges!" he said without thinking and the seaman, who had been peering at him over the barrel of a cannon, ducked down in shame.

"What's that?" Walton demanded, stepping forward.

"This is Hodges," King said, pointing at the man who had the grace to stand and look abashed. "Formerly of my crew, yet now I find him aboard your vessel – why is that?"

"To be present at all he must be a volunteer," Walton announced crisply while beckoning the man over. "We don't use force in the American navy."

"Is that right, Hodges?" King asked.

The seaman stared wide eyed at the officers. "I signed on regular like, but am no runner, your honour," he declared. "They caught me when we was cutting out that slaver last year. Offered me a chance to ship aboard an' I took it so as to stay at sea."

"And would you serve His Majesty again, given the chance?"

"I would, sir, like I says, I'm no runner."

"That's alright, Hodges," King agreed. "There'll have to be an enquiry although I give my word you'll be taken back with nothing said."

Walton stepped closer. "Look here, this is an American warship; whatever the circumstances you've no jurisdiction aboard and definitely no right to help yourself to any of my people."

"I see that," King agreed. "But if Hodges here is willing, how would you take to an exchange?"

"An exchange?"

"One of my men for one of yours. I've a hand who claims to be your fellow countryman, even if the evidence suggests otherwise. What say you take him and I have Hodges back?"

Walton considered. "Is he able?" he asked.

"Able enough, though unwilling," King replied lightly. "I'd gauge you'll find him more compliant."

"What do you say, Hodges?"

The seaman nodded mutely and Walton sighed. "Very well, you're the only one with a boat so will have to make the exchange."

"Then I'll send Knightly over directly."

"You're certain he'll want to come?" Walton checked.

"Oh, he'll want to come," King assured. "I have no doubt of that."

Chapter Sixteen

Of course Croft would have been furious, King decided the following evening as he dined alone. After over a year of almost constant misbehaviour, Knightly had dodged his final punishment and effectively been rewarded. But then Croft had been one of a brand of sea officers that was starting to die out. Their old school methods of rigid discipline and by-the-book procedure might have been the norm in the past but now belonged to the last century.

And he felt there were other changes afoot; currently the talk was of war with America and the campaign against Napoleon was still a long way from over. For most of King's professional life and some time before, Britain had managed to find a war to fight in some part of the world. Such a policy could not go on indefinitely, however, and when it did finally come to an end things would be very different. A new world, one without strife where trade would be allowed to prosper; the prospect seemed incredible yet not totally beyond reach.

Should it materialise, the Royal Navy would not be so necessary, nor as strong. Ships would be laid off and men with them. Regular hands might find employment in the carrying trade and probably a good few officers as well, although he would not be one. Some years back King tried shipping aboard a merchant and had not fared well. Since then, and despite certain aspects of the life that still appalled him, he had been forced to accept he was a man-of-war through and through.

The rabbit pie was delicious, and far too much for one but, after taking several meals with Walton and finally bidding farewell to the *Delaware*, King had wanted to dine alone. Actually the rabbit had been a gift; on one of his frequent visits, King had been shown the vast rack of pens where the creatures were kept and once more the American had extolled their virtues in comparison to the more common shipboard hen. The nett result was his final journey back to *Tenacious* had been in company with a score of the creatures.

Currently they were housed in empty chicken coops on the forecastle although Morales, the carpenter, would be making more secure pens for them as a few had already gone missing.

Memories of the time spent with Walton brought a smile to his face; they might be from different backgrounds yet followed a similar calling so he supposed it natural for them to have become friends. And there was so much they agreed upon; both had the same ethos when caring for their people and ran their ships with due regard to regulations, although not in slavish subservience to them. And both regarded competent seamanship and moral strength as greater attributes to a naval career than family connections. There were some areas where they disagreed, yet these only served to make their friendship stronger. King regarded himself as a nominal Christian – how could he not when society viewed an absence of faith to be a definite stain on any gentleman's character? But Walton was bold in his rejection of religion and regarded formal worship as mere theatrics. More than that, he was not afraid to say so, a stance that had earned King's silent respect for his own experience of death, and the manner in which it can be caused, had long since robbed him of any belief in an afterlife or hope for resurrection.

Then they had talked of more trivial matters, of families and dogs and past Christmases; Walton also had two children, both girls, and there were vague plans for each to visit the other's home if the threatened war failed to materialise. And if it did not, if their respective governments decided physical conflict was the only solution to failed diplomacy, King supposed they would probably end up fighting each other, despite their camaraderie and the swapping of wine and rabbits. He took another mouthful of his meal and suppressed a sigh; at that moment it all made little sense.

And Croft would have seen that differently as well, King supposed as he cleared his plate before furtively considering the rest of the pie. Croft would have seen Walton as an American first and relied upon the political situation to judge him friend or foe. Such an attitude probably had its advantages, it was far easier to be comfortable with your own thoughts if they always followed direct orders or government policy although King had never sought to be quite so controlled. For him, an armed conflict only became acceptable if he believed in the ideals that lay behind it; to go to war on any other basis would be a betrayal of his principles and tantamount to murder. And it was then King realised that, if the worst

178

happened – if war were declared and he was forced to fight – he may not be able to.

It was a chilling thought and one so radical that he was forced to take another portion of the pie. Yet even as he cut a generous slice his resolution remained as strong and was sincerely held, or so he felt. For experience had taught him no principle or belief could ever be counted upon until put to the test. And for many reasons he hoped this particular one never would be.

* * *

"So it weren't intentional like?" Stokes checked. "You didn't choose to run?"

"I didn't choose to because I didn't run," Hodges declared for what must have been the hundredth time. "I were detailed ashore to strike the schooner's moorin'. A couple of fellows appeared before I could make it back and dragged me off even as the prize were pulling out."

Hodges had been brought back the previous day and spent the night in custody. Then, after talks with the captain and first officer, the seaman was returned to his mess and all were supposed to continue as if he had never been away. But once back amongst his peers a far stricter interrogation had begun, and one that he suspected would last for much longer.

"So how come you weren't taken prisoner?" Groom demanded.

"Because we're not at war with America," Bovey informed them gravely from the far end of the table. "We was able to cut the slaver out 'cause she were a British ship an' breakin' British law. The only say the Yanks had in the matter was we were in their waters."

"He's right," Hodges agreed. "Nearhood and I were taken back to the slavin' station and slung in a pen. Next day a bunch of uniforms arrived and started asking questions though they weren't hard on me, more on them that had kept us locked up with the black folk. Said it weren't Christian."

"Navy were they?" Bovey asked, and Hodges shook his head.

"Army, least I think so. They wanted to know where we'd come from and how we knew about the slaver."

"So where exactly were you?" Lovemore this time.

"Like I said, slavin' station."

179

"But they dunna trade in slaves na more," McKenzie protested.

"Then what was a fully loaded slave ship doing in their harbour?" Bovey enquired.

"Well, whether they are or not, the place were full of natives," Hodges continued. "An' all in the same sort of cages though them in the uniforms didn't take no notice. Anyways, we was carried away to some barracks and I were given a choice."

"We?" Stokes checked.

"Told you, Nearhood were with me throughout; they took him an all, despite his being a Jonathan."

At this point Hodges bit into a lump of cheese and began to chew. The past two days had been taxing enough and he had missed his midday meal completely. Now it had been confirmed he wasn't to be tried as a deserter, and his mates weren't giving him too hard a time, appetite was starting to return. On the whole *Delaware*'s scran had been a good deal fresher. But, hard and stale though it might be, he had missed the cheese served aboard *Tenacious* and the table waited expectantly while he finished his mouthful.

"You said you were given a choice..." Lovemore prompted when the food had gone.

"I were told I was free to go 'cept it was several hundred miles to the nearest British station and no help would be given with me reachin' it. I might serve aboard a merchant but that would mean taking the country as me own, and I weren't too keen on that."

"Quite right," said Stokes but Hodges turned on him.

"It's not what you think, Stokie," he declared. "I said before, countries don't mean nothin' to me but I seen what's been 'appening of late. If I were picked up by a British ship they might think me a runner."

"You could have explained," Bovey suggested.

"I'm explaining now," Hodges countered. "And it ain't going down too well, far as I can see."

There was a moment's silence as the mess considered this, then Bovey spoke again.

"Well old Tommo must have believed you, else you'd be in bilboes."

"Captain's a gentleman," said Hodges. "He can tell when a man's tellin' the truth. Can't expect the same from some unknown Yank officer. Or your messmates, if it comes to it."

There was another silence as Hodges ate some more cheese,

then he picked up his story once more.

"Anyway, it seemed I had another course. I was told I could volunteer for the American navy. After the *Leopard* business our lot wouldn't chance pressing from a Yank warship and I'd be safe – least that's what they told me..."

"So you plumped for *Delaware*?" Lovemore suggested.

"I did. Joined her shortly after an' was there when we saved you lot from them cruisers."

"Well we never saw you," said Bovey.

"I made sure of that," Hodges smirked. "Though will admit it felt good to bail you lot out like we did."

"Kind of you, I'm sure," Stokes grunted.

"An' *Delaware* weren't such a bad old tub," the seaman continued. "They did some things different but you'd expect that."

"And how did you find the Yanks?" Johnno, the mess boy, chanced.

"Much the same as us, though you'd expect that as well since a good few come from Britain." Hodges sighed. "Some had only just taken the country but there was no tellin' who. In some ways it were like being at home."

"And Nearhood?" Lovemore asked. "Do you know what happened to him?"

"We spent yesterday's morning watch together," their messmate replied with a grin. "He joined *Delaware* an all."

"So Tommo didn't see him?" Stokes supposed.

"'Parently not," Hodges shrugged. "He probably had the sense to keep well hid; we all did whenever British officers was about – it seemed polite somehow."

"All?" McKenzie questioned.

"Aye, there were a lot more of us aboard the *Delaware*; Dixon's there and Coltrane – Murphy too. As I say, it were like being at home."

* * *

Halifax had changed little in the time they were away. There was more shipping in the Navy Yard anchorage and some building work had been carried out to the fortifications on George Island although that looked to be about it. But as *Tenacious* felt her way along the channel, King was wise enough to know there would be a lot to catch up on when she finally dropped her hook. Even without news of actual war, he would be kept busy dealing with the port authorities and shore-bound officers before revictualling the ship. And if the worst had happened, if Britain truly did intend adding America to her current list of enemies, there would be no end to the ramifications. *Tenacious* must be brought up to a proper war footing, with more hands taken on as well as an additional lieutenant. They could also expect reinforcements from Britain; America might have a tiny navy but her ships were soundly made, as he had seen for himself. With such a vast area to cover it would be impossible to protect British trade without at least doubling their current forces.

And then King realised if he truly were determined not to fight America, none of this need bother him. Should war have broken out it would be a simple matter to resign his commission. With a country estate, a growing family and more than sufficient prize money, no one would be so very astonished and for a man who had already seen more action than most, few would suspect any other motive.

Yet would it really be so simple? He might have found camaraderie with one American, but was that sufficient reason to alter his entire life? And could he really turn his back on his ship, her crew and the officers who had also become friends, and probably closer ones than some former colonial he barely knew?

King took a turn about the deck, conscious of covert attention from those around him, many of whom were probably wondering what particular problem was now bothering their unpredictable captain. And there were quite a few present; he was not alone in having business ashore. By the break of the quarterdeck Manning was waiting with his medical certificates tucked under one arm while Dennison was intending to hand in his papers and would need to arrange for a full survey of the ship's provisions. Over the next few days Cooper was also likely to be fully involved in ship's business so, as Manton was happy conning them in and some of what King would have to do involved his first officer, it made sense to speak to the man during this brief moment of peace.

The subject he had in mind would have been better addressed in the sanctuary of their morning meeting, but *Tenacious* was coming in at first light, and on the previous day it had completely slipped his mind. Besides, in a crowded ship whose very fabric transmitted sound like Wren's Whispering Gallery, where was truly private? And as Cooper stood alone by the taffrail he may as well seize the opportunity.

"I'll be speaking with the C-in-C directly," he said, joining him.

"Of course, sir," Cooper agreed. "Would that be Admiral Sawyer?"

"I assume so. We have been away a fair while, there might have been changes. But whoever it is will want to ask about my officers."

"Do you mean Mr Croft?"

"Not specifically; that sad tale should have been covered by the findings of the board of enquiry. I was thinking more of his successor."

"I see, sir." Cooper's sudden reserve suggested the subject had also been on his mind and now there was definitely tension in the air.

"So, Jack, would you be interested in retaining the premiership?" King asked. "Providing such a position is within my grasp, of course."

"I would, sir."

"Very well." King cleared his throat and looked about in an effort to hide his feelings. On one hand he was pleased Cooper seemed willing to remain, and on the other it would make his leaving the harder to bear should he need to go. "I cannot make promises, but shall press for any officers appointed to be junior to yourself."

"Thank you, sir, I should appreciate that. And if I might also add, we are several light in the midshipmen's berth."

"Yes, yes of course," King agreed. "I expect plenty of candidates, though few will be experienced; we shall have to see what can be found." King went to walk away then paused. "I'm glad you're to remain, Jack," he said. "I think we work well together."

"Thank you, sir," Cooper replied. "I think so too."

* * *

As so often happened, as soon as *Tenacious* was secure she became a hive of activity. King's gig was the first to be lowered but the barge would be close behind as Manning had two patients that required transfer to the naval hospital. And as the smaller craft put out, a positive fleet of bumboats were already approaching from across the water as well as two more official craft. But Cooper could deal with all of that, King had an inkling his forthcoming interview would be significant enough and deserved all his attention. And his suspicions seemed to be confirmed as his boat approached the low stone quay where he noticed a particularly smart midshipman was already waiting for him.

"Captain King?" the officer enquired as King took his first step on land since Bermuda. He considered the man, who was truly no more than a boy, and a dewy-eyed one at that.

"I'm King."

"My name is Green, sir, I'm from the admiral's office. He asked me to meet with you."

"Which you have done." King spoke curtly as he summed the officer up. The child had all the looks of a well-connected prodigy; after a couple of years on land pampering an admiral he could expect to be transferred to a prime vessel. Once there he would quickly find himself made lieutenant and possibly be given his own command not long afterwards. Despite recent changes, this last bastion of the old navy looked like remaining. Interest, which was nothing more than another word for nepotism, may have allowed such stars as Nelson to shine a little earlier, but it remained inherently wrong, and was disliked by most professional sea officers.

"Yes, sir," the midshipman agreed while fumbling for a heavy silver watch that was way above his station. "The admiral requests you join him at Fort George and I fear we are already late."

"Fort George?"

"Indeed, sir." Green was now showing signs of panic. "Our offices have been transferred there while renovations are carried out. If you'd care to follow me the carriage is close by, with luck we may still be in time."

"I was not aware of any appointment," King protested.

"No, sir, but your ship was seen to come in and Admiral Sawyer wishes to speak with you urgently."

King found himself being rushed to where a service carriage did indeed await. Climbing into such affairs was always awkward and he would have preferred the protocol of 'in last and out first' for the senior man to be abandoned. But the deed was finally done without the lad's assistance and soon they were bumping along at a fair lick.

"It's really not far," the youngster announced although King could not tell who he was trying to reassure. He had expected to meet with Sawyer at the Dockyard itself, the alternative would surely have been Government House, a far more convenient venue as it meant he might call on Aimée after speaking with the admiral. Fort George was some distance away on Citadel Hill and, as he settled himself for an uncomfortable journey, King sensed they must already be late.

But eventually the carriage was turning into a long drive that led up to the impressive fortifications and, after clambering clumsily out of the carriage, King stood for a moment and took in the splendid view of Halifax.

"If you'll forgive me, sir, I am to see you straight to the admiral," Green said once he had alighted. The boy was clearly flustered and for the first time King felt a twinge of guilt. Sawyer had been in office for more than a year, but King was absent for much of that time and all dealings had been with his deputy. From what he had heard, the man was not the easiest to work under and an obsession with punctuality was likely to be the least of his faults. Yet as he followed the hurrying youngster towards the fort's main entrance he was also slightly irritated. For it would surely be unfair to blame his escort for their late arrival; however well connected a midshipman might be, he could have no control over how fast a senior captain moved.

Such apparent unfairness only confirmed the impression King had already formed. Sawyer was the son of a distinguished naval officer who had also been fortunate in prize money; throughout his life he would have enjoyed privilege and respect and was probably used to having his smallest wish granted. It occurred to him that, if war truly were imminent, having such a commander would actually make the act of resigning a little easier.

But he must not think so. For all he knew agreement with America had already been reached; the current trade sanctions might have been altered or even revoked and they could all look forward to many years of peace, while he might see out his commission with *Tenacious*. The next few minutes would doubtless tell him much and, if a little hurrying appeased his Commander-in-Chief, it would probably be wise to indulge him.

However, that proved not to be the case. After rushing past armed sentries with little more than an acknowledgement, King was hurried up a large stone staircase before being led to a plain and rather chilly anteroom. And there he was deposited, with Green's assurance that he would be sent for presently. So, when fifteen minutes passed with no summons, he began to grow irritated.

For he was a ship's captain and accustomed to having total autonomy over all he surveyed. To be rushed so, then apparently abandoned, was not the way he was used to being treated while there was also a vague suspicion the delay was intended as some form of punishment for his own lateness. Yet when he finally received the summons all such thoughts were quickly forgotten. King was shown into a large and finely furnished room with an impressive view of Halifax. An ornate mahogany desk faced the window but it was empty; the only other person present sat before it as if he, too, were expecting to speak with the admiral.

And he was one that King instantly recognised. There was perhaps a little more grey at the temples although the face remained finely formed and just as striking. As the man rose to meet him, King noticed the uniform was superbly cut and fitted to perfection but, though it was that of a rear admiral, this was definitely not Sawyer.

"It's good to see you, Tom," Banks told him through the well-remembered smile.

King beamed and crossed the room in three lengthy strides before shaking hands with his former captain. "And good to see you also, Sir Richard."

Chapter Seventeen

"I must say you are the last person I expected to meet here," King announced with an unintended lack of tact. "I'd thought you still on the Cape Town Station."

"I returned about a year ago," Banks explained. "Spent some time in the country with Sarah and the childers and truly considered my days at sea to be over. But you know how it is, the pull can be strong."

King grinned: he knew exactly.

"Admiral Sawyer's been called away though I guessed my former midshipman would be waiting outside so sent for you." The older man indicated the chair next to him.

"I am glad of it," King said, seating himself. "And do you have a ship?"

"In truth I have three, and favour a neat little Lively class for my flag."

"So, a commodore still?"

Banks nodded. "And now of the first class, so have a captain to assist and get to wear the rags of an admiral. My full flag might not come for several years though I am content."

As well he might be, King decided. As commodore, his old friend had been given the power to command a fleet considerably sooner than if he had waited for the automatic promotion to flag rank.

"And what do you intend? Are you staying on station?"

"Well, that is the point," Banks grimaced. "I only put in recently myself and have yet to discover all. But Admiral Sawyer knew you were coming and summoned me to the Citadel when *Tenacious* came into sight. You've had a busy time of it, or so I hears."

"I despatched an interim journal from St George when we were under refit," King stated cautiously.

"Which I have read," Banks said. "And were sorry to learn of James Croft."

187

"It was a sad case," King agreed. "Though the findings of the board of enquiry were copied; there should be nothing to concern the admiral on that front."

"Oh he accepted it particularly well I'd say, however word has reached him of your later dealings and it is those which have wound the old boy up."

King's mind ran back; apart from the storm and meeting with Walton, there was surely little to cause such a reaction.

"*Tenacious* was sighted by the station on Clark's Harbour; in the current weather Admiral Sawyer felt he could estimate your arrival with some accuracy."

"And did I meet his expectations?" King enquired.

Banks frowned. "Actually, no, he had you down for yesterday even' – you may find yourself having to explain that as well."

"I see." The younger man rolled his eyes.

"Tell me, Tom, do you know the admiral?"

"Hardly at all."

"Well I have to say he comes across as a bit of a stickler," Banks confided. "And fear you might have caused something of a rumpus."

"By being a few hours late?" King exclaimed, but at that point the door flew open and Sawyer himself appeared to put an end to further discussion.

The admiral was much as King remembered and probably what Midshipman Green would turn out to be, given time. In his early sixties, still reasonably fit and, unusual in one of his age, not wearing a wig. Consequently a full head of dark, unpowdered, hair was on full display and the eyes and demeanour were that of a far younger man. But as he swung the door wide and barged through there was also that air of privilege – an acceptance of superiority and unearned respect common amongst senior men that always stuck in King's craw.

"Sir Richard, Captain King, you will forgive me I am certain." He swept deeper into the room. "There was an important message from Fort Anne that truly could not be ignored though, when investigated, proved little more than smoke."

"That would be Prince Edward's semaphore, sir?" Banks chanced.

"Indeed," Sawyer agreed, shaking hands briefly with both officers before taking his place behind the mahogany desk. "A wonder of the modern age, I have no doubt, but own there are times when we might do without such foolery. Be seated, will you not?"

King returned to the chair next to Banks and both regarded the senior man expectantly.

"However the reason for my delay was actually relevant to our discussion," Sawyer continued. "There are cold feet everywhere at present and especially so on the western side of the province. One sight of what might be a group of warships and they start ringing alarm bells." He sighed. "I suppose it understandable, Annapolis Royal is a good deal closer to our former colonials than Halifax and there can be no doubt war is in the offing, though I wish they would keep their fears to themselves and not continually bother me."

King's thoughts began to race. If war truly was on the cards this interview may not go the way the two flag officers intended, although meeting with Banks again had also been a surprise, and could alter matters yet.

"So, Captain King, I understand you have recently come into contact with an American frigate?"

"Yes, the *Delaware*," he admitted. "I have run in with her on several occasions; you may recall she engaged *Sparrow* last year?"

"I am aware of that, it is the most immediate contact that interests me. You rendered assistance if I am not misinformed?"

"*Tenacious* encountered a tropical storm on her passage home. While in the midst of it we sighted the *Delaware* and supported when she were partially dismasted."

"Which is exactly what the Jonathans are saying," Sawyer grunted. "Though our intelligence told us as much and the story's in every American news sheet; what exactly were you thinking of?"

"The ship was in danger, Admiral," King replied. "It is every mariner's duty to render aid in such a situation."

Sawyer rocked back in his chair and considered him. "Maybe so, but you must be aware of the current political climate. War is likely, I would go as far as to say inevitable. For the past month every Yankee trader's been confined to port by their own government, yet you went out of your way to offer assistance to one of their warships. Worse, you actually provided them with crown equipment!"

King pursed his lips; Sawyer must also know that men had died during the rescue and fortunately was not choosing to centre on that.

"I allowed them the use of some spars," he admitted.

The Admiral was clearly not impressed and leant forward, fixing King with his eyes. "Really, Captain King, it would be better to

189

remember you are an Englishman first and a seaman very much second. I expect more loyalty from officers under my command."

"I understand, sir," King lied. There was more to say; he might cite the fact that Walton had rescued him in the past and showed a degree of magnanimity over being fired upon by *Sparrow*. But despite the youthful appearance, his Commander-in-Chief was obviously yet another old school officer, and sensed it better not to argue further.

"Very well, Sir Richard has persuaded me to say no more about the incident, even if it is much against my better judgement." The older man relaxed slightly. "So you may thank him that a court martial has been avoided. At present there are more important matters to concern us and I fear America is still very much at the core."

Sawyer paused and regarded them both. "As I have already intimated, it will be war gentlemen," he said. "Nothing is official for now and won't come as soon as our friends at Annapolis Royal seem to imagine. However, it appears inevitable and we must be prepared."

That would have been enough for several seconds of silence although Admiral Sawyer had more to say.

"And to be frank I am surprised, though suppose so young a country is allowed to be a little immature. For years now we have been banned from their territorial waters which is juvenile, to say the least. Why, Denmark has a naval force five times the size of theirs and an army at least ten times larger, yet we might sail up the sound within cannon shot of her shores with total impunity."

He sighed and glanced briefly at the papers on his desk and King was wondering if some comment was required when the admiral began again.

"So, if America wants a war, let them have it – they only won the first bout due to our attention being elsewhere." Sawyer had settled back in his chair now, his eyes seemingly set on a point about a foot above his guests' heads and all King's suspicions were confirmed.

"A short, sharp conflict that ends with a sound drubbing will settle matters and finish this nonsense of calling for liberty! Their so-called union was bound to fail, we shall just have to take the country back and instil some proper government."

This time King chanced a glance towards Banks, and was surprised to note the commodore seemed genuinely interested in Sawyer's words.

"I'd admit the timing is not the best when we have

commitments elsewhere – an army in Portugal and what is left of the Spanish mob to maintain. At least we are now at peace with Sweden and Russia. Those ships previously blockading their ports can be released and, more importantly, trade will resume. And the Swedes are able to supply much of what America offered so we can do very nicely without their business."

"But surely that has been the case for some while, sir?" King chanced and Sawyer, who obviously had not intended this to be a discussion, jerked his head slightly.

"Think you so, Captain?" he demanded.

"The American Embargo Act, and what came after: together they cancelled out a good deal of commerce with England." King was vaguely conscious Banks had begun to shuffle in his chair but, now he had started, it felt better to finish. "With them and our own Orders in Council, trade has been decimated; the only channel not affected is the small amount of contraband that passes through Canada."

"I believe Captain King is forgetting our commitments in the West Indies," Banks remarked and King suddenly went cold. That was indeed the case, he had annoyed Sawyer for no reason and, in the process, made himself look the fool.

"Yet there is an element of truth in what he says," his former captain continued. "Since our market has been closed to them, the Americans have been inclined to supply the French, and that is something that surely counts against us."

King looked his thanks, although the commodore appeared not to notice, while Banks' comments had sparked something further in the admiral.

"Which is exactly why you are here, Sir Richard," Sawyer confirmed, apparently pleased at being handed back the lead. "We expect both American and French commercial trade to resume once war is declared, and possibly increase dramatically. And I need not tell you that those merchants will require warships to protect them."

King released a silent sigh; yet again he had allowed his mouth to carry him away. The Admiral had apparently dismissed him as a nuisance and was now concentrating solely on Banks.

"As soon as your ships have revictualled they will be heading south to cruise the Eastern Seaboard. Once war is declared we shall be mounting a blockade on every viable port; your task will be to collect any outgoing vessels that evade this as well as meeting those incoming from across the Atlantic. Initially most will be American,

191

though the French will no doubt come in force later. You are to take up your station before war is declared and be ready to go into action as soon as hostilities commence. How does that sound?"

Banks seemed pleased. "I should regard that as the ideal commission, sir," he said. "Indeed, it must be every officer's dream."

"I expected you to think so." Sawyer allowed himself a brief smile. "But do not expect to have everything your own way. The Americans have warships of their own – indeed their fleet is actually larger since Captain King's recent act of benevolence. And though their navy may be minor in comparison to our own, several of their frigates are not. Considering your station, it is likely you will chance upon some of these, Commodore. And, should it so prove, they will require careful handling." He paused and this time subjected Banks to his stare.

"Let me make it clear: if met they will be defeated," Sawyer added with emphasis. "Indeed they must; anything else would prove a disaster for this station and can hardly strengthen our position fighting Monsieur Bonaparte."

"I understand, sir," Banks said. "And can I ask what is required of Captain King?"

Sawyer finally turned his attention back to the younger man and King blinked in anticipation.

"Why, King will be attached to your force," he said at last. "Four ships will see the job done more efficiently than three and I understand the pair of you go back some way. But make sure you keep an eye on him, Sir Richard," Sawyer warned. "It appears Captain King is still to learn the niceties expected of a senior officer. And worse, has trouble distinguishing friends from enemies."

* * *

"Corbrite!" Brotherton exclaimed in surprise. "Whatever brings you down here?"

"A fine welcome," the midshipman replied, entering the tiny berth. "And exactly what do you have there? Some form of cat?"

"This is Tommo," Brotherton announced holding the beast up for inspection. "And any educated person would recognise him to be a rabbit."

"Goodness, so it is," Corbrite agreed coming closer. "And a fat one too; would it be for food or friendship?"

"Food!" Godby announced as he swung himself down from his hammock. "Though Brotherton has yet to see it that way."

"You must be Godby," the newcomer told him.

"I see my reputation goes before me," the midshipman acknowledged glumly, "and cannot think the reason."

"All I have heard has been good," Corbrite assured as the pair shook hands. "I look forward to serving alongside you."

"Alongside?" Brotherton questioned.

"Poor old *Sparrow*'s for the knackers," Corbrite said as he seated himself at the table. "She spent an age waiting for the dockyard, then when her turn finally came they found a mass of rot that was missed in survey. Nothing could be done, she were condemned on the spot."

"I'm sorry to hear that. *Sparrow* was a fine sailer."

"Steered like a boat," Corbrite confirmed.

"Though if it means we are to be shipmates it can only be good news," Brotherton continued. "In truth, there are so few of us in the berth I was thinking of rating Tommo."

"Tommo?"

"His rabbit." Godby pulled back a chair and joined them.

"How many are you?" Corbrite asked.

"What you see here, and Vernon of course." Brotherton stroked his pet's head. "He's on deck at present but only a kid really. Be junior to you for sure."

"Three mid.s ain't enough for a ship this size," Godby mused.

"Well it's four now," Corbrite announced. "And I'm bringing Taylor with me."

"Our old third lieutenant?"

"The very same."

"Well, that'll make up a really decent set of officers," Brotherton grinned. "He'll be senior to Summers – I say do you know about poor old Croftie?"

"I were sad to hear of it," Corbrite confirmed and all three looked suitably glum for a moment.

"Here, join us in some tea, it's not totally cold," Brotherton suggested, springing to life once more. "Godby, do the honours, there's a chap – I think old Tommo's got a tick behind his ear."

"So how's Jacky Coops panning out as premier?" Corbrite

asked.

"Could do worse." Brotherton was peering at his rabbit's head. "Mind he'll have to go some to match Croftie's bawdy sense of humour."

"So when did you know you were being appointed?" Godby reached for the pot.

"Only this morning; Captain King arranged it." Corbrite nodded and Godby began to pour a stream of weak tea into one of several battered mugs that littered the table. "Best news I've had in an age; once *Sparrow* were condemned I lost both berth and income. Been living on charity for the past few weeks and forget when I last had a full belly."

"Then we must celebrate!" Brotherton exclaimed. "And a meal would seem the thing!"

"Meal sounds capital," Corbrite agreed. "Has petty warrant begun?"

"Not till tomorrow, in the meantime we have a bite of cheese left over from midday and a little bacon that is not totally beyond redemption."

"We'll have to do better than that." Godby took a sip of his tea, then hurriedly replaced the cup.

"Why so short?" Corbrite asked.

"We failed to stock up sufficiently in Bermuda," Brotherton explained. "Weren't no one's fault, they just didn't have the victuals and we've been running low since."

"And little chance of shore leave," Godby added. "Least, not 'mediately."

"I suppose we might hound the pusser," Brotherton said. "Though understand he's handed in his ticket."

"We should get a replacement directly," Godby pointed out. "And the cove'll be bound to have made some purchases."

"Which will doubtless be sold at a tidy profit." Corbrite picked up his cup and sniffed at it cautiously.

"Do you know the new man?" Godby asked.

"Maybe not, but I do know pussers."

"I say, it wasn't a tick but a flea!" Brotherton beamed in triumph as he held an insect up for inspection."

"Very nice," Godby grunted and the thing was flicked across the berth.

"Look, there is little need to rush," Corbrite assured them.

"We'll eat well enough on the morrow. I had no idea today would find me employment so am already ahead."

"No, a meal it must be." Brotherton had returned to aimlessly stoking his rabbit once more. And then, realising the others had gone quiet, the lad glanced up.

Both midshipmen were staring intently although not at him but the animal resting comfortably against his chest. In a sudden rush of realisation Brotherton clutched the creature closer to him and glared back defiantly. "Absolutely not!" he said.

* * *

"Well, you went down swimmingly with the Admiral," Banks announced when they had quit the Citadel. "Tell me, Tom, where exactly did you learn diplomacy?"

King shrugged. "Sawyer's type annoy me," he said. They were walking down the drive that would eventually lead to Halifax itself and King, at least, was glad of the fresh air.

"By type, do you mean admirals?" Banks asked. "Or flag officers in general?"

"Anyone who behaves so," King replied a little sulkily.

"That would be fine, Tom, I'm all for folk speaking their mind and would never miss hearing your opinion for one second. But in this instance it *was* an admiral," Banks pointed out. "And one who also happens to be our Commander-in-Chief; that is surely a different matter?"

There was silence as the two men passed through the sentry post after which they paused. The town lay sprawled before them and appeared like many other overseas stations. Certain buildings stood out; a church built more in the style of a temple and what appeared to be a theatre, while several of the private houses could have been competing for the most number of square-pained windows. Between these, far more humble buildings had evolved, the majority being shops or small workshops while simpler dwellings, brightly coloured and oddly stark in the spring sunshine, showed where ordinary folk might live. And through all the splendour and confusion, a far more considered grid of streets had been laid to carry wandering civilians, hurrying workers and the occasional narrowed ranks of marching men.

"Are you sure you don't mind not taking a carriage?" Banks checked. "It will be a fair stretch to the dockyard."

"When have I ever objected to walking?" King enquired with a grin, and they set off once more, comfortable in the other's company.

King was especially pleased to be back with Banks. The pair had been through much together, including a momentous march through the heartland of France when prisoners of war. They first met well over ten years ago when the commodore was a junior captain in command of a frigate. There were times when he could be a strange stick, and they had not always seen eye to eye, although Sir Richard remained the closest thing to a father King had known since going to sea, and he usually found it easy to confide in him. Consequently it was relatively early in their journey that his worries began to be revealed.

"This Walton sounds like quite a fellow," Banks said when he had heard some of King's story. "And a New Englander, you say?"

"Indeed, though his parents were born British."

"Then there's hope for the cove!" Banks gave a quick grin.

"That's just it, he is so like us." King paused. "Not in every way, perhaps, but closer than any Frenchman."

"And you don't think we should be fighting him – him and his kind?" Banks clarified.

"I don't. It seems wrong. Wrong on many levels."

"Name some."

King considered for a moment. "Well, what will this war be about? A stack of sanctions that were poorly thought out and no one sought to change. Is that truly a reason to start killing people?"

"And your solution would be?"

"We are on station and know the situation better than any politician many miles away. Gather a few sensible folk together, people like Walton, and we would soon sort out some form of agreement that would keep all sides happy."

"As simple as that?"

King turned to look at his friend. "Does it have to be complicated?"

"You were explaining why we should not go to war," Banks prompted after several seconds had passed.

"I suppose it comes down to what I said earlier; the Americans are not so very different; they speak the same language, have many of

196

the same values, even sing similar songs and worship the same God. The French have been an enemy for most of our professional lives but there has always been cause; even before Napoleon and his atrocities, their government ruled by terror, invading other countries at will and subjugating their people. They even threatened us and our families and are clearly intent on world domination."

"I've no argument there."

"Well, as far as I can see all the Yanks have done is object to our choking their trading, that and the methods we use when reclaiming our countrymen. They do not endanger my home, my household or my country. Fighting them would be akin to a civil war with all the obscenities such a conflict attracts."

"Maybe you're right," Banks allowed after thinking further. "Maybe our politicians have got it wrong, and are too remote to truly understand. But those trade restrictions that upset you so were made with the best intentions. And their purpose was to avoid a war, not create one. That they have failed might be more down to how they were implemented."

"Some captains are definitely harsher than others," King agreed.

"Exactly, you only have to look at the *Leopard* affair, and that of *Sparrow* and *Little Belt*; none of those had anything to do with politicians or government directives but were down to the various commanders taking the law into their own hands. Each were on the spot and frankly should have known better, yet you would have such fools decide our national policy?"

King was silent as he considered this and Banks continued.

"What they – what any of us who wear the King's uniform – can never fully comprehend is the global aspect. World affairs are exactly that: a cancelled trade agreement can have repercussions that affect countries on the other side of the planet."

"There have been times when senior naval officers have needed to act as ambassadors."

"And in the main they did so well enough," Banks agreed. "Though not always; there have been disasters as well as achievements. In truth, few simple seamen fully comprehend political diplomacy. It's not in their remit; such matters should be dealt with by those who truly understand."

King supposed Banks might have a point although he was still relatively new to the station; give him a couple more months – or an hour with Bob Walton – and he might think differently.

"And you speak of this American fellow as being like us – which I am sure he is," the commodore continued. "From what I have read those from New England are; the title is clue enough. Go a little to the west, though, and the population changes dramatically, Federalists decline and are replaced by a different breed that include Democratic-Republican War Hawks."

"Walton has spoken of them."

"From what I gather they are of pioneer stock and used to carving a living for themselves in the harshest of circumstances. And one of the challenges they face is promoted by us."

"The arming of Indians?"

"Indeed, our government have been funding those to the North-West for years. Such measures are hardly likely to promote friendship and trust. Likewise the southerners have developed along different lines and bear far less resemblance to you or me, despite our sharing a language."

King regarded the older man for a moment. "How do you know all this?"

Banks grinned. "It was a rushed deployment," he admitted. "One day I were in my London house, the next aboard *Alert* and at the head of a squadron of frigates. But I did take the precaution of purchasing as much as I could on the subject and have been reading diligently since."

King nodded; that was so like his old captain, and so unlike himself. "So you think we should go to war?" he asked at last.

"To be frank, Tom, it is not up to me and glad I am that is so. I might keep myself informed yet fundamentally remain a King's officer. And as such it is my place to trust those in power and obey their orders."

"And if those orders include fighting a friend?"

Banks stopped suddenly and King had to turn back to face him.

"*I* am your friend." The older man spoke with feeling. "We have been through much and survived, more or less, intact. Your ship has been placed under my command – *you* have been placed under my command. Is it your intention to betray me in favour of some former colonial – a man with whom you have exchanged a couple of favours?"

"I would never betray you," King declared and the older man

relaxed.

"I know that, Tom," he said as they started to walk once more. "Though you get my meaning I am certain. There is nothing wrong in respecting your enemy; indeed it is commendable. And you may even get to like the fellow. But he cannot be your friend, Tom, that must never happen."

Chapter Eighteen

Two weeks later *Tenacious* sailed out of Halifax harbour as the back marker in a flotilla of four frigates. In the intervening time she had revictualled, watered and taken on powder and shot as well as attending to several minor repairs to her rig. The new officers and a replacement for Dennison were also embarked along with a fresh draft of hands while her population of rabbits, of which roughly half proved to have been pregnant on arrival, had steadily increased. And King had come to a resolution.

Banks was right. His knowledge might have been gleaned from books rather than experience but there was possibly greater value in information gained in such a manner. Whatever, the man was certainly far more worldly and King had become used – conditioned almost – to taking his advice. And there was another factor that he was slowly starting to appreciate. With only the briefest of respites, Britain's conflict with France had lasted nearly twenty years. In that time the changes were almost too numerous to remember; whole countries had been lost only to be regained, enemies turned to friends and friends to enemies while the entire face of the world had altered beyond anyone's expectation. Yet that must happen in a war fought between powerful nations with many hundreds of formidable warships and massive armies capable of conquering continents. It was not so with America; her entire fighting navy was headed by a handful of frigates while the United States Army was poorly provided for and truly in no position to defend their own shores let alone invade Canada. Should war between their countries be declared, it could not last long and must surely favour the British. Within a year, probably less, a resolution of sorts would be reached and the chances of encountering Walton in that time were slight, especially as King would be stationed deep in the anonymous wastes of the North Atlantic.

Deciding so came as a relief and the rest of the period ashore had been spent playing with his children or attending those functions that could not be avoided. And, when the time came to leave, he had kissed Aimée, bid farewell to the little house on Princes Street and set off in good heart. There had still been no official declaration of war and many in Halifax were coming to doubt there ever would be. *Tenacious* was due to revictual in three months when that may still be the case. Or the war might have been fought and won, but in either instance he trusted some good would have been served; an agreement reached and the much vaunted War Hawks finally silenced. At which point Britain could return to her proper role, the one he felt he had been born to, that of fighting Napoleon.

"Pleasant weather, sir," Cooper remarked. It was first light on their tenth day out of Halifax and King had come on deck some minutes before, although the first lieutenant wisely delayed speaking until his captain finished inspecting the traverse board.

"It is indeed, Mr Cooper," King agreed as he took station next to the younger man. His previous executive officer would have avoided any conversation beyond a formal greeting unless it were instigated by his captain, but King was not in the mood to find fault. For though his ways were different, Cooper was turning into an excellent second in command and King had to admit the man's more relaxed manner was easier to deal with.

"Signal from flag!" The call came from the foretop lookout and Godby and Brotherton immediately sprang to life. King had decided it would be better to have all their young gentlemen trained in signals and Godby was proving a willing student.

"Sail in sight," he reported with reassuring certainty. "East-sou'-east."

"Probably another merchant," Cooper murmured.

And that was indeed likely; already they had encountered three such vessels all making for the American coast after an Atlantic crossing. King knew little of the details, *Albatross*, an aged jackass frigate and the smallest of their number, having been the intercepting vessel on each occasion. One had definitely been suspected of contravening British trading laws and, after a lengthy inspection, was seen to be making for Halifax. Of the others he was unsure, *Tenacious* had not closed with any and only a minimal amount could be learned through a glass. It was likely one had been carrying British seamen as a second cutter had been summoned before the vessel was allowed to continue her journey.

"Sighting is an American..." Godby reported slowly, "and... And *Albatross'* number has come up."

The announcement caused a muttering of disappointment from those on the quarterdeck although King remained mute. He could understand the frustration; cruising in formation at such a slow speed was hardly the most satisfying of activities and any distraction, even the rummaging of a neutral vessel, would have broken the monotony. But *Tenacious* had yet to be at sea a full fortnight; there were likely to be many such days to come and they may as well get used to the inactivity.

"Traffic only seems to be one way," Cooper commented as the little frigate broke formation and increased sail. That was certainly the case, President Madison's insistence that local merchant shipping should remain in harbour would seem to be holding and overseas vessels could be expected to make for home if a war were truly anticipated.

"If you'll pardon me, gentlemen, that's not what I hears."

King turned and was surprised to see Manton, the sailing master, appear from behind the mizzen; he had not been aware the man was even on deck. "There were no end of stories back at Halifax."

"That would be in Brewer's would it, Master?" Cooper asked with a grin.

"Brewer's is more than a coffee house," Manton agreed unabashed. "You get to meet all sorts and learn much. Word was the Yank's carrying trade would be startin' up again, despite what their president has ruled. Seamen are being offered up to twice their usual wages an' takin' it, far as I could gather."

"Well that's not been our experience," the first lieutenant declared. "Only craft putting out from the west have been fishers, them an' those gunboats that ran as soon as they saw us. I'd say your merchant friends'll need to pay a bit more if they expect honest sailors to go to sea in times like these."

Cooper glanced across at his captain for confirmation but King was disinclined to add to the conversation. If what Manton said were true it made war appear even more unlikely, although to comment on the fact might be misconstrued.

"Well it would seem *Albatross* is in for another haul," the first lieutenant remarked and they all turned to look. The frigate had now left their line and was beating into the wind under a full suit of sails as she made for the still invisible merchant. "Just hope she waits till we're in sight afore closing; be a shame to miss out on a share if it be a juicy one."

Again King held his peace even though he could well remember being an impoverished lieutenant and the difference a small amount of prize money could make. Any contraband seized would be treated in the same way as a capture with additional for every British seaman reclaimed. Not great riches perhaps, and even Cooper's share was likely to be minimal, but still a pleasant contribution to his regular pay.

And there was no doubt Banks was right in despatching *Albatross*, right in stopping all suspect shipping in fact, and right in condemning any vessel breaking British law. In doing so the commodore was simply carrying out his duty even if to King it still felt like a futile, and possibly dangerous, exercise. At the moment they were on the very brink of war, even the smallest nudge could tip them over and a disgruntled ship owner might just be what was needed. He remained convinced that if the politicians truly understood, they would back down, with one or other side revoking their current sanctions and – hope above hope – come to an understanding. If not, the British seemed determined to continue stopping ships and seizing men while American protests were not quite loud enough to hide the need for revenge in some and a deluded desire for Canada in others. The situation might be short of the point when it came to actual fighting and a chance remained it never would, although deep inside King feared otherwise.

* * *

The door to the fore cockpit opened and Wilson, the sailmaker, walked in, still clad in the cotton smock and leather trousers he wore for his work. Morales and Regan were seated at the table and deep into their nineteenth game of brag so welcomed the distraction. The Irishman looked up and nodded in greeting.

"How's about you, Wilson?" he asked.

"Aye, where'st been?" Morales added.

"Ferreting," Wilson announced, slamming a pair of dead rabbits down between them. "Caught 'em comin' out of their coop further aft. Whoever made them pens want's shootin'."

"Would ya t'ink anyone'll miss 'em?" Regan asked as he regarded the corpses.

The sailmaker shook his head. "They'll blame it on the rats," he said, "or one of them mogs."

"Or a midshipman," Morales added.

"Sure, cats, rats and mid.s are a rabbit's worst enemy," the gunner agreed sadly.

"And sailmakers," Wilson snorted.

"S'pposed to be a banyan day." Morales was also considering the beasts.

"S'pposed to be," Regan agreed. "But dat don't need to apply ter us."

"But you know how the 'ands'll kick up if we starts roasting in their oven when all they're gettin' is pap," Morales pointed out. "Though I'd chance we might wait until the morrow..."

"Wouldn't nade ta roast 'em," Regan grunted. "Do nicely in a stew so dey would, or jist boiled up wi' carrots an' onions. An' spuds, plenty of spuds."

"Such fine specimens shouldn't be kept waiting," Wilson agreed. "We could have them for supper an' put what's left in a pot for later."

"Dere won't be too much over," Regan stated with certainty.

They considered a little longer, then the sailmaker cleared his throat. "I'll have a word with the slushy," he said.

* * *

The senior officers had already dined well, although in their case it was on preserved ration beef which had been made into a lobscouse, one of the gunroom cook's specialities. And Sturridge had also excelled himself with their pudding, a prime figgy-dowdy that had gone down extremely well. Now, with more than an hour to go before any of them were due on watch, and as the daily officer was Summers, who also had the deck, the remaining occupants of the gunroom were at their leisure. But that hardly meant ship's business was removed from consideration; the state of their command had been the main subject throughout their meal as well as the relative attributes of every other vessel in their flotilla. And as the food nestled comfortably in their stomachs and a few picked at nuts and fruit to accompany their coffee, they were venturing on dangerous ground and actually discussing their senior officers.

"To my mind it is best that *Albatross* does the rummaging,"

Rushlake, the second lieutenant of marines, declared. "As long as we're in sight, our share remains the same and my lads don't mess up their uniforms clambering in and out of boats."

"As long as we are in sight," Bream, his superior, confirmed thickly before draining the last of his wine. "This morning's capture were nigh on the horizon though I'll bet a penny to a pound that robber Bentley disputes it."

"That's if he's made any seizures," Taylor pointed out. "So far we've heard nothing and only seen one merchant sent into Halifax. For all we know she were making for there anyways."

"But had *Tenacious* been ordered in there probably wouldn't have been no seizures," Rushlake persisted. "When it comes to snagging runners, I've never known a captain so reluctant in claiming what's ours."

"I prefer careful to reluctant," Cooper stated with an air of authority. The current subject concerned him and, if it persisted, he may well have to intervene. As it was his book had long since been abandoned. "If Captain King takes a man you can be certain he has right on his side. Simply dragging off anyone with an English surname is a passage to nowhere. We will not be paid out by the court and the Yanks'll hate us all the more."

"Though it's not just men." Bream was refilling his glass. "Other captains sequester cargo; while we was in Halifax the court paid out generously on a couple of brigs found filled with sulphur. Stuff would have made up into cylinder powder as easily as duck soup, although we never seem to fall on such riches."

"If that's the case we've been unlucky." Cooper again. "But that has nothing to do with Captain King. He'd have jumped on that freight as fast as anyone and, remember, every consignment we've taken so far has been passed and paid out in full."

"Then there was that privateer," Taylor reminded. "We saw a pretty penny from that did we not?"

Cooper nodded. "When Captain King makes an arrest, be it of man or materiel, you can be sure he's acting lawfully. And personally I wouldn't have it any other way."

"Me neither," Taylor agreed. "I've seen the other side of the coin and it ain't as shiny as some might think. Captain Leyton were inclined to seize anything that passed by and little good did it do him."

"Well what about if it comes to more than rummaging?" Rushlake asked. "If this war truly kicks off will he be as reluctant to fight as he is to make a decent inspection?"

"The captain has never been reluctant to search," Cooper stated firmly. "Just more circumspect when it comes to seizing."

"Whatever." Bream had drunk more than any present and waved a hand dismissively as he spoke. "Will he fight? He was pretty close with that Yankee captain – think he might be a sympathiser?"

"Oh, Captain King will fight," Cooper declared. "And I would advise anyone who believes otherwise to keep such thoughts to himself."

"Well that's alright then." Bream reached for his glass. "Because if what I hear is correct this won't be no skirmish."

The senior marine was not the most popular officer on board and had definitely taken a fair measure of wine. Yet his words had the ring of authenticity and suddenly all eyes were upon him.

"What have you heard?" Cooper demanded.

The officer shrugged. "My wife's people are from Baltimore," he said, "and have friends further west. From what they say all are geared up for a rerun of seventy-six."

"The Revolutionary War?" Taylor checked, and Bream nodded grimly.

"Word is they're set to drive us out of Canada and take Florida into the bargain," the marine continued. "Should that happen we lose our supply of timber and a whole lot else, just when we needs it the most."

"Their army's not big enough," Cooper said. "Less than three thousand I hears."

"Regulars maybe," Bream allowed. "Although there are plenty more men willing to fight – men who missed out on the first ruck and are keen to start a second."

"But you could look at it another way," Heather, the new purser, suggested as he abandoned his ledger and joined the conversation. "Wellesley's in Spain fighting what troops Boney's not sent to Russia, yet we can still round up a decent force in Canada. Once we wipe out what the Yanks have to offer there'll be nothing to stop us moving south and taking back the whole damned colony."

"You think that a possibility?" Taylor questioned.

"I believe it to be likely." Heather removed his steel-rimmed spectacles and placed them neatly in their case. "And would make sense of the whole darned show. I'm a man of business and it's money that wins wars. With America under the British flag once more we'll have proper resources and, whether Boney takes Russia or not, he'll have to watch his step."

"Then there's the American navy," Taylor said. "The Jonathans make fine ships; I should know, I've felt their fire."

"No. No they are too few." Cooper was positive. "We have a damn sight more – why this flotilla alone could account for a quarter of their entire fleet with ease, and I hears there are liners being despatched from Britain."

"Which can't come soon enough," Taylor added. "But until they do we'll have to be mighty careful."

"The chances are any Jonathan we meet'll be sailing alone while we shall be in force," Cooper declared. "Though even if it be one-on-one, the Royal Navy have been fighting the French for almost twenty years and is accustomed to combat. Frankly I don't believe there is a British frigate afloat that could not account for an American were the chance provided."

"Well that's alright then," Bream repeated as he filled his glass yet again. "War ain't likely, but should it come we have a captain prepared to fight and the ability to sink anything encountered." He raised his wine and gave a supercilious smile. "So none of us have a jot to worry about."

* * *

The first sign that this was not the case came some while later. Banks' squadron had continued to make gentle southerly progress although the formation had changed to one of line abreast, with each ship roughly three miles from her neighbour. And with clear air and the sky almost permanently empty of cloud a broad path could be swept, one that extended from the most westerly lookout's occasional glimpse of the American coast to almost sixty miles deep into the Atlantic. Such a net was sure to bring in a fair catch and indeed most days saw them meet with at least one westbound merchant. Many proved genuine, Spanish traders returning with a cargo of olives after taking more vital supplies to the Peninsular armies, or sleek British runners that had been granted licence to sail independent of convoy. Mostly they were making for Halifax after being taken off course by poor navigation or the vagaries of the North Atlantic. Only one, a schooner intercepted by *Tenacious* herself quite early in their patrol, had aroused King's suspicions.

The master had been too glib and his paperwork too orderly; a thorough search had indeed revealed a different cargo – one that included munitions that would have been welcomed by any country preparing for combat. The vessel was duly seized and despatched to Halifax under a prize crew of a master's mate and six loyal hands. There it would doubtless return a healthy sum, yet King privately mourned the loss of manpower.

However, the majority of those stopped were actually legitimate and, being as they originated from Europe, lacked hands that could be legally pressed, although there remained a few that were still obviously breaking British trading laws and had to be impounded. Which presented a problem; even in peacetime no warship can afford to haemorrhage trained hands and, as war was likely and may even have been declared, the need for prize crews must eventually compromise the squadron's fighting ability. It was a situation that might have been eased if the eastbound traffic had been correspondingly high; a few American vessels manned by men who might conveniently be considered British would have made up their numbers nicely but, whether due to Madison's decree, or knowledge of Banks' squadron in the vicinity, no outward-bound vessels were sighted. Consequently, though the squadron remained on the lookout for fresh prey – and possibly something of slightly more mettle – they were approaching the time when a lack of hands meant there could be no more captures.

And then, on yet another dry summer's evening when the squadron had been at sea for more than a month, there came a different sighting and from a totally unexpected quarter. *Tenacious* was the first to sound the alarm as the rig of a southbound vessel appeared above the coastline off their starboard bow. And there were three masts, so this was no minor trading brig but a sizeable craft.

In addition to holding the westerly station, King's ship was also leeward of the squadron and when *Albatross*, on his larboard beam, seemed unable to read his signals he considered steering closer to the wind to be sure of passing on the news. For there was much to tell; the sighting had definitely spotted them and was reacting although, again, not in the way he would have expected.

"Definitely tacking," Corbrite, at the masthead, confirmed. "An' now she's settling on a course to close with us."

For a ship to sail so near to the coast suggested she was an American and one that wished to avoid detection, yet when *Tenacious* came into view, she had immediately altered course to intercept; it hardly made sense.

"*Albatross* has responded," Brotherton reported at last.

"Very good, make 'sighting has altered course to close with us' and see they repeat it to the flag."

"Have you no news?" Cooper bellowed up to the masthead.

"Only that she continues making for us, sir," Corbrite replied lamely.

Cooper turned to King. "The course would suggest her to be one of ours."

"It would," King agreed, but without enthusiasm. If Corbrite could not give a positive identification it was likely the sighting would be having the same difficulty distinguishing *Tenacious*. And more than that, *Albatross* was a fair distance off their larboard beam; she and the rest of the squadron might be totally invisible.

"Wait, she's coming clear," the midshipman urged before leaving all on deck hanging in anticipation. Then, "Yes, a frigate for sure."

"And her heading?" Cooper demanded.

"That remains the same."

King knew it would be futile to ask about colours or for any further clarification when Corbrite could only just make out her type, yet for a ship to be steering so was asking a thousand equally unanswerable questions of him. She came from the land and any number of ports were strung along that particular coastline which would confirm his suspicions of her being an American. But then she could also be part of several British inshore patrols that were keeping watch; indeed, if war had been declared, this might be one of a blockading squadron sent to intercept them and pass on the news.

And news was what King wanted more than anything else; the small amount of intelligence provided before sailing was now considerably out of date and even at the time had been vague. Negotiations were underway, there had been meetings in both Europe and America, although little of concrete looked like being agreed. Sawyer had intimated somewhat grudgingly that he feared the British government would climb down, rescind the Orders in Council and press for better relations but nothing had been confirmed and, with the inevitable delay caused by the distance between London and Washington, that might still be the case.

"If she's British and bringing news that we're at war it will be welcome," Cooper remarked with unusual naïvety.

"Or that we're not," King quickly countered and his second in command nodded, mildly abashed.

"Of course, sir."

King supposed it generally known that he was not in favour of conflict – at least his officers must be aware – and the fact that no one had openly challenged him on this was probably a compliment of sorts. For there would have been no need for direct confrontation; he felt his style of command was reasonably relaxed; a word might have been said over meals in the great cabin, during their morning meetings or even the previous week when he had dined in the gunroom as his officers' guest. Political discussion might not be encouraged aboard His Majesty's warships but to deny it occurred was plain folly. And in some ways he was disappointed at the lack of debate for others might share his opinion, as it was he would probably never know. But, although much of the Navy's old regime was gradually being eroded, a captain remained a captain and lord of all he surveyed, so there would always be a perceptible distance between him and his officers. And even if the times were undoubtedly changing, captains were still allowed to be slightly cranky.

"I have her more clearly still," Corbrite announced and once again all on deck hung on his wise words. "Yes, I am certain, or nearly..." the lad floundered. Then: "I'd say she was the *Delaware*!"

The rumble of comment that met this revelation stretched far further than the quarterdeck; even some in the waist and on the forecastle gave wise nods and muttered aphorisms. But further aft King remained silent and, though the man was obviously bursting to speak, he was glad to note Cooper did also.

For his worst fears had been realised and there was much to think about. He had not been in contact with Walton for a good two months, in that time his frigate could have been posted anywhere on the Eastern Seaboard. Or further; should the Americans be set on conflict, it might have been on the other side of the Atlantic by now ready to hound Britain's home trade, or deep in the Pacific and after her whalers. Yet she was there, within sight of his masthead, and heading to close further. And coming from the direction of land – her land – where an efficient semaphore meant news could travel faster than a speeding horse. So if this truly were *Delaware* and Walton still captained her, it was likely that there had been agreement and they were not at war. More than that – King felt his heart skip a beat with the realisation – his friend might have identified *Tenacious* and was intending to pass on the news. He released a long held sigh; the day might yet end in cheerful celebration and expectation of a better future.

But it was foolish to even think so, King told himself, as he did when any hint of optimism appeared to influence his judgement; he was a professional sea officer and should be at all times realistic. He had already decided *Albatross* and the rest of the British squadron would be out of the American's sight, consequently it seemed far more likely *Delaware* was heading for him in order to do battle. And should that be the case his friend would be in for a shock.

Currently King held the windward gauge and, though land lay several miles off, Walton was effectively on a lee shore. Which hardly mattered in a single ship engagement; two frigates fighting it out one-on-one would be manoeuvrable enough to dodge and sidestep the other, at least until significant damage were caused. Yet *Tenacious* was not alone, as the American would soon discover. In a matter of minutes, *Albatross* must come into Walton's view, with *Alert*, Banks' own ship, following shortly afterwards and finally *Mercury* on the easterly station. If they were at war, and *Delaware* held her course much longer, she would find herself to leeward and facing odds of four-to-one; only luck and extraordinary seamanship could prevent her ending up pinned against the coast as a consequence. King closed his eyes and took a deep breath at the new thought, which bore little resemblance to the one that had preceded it. But he did have to be realistic, and it was the more likely outcome.

Chapter Nineteen

Those of the larboard watch were officially below but with such excitement in the air few had any mind for rest. Instead much of *Tenacious'* topsides were crowded with idle hands, men seemingly with no ambition other than to encumber their working shipmates as they competed for places to view the developing situation. And several from Stokes' mess had bagged one of the best; the starboard side of the forecastle where they had a splendid view of proceedings and might still annoy the duty watch.

"They says it's *Delaware*," Bovey remarked when they were settled, "but there's no true way of knowing."

"What about it, Hodges?" Stokes asked. "You was in her long enough."

"I were aboard for sure," Hodges grudgingly allowed, "but that don't mean I knows her from afar."

"Never mind, with the speed she's making, we'll soon be certain."

And Lovemore was right, although still a good distance off and barely in sight from the deck, experienced eyes could already tell much; the oncoming ship was beating towards them on the starboard tack under all plain sail. Providing the wind, and her course, held she would be up with them in under two hours.

"Aye, heading for us with all despatch," Groom, the Yorkshireman, agreed warily.

"Must be carrying an important message." Johnno was all but hanging over the side and had the best view. "Though she's takin' a chance."

"How so?" Lovemore asked and the boy pulled himself in slightly.

"Well, if war's been declared and she's coming to tell us..." his voice trailed away as the men about him began to laugh.

"Give the chit some slack, it ain't such a foolish notion," Stokes

212

told them.

"Aye," Bovey agreed. "'Specially if Knightly's still aboard and they've made him captain."

"Do you think he'll be there, Hodges?" Groom asked and the seaman raised his eyes.

"Now how in 'eaven's name should I know?" he exclaimed. "It's not as if we even served together – he came an' I went. But I will say this, there's a fair few other British aboard. Browning, from the *Shannon*, is one, and that pair we met in the cat house on Barrack Street."

"And Nearhood," Lovemore prompted, "don't forget 'im."

"He ain't British," Bovey pointed out.

"No but he were a mate, it's almost the same."

"I remember yon Browning." Groom rubbed at his chin. "Weren't there somethin' crank about one of his fingers?"

"Aye, part of it were missin'," Bovey confirmed.

"How's that strange?" Johnno demanded and Bovey treated him to a firm stare.

"It were the bit in the middle," he said.

"Pig of a man as I recall," McKenzie added.

"Maybe." Stokes was still considering the oncoming ship, "But he were one of us; it don't do to fight your own."

"Who said anything about fighting?"

"Curly's right," Bovey said. "We can't be sure we's at war. An' if that Jonathan's course's anything to go by, it don't look likely."

"You think he can see yon *Albatross* then do ye?" McKenzie asked and all eyes turned to the British frigate keeping station off their larboard beam.

"Probably not." Stokes reached into his jacket pocket and withdrew a plug of tobacco. "Though if we is fighting, he'll turn tail once she comes into sight."

But no such thing happened. The American ship drew nearer until there was no doubt she could see not only the second frigate but probably *Alert* beyond. Yet still she came, and gained clarity with every yard made.

"Well, that's a turn up." Stokes took a bite of his tobacco before passing it on. "Jonathan gets any closer an' we'll nab him, sure as eggs is eggs."

"Then we can't be at war." Bovey almost sounded disappointed. "Or if we is, she's changin' sides..."

213

"I've never understood that." Johnno scratched at his head. "Why do we call them Jonathans? Or Yanks if it comes to it?"

"Same reason the French are frogs." Lovemore had the plug now and took a nibble.

"And the Spanish, Dons," Bovey added.

"Suppose if we give them odd names we can forget they're persons," Stokes decided with rare insight. "Makes 'em easier to kill."

"Hey up, old Dickie Banks is a talkin'!" Groom was pointing towards *Alert* where a signal had broken out which was soon repeated by *Albatross*.

"Give a lot to know what them's sayin'." Bovey glanced back at the quarterdeck. "It's the pity we didn't put in for carronade work, you gets to hear all sorts of stuff aft."

"Told you, I'm never firing no carronade," Stokes snapped. "Darn things're more dangerous than they're worth; give me a long piece every day."

"Aye." Groom rolled his eyes. "Long guns are as safe as houses."

"Well it looks like we're gettin' some action." Lovemore pointed to larboard once more. *Albatross* was matching their leisurely pace and beyond her *Alert* had added topgallants while, even further off, *Mercury* was raising her royals.

"Squadron's fannin' out." Stokes again. "Ask me they'll hold this course for a while, then bear off and run down on the Yank. With the wind as it is we should catch him long afore 'e touches land."

"And if we don't," Groom added, "we'll simply run 'im aground."

"But if we're not at war..." Johnno began.

"If we're not at war he'll heave to." Bovey tossed the tobacco back to Stokes who caught it with one hand.

But *Delaware* did not heave to and neither did she hold her course, instead the frigate flew into a swift, smooth turn that brought her about in close to her own length. In no time she was heading southerly again and away from the British squadron.

"Well there's a thing," Lovemore commented. "Must 'ave changed 'er mind."

"Smoothly done," Stokes added. "Not many can 'andle a ship so."

"Told you." Hodges again. "They got a lot of British aboard."

"Stunsails are going out now," Groom said and all watched in silence as the distant ship began to pull away under the extra canvas.

"Say goodbye to the rest, lads," Bovey told them. "Topmen are going to be busy."

"We're *all* goin' to be busy." Stokes nodded towards a signal breaking out on *Alert*, "Sir Dickie's getting chatty again."

"So what'll happen?" Johnno asked.

"We're gonna give chase, that's what," Groom replied.

"And will we catch her?"

For a moment all considered the speeding frigate afresh.

"Aye," Stokes finally decided. "I reckons we will."

* * *

"Squadron's fanning out." Cooper unknowingly repeated Stokes' words. "Reckon we'll be turning to starboard afore long, then it'll be 'show all canvas' and a general chase."

King made no comment; he genuinely liked his second in command even if there were times when his tendency to chatter annoyed and this was just such an occasion. They could all see what was happening and did not require explanation or predictions. *Mercury*, the easterly ship, now lay a good quarter of a mile ahead of *Alert*, which was a similar distance in front of *Albatross*. And yes, Banks would order them to starboard shortly; otherwise there was every chance *Delaware* would escape.

Although that did not seem likely; he might not have sailed with the commodore for several years but King still thought he knew him sufficiently. And then the signal came, all ships turned towards the fleeing American, extra sail was added and Cooper gave an odd and mildly conceited grunt as he was proved correct.

"I reckons we'll have the measure of her," the first officer added when they had picked up speed.

"Oh, undoubtedly," Manton agreed. The sailing master had just added stunsails and *Tenacious* was fairly thrashing through the dark waters. The wind was perfect for such sailing, every stitch of canvas could be set and to the greatest advantage; if they could only turn a couple of points the ship might log her best speed to date, although King could not ignore a dull feeling of impending doom. *Delaware* remained a good distance off their larboard bow and Cooper may well be right, only a come-up glass would truly tell them who was the faster and their particular instrument had unaccountably

215

gone missing. Still the land was already very much closer and, even if they failed to catch the American frigate, there was every likelihood she would be trapped, providing Reynolds in *Mercury* played his hand correctly. But he could now be certain of one thing: they were definitely at war with America.

"I wonder why she behaved so oddly," Cooper pondered and King was on the verge of giving a sharp reply when curiosity ambushed him.

"In what way oddly?" he asked.

"Why, she was heading south when we came upon her, and could hardly have been travelling fast or the squadron would never have forereached in the first place. Then on sighting *Tenacious* she turned and made sail in order to close with us. And continued, even after *Albatross* would have been in sight; indeed others in the squadron may have been visible to her. It was only when the Commodore signalled, and we began to separate, that she smelled a rat."

"Belike her lookouts weren't up to scratch." Manton seemed to have joined the conversation and King turned away; at that moment the last thing he felt they needed was a discussion.

However, his officers had been wrong about one thing; *Delaware* was sailing extremely sweetly and might even be extending her lead. Were it not for the dark line of coast that seemed to grow larger with every breath, she would probably escape. But the land was there and Walton would shortly have to change course, that or see his ship run aground. *Mercury* was the nearest to her; although only a thirty-two, the British frigate would be in range within the hour and, even if *Delaware* dealt with her harshly, should cause enough damage to prevent the American's escape. And then it would simply be a case of mopping up; once the remaining British force closed, Walton would have no choice but to surrender. It may even be the first American casualty of the war, in which case King supposed it cause for celebration yet somehow could not summon enthusiasm.

"Perhaps she mistook us?" Manton and Cooper were still bickering about Walton's sudden change of plan – as if such a thing mattered – although King still found himself listening.

"Mistook us for what?" Cooper questioned and the sailing master pulled at his chin.

"A Yank squadron?" he suggested.

Now that was a different matter. If Walton truly had been

looking for friendly vessels it put a whole new light on things.

"You mean there might be other American shipping in the area?" King interrupted and both officers turned to him.

"It would explain much, sir," Manton said. "We thinks he only changed his mind when he saw the Commodore's signals but maybe it weren't that at all. Maybe 'e had spotted *Mercury* by then an' was only looking for three ships, not four..."

For a while no one spoke; it had been reasonable to suppose the fledgling American navy would spread its forces although that need not be the case. There would be everything to gain in forming a battle squadron similar to their own, and suddenly the chance of such a thing being close by looked strong. Of course, no one could say where exactly; Walton might have been searching for several days; they could be almost anywhere along the American coast. But if an enemy flotilla really was on the loose nearby it made it more important than ever to catch *Delaware*. For if she were allowed to meet up with the others, it would truly be a force to be reckoned with.

* * *

"She's wearing!" Corbrite's words cut into King's thoughts, and those of everyone on *Tenacious*' quarterdeck. Once more all eyes were on the distant ship that indeed appeared to be throwing herself into the fastest of turns.

"Neatly done," Manton muttered grudgingly, "an' with stuns'ls set..."

That was the truth, King acknowledged. Walton had turned his ship on a sixpence and was now bearing away northwards. With the change of course it was possible to gauge the American's speed with greater accuracy and she was definitely setting a blistering pace. More than that, as she crept steadily along his beam he knew the squadron must be called to follow, and *Tenacious* would become the operative ship.

"Signal from the flag." Brotherton confirmed his suspicions. "All are to wear and our number has been ordered to close."

"Wear ship!" King's order came without hesitation and *Tenacious* was first into her turn as *Alert*'s signal came down. But it didn't develop into the smoothest of manoeuvres, as all were

217

uncomfortably aware. Whether the hands lacked practice or simply encountered ill luck, they fell badly off the wind and made far too deep a turn. It took seconds – minutes probably – before she was safely back on the wind and even in that short time they lost pace and distance.

"Hardly your best work, Master," King commented when they had regained stability.

"I 'pologise, sir," the sailing master muttered. "It's having the stuns'ls set, makes her unwieldy."

"Of course," King allowed.

"I could take her another point or two to larboard," the older man suggested. "With the wind as it is that'd bring it more on our quarter – might add a knot or two."

King considered *Delaware* as she gamely blasted through the water; now there could be little difference in the two ships' speeds, and yes, turning *Tenacious* more to larboard may give her the slight edge. But that must also make it more of a stern chase, as well as taking them closer to the shore. He glanced around; the rest of the squadron had been far smoother in their turns and were slightly ahead while both *Mercury* and *Albatross* appeared marginally faster.

"No, we'll keep her as it is, Master," King said at last. "How long until darkness?"

"Dusk in just over two hours, sir," Cooper replied.

With luck he supposed *Tenacious* might have closed with Walton's ship by then, her or one of the other British frigates, and once that happened it would all be over very quickly. For the American was a realist; while there lay any chance of escape it would be taken, but King could not see him fighting a losing battle. In which case there was still a possibility they might meet up that day, if not in quite the same circumstances. Walton would be his prisoner, of course, although that would matter little. How could it when the difference between friend and enemy was so hard to define?

* * *

In fact it was nearer three hours later, and the light was failing fast, when *Mercury* fired the first shots. In the meantime both of the smaller British warships had edged their way westwards and taken station behind the fleeing American while *Tenacious* and *Alert*, the heavier frigates, remained to seaward of her and slightly behind. No sound came from *Mercury*'s bow chasers and neither could any splashes be seen but it was extreme range and *Delaware* gave no sign of being hit.

"The Yank's faster than we thought," Manton admitted reluctantly.

"Aye, if we cannot bring her to quickly she'll be lost in the night." Cooper's words rang out about the crowded quarterdeck yet went unanswered. It seemed impossible, but Walton looked likely to pull off one of the neatest escapes in naval history and King could not be sure if he were pleased or sorry.

"Flag's signalling!"

Brotherton was on the ball as usual and able to distinguish flags that King had difficulty even seeing.

"It's *Mercury*'s number, she's being ordered to veer."

"Trying her broadside," Manton supposed. "What would she be carrying?"

"Twelve-pounders," Cooper replied. "Should reach further than her chasers but it'll still be down to luck, and long-range if they are trying for her masts."

"As they should be," Manton stated firmly.

But though the British ship swung smoothly into her turn, then released an impressive barrage that glowed brightly in the gloom of evening, there was still no sign of damage.

"Couldn't expect more, I suppose," Cooper said. "And now night is truly upon us."

"Yet *Albatross* is 'avin' a crack an' all," Manton added.

Sure enough, what had become the leading British ship leant into a stiff turn and released her own broadside. And it was a measure of the dying light that this time the glare from her long guns was positively painful and left a cast over the eyes that remained for some while. Consequently it was impossible to tell if any damage had been caused, for *Delaware* was growing indistinct and must soon vanish into the night.

"Masthead, what do you see there?" Cooper bellowed.

"Light's fading fast," Corbrite replied after a short pause. "I only get the occasional glimpse of the American."

"And was there damage?"

"Nothing I could see, sir. Chase were sailing sweetly immediately afterwards."

"And now? Is she holding the same course?"

Again a pause and this time it was longer before Corbrite's hesitant words.

"I couldn't be sure, sir," he said. "And now she has totally disappeared."

King had to stop himself from stamping on the deck. "What time is the moon?" he demanded.

"Rises just afore three," Manton replied. "Though it is only a quarter full at present and the clouds have been closing in of late."

"*Mercury* and *Albatross* should still be in touch," Cooper suggested and King nodded. That was certainly the case although he was starting to appreciate Walton's skills were not restricted to seamanship. With a properly darkened vessel most competent captains could shake off any tail in the course of a night, and King sensed the American would find such a task simplicity itself.

Chapter Twenty

And so it proved. After several hours of groping about in the dark the slender moon finally rose to reveal an empty ocean. And worse than that, with a starless sky and only dead reckoning to go by, when light did appear it showed *Tenacious* had wandered dangerously close to the shore.

"Would have been a pretty kettle of fish if any ended up there," Cooper remarked when the dull mound of land came into sight.

"Better bear away, Master," King ordered softly. "I've no wish to offend the Americans by invading their waters."

The comment brought only a faint chuckle from those nearby, but then most had been on deck for several hours. And King certainly did not feel like laughing, the past day had brought more than its fair share of misery. Not only had they discovered themselves to be at war, the first enemy encountered had slipped through their fingers. For *Delaware* to have made such an escape when the odds so favoured the British, and capturing her seemed inevitable, was almost as humiliating as losing an action. Worse, the memory of that muddled manoeuvre still rankled.

Manton had handled the ship well enough, King did not think he could have done any better. But Banks would probably have realised the American ship's identity, and known her captain to be his friend. He and Sir Richard went back a long way yet King still wondered if the commodore suspected him of deliberately fudging the manoeuvre in order to let an enemy escape.

And that was definitely how he must now regard Walton; whatever their past, the man had become his adversary and would stay that way for as long as their countries were at war. As an officer in the Royal Navy, King's professional interests must come first and any human feelings a long way second; to behave otherwise was an invitation to madness.

"That would appear to be *Alert* to starboard," Cooper

221

commented and King dutifully looked. Yes, the outline of Banks' frigate was quite obvious and less than two miles off. Throughout the night there had been few signals as any light would have betrayed their presence, but a general chase had been called and, with dawn now imminent, he supposed it would be a case of rounding up the flotilla and reforming. Quite what Banks would do then was another matter; continue southwards as before, King supposed, although knowing at least one enemy lay to the north must be a temptation. But would *Delaware* still be so? None of the British ships had made contact with her and he suspected most, if not all, would have allowed the current to draw them towards the shore as they had been. Walton must know the waters better and may have anticipated such an outcome, in which case it would have been an easy matter to head out to sea and bypass the blundering British. *Delaware* could be several miles to the south now, and may even have met up with the battle squadron King was convinced she had been seeking.

The bell sounded eight times and he waited as the watch below came up to relieve those on deck.

"Gentlemen, I suggest you turn in," King said, addressing the nearby officers.

"I usually stand the morning watch, sir," Cooper replied stoically.

"You have already taken Mr Summers' trick," King reminded his first lieutenant. "Have him stand as your replacement. And the same goes for you, Master, though I appreciate the support you both provided."

"Might you not consider going below yourself, sir?" Cooper enquired.

"Oh, I shall," King confirmed. "Dawn will be fully up in no time; once we are in contact with the flag and have rounded up the rest of the flotilla you shall not see me for dust, nor again for some while."

"Signal from *Alert*, sir," Godby, who had just come on deck, reported. "That's a blue lamp and two red above – we are to close with the flag."

"Very well, starboard three points, and be ready to spill our wind." King turned back to Cooper and Manton who had delayed their departure and now appeared uncertain. "I see Mr Summers is in the waist," he said. "You might ask him to join me here on your way below."

The pair hurried off and were soon replaced by the fresh-faced junior lieutenant. King waited while the lad ordered *Tenacious* to close further on Banks' ship, then brought her to when there was less than fifty feet between the two quarterdecks.

"We must count that as a loss." Banks' voice came over clearly in the still night, although the speaking trumpet gave a strange timbre that made it sound vaguely sinister. "But no matter; it is doubtless war and all ports should be under blockade, she will not get far."

"Indeed, sir," King replied. "Though she might be heading south once more."

"You mean bypassed us?" Even through the instrument, King thought he could hear doubt and possibly something more.

"Yes, sir."

"I think not." Banks' tone was level enough as he continued, although King still felt he could read more into it. "If that had been the case we should have caught her – *Albatross* and *Mercury* are further out to sea – at least they should be."

There was no point in arguing further, the commodore had many qualities but an ability to consider other opinions was not one.

"Don't blame yourself, Tom," he added. "She were a wily customer and had the legs on us all, which frankly came as a surprise."

Again King remained silent. It seemed his previous observations about *Delaware*'s sailing abilities had fallen on deaf ears.

"Dawn is due shortly; we should be able to round up the others and continue as before."

"Very good, sir."

"Though we should speak before. Join me at three this afternoon."

"Me, sir?" King replied, mildly disconcerted.

"No, captains and first officers from all vessels. A council of war is in order; we have a great deal to talk about."

* * *

The words stayed with King as dawn rose. Was there perhaps something more to them? Did Banks feel he had deliberately bungled that turn? If so it would be unfortunate; Manton had been in charge, as could be easily shown, so there would be no official repercussions. Yet for the commodore to even hold such a suspicion seemed to cast

223

a shadow over the many years they had served together.

"*Mercury* has closed up now, sir," Summers reported and King gave a brief acknowledgement. That was the last; the flotilla had reformed and when the sun rose properly it would be on four ships sailing lazily south once more. And once more *Tenacious* was closest to the shore; he glanced out at the grey hills that were about to be kissed by light from the rising sun when suddenly something nearer caught his attention.

"There's a sail," he said, pointing.

"A sail, sir?" Summers enquired politely.

"A sail – a damned sail," King all but spat. "Masthead, what do you see to the west?"

"Sail ho!" That was from the foremast although the main lookout quickly took over only mildly flustered.

"Sail in sight to westward. Five mile off and travelling south; she's two-masted and under all canvas."

"Blighter must have been trying to sneak past in the dark," Summers muttered. "Too bad dawn caught them – and you, sir," the youngster added hurriedly.

"Report to the flag," King ordered. "And summon the watch below." It was simply bad luck on those who would have only just settled in their hammocks, but this had never been intended as a pleasure trip.

"Raise t'gallants and royals," he added as the first of the pink-faced men began to appear. *Tenacious* had been under topsails alone; the gentle onshore wind would take the extra canvas with ease. "And add stays'ls."

"What's about, sir?" Cooper asked. He wore a greatcoat over what was probably little more than a nightshirt yet his face was totally clear of sleep.

"There's a coaster, or similar, to leeward," King snapped. "And it's not getting away…" he bit his tongue; nothing had needed to be added to his first statement.

"Signal from flag," Godby reported. "We're to investigate."

"Acknowledge."

Banks would have ordered that hoist before *Tenacious* began to make sail and King was privately glad. Here was the chance to demonstrate his ship could be fast, and he was very able to handle her.

"A sighting?" Manton asked joining them. "Would it be the frigate?"

"Not the frigate," Summers replied as he peered through the deck glass, "more like a schooner."

"A coaster you think?" The sailing master was raising a small private glass. He too was dressed in a watchcoat and, like the first lieutenant, had bare legs and no boots.

"It's likely," Cooper allowed; he had wrenched the deck glass from Summers and was now studying the sighting. "Though that rig is familiar, it's similar to the slaver we nabbed a while back."

"In which case it would hardly be port-hopping along the coast," Manton grumbled.

"She would if she had just completed a crossing," King found himself adding. Tiredness and his own fool head had lured him into the conversation; suddenly all eyes were upon him and he inwardly cursed himself for not keeping his mouth shut. "Few ships can make that sort of passage and arrive directly at their intended destination," he continued more lamely.

"Then she might be a slaver, sir?" Manton asked.

"I think it a possibility," King admitted.

* * *

"Captain says she's a slaver," Stokes told his mess. "Heard it from Jenkins what heard it from Denning who were dryin' himself off after helpin' cast the log. So there's no doubt about it."

"Well, if it pays out like the last, it'll be welcome," Bovey said. The larboard watch had been called up after barely minutes below but, once they had set the additional canvas and attended the braces, little had been required and they were sheltering under the lee gangway.

"Pays out!" Hodges exclaimed. "We ain't seen a penny for it."

"It'll come," Lovemore assured. "Got a fair price for them earlier seizures, didn't we? And that privateer."

"Aye, three guinea a man for the privateer," Groom said. "Nice bit of chink."

"Is that the case?" Hodges snorted. "Well none of it came my way."

"Course it didn't, you weren't aboard," Bovey chuckled. "Time we was paid out you was larkin' about in some Yank battlewagon getting your forty bucks."

"Well I were about when we tooks the slaver – 'ad to 'ave been, else I wouldn't 'ave been captured. So it's only right I gets me share."

"Well good luck with that," Bovey told him without feeling.

"Never mind, you'll probably get a pull from this one."

"If she is a slaver," Hodges added.

"Oh she's a slaver alright," Stokes confirmed. "Old Tommo said so."

* * *

"Word is we've flushed out another slaver," Morales told Drake as the master-at-arms swung himself out of his hammock.

"A slaver you say?" he asked, although there was little pleasure on his face.

"So they're saying."

Drake yawned, rubbed at his eyes and then reached for the pewter pot. "Tea brewed is it?" he asked.

"'Bout half an hour ago," Wilson replied from his place at the table.

"Should still be warm enough," Amon, also at the table, confirmed.

Drake poured himself a mug of the tepid liquid, sipped cautiously, then downed the lot in one. "So we're delaying, then?" he asked before wiping his mouth on his sleeve.

"A slaver's worth delaying for." Morales also took a seat. "I mean there's no argument, be they Yank or British, they's in the wrong and we got to stop them."

"An' there'll be no shortage of volunteers to board her." Wilson was sucking at a piece of dry biscuit. "Apart from our recent adventure with the Yank, there ain't been much occurring of late. Even rummaging the occasional merchant don't get the blood running."

"My blood's running very well as it is, thanking you kindly," Drake grunted as he helped himself to a biscuit.

"Government pays over an 'undred guineas an head for every slave freed," Amon reminded them.

"Fair whack," Wilson nodded approvingly, "though it might not be as easy as they seems to think."

"'Sright," the carpenter agreed. "We still got to catch her."

"And them on the last didn't go easy," Amon added. "But then

226

they says a slaver's crew fights harder than any national ship, or privateer if it comes to it."

"S'pose they know they're in the wrong." Wilson spoke through the biscuit. "Like pirates."

"Them's worse than pirates," Morales decided. "Much worse."

"Aye, it takes a special kind to be a slaver." Drake finally slumped down at the table, biscuit still in hand and untouched. "You got to be set in your ways," he continued almost meditatively, "and intent only on one thing: yourself."

"I hear the money's good," Morales chanced.

"Oh yes, the best," Drake said as Wilson yawned. "And it ain't hard work as such. But you can't think too deep about what you're doin' or who you're doin' it to; soon as you twig, your days are numbered."

"Twig?" Morales questioned.

"Aye, once you realise them's people you're transporting," he confirmed.

"What happens then?" Amon enquired after a spell.

"Then?" Drake gave a short laugh. "Then the others gets rid of you, or try to."

"What, over the side?" Morales seemed appalled.

"If they can. Them's not the kind to worry over such things. Though a fellow can usually slip away if he's got 'is wits about 'im. That's the best course, even if it might cost a trip's wages."

"It's only been illegal a few years," Wilson pointed out.

"Maybe," Drake allowed, "except slaving has always been a close community; they don't like no one leaving. You gets those who were whalers, or former Trinity men, but you don't come across many who'll admit to having been a slaver."

"True enough," Wilson conceded. "Though I never thought of it before."

"So why's that then?" Morales this time and Drake shrugged.

"Suppose they don't like talkin' about what they did; conditions and the like. Most would rather pretend it never happened."

"So what do they do when someone tries to leave?" Wilson was now munching at his biscuit. "Go after?"

"They might, and if a fellow's got any sense he'll head for a King's ship," Drake stated with apparent satisfaction. "Once aboard he'll be safe and they'll leave him be."

The others considered this. The five men had lived together a fair while and been shipmates far longer. The sense of mutual trust was strong and they held few secrets. But neither did they know much about the other's past lives and occasionally it felt better that way.

* * *

The wind had stayed firm and came across their larboard quarter at the ideal angle; with canvas tight and the sea compliant, *Tenacious* was once more close to her maximum speed and, despite yesterday's disappointment and the wasted night that followed, spirits were high on her quarterdeck. Cooper and Manton had disappeared briefly, but now were back in full uniform and, after drinking his second cup of breakfast chocolate, King was feeling more the thing. And there was just cause, for not only was the ship sailing sweeter than for many weeks, she had a prey before her and actually seemed likely to catch it.

The schooner was now less than a mile off their starboard bow and, although her crew had made every effort with additional canvas, was being overhauled visibly.

"It'll be her bottom," Cooper stated with the air of one who knows. "Probably been skimping on careening and look where it's got them."

"Should have paid more attention," Manton agreed. "Though I'd chance that's not the half of it; she ain't being sailed proper."

"How so, Master?"

"Main tops'l and main tops'l stays'l," Manton nodded towards the craft. "Both are unnecessary and will be putting undue pressure on the hull; without their weight she'd be showing at least an extra knot."

"Maybe so," Cooper allowed although it was clear he respected the sailing master's opinion.

"Neglecting maintenance and seamanship is a mistake," Manton continued. "A slaver relies on speed, both to keep her cargo fresh and avoid being captured."

King closed his eyes and cursed inwardly. They were chasing another topsail schooner, a type commonly used for everything from privateering to general transport. And yes, the last had been carrying human cargo, and yes he had said this might as well. But chances still remained strong she'd turn out a tramp with nothing more valuable aboard than pig iron or soft fruit and then it would be him who looked the fool. With all that had happened over the last day or so it seemed the unkindest blow of all.

"She's turning to the shore," Summers announced and that was indeed the case.

"What can we expect in these parts, Master?" King demanded and Manton pulled a face.

"Bed shelves steeply mostly, though there are shoals and sandbanks aren't unheard of."

The sailing master's assessment had been about as much use as a pastry teapot, although King had other matters on his mind. Land still lay a good three miles off; ample room to bring the chase to.

Cooper turned to him with a salute. "Permission to clear for action, sir?"

King shook his head. "Clear away the main batteries and arm the men," he said. "And ask Mr Bream to join me directly."

Whatever the schooner contained, it would not require the full force of a warship to take it. And, be it slaver or simple merchant, he had no intention of using his main armament, although it may decide to offer opposition and only a fool would approach an enemy effectively unarmed. But the idea of striking down bulkheads and extinguishing the galley fire seemed unnecessary and strangely repugnant. The slight stimulation from the chocolate was wearing off; suddenly he felt tired and longed only for his cot and comfort.

"You sent for me, sir?"

If anything the marine lieutenant looked worse than King felt; his eyes were red and sat amid a pasty face. Whether this was from wine or lack of sleep King could not tell, but clearly Bream was not on top form.

"Yes, Lieutenant, we shall be boarding that schooner directly." He pointed forward.

"Very good, sir. Boat work, will it be?"

"No, I intend pulling alongside. There is a chance – only a chance mind you – that she will be carrying slaves so don't intend firing on her unless I have to. And when you board you will be suitably careful with firearms."

"Very good, sir," Bream repeated. "Twelve men to a party should be sufficient; I'll speak with Rushlake. If we organise groups forward and aft it won't matter if you don't land squarely; either should tell for a tiddler like that."

"We shall endeavour to place her alongside evenly enough, Mr Bream," King told him primly, "and though she may be small I expect her to be well manned so will be supplementing your men with my own."

"Supplementing, sir?" The man appeared confused and possibly offended.

"Six marines per group shall be enough," King stated firmly, "though you may hold others in reserve. I shall be sending a further six seamen under the command of an officer."

If too many tried to board at once it would create mayhem; better by far to allow the first group across and send more if need be.

"I'm sure that is wise sir," the marine agreed. "And shall be leading one party personally."

King glanced at the jaded little officer and wondered what good that would be, but Bream had more to say.

"There may indeed be strong opposition," he continued. "I was forgettin' she were a slaver."

* * *

The time came less than twenty minutes later. By then the schooner had made a final bid for freedom, aiming her bows directly at land and seemingly intent on taking the ground. But *Tenacious* had doggedly followed; at such a speed there was no chance of an accurate depth from the lead although King felt curiously sure of their depth, and it was a confidence that had been bolstered by their recent manoeuvre. To keep in touch with the chase it had been necessary to wear ship and, though they lacked stunsails, the turn was carried out faster than the day before and was as smooth as silk; something that gratified him greatly as the eyes of the flotilla would no doubt have been watching.

And now they were ready to board; Summers was aft with a throng of heavily armed seamen that mingled oddly with the stiffly ornate marines, while Taylor stood at the head of a similar group nearer the bows. King glanced at Manton.

"Be ready to take us alongside," he said.

The sailing master touched his hat and collected a speaking trumpet. There was a chance the older man had been offended when King took the ship through her recent turn and this was one way of ensuring no hard feelings.

"Very good, Mr Regan!"

From forward, the gunner released one of *Tenacious*' chasers and the blank charge echoed loudly in the morning air.

"No response," Cooper murmured.

"Ready lads!" this was Summers at the head of his party and King suspected the lad would lead and inspire his men far more effectively than the staid Bream. A murmur of suppressed excitement flowed about the small group, increasing the tension on the quarterdeck until the entire ship felt taut and brittle.

"Strike royals!" Manton was doing his stuff; the ship was definitely travelling fast enough to cover the remaining distance without the support of their uppermost sails. And there was likely to be damage when the two collided, although that could be rectified later. All King wanted was for *Tenacious* to be brought alongside and her boarding parties despatched.

A faint popping sound was coming from the chase; a group of fools were firing muskets at them, as if lead balls would stave off one of His Majesty's frigates. And then *Tenacious* was creeping up on the schooner's quarter, the frigate's sails catching her wind and causing the smaller vessel's canvas to flutter and crack in the suddenly stilled air.

"Larboard a point... and a point more."

Manton was continuing to bring them in, and doing it well; *Tenacious* was almost alongside but a good way ahead and there was still thirty or so feet between the two vessels. King glanced across and the sailing master seemed totally at ease.

"Two points more, and watch her!"

The British ship still had the lead but, as she made the additional turn, dropped back and off the wind. Her momentum was strong though, and carried her towards the schooner. There was a clatter from above when their yardarms met and tangled, then a grinding noise as the two hulls collided and, with a roar, both British boarding parties began to drop onto the deck below. Manton had done a splendid job.

* * *

Summers was no stranger to boarding vessels, he had done so several times in the past. And, though each were different in their way, all had been ultimately successful, inasmuch as he had survived. Leading was always tricky, however, and having six marines in the party along with a soak of an officer would not make the task easier. But they would be dropping down on the schooner's deck and, as Taylor's lot further aft also seemed to be in reach, he was quietly confident of swamping whatever crew the schooner had to offer.

So it proved, he was one of the first across and, though he stumbled slightly on landing, soon recovered. Then, raising his hanger, the young man began to tear down the schooner's deck. Two seamen were before him, both armed with short swords that really did not seem up to the task. A swift slash from his own weapon broke one in half and its owner's hands swiftly rose up in surrender and supplication. The second was as easily dealt with, and then came a positive crowd that had been hiding behind two upturned boats.

For several seconds it appeared dire, Summers had been backed by marines and the sea soldiers seemed less than happy with the rough house style of fighting. But soon a regular seaman appeared beside him, and was quickly joined by another. Together the trio held back the mob, then began to make inroads until, less than a minute after the two forces had met, there was an uneasy peace.

"Stand to there, stand to!" It was the voice of Bream. Summers looked back to see the marine lieutenant advancing from the back of the pack, his unfired pistol raised. "Bennet, relieve those men of their weapons; Dean some rope, see they are secured, Smith and Chancy help them."

The bemused enemy were duly bound while Bream strutted back and forth as if it had been his actions alone that had won the day. Summers glanced to one side.

"That was well done, Hutton," he said. "And you, Grove; I am grateful for your assistance."

Bream was issuing more orders, clearly he had a lot to do to secure the prize and it fell to one of his abilities to handle such a task, while the two seamen simply knuckled their foreheads in quiet acknowledgement.

A strong odour caught Summers' attention and it was one he knew only too well.

"Pongs a bit, don't it?" Grove was wiping blood from his cutlass although he appeared more concerned by the smell.

"She's a slaver," Summers announced. "I fear it is in the nature of the beast."

"Oh we knew she were a slaver from the start," Hutton declared as if it was the simplest thing in the world.

"How on earth could you tell with the wind on our backs?"

The man seemed surprised. "Well it weren't that difficult," he said, "though in truth none of us could rightly be sure. But the captain said so, and that were good enough for us."

Chapter Twenty One

"*Tenacious* will be returning to Halifax."

It was a blunt statement and one that caused all the men around *Alert*'s dining table to sit slightly straighter. As well they might; Commodore Banks had provided an excellent meal that was amply supported with fine wine and, now sufficiently filled with both, several present had been seen to slump in their seats.

"To Halifax?" King questioned. He had more reason than most to be tired; the brief rest grabbed earlier that afternoon had only been possible due to the slaver's capture, which forced Banks to delay their meal slightly, but still he felt exhausted by the past two days' activities. Consequently, and despite the magnificent spread, he had eaten little and drunk less although Cooper, reclining opposite, appeared to have more than made up for his restraint.

"I'm afraid so, Tom." Banks spoke with apparent sadness. "We've been running low on men for some while and you bagging that Guineaman was the last straw."

"Forgive me, sir, but it would seem unnecessary." Despite the lack of wine, King's head had started to spin; was he being punished for carrying the schooner? Or perhaps the commodore still remembered that rushed manoeuvrer of the previous day? "Were sufficient men taken equally from each ship we may easily raise a prize crew and could continue our patrol."

"That's just it, Tom," Banks sighed. "Those prizes already taken have reduced our people significantly. Given the time again I should not have despatched the earlier captures – they would have been better burned – though there's no going back."

"And we certainly could not consider burning the slaver!" Hopkins, *Alert*'s captain, added with a bibulous chuckle.

King treated Hopkins to a harsh stare; he had disliked the man from the outset, if with little justification other than his position as Banks' deputy. Now at least he had reason for his loathing.

234

"I'm afraid that's it," Banks added. "Although, even if we had the men I would be reluctant to send her to Halifax without an escort. As Adam has intimated, she is inordinately filled; on reaching British soil her slaves will find themselves free once more yet, were an American to intercept, they would have nothing to look forward to other than lives of servitude."

There was a murmur of sentimental concern from the table in general that made King squirm. In all the years he had known Banks, this was the first sign of a compassion for slaves, or any other segment of society if it came to it.

"But as we have already agreed, there may be an enemy squadron hereabouts," he persisted.

"We agreed no such thing!" Bentley, of *Albatross*, interrupted from across the table. "It were your theory, Tom, and a worthy one I am certain though a theory nonetheless and cannot be guaranteed."

"Besides, you were anticipating the Yanks having three ships were you not?" *Mercury*'s captain added cheerfully. "With luck, *Delaware* will have been as unable to find them as ourselves, and I'd wager three prime British frigates more than a match for an equal number of Jonathans."

King went to reply then thought better of it. Reynolds' opinion was by no means unusual and doubtless influenced by earlier American warships that had been little more than converted merchants. Yet the vessel King had inspected – indeed the one he had grown to know well during his frequent visits – was a different proposition entirely. *Delaware* had been thoughtfully designed, soundly built and was extremely well armed. More than that, there were at least six other warships reputed to be larger and presumably more powerful still; were Banks to run into a trio of such monsters he might find it hard to stave them off with four frigates, let alone three. But a single glance about the table was enough to tell him any further protest would be in vain; none of the mildly merry faces would take kindly to hearing an enemy was more powerful than they assumed. All had been brought up with the habit of victory firmly instilled, and reasonably so considering the Royal Navy's record of success in everything from fleet actions to single ship duels. But a secondary effect of such achievement had been to produce senior officers comfortably complacent that nothing other than a fleet of enemy liners could harm a British frigate squadron.

"Tom, you look totally pooped," Banks told him. "Join me for a talk in the morning and we'll sort out the details. Once you've released your charge there's nothing to stop *Tenacious* taking on additional hands and heading south once more. I'm sure we could all use a draft of fresh men, isn't that right gentlemen?"

A chorus of drunken affirmations neatly punctuated the commodore's statement and King felt utterly beaten.

"Then we'll say no more for now," Sir Richard concluded. "At the pace we've been making you should be back with us within a month."

"And if we raise a bunch of Jonathans in the meantime, we'll be sure to save one for you," Reynolds assured them all to general laughter.

King looked from one face to the next; even Cooper was too far into his cups to give support, and the rest were clearly content in their superiority. He remembered a maxim from his school days; it was Euripides' statement about those who God would destroy he first makes mad, and at that moment it seemed wholly apt. Although arrogance was possibly more dangerous than insanity.

* * *

"*Bristol Pride*," Lovemore read the name on the slaver's transom as their boat drew nearer. "Now there's a title and no mistakin'!"

"Be interesting to see what made Bristol so proud," Stokes muttered from the launch's stern. "From what I know of Guineamen there won't be much to shout abart."

"Takes a special kind of seaman to work a slaver," Bovey announced. "Not everyone can do it."

"Not everyone would want to." Lovemore spoke under his breath.

Almost as soon as the schooner was secured she had been cast loose from *Tenacious* for fear of further damage; now she lay less than a cable off and wallowing gently in the slight swell. They were still uncomfortably close to the American coast but careful soundings had shown the bottom to be deep enough for safety while still being in comfortable reach of their anchor cables, and both ships were riding at a single bower.

"Well, this looks to be home for the foreseeable," Groom

grumbled as their boat pulled alongside. "An' I must say it don't smell too choice."

"That'll be down to her cargo," Stokes told them levelly. "Dare say we'll get used to it."

"Bleedin' 'ope so," another added.

"Told you, it takes a special kind of seaman to work a slaver," Bovey reminded them.

"Aye," Stokes agreed. "One with no nose."

* * *

It had been a busy morning; the interview with Banks had taken two hours yet produced little other than his superior expressing regret that *Tenacious* would be leaving. However Sir Richard had seemed genuine, there was no talk about the frigate missing stays or their failure to catch the American although King's success in snaring the slaver may have made up for all that. Then, as soon as he returned, there was the briefest of meetings with Cooper. The first lieutenant had little to say other than list the wounded from the previous day's action; none had died but two were critically injured and seven less seriously so, including a marine who had managed to slice off a finger while cleaning his bayonet. The ship had suffered little damage other than a foreyard which might have been weakened by impact with the slaver. Cooper was not quite himself but King glossed over that; Banks' table the previous evening had been generous indeed and, with the tension all had been under of late, he almost envied the man's ability to find relief in a surplus of wine.

But when King recalled his first lieutenant to the great cabin later that day, this time to speak with Summers, he seemed much more the thing and even had a little colour in his cheeks. And there was certainly plenty to cheer them in their junior's report. The lad had been most diligent in surveying the schooner and, slightly self-consciously, produced a full inventory of her stores as well as the prisoner list and a rundown of her live cargo.

"Nigh on four hundred in all," the third lieutenant summarised as King was still reading the latter. "Made up of two hundred and forty adult males, eighty women, forty-nine children and a dozen babies – although that might soon change as one of the women appears heavy with child."

237

There was silence as the news was imparted, then Cooper accepted the list from King, glanced at it, and cleared his throat.

"Quite a family you have inherited," he said.

"It would seem incredible," King began, "impossible even, to pack so many below."

"They are indeed crammed," Summers agreed and the look on his face said much. "It would appear to have been a successful passage with few losses."

"And are you able to cope?" King asked.

"I am, sir. I retained the boarding parties from last night and Mr Cooper has allocated more men today." Summers nodded towards the first lieutenant. "There are also several from the slaver's crew willing to assist with the feeding and basic... basic necessities."

"I understand," King assured him. He had no intention of visiting the slaver himself yet could easily imagine the conditions.

"I've already had a few up in the open air," Summers continued, "mainly mothers and their children; until we can get a proper guard mounted I didn't wish to press matters."

"Lieutenant Bream will have provided marines," Cooper assumed.

"He has, but those involved in the action were called back."

"Called back?"

"Mr Bream considered they had exerted themselves sufficiently," Summers explained. "Others have been sent as replacements."

"And are the marine lieutenants still aboard?" Cooper asked.

Summers shook his head. "They have returned to *Tenacious* also, sir; a sergeant is in charge."

"I see," King replied and Cooper made a short note. "Well we shall ensure you are properly manned before the end of the day. Further marines will be provided and I shall make certain both Mr Bream and Mr Rushlake pay a more lengthy visit," the captain added. "It may benefit them to realise the conditions their men are working in."

"Might not they accompany them aboard the slaver?" Cooper suggested with a wicked glint.

"A capital idea!" King boomed, but Summers was not so sure.

"If you'll forgive me, sir, the marines were not a great deal of use last time," he said. "They obeyed orders and I have no complaints as such, although..."

"I would imagine the average leatherneck is not the best at caring for tightly packed humanity," Cooper supposed.

"Exactly, sir. I should prefer regular hands."

"No marines at all?" King questioned. "They are a disciplined bunch and can be counted upon to instil order."

"I realise that, sir, but they really did not take to it last time and, you will pardon me, it might be awkward having the marine lieutenants aboard."

King cursed himself for a fool for not thinking of that before; Rushlake was roughly Summers' age and an upstart if ever there was one while Bream certainly would not take kindly to taking orders from a younger officer – as would have to be the case.

"Very well," he said, "though we will have to do something about security."

"I would welcome Mr Drake," Summers suggested. "Him and a few of his corporals would keep my lot in order and I think the rest would respect his natural authority."

King could not dispute that; with his stocky frame and commanding voice their master-at-arms was a born disciplinarian. Since his appointment there had been few outbreaks of trouble on *Tenacious*' lower deck. However, the schooner would require a reasonable crew in addition to those caring for her cargo and he was reluctant to give up quite so many seamen.

"Very well," he finally agreed. "Though you are aware we are short of hands. Should *Tenacious* need to go into action I shall have to claim them back."

"Of course, sir."

"I understand Mr Amon and Mr Morales have inspected and believe the prize to be seaworthy?"

"They do, sir, apart from her bottom which is badly encrusted."

"There is little we can do about that, she can still show a reasonable pace, I assume?"

"I believe so, sir and should raise Halifax safely."

"And do you have any preference regarding the officers that accompany you?"

King waited as Summers contemplated his question. Considering the young man's previous experience it had been logical to appoint him to lead the prize crew once more. Such an assignment was actually a compliment although Summers might not regard it as such and could be forgiven for regretting his past good performance. But he had responded well to the responsibility with sensible suggestions and a mature attitude that would have credited many older officers.

"Brotherton and Vernon, as before," the lad decided at last and Cooper duly made another note. "Though thinking further I may not need both."

"Just Brotherton?" King questioned.

"Indeed, sir. With Drake aboard there should be no trouble from the hands, and Brotherton and I can share watches."

"It could be a long voyage," King reminded. "Watch and watch about is tiring in the extreme."

"I realise that, sir, although *Tenacious* is hardly well off for mid.s either – if I take two it will leave you short."

"Very well, as long as you are certain. And what about any extra provisions, did you have sufficient last time?"

"I had enough," the youngster replied. "Though water became a little scarce. And I should like apples and perhaps some peas."

"Peas?" Cooper questioned, his pencil held above the page.

"Yes, sir. There were none aboard the *Sapphire* and I reckon they might prove popular. Apart from fruit the last lot would only eat horse beans; a few peas might make for a more varied diet."

Cooper raised his eyebrows but wrote, and King cleared his throat.

"We can arrange for that and I shall speak to Mr Drake. Have you anything to add, Mr Cooper?"

"The first lieutenant leaned forward. "I was just wondering about Mr Brotherton," he said. "When he accompanied Mr Summers last time he was our main signals officer. You may remember, sir, it made communication between vessels and announcing our arrival at Halifax awkward. Mr Godby is currently training up but should serve for passing messages between us both; might I suggest Mr Summers takes him and we retain Mr Brotherton?"

"What do you say, Michael?"

"That would be fine, sir, though he is black."

"I'm aware of that," King grunted, "and also a warrant officer in His Majesty's Navy."

"Of course, sir."

"Perhaps you are thinking the slaves will resent being effectively contained by one of their own?" Cooper suggested.

"Indeed, it was something I had not considered," King admitted quickly. "In which case you had better take Brotherton after all."

"No." Summers was positive. "No, thank you, sir. I get on equally well with both and would be just as happy with Godby. I'm sure he will prove a worthy support."

* * *

Drake's stance on the slaver's main deck lacked its usual self-assurance but then he was not exactly comfortable. For so much was familiar, so little had changed, that he felt disconcerted and ill at ease; conditions that were strangers to the revered and normally confident warrant officer. Still, simply being on board such a vessel again was enough to bring the memories back; the sleek lines and slender masts reminded him of long days and dark nights when every stitch of usable canvas was raised to ensure the fastest of passages. He recalled the sense of desperation when fleeing from any sail that threatened and a continual tension that came with existing amongst men living with the fear of capture, yet content to subject their fellows to the most inhumane confinement imaginable.

Since Drake had last stood on such a deck, so much had happened; he had joined and become part of a very different service, one where he was immediately accepted and soon prospered. In his new position – his new life almost – he had found both purpose and station. Now he was a respected member of a ship's company and addressed by all with deference – why even the captain called him mister. But just to be aboard a slaver, to feel her motion and scent her air, was enough to wipe all that away and the horrors he had sought to suppress for so long came rushing out like water from a sprung cask.

A movement caught his attention; someone was approaching and Drake urgently sought to regain a degree of composure.

"Hands is berthin' for'ard," Worth, one of his corporals, informed him. "I reckon we'd better bed down with them, just to be safe."

"So be it," Drake's response was brusquer than usual although Worth was hardly surprised; the Jaunty had never been known for his sensitivity.

241

"I weren't meaning you, Mr Drake; plenty of space for officers aft, I'm sure you'll find a spot. There's a lot of blacks 'twix the two, mind, but they're all properly secured an' most ain't got no life in them," the corporal confided. "Keep 'em locked down tight an' I reckons we'll all be safe enough."

"I'll berth for'ard an' all," Drake snapped. Though nothing like the luxury of *Tenacious*' fore cockpit, sleeping amongst regular hands was no novelty and his would hardly be the worst pitch in the ship. Besides, it should not be a long trip; some reckoned two weeks – three at the most – but with luck and a favourable wind it might be done in little more than one. And three weeks living amongst slaves was surely insignificant when he had spent much of his early life in such company, yet still it felt strangely uncomfortable being in their presence.

Even now there was a group forward; mothers feeding emaciated babies in the shade of a hastily rigged awning while a dozen or so kids sat oddly silent under the awkward eyes of a pair of armed waisters. The slaves needed feeding twice a day, Drake remembered. They should also be watered three times although mucked out far less often. A few, the sick mainly, might be allowed on deck when they were on passage but most would spend the entire voyage below, as had the current lot. Really they were doing the poor devils few favours by diverting so; if the slaver had been allowed to land as intended, they might all be in the open air by now. Though not free, it would simply be a moment of grace before the beginning of a lifetime's toil. And things might not be a great deal better when they finally raised Halifax.

Due to his earlier involvement with the trade, Drake had followed the progress of freed slaves with clandestine, and faintly macabre, interest. Government promises had been generous and prolific, but the majority quickly withered and were now almost forgotten. A few of his current charges might find a better life in Nova Scotia – or Sierra Leone, if they opted for there instead – although all would have been better left where they had been taken from, and where they could never now return.

Worth had wandered off to see about their accommodation while Drake steeled himself to consider the group of women once more. Earlier he had inspected the slave's quarters but, so vivid were his recollections, little new had been taken in. And it was not just memories of the atrocious conditions that he remembered; there had been bad behaviour on behalf of the crew and, though it pained him to admit it, himself.

With the Royal Navy now firmly in his blood, and life as a disciplinary officer so much a part of him, it was hard to remember the young man that at times had been sensitive and at others cruelly not. That person had disappeared many years before only to be replaced by something more constant, if almost comically severe; a man amongst men who took no nonsense and was grudgingly admired by even the hardest of cases. Drake supposed he could maintain that persona a little longer, although at that moment three weeks seemed an age. And if he were forced to live alongside echoes from his past and the reason he had evolved so, he feared it would prove beyond him.

* * *

Later that afternoon, when the slaver had still only been in British hands little more than a day, *Tenacious* and her prize bid farewell to the rest of the squadron and headed north. Standing on the quarterdeck, King inspected the prize with his personal glass. Summers had opted for an ideal sail pattern and, despite her barnacled hull, the schooner was making good speed. With luck, and barring any unforeseen encounters, they should be raising Halifax by the end of the month. Before then they must pass several major American harbours; all should be well guarded by a British blockading force but the thought of at least one major enemy squadron being at sea still haunted him. And Bob Walton might also be out there, although King still felt it more likely he had bypassed Banks' search and was heading south. It was odd but, now he knew them to be at war, all traces of friendship had been suspended. He still liked the man, indeed was in little doubt they shared an affinity yet, while hostilities existed between their countries, he could only ever be an enemy.

"Pretty little thing, ain't she?"

Cooper's habit of appearing unseen and launching into conversation was starting to annoy but King let the matter rest. And yes, with the falling sun setting the schooner's sails aglow and a faint cloud of spray rising from her bows, there could be few things on the water more beautiful.

"Summers did a good job last time," Cooper continued, "so no reason he shouldn't do so again. And with Drake and the mid. alongside it should be pips."

"Indeed." King's reply was purposefully flat but Cooper was not to be put off.

"I noted Godby and Brotherton exchanging signals earlier on," he chuckled. "Goodness knows what the pair were saying to each other and probably best if we don't enquire, but they seemed happy enough. And why not? *Tenacious* will be raising Halifax in no time, then just take on some extra hands and a drop of water and we'll be back with the commodore afore we knows it."

Cooper was right, or at least close to the mark, although King could not share his enthusiasm. There were still several hundreds of miles to cover along a coast they had always regarded as inhospitable but had now become positively hostile. And something else; King had served with Sir Richard Banks for much of his professional life, yet the last few weeks had been different and, for the first time, he had worried about displeasing the fellow. Then there was Bob Manning – probably his best friend in the world – and how strange that he should share a Christian name with the American. They still got along professionally but there was no doubting the surgeon had been noticeably distant of late. Even Cooper, his second in command and a man he was steadily growing fond of, had started to annoy. James Croft was long gone, Summers, the youngster who had shared so many past adventures, would be commanding another vessel for the rest of this passage and as for Bob Walton... It was almost as if he were steadily being robbed of all his friends.

* * *

Aboard the schooner Stokes' mess were taking their evening meal, and much was different to when they ate aboard *Tenacious*. For a start only four members were present: due to the relatively large prize crew – more hands being needed to tend the ship and care for its cargo – half their number were being fed at a time. And it was cold food, basic banyan provisions of cheese, onions, biscuits and pickled cabbage, without even the consolation of a boiled pudding to follow. But at least those eating could choose between being on deck, or below in their dark quarters forward. Stokes' lot had opted for the latter although this was totally on account of space; the area allocated to them was small enough but, with upwards of sixty natives currently on deck, it was equally crowded topsides. Besides, all were glad of the chance to talk in relative privacy. And there was much to discuss; despite only having been aboard the schooner a short while they had already learned a good deal and most were of the same mind.

"I'd heard life were grim aboard a Guineaman, but never chanced it being quite so low," Longdon admitted through the onion he was munching. "Them blacks got it rough and no mistakin'."

"Least we's doin' what we can to help," Lovemore assured his tie mate, "though heaven knows it ain't much."

"That's about what they thinks," Bovey, the sea lawyer, butted in as he reached for a piece of hard tack. "I spent all afternoon seein' 'em up an' down, then muckin' out their quarters an' most behaves like they was doin' me the favour."

"None of 'em asked to be here," Stokes pointed out. He had barely eaten any food; even the apples brought with him from *Tenacious* held little attraction.

"Neither did we," Bovey glanced about at their temporary quarters. "Rather be back aboard the barky any day of the week."

"We'll be home soon enough," Lovemore assumed. "Though that's more than can be said for them blacks."

"They'll be alright." Bovey had been tapping his biscuit on the tabletop. "Freed slaves get treated well in Halifax. Government'll even give out land if they asks for it. All they got to do is put in a bit of effort and they're set for life."

"I heard all that stopped a long time since," Stokes said. "And even then what they got were nowt but rock an' forest; cove would've had to be a magician to make anything from rubbish like that."

"An' they ain't even slaves," Longdon added with unusual intensity. "Most can't speak the King's English so how they gonna make a livin' in a place like Nova Scotia?"

"Well they don't have to stay." A fair number of weevils had been encouraged from Bovey's biscuit; he picked one up on the tip of his finger and considered it as he continued. "Any that don't like it can go where they chooses."

"Even if they starves doing so," Lovemore sniffed. "At least a slave gets fed."

"No, I'm straight," Bovey insisted despite a mouthful of hard tack. "Drake were tellin' me earlier."

"What does the Jaunty know about slaves?"

"Aye, it's hardly a regular subject for a master-at-arms."

"Old boy seemed quite the authority," Bovey assured them with what might have been respect. "An' he handles them surprisingly well."

"I noticed that an' all," Longdon agreed. "Better than 'e treats any of us."

"Anyway, it seems a load of bible-bashers have got together and are sending them back to Africa." Bovey had swallowed his mouthful and was eyeing the rest of his biscuit speculatively. "Waste of effort if you asks me, though it don't do to judge how others get their jollies."

"Back to where they comes from?" Stokes asked doubtfully.

"Not exactly, but it's the same country." He took another bite. "From what he said I think I'd rather take my chances as a slave."

Chapter Twenty Two

They sighted the *Delaware* just over a week later when the coast of Nova Scotia was barely over the horizon. Until then it had been a surprisingly fast and incident-free passage but when a rising sun revealed the American frigate less than five miles off their larboard beam all knew their run of luck had come to an end.

King barely glanced at Walton's ship before turning to Brotherton. "Make to the prize, 'enemy in sight to windward, steer east with all despatch'."

By unspoken agreement Summers' command had been referred to in that way as the slaver's true name, *Bristol Pride*, stuck in everyone's throat.

"Mr Manton, kindly take us to starboard and make all sail commensurate with the weather."

Due to the American's proximity, Cooper had immediately summoned King and the sailing master. Both had come on deck with a good idea of what would be needed and Manton bellowed out the orders with little hesitation.

Tenacious had already been under topsails, topgallants and stay's so the addition of royals might only add a fraction of a knot to her speed although, as they would be taking the wind more on the quarter, she should still be able to show a clean pair of heels. And King had no doubts that the prize would keep up; despite the state of her bottom. Summers was sailing her extremely well, there had even been times when he needed to restrain his charge to remain with the more ponderous frigate.

"Mr Summers has acknowledged, sir," Brotherton reported. "And he's already altering course."

As was *Tenacious*. Less than five minutes since *Delaware* had been identified, the British frigate had turned away and was heading for the deep waists of the North Atlantic. But that could not continue for long, King told himself, even as the ship settled on her new course.

If the American offered combat, as would seem likely, they would be in for a hard old fight and having the prize to consider would not make it easier. Consequently he would be hoping for support; by Manton's workings, Halifax was less than a hundred and fifty miles off so there was every chance of meeting with at least one British warship. And one was all it would need; another frigate, or even a well-handled sloop, and Walton's ship would be captured for certain.

He strode to the taffrail and looked back. *Delaware* remained in plain view and was under topsails alone; with the current wind she could barely be making steerage way. And still heading south, possibly after nosing about the coast of Nova Scotia or, more likely, Halifax itself, King decided with a private smile. It was just like Walton to beard his enemy in its den. *Tenacious* was bound to have been spotted and probably identified, although, even if the American were still unsure exactly who lay to leeward of him, he must know them to be British.

But there was still no change in *Delaware*'s sail pattern and her heading remained the same. For a moment King wondered if Walton were deliberately ignoring them; turning a blind eye was not an exclusively British prerogative after all. However, *Tenacious* was obviously escorting a prize and, with this also in sight, he would be less able to ignore their presence.

And so it proved; even as King watched, extra canvas finally started to appear on the warship, topgallants and royals were raised and soon she had increased her pace and would be showing a fair rush of water from her prow. And then came the time he had been waiting for – dreading even. Slowly, and with apparent care, *Delaware*'s helm was put across and she began to flow into a gentle but slick turn. Then the two frigates were on the same tack; the American was making for him in earnest and it had suddenly become a chase.

* * *

"What do you see there?" Summers bellowed.

"Nuffink new," Stokes roared in reply. He could give the young lieutenant a good fifteen years and had already answered the same question five times. "Yank's headin' for us," he added, "or rather headin' for *Tenacious*. Can't see if he's forereachin' though there's still a tidy gap between the pair."

Summers released a long-held breath. He had reckoned that distance to be upwards of five miles, add a couple more for their lead on the British frigate and his little command was relatively safe. And could be made more so, he reminded himself. There was still an extra jib and staysail that could be added. Once those were set he could happily wave goodbye to both warships, even with a fouled hull. And then? And then he would wait until darkness and maybe an hour or so beyond before, ever so carefully, altering course. Perhaps another fifty miles to the north to really be certain, then turn back and make straight for Halifax. He would be alone, of course, although the skies had been reasonably clear of late. With luck he might make harbour in a couple of days – possibly less – and have his precious cargo safely ashore by the weekend.

But that could not be; Captain King had been generous in his allowance of hands and they were men *Tenacious* could not afford to lose, especially if there were the chance of a fight. And with that possibility now likely, they would have to go through the measures previously planned and agreed upon, however frustrating that might be for him.

"Beggin' your pardon, sir, can I start bringing the first batch up?"

He turned, there was the master-at-arms with his regular morning request. Yet this was no regular morning, they were likely to be going into action before dusk and Summers had to stop himself from laughing out loud.

"I fear not, Mr Drake," he said. "Do you not know of our predicament?"

"Been below, sir," the warrant officer admitted, "though gather we've company." Summers recognised the earnest look on the man's face. Drake's attitude to the captured natives had surprised him during his brief time in command. Rather than the cantankerous disciplinarian, a different side to the man had been revealed. From the start he had taken their live cargo under his wing and, with support from Godby and three of the hands who had also shown a special interest, become both their carer and unofficial advocate. Just why the old bullet-head should behave so was beyond him, although Summers was grateful and recognised that, despite it being larger, this current batch of slaves was proving far easier to manage.

"There were a bit of trouble," Drake was explaining. "Nothing to worry about though one of the women is not too good."

"Illness?" Summers was suddenly alert but the man shook his head.

"Hardly that, sir, least not in the normal way. I should say she's about to pop."

For the second time Summers had to suppress laughter. Not that the circumstances were in any way amusing, of course, but in a situation already complex enough, this was surely the most ridiculous complication.

"But we thought she'd make Halifax..." he began before realising the futility of what he was about to say, and coming to an abrupt halt.

"We did," Drake agreed, "'cept the Judy had other ideas. I'm afraid there's no doubt."

"Deck there! I reckons the Yank's changin' her rig – settin' stuns'ls p'raps?"

That was very likely, and an example Captain King would probably follow. And though the schooner would also be able to increase speed, it must bring forward the time when they made their next move.

"I'm truly sorry to hear of the problems," Summers said. "But am anticipating a signal from *Tenacious* at any moment. You know the provisions made were an enemy sighted; we have twenty hands aboard as well as several key officers, yourself included. As soon as Captain King gives the order we shall be abandoning the prize."

"Abandoning, sir?" The man seemed confused yet Summers knew for certain he had been aware of what might happen.

"As was agreed," he said. "They'll be sending a boat and we shall evacuate. Some of the original crew are secured below, they can be set free but all major lines must be cut and the tiller removed. With luck *Tenacious* may even recapture us when the present emergency has passed.

That was assuming much, of course; *Tenacious* might not even engage the American frigate; it was far more likely the chase would continue until dark, when they lost each other entirely. Were that to happen the schooner would be left many miles in their wake, and only luck and good seamanship on the part of her original crew would see her to a port.

"Very good, sir," Drake replied like the solid warrant officer he was, although Summers sensed his heart was not behind the words.

"How is the patient at the moment?" he asked.

"Well enough, I believes, sir." The man lowered his head in mild embarrassment. "The women are takin' care of her mostly, I've seen some released from their bilboes and Mr Godby is keepin' watch, subtle like. They got everything we thinks they might need."

"Then that's all we can do," Summers said. "Mr Godby can remain below for now, but I shall need the crew organised; when Captain King signals, we'll have to move quick."

"Of course, sir."

"Summon all hands," the lieutenant continued. "I shall address them, then we can make provisions to start the evacuation."

"Very good, sir," Drake repeated and, once more, Summers could not be certain he meant it.

* * *

"She's surely gaining, sir," Cooper declared, "though that comes as no surprise..."

King noted the mild criticism; since *Delaware* had set her stunsails the first lieutenant had been itching to add their own. Yet still he could see no reason to rush; they would have to be stopping shortly to collect the slaver's crew, until then King was more interested in seeing how the American frigate behaved.

In their last encounter Walton had outsailed four British frigates in conditions not dissimilar, so an all-out chase would probably end with the pair meeting – something that, for a number of reasons, King was keen to avoid.

"I'd be obliged if you would prepare the quarter boats, Mr Cooper," he announced, after considering a long enough pause had been left to show he had ignored the officer's comment. Then, to Brotherton, "Make to the prize, 'heave to and prepare to receive our boats'."

The schooner was a good two miles ahead, which should give Summers plenty of time to assemble his prize crew and disable the small craft. Once they were safely back aboard *Tenacious* he might think about those stunsails although it was quite possible that by then they would not be needed.

Of the two, *Delaware* was probably the more stoutly built and undoubtedly matched them in armament, yet King still felt his ship to be better served with a more experienced crew. But of one thing he was certain: if the pair were to meet in combat it was unlikely to produce a positive outcome for either. And Walton was no fool, he must realise the Royal Navy could afford to lose a frigate, whereas America most certainly could not. Even if *Delaware* proved victorious, the likelihood was both ships would require extensive repair that called for facilities Walton's navy simply did not have. With that in mind he had a strong suspicion the abandoned slaver might prove too good a distraction to ignore.

"Prize has replied 'affirmative', sir," Brotherton reported. "And she's starting to take in her canvas."

"Very good."

"Cutters are prepared." Cooper this time. "I have their people standing by."

King glanced back and noticed a group of stout seamen by each boat with Vernon and Corbrite alongside. It was a minimal crew but more would not be necessary as they should be returning fully manned. Besides, he did not intend leaving a great distance between his ship and the slaver. If all went well they should have collected the prize crew and their officers and be up and running again in a matter of minutes. And then they could really start to put *Tenacious* through her paces.

Or not, for there was still something lurking in the back of King's mind that might even save the day. If Summers did his job properly the vessel would be left temporarily unable to sail. *Delaware*'s crew could put her to rights in a matter of hours, of course, after which they might accompany the schooner back to New York in triumph. King had no idea what would become of her then but was sure the capture would be well publicised, which might see the slaves better provided for than if Walton had not claimed them from the evil British. And there was another consideration; retaking their prize would give the American every reason not to bring him to combat. Should he decide otherwise and ignore the positive gift *Tenacious* would be leaving in her wake, King could hardly refuse action. Yet for two warships – captained by men who once had been friends – to pound themselves to pieces for no apparent purpose seemed utterly senseless. Even if it did serve as an excellent metaphor for the current war.

* * *

His prize crew were mainly on deck and the schooner was virtually bereft of canvas. Without the wind's steadying pressure her small hull pitched and rolled alarmingly in the swell making even standing upright a physical trial. But *Tenacious* was coming up fast; Summers reckoned her less than a mile off and she appeared to be positively eating up the remaining distance.

"Very well," he roared. "Sever all halyards, lifts and braces; then we can look to the shrouds and stays."

It went against the grain to wreck a perfectly usable tophamper and every seaman hesitated, their knives and hatchets poised before starting the terrible work. Which gave just enough time for the master-at-arms to come clambering up from below with Godby close behind.

"Belay that!" Drake ordered and all gratefully drew back.

"What's the meaning of this?" Summers demanded, directing his question at the midshipman, who was at least a quarterdeck officer.

"There's a woman in the midst of givin' birth..." Godby began but was quickly overridden by Drake.

"Though that ain't the problem," he said. "If we're taken, the slaves will remain captives; there are nearly four hundred of 'em and some are entire families, we can't let that happen."

"You know the reason and have your orders," Summers snapped and was turning to address the crew once more when Drake continued.

"There's another way, mister," he said, drawing uncomfortably near. "We can keep this ship in the wind and sail her away; different course – split her from the barky."

"No!" Summers shouted. He looked back; *Tenacious* was now less than half a mile off; if they did not start disabling the rigging soon the job would only be half done. He turned his attention back to the men: "Carry on with your work."

"I said wait!" Drake, in bellowing directly into the younger man's face, was risking demotion at the very least. "The Yank can't chase both, our way there's a chance we'll make Halifax and can let the poor buggers go."

"You are needed aboard *Tenacious*," Summers replied angrily. "We all are. Now stand aside; the tophamper must be disabled. Both of you go down to the for'ard lazarette and bring up the schooner's original crew. See they're roped hand and foot, they'll fight their way free in time."

"We're not going," Drake announced and his expression was repeated on the midshipman's face.

"We don't need to go, Michael," Godby almost pleaded. "What Drake says is right, there's a chance we can avoid being captured. Leave us here, we can set enough sail to bear away."

"The pair of you?"

"That's right," Drake confirmed, deadly serious. "We can start with the fore' and add the main; or you can raise them afore you go if you've the mind. Once they're set it'll be one to the tiller and the other can attend to any more. Might get a few blacks a helping an' all, they trusts us and some have picked up a bit of our lingo."

"Besides, three of the hands intend staying as well," Godby added. "They got it into their heads that, as long as they can avoid being recaptured by the Americans, the natives will be shipped back to Africa."

"As well they might," the master-at-arms confirmed, his arms now firmly crossed.

Summers could hardly believe what he was hearing; his experience of command had been so very limited, surely he should not expect to face a mutiny this early on? His glance returned to *Tenacious* now desperately close and preparing to spill her wind while the quarter boats were ready to launch. The best he could manage would be to sever a few of the lighter lines.

"Very well, damn it," he shouted. "Though both of you can say goodbye to any future in the Royal Navy."

"That's fine, mister," Drake snorted. "Some things is more important."

* * *

"Prize crew appears to be safely aboard, sir," Cooper reported cautiously, "an' the second cutter's been cast off."

To save time both boats returned to the frigate's waist and had been abandoned as soon as the last hand scrambled home.

"Have Mr Summers report to me this instant!" King snapped as he glared at their former prize. Not only was her tophamper in perfect order, she was actually showing sail and preparing to get underway.

"You wished to see me, sir?" Summers announced, approaching.

254

"What the hell is that about?" King demanded, pointing to the schooner slowly taking to the wind off their starboard beam.

"Godby and Drake refused to leave," the young lieutenant admitted. "Three of the hands did likewise; Longdon, Lovemore and Stokes. They plan to take the prize to Halifax independent of us; reckoned the American can't engage both an' there were a chance they might get the blacks to safety."

King's head was spinning with rage and the words simply would not come; he felt betrayed, gulled – bobbed even. Apart from the harm they had done themselves, and the fact that surrendering the prize might have avoided *Tenacious* going into action, the fools must realise that what awaited slaves in Nova Scotia might be every bit as bad as any fate further south. There was nothing to be done, though, sending a boarding party would only eat up time; as it was the American lay less than three miles off their stern and they had yet to return to the wind.

"Bring her back, Master!" he snapped. "And rig stuns'ls aloft and alow!"

That should at least maintain a reasonable distance between the two, and give him time to think. *Tenacious* found the wind quickly and soon began to gather speed. He looked back at the schooner, now gamely taking the breeze on her starboard quarter and steering directly away. He supposed all was not entirely lost, Walton could hardly take both, although whatever persuaded young Godby to behave so remained a mystery. Of course that might be partly his own fault for appointing a black man to be in charge of slaves. But Drake – a seasoned warrant officer, hard as nails yet the best at his role King had encountered – why he should be showing sympathy for a bunch of natives was totally beyond him.

However, the cards had been dealt and he could do no more. His glance shifted to *Delaware*, now apparently being kept at bay by his own ship's extra canvas. Chances were strong Walton would still try for the slaver, in which case the sentimental idiots had done nothing other than make the American's task easier. It was even possible Walton would do no more than send a prize crew before continuing in pursuit of him. But one thing King had learned since taking up command was to play the hand he held. And though there might be every reason to feel betrayed, a few aces remained that could still grant him victory.

Chapter Twenty Three

Godby was aware of what he had done yet felt oddly unconcerned. And in this he was reassured – bolstered even – by Drake. Aboard *Tenacious* the pair had little to do with each other with Godby actually marking the man down as one who distrusted or disliked those of his colour. But in the short time they had been aboard the schooner and caring for their captives an understanding had developed that came close to respect. And they were not alone; forward, the three seamen that also opted to remain sat with a group of natives who had just finished their wash. The deck steamed in the strong morning sun; Godby guessed the hands had considered it hot enough to allow the rays to dry them. It was yet another example of the way they treated their charges and he sensed it was appreciated. Whether any knew the risks their guards were taking to ensure their eventual freedom was more doubtful, although the midshipman suspected a few might have an inkling.

But he definitely knew of the danger, and it was one that stretched further than mere professional ruin. Although matters could have been worse, for behind him the American frigate was still in sight yet thankfully not in pursuit; instead it chased *Tenacious*. Both were on the opposite tack and heading for the northern horizon, already the British ship was growing indistinct and the sight made Godby indescribably sad, even if it also instilled a feeling of relief.

The warships were effectively blocking his route to Halifax, yet still Godby felt in no need to rush. The day was young; he could afford to maintain their current southerly course for several hours, and then make for the east. By nightfall he hoped to be a good way out to sea; only then would he turn north and ultimately to the west. The schooner's charts only extended as far as New York but by simple dead reckoning he was confident of raising the northern coast of Nova Scotia, after which it should be a simple matter to follow it south until they fetched Halifax.

And once there the problems would surely begin. The least he should expect was to be dismissed the service, as must Drake, while the seamen would be lucky to escape a punishment far worse. However, Godby was no stranger to conflict and, should *Tenacious* make harbour safely, privately hoped their little escapade might yet be excused. After all, he intended delivering a prize that would otherwise have been retaken by the enemy, as well as freeing the four hundred odd souls it held. But then if *Tenacious* brought the American frigate to battle it could be a different matter. Should such a thing occur his conduct could be considered desertion in the face of the enemy, and they might all forfeit their lives.

That was for the future, though, for now all Godby had to consider was keeping the schooner steady and as far away from any fighting as possible. The next few days would not be easy and handling so many captives with just five men must mean little rest for all. He had considered releasing the seven that were part of the slaver's original crew before deciding the risk not worth taking, at least for the time being. There may come a need for extra manpower although that moment had yet to arrive, for now they were in charge of the situation, and hopefully would remain so.

* * *

King had begun to edge away northward over an hour before and, predictably enough, Walton duly followed. And now both ships were firmly on the larboard tack he felt slightly more confident; after all *Tenacious* was heading roughly in the direction of her base and presumably safety. And even though the American frigate solidly gained on them, every foot would be taking her further from home and deeper into British held waters. As it stood he reckoned the two ships would be within range of the other within three hours; by that time the heat of the day would be dying and he could expect a more reliable wind for any fancy sailing. They would also be several miles closer to Halifax and several times more likely to chance upon another British ship, which remained King's key hope.

Of course he would still have no hesitation in meeting Walton in battle, indeed part of him was wickedly interested to see who would perform the better. But if another Royal Navy warship appeared, one able and willing to join the fray, it would make all the difference. Walton was a practical man and, with the odds so decidedly against him, would run for certain. And should he make yet another escape, King supposed it would not be such a terrible end to matters.

"Take her three points to larboard," he muttered, and Manton touched his hat before giving the necessary orders. They were still heading for Halifax although the change of course would bring them closer to land and, more to the point, it meant *Tenacious* must take the wind slightly forward of her beam. It would be interesting to see how the change affected the American. The two ships might be similar in size, but their beam and bows were very different. Walton had escaped from the flotilla with the wind on his quarter; King suspected *Delaware* would not be so suited to sailing close-hauled. Should this be the case and *Tenacious* were finally able to maintain her lead – or even draw ahead slightly – he might take her closer still until she was positively clawing. They would still be heading roughly for home but closing with the land earlier would increase the chances of meeting with a friendly warship.

He looked around, the quarterdeck was crowded yet remained remarkably quiet. After all, they were being chased by an enemy frigate, something that would normally provoke any amount of speculation amongst his officers. Admittedly King might have been unreasonably touchy for some while, although his anger had nothing to do with anyone aboard *Tenacious* and he wondered why it should bother them so.

Besides, he had every reason to be cross; the incident with the slaver still rankled, especially as exactly why Godby and Drake had behaved in such an extraordinary way remained a mystery – one that even the stammering Summers had been unable to explain. Godby he could understand to some extent but Drake, their master-at-arms, was another matter entirely.

The man had been a replacement for Guppy, a deplorable specimen that King had almost been pleased to see on the casualty list. As soon as Drake took up his duties as principle disciplinary officer the lower deck had shown a noticeable improvement in both morale and spirit, for he had a natural gift when it came to managing men. Drake could bellow and badger with the best, yet there was also an understanding rare in his type. Complaints of bullying within messes had almost disappeared overnight and more hands were put forward for advancement than at any time during *Tenacious'* commission. For one such as him to turn so, and actually defy authority for the sake of a few hundred slaves, really made no sense

258

whatsoever.

Cooper had finally uncovered the come-up glass and was studying the pursuing American through it.

"How is she?" King enquired.

"No change, sir," the first lieutenant replied.

"Do you mean she still gains, or we are maintaining our lead?"

"I-I mean she closes, sir," Cooper mumbled. "B-but possibly not by so much."

King nodded and resisted the temptation to say more even if it was somewhat galling that his previous ill temper should have been taken as a personal rebuke. He would not allow it to bother him though; a little silence would actually be welcome and, besides, captains have a lot to think about so are permitted to be grumpy from time to time.

* * *

Now that he had sole charge of the schooner, Godby was starting to experience the loneliness of command. Drake remained aboard, of course, and was actually in sight as he trimmed the jib, yet there was a deal of difference between a master-at-arms and a midshipman, even in a captured slaver that had effectively been stolen by its prize crew. Both might be warrant officers but only Godby had the right to walk a quarterdeck and, in theory at least, was expected to progress to commissioned rank; of the pair he must undoubtedly be the leader.

They might discuss their course and even call the hands in for an opinion, as their eventual destination would affect them all, but as to whether they had done the right thing in defying Summers, or exactly what might become of them now the deed was done, would be a closed subject. And one that was made worse by necessity as each man was forced to work alone. For the past hour the wind had been fluctuating and Drake was kept busy attending the sails while Longdon guarded those natives allowed on deck and Lovemore watered the main body below. Meanwhile Stokes was at the maintop acting as lookout and Godby himself manned the tiller. When Lovemore had finished, he and Longdon would see a fresh batch of captives up to replace those currently on deck, after which there may be a change in duties. And presumably they could continue in such a way for some while, or so he hoped. At night, when all the natives were safely below, two might take what rest they could in turn. Such an arrangement would last long enough to see them to their home port and then it would be up to Godby, and Godby alone, to explain their actions.

"Deck there!" the height of the schooner's main was low enough for Stokes' call to be almost conversational. "There's sommat on the eastern horizon. Comes and goes a bit though its gradually getting stronger; I'd say whatever it might be is closing."

"A sail?" Godby asked and he could see the seaman shrug.

"More like a body of shipping. Convoy or similar."

"Or a fleet..." It wasn't meant to be a question, Godby had been thinking out loud, yet Stokes heard easily enough.

"Yup, might be a fleet at that."

A convoy arrived from Britain roughly every two to three weeks although, now war had been declared, more could be expected. But this might be something else, something far more valuable: this might be the promised reinforcements.

A wild idea came to him; were that the case they could intercept, make contact and report *Delaware*'s presence. It was by no means guaranteed but, should they be able to summon assistance for his former ship, and capture the American into the bargain, it might alter the way their act of defiance was regarded by those in authority.

"Drop down, Stokes," he ordered. "Mr Drake, I believe we should change course; do you need Lovemore from below?"

"Nah, we should manage fine," Drake replied. "'Specially if Longdon lends an 'and."

They looked to the captives currently on deck, all were women and included the one who had given birth only an hour or so before, along with her baby, strangely quiet. In fact none looked exactly threatening and should give no trouble while they carried out a simple manoeuvre. And as Stokes had arrived on deck they may as well act immediately.

"Ready about!" Godby called as he pressed the tiller to starboard. The schooner turned instantly and no speed was lost as skilled hands kept the sails filled. Then, at the critical time, boom and jib were laid across and she came neatly onto the opposite tack. The midshipman instinctively glanced at the compass although no accurate course was needed, their current heading should roughly intercept Stokes' sighting. He wondered for a moment about adding extra sail but the wind had been steadying of late and was now holding strong; they were making a fair pace even with a fouled bottom. Adding more, then having to strike, would only complicate matters.

"Looks like things is on the up," Stokes muttered as he made for the shrouds to resume his place and Godby found himself smiling a little in agreement. Maybe matters would turn out right after all.

* * *

The call to clear for action had come and Morales was suddenly one of the busiest men in the ship. In addition to many smaller tasks, the carpenter and his team had to supervise the removal of all temporary bulkheads including those in the captain's quarters, gunroom and midshipmen's berth. These were either struck below, along with important pieces of furniture, or folded to one side. And the work had to be done quickly to allow free access for other tasks, such as clearing away cannon and establishing an emergency sick bay. But once all was well advanced he excused himself and made his way forward, as there was one job he always performed himself.

Throughout its brief existence, the unofficial fore cockpit had been struck on several occasions; indeed Morales had paid particular care with its design and construction to see this could be accomplished easily. But this time, as he made to carry out the task, it was as if it were somehow different. He dropped down to the orlop and made his way forward then, on reaching his shared home, secured the door before swiftly releasing each latch that held the entire partition in place. The structure was hinged at the top and swung up easily to the low deckhead where a line of bolts waited to secure it. With that simple act their private space had been opened up for the perusal of all; the individual piles of fresh laundry, neatly stowed hammocks and table already laid for the next meal looking mildly pathetic in the light of public glare.

Morales determinedly closed his mind to such things; in action, additional access was needed to the forward filling and light rooms and even the forepeak may need to be reached. He piled the clothing into a spare chest and removed the two pictures of woodland scenes that had made the place more homely still. The table's legs slipped out and fitted neatly into its top which was then placed alongside the scantling and secured by clips of his own design. Then each of the five chairs folded into themselves and were slipped into their individual pockets set between the beams of the deckhead. Each

261

of the hammocks were stowed in a similar way and it was done; within minutes their private lair had been dismantled and might never have existed. Of course, it could be rebuilt in the future and, if all survived, their previous life might resume. But Drake had already absented himself, and none of the remainder could be certain of surviving the next few hours. In fact the chances were strong their little community was gone for good and, even amid the confusion and expectation of a forthcoming action, the thought made Morales unutterably sad.

* * *

"I'd like to bring some more darkies up," Drake announced and Godby looked at him in surprise.

"Darkies?" he repeated.

"Didn't mean no disrespect," the warrant officer added hastily. "Only I don't like callin' 'em slaves all the time. It's not as if they've ever been put to work, an' the poor buggers didn't ask to be 'ere."

"No," the midshipman accepted. "I suppose not. And yes, you can allow a further group on deck by all means."

They had been heading towards the eastern horizon for some while and the sighting was turning into something far more distinct. It did indeed appear to be a battle squadron, possibly even a fleet, though warships for certain. Of course they could be the old enemy – a scratch group of French rounded up to torment the British in their new theatre of war – though the likelihood was small. But either way Godby could hardly have cared less; he still hoped his previous behaviour might be excused even if the doubts were now mounting.

If he could direct a suitable force to *Tenacious'* aid it may yet be to his favour, although such an act now seemed unlikely. Both frigates had been out of sight for some time, he only had the vaguest idea of their current whereabouts and must still close with the sighting. That being the case it was likely Captain King and the American would settle their differences undisturbed, leaving him to answer for his own actions. And, given the choice of disgrace and punishment at the hands of his own country or being a prisoner of the enemy, he knew which he preferred.

* * *

262

The afternoon seemed to be stretching on inexorably and was not going entirely to plan; certainly King's theory about *Tenacious* being the better sailer close-hauled lay in tatters. They had made their final turn some hours before and begun clawing towards the distant coast, but the move had not shaken *Delaware* off and neither had it left her in their wake; whatever the shape of her prow or width of her beam, the American was proving as good on a wind as before it, and possibly better. Currently she lay about a mile off their larboard quarter and had been steadily creeping up; at any moment he expected Walton to open fire, at least with his bow chasers.

Which must not happen, King decided, strangely resolute. It was rare for him to have any knowledge of the enemy he faced, yet Bob Walton was a man he knew well; why, they had even exchanged wine and rabbits. More than that, they agreed on so much and both were experienced frigate captains who appreciated the importance of instigating an action. Consequently King had the uncomfortable feeling that, should the American be allowed to fire first, it would quickly become an uphill struggle.

"I intend to bear off to larboard," he announced and Manton alerted the waisters and forecastle men while Cooper warned the gunners. Walton was unlikely to submit to even a long-distance raking, yet King knew his lead was steadily diminishing; he must take advantage of what remained before it became too late.

"Simultaneous broadsides if you please, Mr Taylor," he added in his own hoarse bellow. "And at all times keep your sights low."

It was too great a range for anything else, but King also wanted to make an impression on the enemy frigate. There was something about that hull; even at a distance it appeared soundly made and apparently impervious to shot. He had to prove it otherwise and quickly. All gunners able to move were in position at the larboard battery; everything seemed ready and, with a heart suddenly heavy, he ordered the helm across.

Yet almost as soon as the rudder began to bite, a rumble of comment drew his attention; King turned and caught the last of two puffs of smoke that had erupted from the American's bows, then suppressed a smile. The cove had beaten him to it, a pair of six-pound round shot might be nothing to what King would shortly be sending in reply, but a point had definitely been made.

There was a brief whine as Walton's salvo whipped past while the British frigate leant into her turn. Then *Delaware*'s bows began to

263

edge into *Tenacious'* arc of fire.

"Meet her!" Manton grumbled and the quartermaster finished the job. King waited; it would take a moment for the ship to stabilise at which point her gunners could adjust to the new motion.

"*Delaware's* turning as well," Cooper warned, and that seemed to be the case. Walton was following his example and falling off to larboard; there was still a chance to catch the American's bows, but it must be taken quickly.

"As you will, Mr Taylor!"

"Fire!" The order came even before King had finished speaking and *Tenacious* rocked gently as her main larboard battery roared out.

"Back to starboard, sir?" Manton needed to bellow as all on the quarterdeck had been deafened by such close thunder.

"No!" King shouted in return, and would have done so even without being partially stunned. Returning to the previous course might restore their lead and increase the chances of meeting with other vessels but, if Walton were offering a broadside, the last thing he should do was present his stern as a target. "Keep her as she is."

Taylor's men were throwing themselves into reloading and those tending the sails had secured the braces but King, Cooper and Manton's attention was solely on the American frigate, roughly a mile off their beam and still in the midst of a sweeping turn. And when the British barrage landed it was not a disappointment.

Their target had been moving at speed so, with smoothbore ordnance that boasted only the most basic of sights, there was every excuse for some wild shooting. And several did go horribly wide while most landed aft, as might be expected. But a favourable grouping appeared to have struck Walton's ship and King was satisfied. Quite how the fellow would phrase his reply was another matter, although he sensed they were about to find out.

As they did, barely seconds later. The enemy's broadside was released in a slow ripple of fire that spread from bow to stern with measured menace. Even as *Delaware's* aft carronades were being despatched, her forward shot was biting into *Tenacious'* timbers and doing so with devastating effect. The British frigate's hull was punctured in several places with two shots breaking through her upper bulwarks and carving chunks from the neat line of marines posted alongside.

Number three gun was struck and sent back against its breaching rope even as its servers fought to reload. And there were other hits to flesh and fixtures that produced a veritable cloud of dust, splinters and detritus far worse which was liberally distributed about the frigate's waist. The quarterdeck was similarly treated; the binnacle exploded into a thousand pieces throwing out more sharp shards laced with spirit and oil, while three hands from a larboard carronade fell to the same deadly ball.

"Keep her as she is," King repeated, more to assert his authority although it was doubtful if any truly heard. Yet throughout the confusion and fear, the larboard battery continued to be served and, less than a minute after the first enemy shot had struck, gun captains began signalling their pieces ready to reply.

"Target, sir?" Taylor shouted up from the waist.

"Keep your sights low!" King bellowed in reply.

Delaware remained marginally off their larboard quarter but was coming up fast; she was also steering slightly to starboard and so closing the distance between them. There was now every chance, and every reason, to aim for her tophamper though King remained set on targeting the ship herself. A mast might still be wounded from below but his motives went deeper; there remained something about that smooth, slightly rounded hull that made him want to dent it.

"Fire!"

Taylor had taken the initiative, which was fine, the man was in far closer touch with his gunners. And this time they made better practice; actual damage could be seen; what might be a hole appeared just above *Delaware*'s waterline and he was reasonably sure her starboard mainchains had been struck. But there was no apparent change to the frigate's sailing abilities, and King knew he could not afford to continue simply exchanging broadsides.

"Prepare starboard battery!"

That was the only way. It meant slowing the reloading of their own larboard guns and almost committed him to his next move, which was never wise in single ship duels. Yet they had to force a closer action and there was only one way he could see of doing this.

"As soon as they release their next barrage, I want us to bear off fully to larboard."

"To larboard, sir," Manton repeated deliberately as if learning lines for a forthcoming play.

King considered his opponent again; *Delaware* was holding her course and, though *Tenacious* still held a small lead, catching up fast; if he left it too long she would be level and then ahead. And

Walton was no fool; as soon as King turned he would also manoeuvre although there should still be time to land a glancing blow on the American frigate's stern. But before that could happen he must wait for the enemy to speak; only then, when her venom had been drawn, could he risk exposing *Tenacious'* bows.

The expected broadside came seconds later and proved even more devastating than the first. Their larboard bower was struck and sent on a one-way trip to the seabed and another shot clipped the foremast just below the fighting top. A second gun was hit and more deep belly blows thundered into the British frigate's side, although the most important damage was caused to her steering. And it was not material, instead their aged quartermaster and his two helpers were struck by the same deadly ball, leaving the wheel miraculously untouched but deserted and turning of its own volition.

"Watch her!" Manton yelled in rebuke before realising the reason for such apparent inattention and rushing to the wheel himself.

"Brotherton, assist there!" King ordered, although the midshipman was already on his way and, joined by a seaman from one of the starboard carronades, the ship was brought under control.

"Do you still wish to turn, sir?" Manton asked without taking his eyes off the sails.

"I do," King replied. "Are you able?"

The sailing master nodded once, then yelled out to those at the braces before heaving the wheel across. Slowly, and with greater care than was usual, *Tenacious* began to bear off until she was running before the wind with her tophamper mercifully intact and holding.

"Penrose, Biggins, lend a hand here!" Manton ordered and two seaman came aft from the waist. "You boy, drop down to Mr Duckworth in the gunroom," he added to the messenger. "Ask him to come up and be quick about it."

King turned his attention to the American. *Delaware* was definitely reacting to their turn; Walton had also thrown his helm across and apparently intended keeping pace with them.

"Can we wear?" King enquired cautiously.

"We might, sir," Manton replied. "Once Duckworth replaces me here."

The quartermaster's mate appeared at that moment and, taking the situation in at a single glance, stepped over the body of his late superior and up to the wheel.

"Very well, sir." Manton was wiping his hands on his tunic as he moved away. "You wished to wear ship?"

"Mr Taylor, we are turning further," King bellowed. "Be ready to fire as we go!"

It was asking a lot of a ship and her crew that had already taken a pounding, but King felt it vital to keep moving and, more to the point, keep his opponent on the move. Taylor replied with a wave of his hand and King could see all at the starboard guns were ready.

"Very well," he said. "Take her round!"

* * *

"What's goin' on here?" Midshipman Kenard demanded as he clambered up the side of the schooner. He was not unduly surprised by what he saw, the vessel had the looks and smell of a slaver and there were black faces all about with most, if not all, in chains. And the lad had encountered slavers before, though never with what looked like half their cargo on deck. If it weren't for the shackles he'd have guessed some form of uprising had taken place and, despite all appearing secure, drew his hanger and held it at the ready.

"This is the slave ship *Bristol Pride*," a voice declared and he turned to see yet another black man, although this time wearing a uniform similar to his own. "She is the prize of HMS *Tenacious*, Captain Thomas King," the figure continued, "and we are seeing her to Halifax."

"Then you're heading the wrong way." Kenard's reply was instinctive and curiosity soon got the better of him. "Where d'ya get that uniform?"

"Same place you got yours, mister."

This time it was a white face and Kenard felt a wave of relief and even camaraderie.

"Name's Drake, master-at-arms," the man announced approaching. "And this here's Mr Midshipman Godby. He's in charge of us all and has done a damned fine job. You'd better listen to him, if you knows what's good for you, 'cause 'e's got something mighty important to say."

* * *

"Wear ship!"

All had been expecting the order and *Tenacious* flew into the manoeuvre with far more fluency than her last. King watched, spellbound. They had already proved her shaken tophamper was relatively stable, but the next few minutes would show if she were truly up to the rigours of combat. *Delaware* was starting to follow her example and currently lay ahead of their turning bow, although that would soon change. *Tenacious* continued to manoeuvre as if on oil; in no time she was heading to pass the American and her gun captains were signalling the enemy in reach.

"Fire!"

Taylor's order rang out and was immediately followed by a thunderous discharge that echoed throughout the ship; the starboard battery was complete and, until then, unused; their captains must have been itching for the chance to add to the fray.

"Continue around," King ordered, "though be prepared to turn back."

Walton would have enough on his hands dealing with that broadside so King must press home the advantage while he held it. Yet it seemed that, however well-laid their fire – and the American ship had been comprehensively peppered – *Delaware* was able to ride it. She came onto the same tack only a few minutes after *Tenacious* although that brief time had given the British back their lead and, more importantly, should allow for his next move.

"The Yanks seem to be on their toes," Cooper commented wryly and King could only agree. But then he had expected nothing less; everything learned about the American ship and her people suggested she would perform well. For years Britain had been fighting navies demoralised by defeat and poor supplies; their subsequent victories had encouraged a sense of superiority that was now being soundly challenged.

King glanced up at the sails that were well filled; the ship had settled to her new heading while those at the starboard battery were advanced in serving their cannon. *Delaware* was on roughly the same course but still considerably behind, although that could not continue; he now accepted Walton had the faster ship, in which case he must act immediately. "And back, Master!" he ordered.

Once more *Tenacious* did not disappoint; she bore round easily and was soon running with the wind and threatening to cross her opponent's bows. In no time the American's prow was almost on her beam and it was tempting to order those guns already primed released. But Taylor knew his business and, barely seconds later, another full broadside rolled out.

And again it was on target and seemed well laid. King watched as the iron balls rained down, waiting for the flutter of canvas that would be the first sign they had hit the base of one of the American's masts. But despite a deal of dust and debris being raised, and a couple of wild shots causing neat holes in her canvas, *Delaware* came on.

King glanced at Cooper; there seemed nothing they could do to wound this particular beast. And worse, it would soon be in a position to retaliate although, rather than following them to starboard, Walton was holding his course and trying for a rake.

"She's coming in close!" Cooper remarked, and that did appear to be the case.

"Continue around!" King ordered. There should be time to wear once more, then be pulling away on the opposite tack when the American arrived, but that was by no means guaranteed. And even if so, Walton would be in an ideal position to turn also; if he kept his head they would become entwined in a deadly spiral that could only end in collision.

Were that to happen it might signal a boarding, and King's instincts rebelled against the thought. His marines were a reliable body of men, and many of the lower deck were practised in hand-to-hand combat, however the American ship boasted a larger complement and he knew in his bones she would never be carried in such a way.

Tenacious was well into the turn now with *Delaware* speeding towards her. King held his breath, there was still time to complete the manoeuvre and meet the American broadside to broadside although it would be close, damned close.

And then the unthinkable happened. Even as the British frigate began to take the breeze to starboard there came a deadly crack from forward. The sound travelled freely about the ship but reverberated most strongly in every man's skull as the foremast, damaged earlier, finally began to tumble. King realised in an instant what had happened but had to tear his eyes from the sight to consider the approaching American. *Delaware* was simply too near; he might coax a little movement from his own command yet nothing less than a miracle would be needed if they were to avoid a thorough raking.

Chapter Twenty Four

King could see Cooper – the man must have rushed forward at the first sign the upper mast was falling and had already begun supervising its removal. Under his direction topmen began hacking at innumerable lengths of taut and limp line while others gathered up the strips of torn canvas that almost enveloped their prow. The severed portion of the mast was suspended above them, surrounded by several separate bundles of splintered spars and shattered tackle that could so easily fall and cause further injury. But the first lieutenant remained calm and the wreckage was finally manhandled over the side.

The American ball had actually struck slightly below their foretop, taking the lower yard with it, as well as all support from the shrouds; even if they were to rig a jury spar any square sail could only be of negligible size. Then King noticed Amon and his team; the boatswain was assessing the damage and hopefully planning an additional head or staysail to balance the pressure from main and mizzen. Until that could be done, King knew he would have to strike some canvas aft, and *Tenacious* would be virtually unmanageable, at least as far as further combat was concerned.

His head had started to hurt and a general feeling of despair was building and threatening to take him over. Yet there was no time to think about himself, he turned to Manton. The sailing master appeared fascinated by the damage forward and started visibly at his captain's shout. But there was no delay in issuing the necessary order, and soon topmen were taking in their main topgallant.

"Will she steer?" King bellowed to Duckworth at the wheel. The replacement quartermaster was younger than his predecessor but appeared competent enough.

"I've had her over f'ra while, y'r honour," he said, eyes fixed on the leech of the main topsail. "Though the wind's dropped somethin' rotten and we didn't have much speed in the firs' place."

"Very good." There was little else that could be said and, as the

270

thumping in his head increased, King braced himself to consider *Delaware*, now closing on their starboard bow. The small amount of headway *Tenacious* could make was being heightened by a subtle change of course on behalf of the American; Walton was steering to close as tightly as possible. Those of *Tenacious'* starboard guns that could reach were letting off individual shots, but there was no reply; *Delaware*'s broadside was being saved for a more tempting target.

King knew he would have to strike; within minutes the enemy frigate would be stationed off their prow and could begin a regular close-range raking that would destroy his ship whilst killing a good proportion of her crew. It was unfortunate, but there could be no avoiding the fact. And then, as he looked about for someone to lower their ensigns, two things happened, and in such quick succession they might have been ordained.

First the wind returned; it started as a slight gust which soon grew, bold and firm. The canvas above cracked loudly before billowing out and there was a sigh of relief from the quartermaster's mate. Then, as if on cue, a call came from the hand at the main masthead.

"Deck there! I've something to the east. Not clear at present, barely over the 'orizon, but I'd say it were a bunch of shippin'."

King glanced round to see Cooper returning; his face grimy and streaked with sweat yet he also carried a look of hope.

"A fleet!" he said in wonder. "An' they may be ours!"

"They may," King agreed, yet that hardly solved the present predicament.

Delaware was still closing and seemingly intent on delivering the first of several deadly blows. But *Tenacious* could now steer and, as Duckworth leant heavily on the wheel, King knew they should avoid a full raking. Taylor had stopped any further pot shots from his starboard gunners and those that had already fired were frantically reloading although there would be no full broadside to send in reply.

King caught Cooper's eye; the first lieutenant was equally mindful of their situation and his expression had changed to one of concern.

"I might still strike," King said as softly as was practical.

"You might, sir, but with what should be warships in sight..."

"They won't get to us immediately."

"No, sir. But if we can delay the American even a little it will make her capture the more likely."

"It would," King sighed, just as *Delaware* came into position.

And he had made up his mind even as she opened fire.

* * *

Godby had been relieved of his command, the *Bristol Pride* was now in the hands of Kenard, the midshipman who first boarded her, while he, Drake and the three hands had been struck below. All five were secured in a tiny store room next to that which housed part of the schooner's original crew yet he was not downhearted. By the time his message had been sent to Kenard's ship, and then on to the flag officer commanding the battlefleet, smoke from the frigates' engagement had already been spotted and scouts were being sent to investigate. So perhaps his action – their action he reminded himself quickly – had turned out to be a waste of time. Maybe there had been no need to defy authority and effectively steal the schooner; maybe it would have been better to let her go, and be taken by the American. Her cargo would hardly be any worse off; what awaited them in Halifax was probably little better than the life of a slave further south. But still the sense of satisfaction was strong and, he suspected, one he shared with Drake and the men. None of them could tell how matters would pan out; the future might see them hailed as heroes or tried for desertion but, whatever happened, he felt at peace with himself. And the feeling was a good one.

* * *

Delaware's broadside had done considerable damage; the shots were taken low on *Tenacious'* starboard bow and several killing blows to the forward hull must have weakened her frame drastically. The dead and dying now littered her upper decks and a number of her cannon were permanently out of action. But to some extent she still remained viable and King was focusing his mind on that, with perhaps a little room for the good news.

For they had struck back and struck back hard. Being able to turn slightly had allowed Taylor's cannon to speak and the last broadside – a derisory barrage from a weakened battery – had actually brought results; *Delaware* was severely injured and now lay several cables off while she licked her wounds.

"Take a while afore she sorts that little lot out," Cooper declared as the pair of them surveyed the American. Her mizzen had fallen completely, the entire mast having been taken down by a chance shot that had struck low and hard. And there was more: when it fell it had carried the frigate's main topmast with it.

So now the race was on; Walton would be battling to remove as much of the wreckage as possible while King's boatswain and topmen rigged additional forward canvas to give *Tenacious* much needed manoeuvrability. It was not clear who would win; the American was definitely favourite as she should be able to sail adequately enough powered by her foremast alone, whereas at best *Tenacious* would be limp and sluggish. But then all King had to do was buy time; already the oncoming warships were in sight from the deck; in a matter of hours they would be alongside when *Delaware* must be taken for certain.

Although he hoped it would not come to that. He hoped Walton would see sense and, once his ship was clear of the sea anchor his fallen tophamper had created, make off. *Delaware* may not be capable of great speed yet would have a head start and, with her own coast close at hand and New York harbour not so far away, might still make good her escape.

One of the boatswain's team approached and knuckled his forehead.

"Mr Amon reports main topmast stays'l is rigged and drawing. An' he hopes to 'ave some form of jury heads'l ready presently."

King's brain continued to pound and there was a strange taste in his mouth but still he peered forward. *Tenacious* was indeed making steady progress away from *Delaware*; with extra canvas he would be able to increase his speed further or turn to take on the wounded American and at that moment he was not sure which would be the right path.

Then the decision was made for him; a shout from Manton drew his attention. The Americans had finally cast off the last of their wreckage and *Delaware* was taking to the wind again. The next few seconds would tell if they intended making for him, or running for safety, although he had already made up his own mind. Should Walton take the sensible course, he would not pursue; the pair had done enough; were this a duel, the seconds would be stepping in to call a halt, for honour had been satisfied.

But, probably for the first time, it seemed he and Walton were not of the same mind. King watched in silent wonder, but there was no doubt about it; *Delaware* was definitely entering into a turn and it was away from safety. Instead the frigate would soon be making for them; it seemed his former friend would only be content with an outright victory, however temporary, and King now knew this must be a fight to the death.

* * *

"Ready larboard battery!"

The last American broadside had dealt so decisively with *Tenacious'* starboard guns that this was undoubtedly the best strategy. Amon and Wilson were still attending to a particularly ambitious jury headsail; a line had been rigged from the main topmast although, even if they proved successful, King doubted it would give sufficient speed to avoid *Delaware*. But it seemed the stream was favouring them so Duckworth gently eased the ship back to larboard under what canvas they had, while Taylor's gunners prepared themselves. *Delaware* was considerably less than half a mile off and steadily picking up speed. King reckoned they might despatch two broadsides – three at the most – before she was on them.

"I suppose I might strike now," King remarked and was surprised by Cooper's immediate look of horror.

"But we can still fire on her, sir!" he exclaimed. It was clear the young man's blood was up; King had the unsettling impression he would probably now wish to fight until he dropped. "And with a British fleet in the offing..."

"Which will not be in range for some time."

"Though we must try," Cooper implored. "There remains every chance the American will be totally dismasted."

King turned away; the pounding in his head made rational thought impossible although inwardly he knew the man was right; it would only take one well-placed shot on the American's fore' to totally disable her. Then they might rightly claim victory and be ready to hand over a prize when rescue did arrive. Yet that same shot might as easily kill several while adding further damage to what had so recently been a beautiful ship. Suddenly the whole business made no sense at all and he felt physically sick. Then *Tenacious* came fully to larboard and her broadside rolled out.

* * *

It caused no perceivable damage and, apart from totally wrecking the enemy's hawse, neither did the second. Then the American was close enough for *Tenacious'* marines to start sniping, but still the warship came on. King watched, transfixed; there was no fire from her bow chasers, presumably both guns had been wrecked. He tore his eyes away and sought out Bream, his senior marine lieutenant, and found him shamelessly sheltering behind the mizzen.

"Mr Bream, order your men to stand down and secure themselves!"

Taylor's guns had only just fired, there would be no time for a third broadside before the American took up a raking position and, when he noted Walton was steering for their stern, he almost felt relieved.

"If you'll pardon me, sir, I think we might strike now," Manton said a little tentatively and King could sense his fear. But then a powerful frigate was about to deliver a raking broadside; one that would probably tell for their ship, and those on the quarterdeck would be the first to meet it. King's eyes flashed to Cooper. His first officer was staring resolutely at the oncoming ship; literally looking death in the face. The two men were poles apart and he stood between, conscious only of the worst of all headaches and a lack of direction that might tell for them all.

And *Delaware* was indeed drawing horribly close, although the marines manning her bulwarks were also holding their fire. As King suddenly sensed Walton's cannon would; the American was taking up an unassailable position off their stern but it would not be exploited. This was merely the point of a rapier held at an opponent's throat; Walton was proving victory beyond doubt and who could blame him? And then, through the chaos of the frigate's wrecked quarterdeck, he saw the man himself.

Bob Walton was standing alone and appeared unusually immaculate amid the smoke and carnage of action. King smiled to himself – the fellow had even managed to retain his hat and they were close enough for him to see that familiar smile. And then he had to laugh out loud for the American was holding up a glass of wine as if in a toast.

"Very well, Mr Cooper," King said, touching his forehead in response. "You may haul down our colours."

* * *

The young officer that boarded them a few minutes later was no stranger and as King shook hands with *Delaware*'s first lieutenant it was hard to keep the welcome from his face.

"You fought well, Captain," Seymour told him.

"Though you did better," King replied, reaching for his sword and proffering the hilt.

"I have no need of that, sir." Seymour brushed the weapon away. "And would not, even if your rescue were further off."

They both turned; two British frigates were now in plain sight with a trio of liners following behind. It was exactly as Seymour had said, the American victory would only last a short while. But a victory it would remain; probably the first in this needless war and likely not to be the last.

"I would speak with your captain," King announced. "We have much to discuss and, I'd wager, a bottle of wine to finish."

But the young man did not answer his smile, instead he assumed a look of abject sorrow.

"I fear that will not be possible, sir," he said. "You see, Captain Walton was killed quite early in the action."

* * *

"But I do not understand." Aimée dabbed at her mouth with a napkin. "You saw this Captain Walton on his ship and he was alive, no?"

"I did," King agreed. Aimée had been the first he dared tell of the incident and was already regretted doing so. "I was tired, confused; my head ached and I could not have been thinking clearly."

"But you saw him, Thomas, and are not a man to imagine such things. Especially..."

"Especially what?" he demanded, possibly too sharply.

"It is no matter," she told him quickly before calmly helping herself to another potato. King closed his eyes and drew breath; he must not be cross with Aimée, she was hardly responsible for his cranky brain. It would indeed have been better to say nothing, at least until there was chance to rest and properly consider the situation.

There would be little possibility of that for some while, though. *Tenacious* had only put in that morning and, though their journey to Halifax had been short, his frustration would have been as great if the liner towing them had made double the speed. And, now back, there was so much to do – so many people to see. Even the meal they currently enjoyed would be cut short as he had an important appointment with Admiral Sawyer within the hour.

One of his main concerns was Godby and the remainder of *Tenacious'* prize crew; the schooner had also made harbour and all were confined, and would remain so until a full investigation could be launched. He must make reparations; do whatever was necessary to see they received a fair court martial although there was surely a case for the incident to be conveniently overlooked. Certainly, were he in overall charge, King would have little hesitation in turning the Nelsonian blind eye and order their release; he simply had to make Sawyer and his like agree. And it would not be for personal gratification, but the good of the service.

Three years before the crew of HM Brig *Columbine* had mutinied less than two hundred miles from where he sat. It had been a particularly unpleasant affair that involved British seamen attempting to desert to America and ended with a warrant officer, three hands and two marines being put to death at the entrance to Halifax harbour. But the ramifications had spread far wider and were reverberating still. Were Napoleon to hear of a second instance of insurrection on the same station, and one with the added variance of a black officer and captured slaves, the Navy and Britain in general would be held up to ridicule; the consequential damage to prestige and confidence might easily lengthen both wars.

Besides, to King's mind at least, prosecuting the men would be unjustified for a far more tangible reason. Their wilful disobedience had been annoying in the extreme at the time but now he was less certain. Had they not acted so the schooner must surely have been recaptured with those aboard her now facing the prospect of lifelong servitude although, more significantly, *Delaware* would also still be at large. As it was, the United States was down by one frigate, which represented a major part of her navy, while *Tenacious,* a minor cog in her own navy's complex machine, was likely to return and fight again. He would be speaking with Sawyer shortly; the admiral might be something of a stickler but King was quietly confident of convincing him to see sense and grant an informal pardon before things became too official.

Of course *Tenacious* would need a deal of attention and quickly – news had come in of further engagements with American warships – rather than at home, he should be with Banks' squadron seeking out the enemy. But, even as he sat at his dining table in

277

comfort and security, he knew part of him remained at sea. The action with *Delaware* had only taken place three days before and it was hard to separate himself from the stress and terrors of battle, where death could come in an instant and strange aberrations might almost be expected.

He glanced up and noticed Aimée regarding him with concern, then realised he had been quiet for too long. "You were about to say something," he prompted gently.

"Only that what you saw seems even more unusual."

"Unusual? How so?"

"You mentioned Captain Walton as having no faith," she continued.

"I said the fellow did not believe in an afterlife," King corrected, "though yes, I suppose he was hardly spiritual. Yet you can never be certain," he added after considering for a moment. "Combat does strange things to people and I really did not know him well; a few chance meetings and an exchange of favours, no more..."

"But there *was* more, Thomas," Aimée insisted. "You and I have been together for long enough for me to be sure of that."

"I wish you had known the cove," King sighed, "but you were talking with so many at the reception and there was never the chance for our families to meet." He paused to suppress a sudden wave of emotion, then added more softly, "And now they never will."

He glanced up, she was considering him and there was understanding as well as love in her eyes.

"Perhaps not, but from what you say I think I would have liked him."

King reached across the table and took her hand. "I think you would as well," he said.

Character List

HMS *Tenacious*

Thomas King	Captain
James Croft	First lieutenant
Jack Cooper	Second lieutenant
Michael Summers	Third lieutenant
Manton	Sailing master
Bream	1st Lieutenant of marines
Rushlake	2nd Lieutenant of marines
Dennison	Purser
Heather	Purser
Robert Manning	Surgeon
Joseph Morales	Carpenter
Wilson	Sailmaker
Patrick Regan	Gunner
Timothy Amon	Boatswain
'Francis' Drake	Master-at-arms
Worth	Corporal
Duckworth	Quartermaster's mate
Brotherton	Midshipman
Hanson	Midshipman
Simon Vernon	Midshipman
David Godby	Midshipman
Sturridge	Gunroom cook
Stokes	Able seaman
Groom	Able seaman
Bovey	Able seaman
McKenzie	Able seaman
Knightly	Ordinary seaman
Nearhood	Ordinary seaman
Hodges	Ordinary seaman
Lovemore	Ordinary seaman
Longdon	Ordinary seaman
Johnno	Boy

HMS *Sparrow*

William Leyton	Captain
Taylor	Lieutenant
Hudson	Sailing master
Corbrite	Midshipman
Rogers	Boatswain

USS *Delaware*

Robert Walton	Captain
Seymour	First lieutenant

HMS *Albatross*

Bentley	Captain

HMS *Alert*

Sir Richard Banks	Commodore
Adam Hopkins	Captain

HMS *Mercury*

Reynolds	Captain

and

Aimée Silva	King's common law wife
Sir George Prévost	Lieutenant governor of Halifax
Sir Herbert Sawyer	Commander-in-Chief, North American Station

Selected Glossary

Able seaman	One who can hand, reef and steer and is well acquainted with the duties of a seaman.
Back	Wind change; anticlockwise.
Backed sail	One set in the direction for the opposite tack to slow a ship.
Backstays	Similar to shrouds in function, except that they run from the hounds of the topmast, or topgallant, all the way to the deck. (Also a useful/spectacular way to return to deck for a topman.)
Banyan Day	Monday, Wednesday and Friday were normally considered such, when no meat would be issued.
Barky	*(Slang)* Seamen's affectionate name for their vessel.
Barrack Street	Area close to the Citadel that was a favourite haunt of seamen and soldiers.
Barrel fever	*(Slang)* Illness brought about from excessive alcohol consumption.
Beakhead	Area forward of the forecastle.
Becket	A secure hanging place for weapons or equipment.
Bilboes	Iron restraints placed about an offender's ankles, allowing him to be of some use, picking oakum, etc.
Binnacle	Cabinet on the quarterdeck that houses the compass, deck log, traverse board, lead lines, watch glass, speaking trumpet, etc.
Block	Article of rigging that allows pressure to be diverted or, when used with others, increased. Consists of a pulley wheel, made of *lignum vitae*, encased in a wooden shell. Blocks can be single, double (fiddle block), triple or quadruple. The main suppliers were Taylors of Southampton.

Boatswain	(Pronounced bo's'n) The warrant officer in charge of sails, rigging, canvas, colours, anchors, cables and cordage etc.
Bob/bobbed	*(Slang)* A trick/tricked.
Boom	Lower spar to which the bottom of a gaff sail is attached.
Braces	Lines used to adjust the angle between the yards, and the fore and aft line of the ship. Mizzen braces and braces of a brig lead forward.
Brig	Two-masted vessel, square-rigged on both masts.
Bulkhead	A partition within the hull of a ship.
Bulwark	The planking or wood work about a vessel above her deck.
Bumboat	*(Slang)* A shore-based vessel used to supply seamen with small luxuries.
Butterbox	*(Slang)* Dutchman.
Canister	Type of shot, also known as case. Small iron balls packed into a cylindrical case.
Careening	The act of beaching a vessel and laying her over so that repairs and maintenance to the hull can be carried out.
Carronade	Short cannon firing a heavy shot. Invented by Melville, Gascoigne and Miller in late 1770s and adopted from 1779. Often used on the upper deck of larger ships, or as the main armament of smaller.
Cathead	A beam extending from each side of the bow and used to carry and raise an anchor.
Cat house	*(Slang)* A brothel.
Caulk	*(Slang)* To sleep. Also caulking, a process that seals the seams between strakes.
Chink	*(Slang)* Money.
Chips /chippy	*(Slang)* Traditional name for the carpenter. Originally from the ship builders who were allowed to carry out small lumps of wood, or chips, at the end of their shift.
Chits	*(Slang)* Children.
Clod	*(Slang)* A fool, especially a landsman.

Close-hauled	Sailing as near as possible into the wind.
Come-up glass	A device that uses prisms and lenses to detect whether another vessel is gaining or falling back.
Companionway	A staircase or passageway.
Counter	The lower part of a vessel's stern.
Course	A large square lower sail, hung from a yard, with sheets controlling and securing it.
Cove	*(Slang)* A man, occasionally a rogue.
Crows of iron	Crow bars used to move a gun or heavy object.
Cull	*(Slang)* A man.
Cutter	Fast, small, single-masted vessel with a sloop rig. Also a seaworthy ship's boat.
Daily officer	The Georgian Royal Navy equivalent of officer of the day.
Dead reckoning	Calculating a position using previous information and incorporating estimations for speed, current, direction, wind etc.
Ditty bag	*(Slang)* A seaman's bag. Derives its name from the dittis or 'Manchester stuff' of which it was once made.
Driver	Large sail set on the mizzen. The foot is extended by means of a boom.
Felo de se	Literally felon of the self; suicide.
Fetch	To arrive at, or reach, a destination. Also the distance the wind blows across the water. The longer the fetch the bigger the waves.
Figgy-dowdy	A pudding (rich in fat and raisins).
Filch	*(Slang)* To steal.
Filling room	Part of the magazine where cartridges are made up.
Forebiter	A song sung by seamen when at leisure.
Forereach	To gain upon, or pass by, another vessel when sailing in a similar direction.
Forepeak	An area in the bows, often used for storage.
Futtock	A lower frame in the hull of a ship (similar to a rib). Futtock shrouds run from the edge of a top to the mast below.

Glass	Telescope. Also, hourglass: an instrument for measuring time (and hence, as slang, a period of time). Also a barometer.
Guineaman	A vessel used in the slaving trade.
Gulled	*(Slang)* Fooled.
Gun room	In a third rate and above, a mess for junior officers. For lower rated ships the gun room is the equivalent of the wardroom.
Go about	To alter course, changing from one tack to the other.
Halyards	Lines which raise yards, sails, signals etc.
Hanger	A fighting sword, similar to a cutlass.
Hard tack	Ship's biscuit.
Hasty pudding	The British version of grits.
Hawse	Area in the bows where holes are cut to allow the anchor cables to pass through. Also used as general term for bows.
Hawser	Heavy cable used for hauling, towing or mooring.
Headway	The amount a vessel is moved forward (rather than leeway: the amount a vessel is moved sideways) when the wind is not directly behind.
Heave to	Keeping a ship relatively stationary by backing certain sails in a seaway.
Holder	One aboard ship who spends much of his time moving stores in the hold.
Housewife	A case or pouch containing needles, cotton and grooming items.
Idler	One who, through his duty or position, does not stand a watch, but (usually) works during the day and can sleep throughout the night.
Interest	Backing from a superior officer or one in authority, useful when looking for promotion.
Jackass	*(Slang)* A frigate of the sixth rate. Also Jackasses; tapered canvas bags that can be used to plug the hawseholes (and were secured by bucklers).
Jaunty	*(Slang)* The master-at-arms.

Jib boom	Boom run out from the extremity of the bowsprit, braced by means of a martingale stay, which passes through the dolphin striker.
John Bull	The personification of Britain and, in particular, England.
Jury mast/rig	Temporary measure used to restore a vessel's sailing ability.
Larboard	Left side of the ship when facing forward. Later replaced by 'port', which had previously been used for helm orders.
Lazarette	Small compartment usually used for stores.
Leatherneck	*(Slang)* Derogatory term for a marine.
Leeward	The downwind side of a vessel.
Leeway	The amount a vessel is moved sideways by the wind (as opposed to headway, the forward movement, when the wind is directly behind).
Light room	A small glassed-off compartment that held a lantern to shed light into the magazine and filling room.
Liner	*(Slang)* Ship of the line (of battle). A third rate or above.
Lobscouse	Preserved beef stewed with vegetables.
Luff	Intentionally sail into the wind, perhaps to allow work aloft. Also the flapping of sails when brought too close to the wind. The side of a fore and aft sail laced to the mast.
Lye	An alkali solution used for washing, often made from ashes or urine (as in chamber lye).
Martingale stay	Line that braces the jib boom, passing from the end through the dolphin striker to the ship.
Materiel	Military equipment.
Monkey suit	*(Slang)* A midshipman's uniform.
Oldster	*(Slang)* A midshipman who has missed the chance of promotion.
Orlop	The lowest deck in a ship.
Paunch mat	Thick matting made from rope and used to stop spars from chafing.

Penny gaff	*(Slang)* Theatrical entertainment, usually in a form of primitive music hall.
Pips	*(Slang)* Easily achieved.
Preventer	Additional reinforcement for backstays, shrouds etc.
Pushing school	*(Slang)* A brothel.
Pusser	*(Slang)* Purser.
Quarterdeck	In larger ships the deck forward of the poop, but at a lower level. The preserve of officers.
Ratlines	Lighter lines, untarred and tied horizontally across the shrouds at regular intervals, to act as rungs that allow men to climb aloft.
Reef	A portion of sail that can be taken in to reduce the size of the whole.
Rigging	Can be roughly divided into standing (static) rigging which is line that support masts and running (moveable) rigging that, with the aid of blocks and other tackle, controls spars. Also *(Slang)* clothes.
Rondy	*(Slang)* Rendezvous. A recruitment point and base for press gangs and regulating officers.
Running	Sailing before the wind.
Salted bird	Superstition has it that putting salt on a bird's tail makes it unable to fly, and so run quickly.
Schooner	Small craft with two or three masts.
Scran	*(Slang)* Food.
Scantlings	Officially refers to the dimensions of a vessel's inner timbers but usually used to define them.
Scupper	Waterway that allows deck drainage.
Scuttlebutt	Literally where seamen can obtain drinking water, but often used as a slang for gossip. (Think modern day water cooler...)
Seven bells men	Senior hands who dined early and took control of a ship during general mealtimes.
Sheet	A line that controls the foot of a sail.
Shellback	*(Slang)* An elderly seaman.
Shrouds	Lines supporting the masts athwart ship (from side to side) which run from the hounds (just below the top) to the channels on the side of the hull.

Slushy	(*Slang*) The cook. So called because one of his perks was to skim the fat from boiled meat. This 'slush' could be sold, the money raised being his slush fund.
Small clothes	Underwear.
Smoke	(*Slang*) To discover, or reveal something hidden.
Snowball	(*Slang*) A black man.
Staysail	A quadrilateral or triangular sail with parallel lines hung from under a stay. Usually pronounced stays'l.
Stern sheets	Area of a ship's boat between the stern and the first rowing thwart and used by passengers and officers.
Stingo	(*Slang*) Beer.
Strake	A plank.
Swivel	A light gun mounted on smaller warships and merchants.
Tack	To turn a ship, moving her bows through the wind. Also a leg of a journey relating to the direction of the wind. If from starboard, a ship is on the starboard tack. Also the part of a fore and aft loose-footed sail where the sheet is attached, or a line leading forward on a square course to hold the lower part of the sail forward.
Taffrail	Rail around the stern of a vessel.
Taphouse	(*Slang*) A lower class hostelry.
Tompion	A wooden plug placed in the mouth of a cannon to protect the barrel.
Tophamper	Literally any weight either on a ship's decks or about her tops and rigging, but often used loosely to refer to spars and rigging.
Traverse board	A means of recording the ship's speed and direction during a watch.
Trick	(*Slang*) A period of duty.
Turncoat	(*Slang*) One who betrays his country or friends.
Van	Abbreviation of vanguard, i.e. at the head.

Waist	Area of main deck between the quarterdeck and forecastle.
Watch	Period of four (or in case of a dog watch, two) hours' duty. Also describes the two or three divisions of a crew.
Watch list	List of men and stations, usually compiled and carried by lieutenants and divisional officers.
Wearing	To change the direction of a square-rigged ship across the wind by putting its stern through the eye of the wind. Also jibe – more common in a fore and aft rig.
Wedding garland	An actual garland that would be raised when a ship was expected to remain at anchor for some while. It signified that the ship was not on active service and women were allowed aboard. This was considered a preferable alternative to granting shore leave, which often led to desertion.
Windward	The side of a ship exposed to the wind.

Author's notes

To describe **the war of 1812** as unnecessary is misleading, if only because it suggests the opposite is more common; avoidable is probably a better term although both naturally invite contention and strongly held opinions which some could argue are the true seeds of war. Certainly I found examining the various causes, along with what might have been done to avoid conflict, to be both intriguing and vaguely depressing as the rigid stances, bluster and posturing common during the overtures have been repeated in many subsequent disputes. Then, as now, the intention was to avoid conflict; Churchill's later assertion of jaw-jaw being better than war-war would have been just as valid. However, sanctions of any kind will always a powerful tool and, as with many tools, they make equally effective weapons so I was left without doubt that an economic war can be almost as deadly as the physical variety to which it often leads.

And, though others may disagree, to my mind there were no winners, and neither did any country show up in a consistently good light. There were reasons for this, of course; as a new nation America was relatively inexperienced when it came to diplomacy while for many years Britain had been fighting a drawn-out conflict elsewhere and had become stale and jaded. She was also accustomed to being victorious at sea, something that had induced a measure of arrogance which was heightened by Wellesley's more recent performance on land. To be presented with what many of the old guard viewed as rebellious colonialists must have felt like the last straw although that in no way excuses the practice of illegally seizing men that was a major factor in starting the conflict.

Finally, much can be blamed on communication; of late we have grown accustomed to the immediate reporting of facts and an ability to respond instantly, even over great distances. But when correspondence could take months, complex negotiations were far more challenging and mistakes could almost be expected. As it was, when America finally did declare war, a principle reason, Britain's Orders in Council of 1807, had already been rescinded, although news of this had yet to reach Washington, while the later Battle of New Orleans was fought when the Treaty of Ghent had already been signed.

With regard to the **Trade Sanctions** mentioned, these can

290

briefly be summarised thus: **Britain's Orders in Council (1807)** effectively forbade Great Britain, its allies, or – specific to this book – neutral countries to trade with France. Any ship not scheduled to call at an English port was liable to be inspected on the high seas and, should their cargo be considered liable to aid the French war effort, it would be seized. This came as a direct response to the French **Continental System** which was made up by the **Berlin Decree of 1806**, and the later **Munich Decree** which similarly enforced a total worldwide prohibition against British trade, while America's **Embargo Act** brought a general halt to all American exports. The latter inevitably affected their own industry dramatically whilst also signalling the end of the previously prominent Federalist Party that had promoted it. It was swiftly replaced by the delightfully named **Non-Intercourse Act** which lifted all restrictions on American shipping except when dealing with Britain or France. **Macon's Bill Number 2** that followed allowed universal trade for a limited period on the understanding that if either Britain or France continued to disrupt American commerce, sanctions against that country would return. Napoleon exploited this by agreeing to the terms but continuing to seize and impound American merchant shipping.

      Quakers. The reference to early members of the Society of Friends keeping slaves is correct although, so much had the practice become accepted, it was initially followed by every religious group. The more popular concept of their leading the movement against slavery was established by early abolitionists including John Woolman who was supported by politicians such as William Wilberforce (being classified as dissenters, Quakers were banned from standing as members of parliament themselves). After the passing of the Slavery Abolition Act, the Society went on to instigate prison reform, improve social justice and promote radical changes in conditions for factory workers as well as helping to establish organisations such as Amnesty International, Save the Children, Oxfam and The Child Poverty Action Group amongst many others. Quakers still campaign against modern slavery, the arms trade and other related causes although the faith keeps a low profile and has a relatively small number of members with the overwhelming majority being pacifists.

      The Slave Trade Act of 1807 (officially An Act for the Abolition of the Slave Trade) was introduced in British Parliament in January 1807 and came into force at roughly the same time as the

United States' **Act Prohibiting the Importation of Slaves**. Neither abolished the practice as such but were intended to stop the importation of fresh slaves (and encouraged other counties to do likewise). Slavery was finally banned in most parts of the British Empire with the introduction of the **Slavery Abolition Act of 1833**, although even this allowed the practice to continue in territories under the control of the East India Company.

The Little Belt Affair was a naval action fought in May 1811 between the frigate USS *President* (44) and HM sloop *Little Belt* (20). The *Little Belt* (originally the Danish *Lillebælt*) was sighted and believed to be HMS *Guerriere*, a frigate that had recently illegally impressed an apprentice sailing master who was a citizen of Maine, from an American brig. After both ships refused to identify themselves and with the American still under the impression they faced a frigate of roughly equal size, action commenced although precisely who fired the first shot was never established. After fifteen minutes, *Little Belt* was unable to fight further and the *President* withdrew. The following morning officers from the *President* offered repair facilities to the British vessel but these were refused and *Little Belt* finally made Halifax in company with another sloop. Over a year later when HMS *Guerriere* and the USS *Constitution* met in combat, men aboard *Guerriere* painted "Not the *Little Belt*" across their foretopsail.

Alaric Bond
Herstmonceux 2021

About the Author

Alaric Bond has written for various periodicals as well as television, radio and the stage but now focuses on historical nautical fiction with seventeen published novels, fourteen of which being in his acclaimed 'Fighting Sail' series.

He lives in Sussex, is married and has two far taller sons. Apart from researching nautical history he enjoys cycling (in gumboots, rather than lycra), sailing and carpentry as well as jazz, blues and dance band music from the thirties onwards. He also collects musical instruments and 78 rpm records.

www.alaricbond.com

About Old Salt Press

Old Salt Press is an independent press catering to those who love books about ships and the sea. We are an association of writers working together to produce the very best of nautical and maritime fiction and non-fiction. We invite you to join us as we go down to the sea in books.
Visit the website for details of all Old Salt Press books:

www.oldsaltpress.com

The Latest Great Reading
from Old Salt Press

Rick Spilman
Evening Gray Morning Red

A young American sailor must escape his past and the clutches of the Royal Navy, in the turbulent years just before the American Revolutionary War. In the spring of 1768, Thom Larkin, a 17-year-old sailor newly arrived in Boston, is caught by Royal Navy press gang and dragged off to HMS *Romney*, where he runs afoul of the cruel and corrupt First Lieutenant. Years later, after escaping the Romney, Thom again crosses paths with his old foe, now in command HMS *Gaspee*, cruising in Narragansett Bay. Thom must finally face his nemesis and the guns of the *Gaspee*, armed only with his wits, an unarmed packet boat, and a sand bar.

V E Ulett
Blackwell's Homecoming

In a multigenerational saga of love, war and betrayal, Captain Blackwell and Mercedes continue their voyage in Volume III of Blackwell's Adventures. The Blackwell family's eventful journey from England to Hawaii, by way of the new and tempestuous nations of Brazil and Chile, provides an intimate portrait of family conflicts and loyalties in the late Georgian Age. Blackwell's Homecoming is an evocation of the dangers and rewards of desire.

Seymour Hamilton
Angel's Share: A Story from the World of The Astreya Trilogy

Angel, a very old man who once was a Man of the Sea, recalls his boyhood and how he helped five men, a dozen widows and their young children, all led by the charismatic Abner, reach safety at an abandoned Fort, where they hope to escape the breakdown of society in a community guided by hope, faith, loyalty, and peace. Among the children is a girl with sea-bright eyes, and her little sister. More than twenty years later, Angel returns in his own ship to find out how they all fared. Unexpectedly, he triggers murderous violence that threatens to destroy the little community and Angel with it.

Joan Druett
Tupaia, Captain Cook's Polynesian Navigator
Tupaia sailed with Captain Cook from Tahiti, piloted the *Endeavour* about the South Pacific, and was the ship's translator. Lauded by Europeans as "an extraordinary genius", he was also a master navigator, a brilliant orator, an artist and mapmaker, and a devious politician. Winner of the New Zealand Post General Non-Fiction Prize.

Antoine Vanner
Britannia's Morass: The Dawlish Chronicles September - December 1884
1884: Florence Dawlish remains in Britain when her husband, Captain Nicholas Dawlish, leaves for service in the Sudan. She faces months of worry about him but she'll cope by immersing herself in welfare work for Royal Navy seamen's families at Portsmouth. It'll be a dull but worthy time

. . .

. . . until the suicide of a middle-aged widow whom Florence respects. Left wealthy by her husband, this lady died a pauper, beggared within a few months, how and by whom, is not known. The widow's legal executor isn't interested and the police have other concerns. Lacking close family, she'll be soon forgotten.

But not by Florence. Someone was responsible and there must be retribution. And getting justice will demand impersonation, guile and courage.

Alaric Bond
Lone Escort
(The Fighting Sail Series)
The North Atlantic in spring is a perilous place and, with a valuable convoy to protect, HMS *Tenacious* has a tough job ahead. But she is fresh from refit, fully manned and seemingly up to the task; the only factor likely to invite defeat is her captain.

Linda Collison
Water Ghosts
Fifteen-year-old James McCafferty is an unwilling sailor aboard a traditional Chinese junk, operated as adventure-therapy for troubled teens. Once at sea, the ship is gradually taken over by the spirits of courtiers who fled the Imperial court during the Ming Dynasty, more than 600 years ago. One particular ghost wants what James has and is intent on trading places with him. But the teens themselves are their own worst enemies in the struggle for life in the middle of the Pacific Ocean. A psychological story set at sea, with historical and paranormal elements.

Made in the USA
Las Vegas, NV
26 June 2021

25487364R00166